MYTHIC JOURNEYS

OTHER ANTHOLOGIES EDITED BY
PAULA GURAN

Embraces
Best New Paranormal Romance
Best New Romantic Fantasy
Zombies: The Recent Dead
The Year's Best Dark Fantasy & Horror: 2010
Vampires: The Recent Undead
The Year's Best Dark Fantasy & Horror: 2011
Halloween
New Cthulhu: The Recent Weird
Brave New Love
Witches: Wicked, Wild & Wonderful
Obsession: Tales of Irresistible Desire
The Year's Best Dark Fantasy & Horror: 2012
Extreme Zombies
Ghosts: Recent Hauntings
Rock On: The Greatest Hits of Science Fiction & Fantasy
Season of Wonder
Future Games
Weird Detectives: Recent Investigations
The Mammoth Book of Angels and Demons
After the End: Recent Apocalypses
The Year's Best Dark Fantasy & Horror: 2013
Halloween: Mystery, Magic & the Macabre
Once Upon a Time: New Fairy Tales
Magic City: Recent Spells
The Year's Best Dark Fantasy & Horror: 2014
Time Travel: Recent Trips
New Cthulhu 2: More Recent Weird
Blood Sisters: Vampire Stories by Women
Mermaids and Other Mysteries of the Deep
The Year's Best Dark Fantasy & Horror: 2015
The Year's Best Science Fiction & Fantasy Novellas: 2015
Warrior Women
Street Magicks
The Mammoth Book of Cthulhu: New Lovecraftian Fiction
Beyond the Woods: Fairy Tales Retold
The Year's Best Dark Fantasy & Horror: 2016
The Year's Best Science Fiction & Fantasy Novellas: 2016
The Mammoth Book of the Mummy
Swords Against Darkness
Ex Libris: Stories of Librarians, Libraries and Lore
New York Fantastic: Fantasy Stories from the City that Never Sleeps
The Year's Best Dark Fantasy & Horror: 2017
The Year's Best Dark Fantasy & Horror: 2018

MYTHIC JOURNEYS
RETOLD MYTHS AND LEGENDS

EDITED BY
PAULA GURAN

NIGHT SHADE BOOKS
New York

For Neil Gaiman,
with thanks.

CONTENTS

CONTENTS

INTRODUCTION:
A MAP OR MAYBE NOT

PAULA GURAN

"Myth is the nothing that is all."
—Fernando Pessoa, "Ulisses"

The definition of myth has been much debated and written about, so I'm not going to dive into that deep and murky pool. The difference between myth and legend is similarly mootable. (Not to mention, as a character in a story contained herein says, ". . . when legend and myth meet . . . (e)verything gets tangled.")

In *A Short History of Myth*, Karen Armstrong states:

> In the pre-modern world, mythology was indispensable. It not only helped people to make sense of their lives but also revealed regions of the human mind that would otherwise have remained inaccessible. . . .

She eventually concludes (along with much more) that myths are narratives and novels now do what myths once did. Armstrong asks what "else have novelists been doing these past 400 years, if not telling those timeless stories of loss, struggle and homecoming; of exile, sacrifice and redemption; of fertility, death and renewal, over and over again?"

Armstrong's view has, of course, been challenged. ["Armstrong has been misguided in the conception and production of this book." (Simon

Goldhill, *New Statesman*) "She falters once, when she speculates that today it is novelists who can partly fill the void left by myth." (Caroline Alexander, *The New York Times Book Review*).]

I've already mentioned the definition of mythology is a point of contention. Let's amend that: any consideration of mythology tends to inspire some argument.

We can all agree there's currently a great deal of cultural interest in old myths, including that displayed by TV/online dramas [*Atlantis* (2013-2015), *Troy: Fall of a City* (2018), *Vikings* (2013-present), and *American Gods* (2017-present), based on Neil Gaiman's 2001 novel)] and films like *Immortals* (2010), *Thor* (2011) and its more recent sequels, *Wonder Woman* (2017) and its forthcoming sequel *Wonder Woman 1984*, *Clash of the Titans* (2010) and *Wrath of the Titans* (2014), *Hercules* (2014), *The Secret of Kells (2009)*, *Gods of Egypt (2016)*, and *Percy Jackson and the Olympians: The Lightning Thief* (2010) and its 2013 sequel, based on a series of children's books by Rick Riordan.

The influence of legend and mythology on all forms of gaming is so pervasive (if often derived from literature or film), I won't go into it except to note references to Norse mythology are currently popular.

In recent literature, Kamila Shamsie's novel *Home Fire* (2017) reinvents ancient myth in a modern context, while Madeline Miller's *Circe* (2018) and *The Song of Achilles* (2012) both retell the original myths as does *The Silence of the Girls* (2018) by Pat Barker. *Gods Behaving Badly* (2007) is a hilarious take on the Olympians by Marie Phillips. Phillips treats Arthurian legend in the same way with *The Table of Less Valued Knights* (2015). Margaret Atwood's *The Penelopiad*—a novella of the Odyssey told by Penelope, Odysseus' wife—is a bit older (2005), as is *Anansi Boys* (2005) by Neil Gaiman (which weaves African myth with the modern day), but I'll throw them in too.

And one must mention the literary retellings of *Norse Mythology* (2017) by (again) Gaiman.

When it comes to science fiction and fantasy, modern authors often use myths and legends as inspiration or in retellings. Genre novels based on or heavily influenced by myth and legend are too numerous to mention, as are graphic novels, manga, and comic books.

Writers constantly invent mythologies and legends, but no matter how "new" they are, they are connected to ancient tales by the enduring human equation. The truths such fiction express is always relevant to human nature and society.

And for all the deeper meanings and uses of myth and legend, let's not forget they are also entertaining stories.

Novels offer authors a great deal more room to work with, but I hope *Mythic Journeys* provides the reader with a least a glimpse of some modern myth and legend in speculative fiction's short form.

In Western culture, Greek myth resounds with the loudest clang. It shouldn't be surprising to find it by far the most commonly evoked in speculative literature. There are many fine stories to choose from, and this volume could have easily been nothing but stories with Hellenic roots, but that would have not been a fair reflection of either modern society or literature, so I sought out stories from other traditions as well.

That said, this anthology is lacking in myths and legends from many ancient cultures: Egyptian, Babylonian, Arabian . . .

Mythic Journeys is *far* from a comprehensive survey of speculative fiction based on the vast diversity of world lore, but I hope you'll find enough of an assortment to give you some idea of the wonders that abound.

One more thing: ancient myths, or at least those that have filtered down to us, are often grounded in patriarchal societies. Myths themselves were tools men used to reinforce the message that women were subordinate to their male counterparts. Not surprisingly, a number of these modern stories provide a female point of view, reinterpret, or otherwise subvert the old standards to reveal new ideas.

Since not everyone will be familiar with all the myths and legends used in these stories, I thought I'd provide some notes, a sort of a map—albeit far from complete and often tangential—to our journeys. I hope there are no spoilers, but I've decided to group these story introductions here, at the end of my introduction instead of before each individual story, so that if you are particularly sensitive to even inadvertent information, you can more easily avoid the notes below.

We start—somewhere—with a beautiful retelling of the story of Persephone in "Lost Lake" by Emma Straub and Peter Straub. Demeter, the Greek goddess of the Earth's fertility, is one of the oldest of the gods; the story of a goddess abducted to rule the underworld—like Demeter's daughter Persephone—pre-dates the Greeks.

There are many myths and legends about Coyote—as a trickster, creator, lover, and more—found in various cultures of the indigenous

PAULA GURAN

people of North America. The hero/trickster is featured in modern novels like *Coyote Blue* by Christopher Moore, *Summerland* by Michael Chabon, and various shorter tales, but none is quite like Catherynne M. Valente's "White Lines on a Green Field."

As one can suppose from the title, there is another trickster in "Trickster" by Steven Barnes and Tananarive Due: Kaggen, the creator god of the San of southern Africa. But it is quite different from Valente's. It is set in the future in the Kalahari, a vast, arid plateau in southern Africa. Kaggen's ability to shapeshift into a mantis is mentioned, but in old stories he has also been known to become a snake, louse, caterpillar, or eland.

The beings in Brooke Bolander's "Our Talons Can Crush Galaxies" are somewhat akin to the Erinyes. Although their attributes changed from pre-Greek times through Aeschylus' depiction in the *Oresteia*, it's fairly safe to call them chthonic deities of vengeance and retribution.

Speaking of the *Oresteia*, a trilogy of tragedies that tell the end of the house of Atreus, it is the story of what happens a decade or so after the events Rachel Swirsky interprets from the viewpoint of Iphigenia in the fascinating "A Memory of Wind." *The Oresteia* is not a gentle tale.

The Leda of M. Rickert's story of the same name is, indeed, a modern variation of the Leda mentioned (as Helen and Clytemnestra's mother) in "A Memory of Wind." That said, it is a very "realistic" look at one of the more implausible of Zeus' many rapes of women, mortal and immortal alike.

We take a break from the violence of Greek myth for a bit with Neil Gaiman's charming "Chivalry," one of two stories in *Mythic Journeys* loosely connected to Arthurian legend. This one concerns the Holy Grail, the vessel supposedly used by Christ at the Last Supper, then used by Joseph of Arimathea to collect Christ's blood and sweat while he tended him on the cross. According to legend, Joseph immigrated to Britain and—centuries later—his descendants somehow lost track of the Grail. At Arthur's court it was prophesied that the Grail would one day be rediscovered by the greatest of all knights, and a quest to find the relic began.

We will continue to stay away from the Greeks with "The God of Au" by Ann Leckie. Some contend that speculative fiction itself is a particularly effective type of contemporary mythmaking. That fantasy and science fiction fulfill modern humanity's need for myth. Leckie's story is an example of a story that's not directly related to known myths (although the twins Etoje and Ekuba might remind one of Romulus and Remus, the legendary founders of Rome, as well as Cain and Abel of Judeo-Christian tradition) but its theme is mythological: people making deals with a god. Generally, mythology teaches us over and over that one should be cautious when dealing with gods.

"Faint Voices, Increasingly Desperate" by Anya Johanna DeNiro is a story of lust and jealousy related to old Norse myth but set in the present day. A form of Freyja (or maybe Frigg) is the central character. (Even goddesses get mixed up in stories that evolve over centuries.) Briefly mentioned are Freyja's "falcon cloak, her two cats, her boar, and her jewelry." Freyja owned a cloak (or maybe a skin) of falcon feathers that enabled her to fly. If she wanted to travel by chariot, she had one drawn by two cats. Or she could ride her boar, Hildisvíni ("battle swine"). Her most famous piece of jewelry was a necklace: Brísingamen. The magical torc (or neck-ring) was made by four dwarves. Freyja may (or may not) have obtained it by sleeping with each of them.

There are stories within stories in Sofia Samatar's "Ogres of East Africa." It is 1907 and a Pakistani-Kenyan clerk employed by a repulsive "great white hunter" is cataloging different types of ogres as told to him by Mary, a woman of the highlands. Having killed every type of animal he knows of in the area, the hunter now wants to shoot ogres. Are the ogres real monsters or are they legends? How can the powerless fight the powerful?

We journey north (but not quite as far north) from Africa for "Ys" by Aliette de Bodard. Ys is a mythical city off the coast of Brittany built by Gradlon, King of Cornouaille. Or maybe it was founded two millennia before the legendary king. Gradlon may have been an upright sort or maybe not. But his daughter Ahez (if he had a daughter) was—as de Bodard vividly portrays—wickedness incarnate. The stories all agree she was a bad one and Ys (for one reason or another) was lost to the sea.

Tanith Lee takes us to an island off the coast of Greece for "The Gorgon," a story about Medusa, a powerful icon of Greek (and earlier) myth. One of the three Gorgon sisters, most think about her only as the snake-haired monster who turned men to stone with her gaze. Perseus, with the help of Athena, beheads her. There's a great deal more to even the most basic story of Medusa, though, and many rich interpretations of her symbolism abound. Seek them out.

We abandon the warmth of the Mediterranean for Ottawa in Charles de Lint's modern-day glimpse of a mythic character central to Arthurian legend with "Merlin Dreams in the Mondream Wood." (The character, a fusion of historical and legendary figures, actually appeared in separate legends before he was blended into Arthur's story.) Sara Kendall, the protagonist of de Lint's tale, is also featured in de Lint's novel *Moonheart* (1984). Celtic and Native American mythologies are the core of this now-classic fantasy.

Back to Europe we travel for "Calypso in Berlin" by Elizabeth Hand, which wonderfully updates the story of Calypso in a darkly magical way. In Homer's *Odyssey*, Calypso is a nymph who entertains Odysseus for seven years on her idyllic island of Ogygia, but even her promise of immortality cannot keep him. There are a lot of nymphs in Greek myth: water nymphs, land nymphs, tree nymphs. They aren't exactly deities but they are deeply connected to specific places in nature.

Choosing just one story from Lisa L. Hannett and Angela Slatter's collection *Madness and Moonshine* proved a challenge. I wound up re-reading the entire book—not that I minded—before finally choosing "Seeds," the first story. In it, Mymnir flees the devastation of Ragnarok, hoping to escape all that bound her to Ásgarðr. *Madness and Moonshine*'s connected tales tell of Mymnir's Fae and part-Fae descendants in her new realm in the New World. Mymnir is a version of Muninn, one of Odin's two ravens. (The other is Huginn.) Odin sends the ravens out and they gather information for him, but they are more than magical spy birds: they are parts of the Allfather, so he sometimes frets about them flying away and not coming back.

Nisi Shawl's "Wonder-Worker-of-the-World" takes us back to Africa. Shawl has stated her story "strongly mimics the storytelling voice found in translated West African folktales." She has also mentioned how what we now know of African myth and legend is often distorted. This is touched upon in Sofia Samatar's story: African myths are mostly an oral tradition. What we read were collected and transcribed by Westerners who saw Africans as inferior. How accurately could such racist sources be? Still, the stories resound. Untombinde, which means "the tall girl," appears in several guises we know of. The best known is as the daughter of a king who must deal with a monster to gain her bridegroom.

Priya Sharma's "Thesea and Astaurius" is a fresh look at the myth of Theseus, the Minotaur, the Labyrinth, Ariadne, and Daedalus. In the original story, Ariadne helps Theseus by giving him a ball of thread that helps him navigate inside the Labyrinth and escape from it. As promised, Theseus marries Ariadne. But, at the first landfall their escape ship makes, the island of Naxos, Theseus deserts Ariadne. Ariadne either hangs herself or marries the god Dionysus. The goddess Artemis may have killed her the moment she gave birth to Dionysus' twins. Or maybe not. The original story is said to represent ideas about the civilized versus the uncivilized or natural versus the unnatural. But Sharma takes us much further—out of space and time.

"Foxfire, Foxfire" by Yoon Ha Lee deals with a fox spirit. The concept began in China, but drifted into most Eastern Asian cultures. (It is also found in a lot of modern speculative fiction; I know of quite a few examples.) The details of the cunning shapeshifter—called *kitsune* (fox) in Japan, *húli jīng* (fox spirit) in China, and *kumiho* (nine-tailed fox) in Korea vary, but the entity usually likes to take the form of a beautiful woman. Depending on the tradition, the fox can be a mischievous trickster, benevolent, malicious, or downright evil. (By the way, *baduk* is the Korean name for the board game Go; *yut* is another board game.)

Although some traditions see the owl as wise and enlightening, in many Native American cultures—as in "Owl vs. the Neighborhood Watch" by Darcie Little Badger—the nocturnal avian is considered an omen or messenger of death. Similarly in ancient Rome, an owl's hoot predicted imminent death. In India and China owls are harbingers of misfortune. In England, even as late as the eighteenth and nineteenth centuries, the owl was associated with death.

Atalanta, in Greek mythology, was a fleet-footed huntress. In Tansy Rayner Roberts's clever "How to Survive an Epic Journey," she also becomes an Argonaut, one of the heroes on Jason's ship the *Argo* who sought the Golden Fleece. Here we get a woman's viewpoint of the search for the Golden Fleece and what came after.

You'll find some sort of solar deity in most ancient mythologies. Many of them are humanoid and ride in or drive a vehicle across the sky. Ekaterina Sedia draws on Eastern Slavic myth in "Simargl and the Rowan Tree" to tell us of a mortal who dies, becomes the guardian of heaven, and does a good job of trotting along behind the sun god's chariot. When he's free of that responsibility, he has time to get into trouble.

"The Ten Suns" by Ken Liu is another science fictional myth. But you'll find the same elements in many ancient tales: an inquisitive hero who can't abide commonly held belief, a sidekick with a special power, and a mystery/problem to solve.

Any body of mythology has maidens in it. They are young and beautiful and—unless they are divine—powerless. Sometimes they go on to live happily ever after. Sometimes they don't. Like the title character in "Armless Maidens of the American West" by Genevieve Valentine, they may become legends, even while they still exist in the flesh.

Labyrinths and monsters are potent symbols. We've already encountered one set, but "Give Her Honey When You Hear Her Scream" by Maria Dahvana Headley is a profoundly different story.

Did I mention monsters? "Zhuyin" by John Shirley, the only previously unpublished story in this anthology, is an outright scary monster tale. The original serpent-bodied Chinese celestial deity (known in English as the Torch Dragon) that inspired the author may *look* terrifying, but is not really menacing. According to *Shanhaijing* (translated by Anne Birrell): "When this deity closes his eyes, there is darkness. When the deity looks with his eyes, there is light. He neither eats, nor sleeps, nor breathes. The wind and the rain are at his beck and call. This deity shines his torch over the ninefold darkness."

As Rachel Pollack explains, "The story of 'Immortal Snake' was inspired by a very old tale, published early in the twentieth century by the mythographer Leo Frobenius . . . 'The Ruin of Kasch'. . . Kasch was an actual place in the ancient world, its location in Africa precisely known. The modern name for the land of Kasch is Darfur."

"A Wolf in Iceland Is the Child of a Lie" by Sonya Taaffe ends our journey. It is related to Norse myth. Maybe this is a good place to mention that J. R. R. Tolkien acknowledged his fantasy was heavily influenced by the myths of the Northern Europeans. His work became popular—in fact, fantasy as a genre was initially dominated by imitations of Tolkien. Elements of Germanic and Nordic mythology are often found in some forms of fantasy and far too many video games and MMORPGs.

Enough of my cartography. Hope you enjoy our *Mythic Journeys*. May the gods be with you. Or maybe not . . .

—Paula Guran
Written on a Týr's day in the month of November 2018

"LOST LAKE"

EMMA STRAUB AND PETER STRAUB

Eudora Hale spent the warm months in Fairlady with her mother, and the cold months in Lost Lake with her father. That's how it seemed, at least. Now that she was old enough—nearly thirteen—Eudora knew that whatever the time of year the sun would never reach Lost Lake the way it did Fairlady. Some parts of the world were difficult to find, even for beams of light. Sometimes Eudora thought she was the only person in the country who traveled back and forth between the two cities; her train car was always empty, with the uniformed ticket-taker her only companion for the halfday journey. When she reached her destination, her mother or father would be waiting in an otherwise uninhabited station. Eudora assumed that the train tracks still existed as a polite acknowledgment to the days when people still used to go back and forth between the two small cities.

Dawn Hale's white house stood on a corner lot in the neighborhood closest to the center of Fairlady. There were window seats in all the bedrooms. The wide lawn ended at the rounded cul-de-sac. Eudora and her mother were never in the house alone—Dawn had two friends who had their own bedrooms in the house, and their daughters shared Eudora's large room overlooking the smooth asphalt of the street and the houses on the other side of the circle. For half the year, Lily and Jane were Eudora's sisters, her playmates, the ears on the receiving end of her whispers. Sometimes the girls took their pet rabbits down to the cul-de-sac and let them hop back and forth, knowing that they would never run away. A porch wrapped all the way around the house like a hoop skirt with a latticed hem, and when Eudora was in Fairlady, she liked to crawl underneath it and dig her fingernails into the rich dirt until they were black. Eudora loved Lily and Jane, both of them blond like their mothers, but she also loved being alone, underneath the house, where the soil was cool and dark.

The custody agreement was unusual: none of the other children ever left Fairlady, even if their fathers were elsewhere. Eudora had pleaded to go back and forth between Fairlady and Lost Lake, and the judge had been persuaded by her tears. Half the year exactly, split down the middle. Her school in Fairlady had finally accepted the situation, and dutifully handed out reading lists for the months she would be away. There was a library at her father's, in a room they called the fortress, and Eudora knew where to find what she needed. When it was Den Hale's turn with his daughter, he was more likely to show her how to aim a pistol, how to shoot an arrow into the center of a target, how to remain unseen using leaves and branches, how to build a fire using only her bare hands.

The night before she was due to go to Lost Lake, Eudora sat in the kitchen with her mother and their friends. The women were baking pies; the girls, breaking off the ends of sweet green beans. Lily and Jane sat on either side of her, all of them dumping the beans into a large, shallow bowl in front of Eudora.

"Did I give you the list of books for school? Have you packed your new sweater?" Dawn asked the questions to the whole room, clearly going down a list in her head. "Where is your toothbrush? Do you have clean socks?" Dawn didn't know anything about Lost Lake—she hadn't ever been, but Eudora knew that though her mother had agreed to the arrangement, it rattled her nerves.

"Yes, Mother," Eudora said. Her small suitcase was already packed, mostly with books. The clothes she wore in Fairlady would be of little use to her in Lost Lake. When she was very small—*a pip*, her father liked to say—Eudora didn't notice all the empty space around her, the air in between what people said and what she knew to be the truth, but now she could see it everywhere. She kept snapping the ends of the beans until the room filled with the smell of warm apples and sugar and then she too felt sad about leaving.

After dinner, when the girls had been sent to bed, Lily and Jane climbed into Eudora's bed.

"*Promise you'll come back,*" Lily whispered.

"*Don't stay away too long,*" Jane added, her mouth only inches away from Eudora's cheek. She was the eldest of the three, already fifteen, and tended to worry.

"*I always come back,*" Eudora said, and that satisfied her friends. They slept in a pile with their arms and legs thrown over each other, hearts beating strong and safe inside their chests.

On the train the next day, she was as alone as she had expected to be. The conductor who sat slumped into his blue uniform far back at the end of the car could not be counted as company, nor did he wish to be. Boredom and resentment clung to him like a bad smell. For the first time on one of these journeys to Lost Lake, being alone made her feel lonely. A wave of homesickness rolled through her, though she had been away from home no longer than an hour. She missed the white house, she missed her friends tumbling like kittens around her, and she missed her mother, who started worrying about Eudora as soon as she took her suitcase from the closet and opened it up. You would almost think Lost Lake was a dangerous place, you'd just about have to think jaguars and leopards and madmen with straight razors came stalking out of the forest to flit through the alleyways and little courts of the town. . . . Eudora realized that she felt guilty about having caused her mother such anxiety. She couldn't even talk her out of it, because Dawn refused to hear anything about Lost Lake. If you didn't close your mouth, she closed her ears.

Lily and Jane weren't much better, and their mothers were the same. They all acted like Lost Lake was a childhood nightmare they had sworn to keep out of mind. At home—the clean, white house, fragrant with fresh, warm bread and cut flowers, which she missed so piercingly at this moment—when Eudora spoke her father's name or that of his community, Lily and Jane, and their blond mothers, Beth and Maggie, looked at the ground and swiveled back and forth, like shy bridegrooms. Suddenly errands were remembered; something in another room, a book or a sewing basket, had to be fetched immediately. No one was going to tell her not to mention Den Hale or his remote northern world; yet it was clear that she was not supposed to say anything about that side of her life. (In Lost Lake, such strictures did not hold. Eudora had the feeling that people in Lost Lake spoke very seldom of Fairlady only because they found it completely uninteresting.)

One other person she was aware of traveled regularly between her mother's world and Den's, and that person made the journey much more frequently than she. It occurred to Eudora that the conductor, as unpleasant as he was, might be uniquely placed to answer questions that until this minute she had not known she needed to have answered. Eudora turned around in her seat and in a loud voice called out, "Excuse me! Hey! Conductor!"

The man opened a sleepy eye and took her in. He shuffled his upper body within the baggy uniform, lifted his cap, and rubbed the top of his head, still regarding her. He appeared to be either shocked or profoundly angry.

"My name is Eudora, hello. I want to talk about you, Conductor. For example, where are you from, where do you live? Which end of the line?" She had never seen him in Fairlady, so he almost had to live in Lost Lake, although he did not much look like the kind of person you met in and around her father's town.

"Neither end. Wouldn't have a thing to do with them places, nope. Don't like 'em. Don't believe they're very fond of me, either. Nope. *That's* been tested out and proven true."

She squinted at him.

"Do you live in some town in between?

"There *ain't* no towns between Fairlady and Lost Lake. All the civilization in this state's a hundred miles to the east. In here, where we are now, this part's pretty empty."

"Well then, where *do* you live?" The second she asked her question, she knew the answer.

"I live here. In the second car up."

"Are there ever any other passengers?"

"Maybe three-four times a year. Someone's car broke down, that's usually the reason. Or sometimes there's official business, where a couple of big shots ride back and forth, whispering stuff they don't want me to hear."

For a moment, Eudora contemplated this picture, trying to imagine what kind of "official business" would demand so much in time and secrecy. Then she remembered the real reason she had wanted to get into the conversation.

"Conductor, you spend your whole life on this train, but most of the time, you never have any tickets to collect because you're here all alone. I'm your biggest customer, and you only see me twice a year!"

He sneered at her. "You think I'm just a conductor, but I'm not. There's more to this train than you, young lady. It isn't really a passenger train, not mainly—did you never look at the other three cars?"

"I guess not."

Eudora could summon only the vaguest, blurriest images of the other cars. Ranked behind the lighted windows of the passenger car, they had seemed dark and anonymous. It had never occurred to her that they might be anything but closed, vacant versions of the car she always used.

"There's *freight*, in there. Most every morning and night, people load boxes into those freight cars. Big ones, little ones. I don't know what's in 'em, I just know it's worth a lot of dough. And I'm the guard over all that stuff. I'm security." The conductor checked to see if she had taken in the immense gravity of what he had just divulged. Then he slid off his seat and began to saunter toward her.

Eudora paused, a little unsettled by the conductor's approach but not much caring about the freight. What was the big deal about some boxes? "I want to ask you another question. You must hear people talk sometimes. Have you ever heard anything about a man named Den Hale?"

"Dennhale? No, I never . . . Oh, Den *Hale*. You said Den *Hale*, didn't you?" He had stopped moving. "Right?"

"Yes," she said, wondering. "Right."

"You work for him, or something?"

"No, I . . . no. He's my father. He picks me up at the other end." The conductor's narrow head moved forward, and his shoulders dropped. For a long moment, he looked as though he had been turned into a statue. Then he wheeled around and moved swiftly down the polished wooden aisle. At the end of the car, he hit the release button and moved across the dark, windy passage into the next car. Resoundingly, the doors clanked shut. Eudora was not certain of what had just happened, but she did not think she would see her new friend again on this journey, nor did she.

Just past ten at night, eight hours after her departure, the little train pulled into the Lost Lake station. Eudora expected to see her father waiting on the platform, but the man occupying the pool of light from the nearest hanging lantern was not Den Hale but his friend, Clancy Munn. A tough character, Munn was roughly the size of a mailbox, squat, thick, and at first glance all but square. It was funny: when in Fairlady, she all but forgot about Clancy Munn—he was unimaginable

in her mother's world—but here in Lost Lake, he felt like reality itself.
Clancy's daughter, Maude Munn, was Eudora's closest friend in Lost
Lake. She was more fun to be around than the girls in Fairlady, with
their sweet breath and brushed hair. It was as if the big strawberry
birthmark on Maude's left cheek had cranked up all her inner dials,
making her louder, faster, and more daring than most other people.
Eudora knew no one more alive than Maude.

When Clancy and Eudora left the shelter of the platform, the slight
breeze, already much colder than the air eight hours to the south,
whipped itself into a strong wind that cut through the summery jacket
her mother had bought for her as though it were tissue paper. Eudora
leaned in close to Clancy's thick body.

"It's always so *much* colder here."

"You like it this way, only you forget."

She laughed out loud, delighted. It was true: the details and sensa-
tions of Lost Lake were falling into place all around her like a jigsaw
puzzle assembling itself, reminding her as they did so how much she
enjoyed being here. She *liked* cold weather, she *liked* seeing snowflakes
spinning erratically through the air . . . she *liked* the huge fireplaces, and
the thick wooden walls, and the great forest.

Clancy turned on the heat in the cab of his truck, and they drove in
contented quiet the rest of the way to Eudora's father's house.

Eudora asked for news of Maude, chattered about the conductor, and
fell asleep on the last section of the journey. She came half awake only
after the pickup had passed through an automatic door and entered a
vast underground parking space. "We're here, sweetie," Munn said, and
gently shook her shoulder.

Eudora swam instantly back into consciousness and looked around at
all the empty parking spaces on both sides. Munn smiled and left the
cab. Far off to her right, three men in black coats were dragging long,
narrow boxes from the back of an old van and stacking them against the
wall. Eudora had seen this activity, or others like it, every time she returned to Lost Lake, but had never before wondered what it meant. She
scrambled out of the cab and trotted toward Munn, who was already
twenty feet in front of her, carrying her heavy suitcase as if it were empty.

"Hey, Clancy," she said, and he looked back over his shoulder, grinning. "What are those men doing, next to the wall over there?"

"What does it look like they're doing?" He had not stopped moving
forward, and was no longer smiling at her.

"Yeah, but what's in those boxes?"

Struck by a sudden, most curious idea, one wrapped in the aura of the forbidden, she stopped and regarded the faraway stack of containers. Eudora thought of the train conductor and his precious cargo. The boxes were long and narrow, each one the size of a person. Munn stopped moving, too, and turned around to look at her.

"Could be anything inside those things. Don't think too much about it, kiddo. Let's see if your old man is ready."

He picked up her case and led her up three flights of stairs, into a wide corridor and past several sets of doors. Asking him anything would have been a waste of time, she knew. As if in compensation, music and the smell of food drifted to her. Munn opened a door, looked at her for a second, then said, "Keep quiet and stay behind me."

She nodded. Her heart was beating faster, and she felt flushed with anticipation.

Munn slipped through the door, Eudora directly behind him.

Over his shoulder, she saw the great fire at the back of the room, the massive table where the remains of a roast sat amidst scattered plates, glasses, pads of paper—the ruins of a working dinner. The fire and the low candles on the table provided the only light.

A group of men, her father's friends and business partners, were seated on stools and sofas and easy chairs off to the side of the table. They were attending to the conversation in progress as if nothing could be more crucial to their futures. In fact, each of these nine or ten men was staring at her father as if he alone were the key to whatever lay ahead. They were dependent upon Den, she saw; he was at their very center. Den turned his head toward Munn and at last found that Eudora had come into the enormous room. Even at her distance from him, even in the dim, flickering light, she saw joy flare up into his eyes. He moved swiftly toward her, his arms held wide. Behind him, the other men watched his progress with the patient curiosity of dogs. Quickly, he pulled her into his embrace and began to apologize for failing to pick her up at the station. The men dared not move until he looked back and gestured.

Imagine, Eudora thought, *it took me my whole life to notice that he's the king around here.*

Six months later, Eudora and Maude Munn had many times ridden their horses through the town and raced them over the fields. After long secret consultations and hilarious conversations; after luxurious

meals and hurried, impromptu meals because she had to get back outside into the cold twilight to track rabbits through the fresh snow; after
snowball fights with half the girls in town; after hours of lonely study;
after occasions of ecstasy at the suddenly apprehended fact of really being *there*, wrapped in dark furs at the edge of the forest as light snowfall
skirled down from the gray, shining sky and the hints of a thousand
adventures seemed to shimmer before her; after long conversations
with her father; after all of this, it had become her last full day in Lost
Lake. Eudora and Maude were taking their final ride together on their
favorite horses, and they came again to the edge of the forest no one
was ever supposed to enter.

Maude's horse was brown and white, with spots of dirt on his belly
that she would have to comb out later on. The horse whinnied, and
Maude settled him with a few pats on the neck.

"I don't think even he wants to go in there," she said. Maude shifted
on the horse's back, uneasy. It wasn't like Maude to hesitate. When they
had leaped off the roof of an abandoned building into a bed of cardboard boxes, it had been Maude's idea. When they had dropped water
balloons onto the backs of Den's men, it had been Maude's idea. When
they had spent the night together, curled up like she used to with Lily
and Jane, but somehow even closer, it had been Maude's idea. But she
wasn't feeling bold right now, that was clear. Eudora watched as Maude
turned toward her; her strawberry birthmark looked brighter, pinker
than usual. It was her stoplight, Maude liked to say, and it didn't like the
cold. Eudora thought it didn't like the forest, either. Kids in Lost Lake
liked to make up stories about the lake itself, how it was haunted, but
Eudora didn't believe them, and Maude had never acted like she did,
either. Anyway, she'd never even seen the lake. For all she knew, the lake
itself might be a myth, no bigger than a mud puddle after a rainstorm.

"How scary can it be?" Eudora said, and urged her horse on. The forest was thick, but there were pathways—roads, almost—that indicated
they wouldn't be the first, maybe not even the first that day. Maude
nodded, and squeezed her horse, and into the forest they went.

Dark, empty branches stretched skyward over their heads like the
skeleton of a ceiling—all beams and bones, no connective tissue. The
leaves were gone. The girls stopped talking, and the only sounds were
the horses' hooves on the dirt, the wind in the branches above them,
and their own heartbeats. Eudora knew they weren't supposed to go

into the forest, but it sounded like advice they'd outgrown, didn't it? She was sure it did. It wasn't safe for children, of course, but she and Maude weren't children anymore. They could take care of themselves. She felt bolder with every step the horse took, until a man in black clothing like a uniform without badges or insignia stepped out from behind a great oak and held out his hand to stop them, and as silently as smoke other men in faceless uniforms, each with an ugly automatic weapon in his black-gloved hands, appeared on both sides, and they stopped their horses, having no real choice, and their audacity momentarily shriveled.

Maude gasped, and Eudora reached out to take her hand. Maude's palm was sweating already. The guards stepped toward them, spooking Eudora's horse.

"Turn around, girls," the guard said. Eudora looked to Maude, who had gone completely white. *What is she so afraid of*, Eudora wondered. They would turn back if they had to, of course, but why was Maude so frightened?

"I'm Den Hale's daughter," said Eudora, "and she's Clancy Munn's daughter. We just want to see Lost Lake." She was sure that her father's name would grant her access to whatever was hidden in the trees.

The guards didn't smile or soften the way Eudora thought they would. "Turn around, girls, and ride back freely, or we'll walk you back, like prisoners," the guard said. "You choose."

Surprised and slightly shaken, Maude and Eudora rode back through the trees and across the ring road and left the horses in their stables, and hugged each other, and promised themselves that the following year they would figure out how to get to Lost Lake. When they parted at Den's door, Eudora thought Maude lingered a little bit, the horse's reins still tight in her hand.

"What is it?" Eudora asked.

"Nothing," Maude said. She shook her head, as if trying to convince herself. "Nothing." Then she clicked her tongue and turned around and went home by herself, back to Clancy's house on the next block. Eudora stayed outside, listening, just in case her friend came back. The following day, when Eudora took the little train back to warmth and Fairlady, a different conductor accepted her ticket, punched it, plodded to the end of the carriage, and disappeared. When Eudora closed her eyes and fell asleep, she dreamed of horses and leaves and men with guns tucked into their waistbands; she dreamed of Maude's hair blowing across her cheek; she dreamed of a vast lake that stretched all the way to the horizon.

Dawn was waiting when the train arrived, a basket of food hanging from her arm. She'd baked biscuits for the short ride home from the station, and brought some freshly made juice the color of a sunrise.

"How was the trip?" Dawn asked, smiling. Her eyes looked glassy, which could have been from the breeze coming through the leaves and the grass. It was spring again, and there was pollen in the air.

"Good," Eudora said, knowing that her mother wouldn't want to hear more. "Fine."

"If it was good for you, it's good for me," Dawn said, and hooked her arm over Eudora's shoulder and turned toward home. After six months in Lost Lake, Fairlady looked like a film set—there was no trash or leaves in the gutter, no eyesore vehicles, not a broken window or an empty building. Even by the train station, the streets were as clean as if they'd just been mopped with bleach.

"How is everyone?" Eudora asked, expecting more of the same, easy answers to easy questions. She loved her mother, but Dawn didn't like to go beneath the surface. Everything was always fine, no matter what.

"Lily's got the bunnies in the living room—there are more of them now, the big one had some more babies. She wanted to show them to you."

"And what about Jane?"

Dawn didn't stop walking, didn't shift her gaze from the clear, even sidewalk. "Jane's living with her father now."

Eudora tried to stop, but Dawn kept moving. "What?!" This had happened to other girls in Fairlady, older ones who were as pretty and blond as Jane. One day they'd be at school, practicing their choreographed routines in the hall, all white teeth and unblemished skin, and then next day, they'd be gone. To their fathers, whom no one had ever seen.

"She wanted to, Eudora. Just like you want to live with your father. Doesn't Jane get to make a choice, too?" Dawn's voice was as even as the sidewalk, with not a single crack.

Eudora thought of Jane's whispered pleas, her soft cheek resting against Eudora's shoulder the night before she left for Lost Lake. That night, Jane hadn't wanted to go anywhere. Eudora wondered when her friend had changed her mind. "Sure," she said. "Of course." When they made it back to the house, all the lights were on and Lily sat in the middle of the living room floor, surrounded by little moving puddles of white fur, smiling as if nothing was different. Even Jane's mother grinned, so happy to see Eudora home again.

The months went quickly—Eudora went back to school, where she read familiar stories and took familiar tests. She ate her mother's beautiful, rich food and helped clean the kitchen. Lily stayed close to her in bed at night, the two of them singing the kind of children's songs that were harmless until you actually listened to the lyrics, which were about hangmen and rotting earth. The summer came and all the playgrounds were full of children. She washed her hair and braided it while it was wet, which left wrinkles of curls behind after it dried, which reminded her of Maude. In the fall, just before Eudora was heading back, Dawn began to pick at her cuticles, which she'd never done before. Once, Eudora was walking by the bathroom and saw Dawn plucking her eyebrow hairs with her fingers, her sharp nails acting as tweezers. Her mother looked completely unlike herself—Dawn looked pale and frightened, but determined, too. Eudora stepped on a noisy floorboard, and Dawn looked up, catching Eudora's eyes in the bathroom mirror. Instantly her face went back to normal, the corners of her mouth perking back up into a smile. She smoothed her fingers over the reddened stripes over her eyes. "Time for bed!" she said, her voice trilling upward like a happy bird.

Eudora stayed awake on the train—she wanted to know how far it really was in between the two cities. There were tunnels she'd never noticed before, long stretches of time underground. Eudora stared out the window, sure that she would pass something that would explain the difference between her mother's house and her father's, between the way she felt in her two bedrooms, the difference between Lily and Jane and Maude.

This time, it was her father who picked her up from the train. He walked up the platform smiling at her, and she took in again that he was actually a small, compact man who moved with a wonderful economy and efficiency you never noticed until he was coming straight at you and you had no choice. Den walked, she realized, like a dancer. He sauntered, he strolled, he more or less glided up to her and hugged her close and kissed her forehead. Her father was just about the same height as Dawn. In a few years, she would probably be taller than both of them. Eudora slid her face into the collar of his old brown leather jacket and, to keep her childhood from vanishing completely away, inhaled the fragrance of Lost Lake masculinity, minus the smell of horses—Den never spent much time in the stables—but with some sharp extra smell like that of a winter evening growing dark. It was the smell, she suddenly felt, of cold water.

"Ah, you're glad to be back," he said. "That's always good to know. And you're not too softened up from six months in Fairlady, I hope."

"I'm always glad to be back here," she said. "Last time, Clancy said it used to take me a couple of days to remember that I really like being in Lost Lake, but when he picked me up I remembered it instantly. This time, too. But when I go *there*, back to Fairlady, I miss this place so much I think I mope around for weeks."

All in one smooth, unbroken motion, he hugged her more tightly, patted her on the back, picked up her traveling bag, and began to escort her down the platform. Eudora realized that she had never before said so much about Fairlady when in her father's world. "Must be hard on your mother."

"Maybe. But you know Mom, she's always so cheerful and upbeat. That's what makes her so wonderful!"

"That's true," he said. "Very true. But you always bring some of that cheer to us, you know."

"Jane must do that, too. She's here now, isn't she? My friend Jane Morgan, from Fairlady?"

"I don't know any Jane Morgans from Fairlady, honey. Sorry." He smiled at her, then turned to hoist her suitcase into the back of the pickup.

"But . . . she left to live with her father. Mom said."

Still smiling, Den gestured for her to walk around the cab and get in on her side. "I know a couple of Morgans, and neither of them has a daughter. Abel Morgan is so old he can barely walk, and his son, Jerry, who never married, is a captain in our security force. Your friend probably moved to one of those little towns on the other side of the state, Waldo, or Fydecker, one of those. Or maybe Bates, way south of us, that's a good-sized city. Probably a ton of Morgans in Bates."

Den turned on the engine, gave Eudora a reassuring pat on the knee, and twisted around to back up into the aisle.

"Daddy . . ."

"Something else?" He raised his eyebrows.

"Why do you need a security force? Fairlady doesn't have one."

"That's a big question, honey." For a short while, he negotiated the turns needed to get out of the lot and on the road to Lost Lake. "Fairlady's a special place. There are policemen, but you hardly ever see them, and the town has next to no crime. We don't have much, either, but some of that is due to our security force. We're a much busier place than Fairlady. We do have a jail, and there's almost always one or two idiots in a cell. All kinds of things go on here in Lost Lake—and besides, this is the North. Things are different in the *North*. We wouldn't live in Fairlady if you paid us." He gave her a look that was both amused and fond. "I hope you'll feel the same way, next year."

Here it was, thrust in front of her face like a burning torch, the matter she tried never to think about while knowing it could never be very far from her mind. The judge at her custody hearing had ordered that Eudora would have to decide between her mother and her father, between Fairlady and Lost Lake, by the date of her sixteenth birthday, now only two seasons away. After that, her trips back and forth would cease, and she would become a permanent resident of one city or the other, of her mother's world or her father's. There was no in between. This abrupt, unwelcome reminder of the decision she somehow would have to make made her stomach cramp in on itself, and for a moment she feared that she would have to vomit onto the remarkably clutter-free floor of the cab, which Den had almost certainly cleaned up for her arrival.

Some of what she was feeling must have been printed on her face, because her father immediately said, "Shouldn't have reminded you like that. Sorry. I'm sure your mother feels as strongly as I do about this thing."

Eudora thought, *My mother would never have done that to me.* Then: *My mother wouldn't say anything about it even if we were about to go before the judge. Instead, she'd ask how I liked her new brand of oatmeal. Dawn kept everything locked up tight. Too tight, maybe.* Eudora inhaled and said, "How's Maude? I can't wait to see her."

"Maude's probably fine, you know, but she isn't in Lost Lake right now. She won't be back before you have to leave again. I'm sorry about that, too. I know what great friends you were." He used the past tense—*were*.

"No," said Eudora. "No, she would have told me. Where is she, anyhow?" A dreadful thought occurred to her. "Did you do this? Did you send her away?"

"She's on a special trip with Clancy. Town business. She wanted to be more involved! Did I send away your best friend? Of course not. I don't have the power to do that."

"In Lost Lake, you can do anything you like. Last year I finally noticed how everyone acts around you. All those men, they need you to tell them what to do. They look up to you. You're the mayor, or the boss, or whatever."

"Don't you think Clancy decides what Maude does, not me?"

"Clancy especially would do anything you told him to do."

Den frowned at her and without warning swung the wheel sharply to the right, pulling the vehicle off the road and onto the weedy bank. He jerked to a stop, jammed the shift into neutral, and swiveled to face her. His eyes seemed flat, blank, empty. For a second, fear flashed from the center of her chest and sparkled through her nervous system. A gust of cold wind struck the pickup with an audible slap. They were still a mile or two out of town. The nearest building was a little run-down farmhouse about a hundred yards away across an empty field, and it was probably abandoned.

Some feeling came back into Den's eyes. "Look, Eudora. This is how it goes. All right? Lost Lake doesn't have a mayor, and there isn't any boss. When we need to discuss something, we get together, and we work it out. The men in my place, sure, they work for me, but we talk everything over, and everyone has a say in what happens."

"But what do you *do*?" she asked.

"About a million different things." Den paused. "I really thought Maude would let you know, sweetie."

She felt deflated. "Okay. Thanks. I'm sorry. I didn't want to make you angry."

"It takes more than that to make me angry. But if you were thinking, did I send Maude away because the two of you tried to sneak through the forest last year, the answer is no. The guardsman who ordered you back told me about the two of you, however. You were thoughtful enough to give him my name, and *he* was thoughtful enough to come to me afterward. Lost Lake is dangerous, honey, and so is the forest around it. We keep people away for their own good."

Eudora felt her face heat up, and she looked away. Her father was lying to her, she was sure of it. There was no way Maude would have gone away without letting her know. There was something off—first Jane, now

Maude. Eudora thought of all the girls in Fairlady who had left school abruptly, all the pretty girls who had never been heard from after boarding the train north. Her father knew the truth, but he wasn't telling.

"Now that we understand each other, let's get into town and have a nice time, okay?"

"If you say so," she said.

Eudora looked through her window and watched scrubby wasteland yield to rows of shacks and pawnshops and liquor stores. They drove between two massive strip clubs that faced each other across the two-lane macadam road. Past the neon of the clubs, the town of Lost Lake began to assemble itself and display what it was really about. A street of morose one-story houses with tiny lawns led to a huge brick structure that ended at a square from which narrow roads wound this way and that through and into a clutter of shops, taverns, restaurants and supper clubs, foundries, courtyards and town squares, movie theaters (all but one shuttered), tiny frame apartment buildings, streets of diminutive factories, a cemetery, and finally, the area on the north end of town where stood Den's huge blank building with concealed vents and hidden windows and multiple entrances, with uncounted chimneys—a building with comfortable living space for twenty people, an underground pool, a shooting range, the library called the "fortress," a dining room, two kitchens, and all of the hearths, fireplaces, and woodstoves beneath the uncounted chimneys. Described this way, the town sounds enormous, but many of the buildings were of no great size, the streets were narrow, and most of the squares had a toylike quality, not unlike parts of Fairlady. Past Den's realm lay the tremendous forest, and within the forest glinted the immensity of Lost Lake itself, forbidden to all but a few of the town's satraps, rajahs, magi, and sultans. Or so Eudora gathered. Maude had promised her to make another foray side by side into that forbidden territory, and that idea overflowed with equal amounts of the fear of capture, the thrill of outrageous adventure, and joy—the blazing joy of sharing both the risks and the adventure with Maude Munn.

It was possible, of course, that Eudora had always liked Maude more than Maude had liked her, that the friendship had been formed out of familial duty. It was possible that Maude was having the time of her life off wherever she was with Clancy, and that if Maude ever thought of Eudora at all, it was with a gentle nostalgia for her childhood, as if she were an old stuffed monkey found discarded at the back of a closet. This consideration had two effects on Eudora: it aroused a sharp, painful shame that seemed centered in her actual heart, and it made her feel that she, too, should move into a more adult phase of her life. Having no choice in the matter, Eudora decided to become a more independent young woman, and took to riding a horse through town by herself; spending hours alone in the "fortress," reading whatever looked interesting, as long as it also seemed unambiguously grown-up: over a single week, she read *Jane Eyre, We Have Always Lived in the Castle*, and *The Bloody Chamber*. All the other children in Lost Lake seemed like simply that—children—whereas Eudora herself felt like nothing of the sort. She was somewhere in between the kids and the adults, and therefore profoundly lonely. Eudora had never before really noticed the extent to which she and Maude Munn had split away from the others to create a self-contained, self-sustaining society of two. She could almost imagine that her friend had been protecting her from the rest of Lost Lake.

On Eudora's tenth night back in her father's realm, Den and most of his merry men stayed up very late drinking—it was hard to tell if they were celebrating or mourning, the cries and cheers too loud and too blurry for Eudora's ears to differentiate. Either way, she knew that it would be a late morning for all of them, even the guards. It occurred to Eudora that she would probably never have a better chance all winter to slip into the forest unseen. Without Maude did she dare, did she even want to dare? Lost Lake might as well keep its secrets, she thought. Secrets seemed to be the world's principal currency.

Two days earlier, she had been dawdling bored past the big conference room, peeked in through the half-inch opening in the doorway, and seen, far back at a little table near the enormous fire that filled the hearth, her father in the act of counting the money he was transferring from a knee-high metal safe on the floor into a bunch of shoeboxes piled up on the side of the table. He was not counting bills, he was counting stacks of money, bundles of cash held together with thick paper bands. Behind him and closer to the fire, an oversized guard in a black uniform without any identifying symbols stood with his arms crossed over his huge chest. The clearest thing about this tableau was that it *was not supposed to be seen*. A kind of dirty intimacy surrounded it. Eudora had moved away as swiftly and as quietly as she could manage. Yet Fairlady, too, had its dirty secrets. When she sat in her mother's pretty kitchen sometimes, shelling peas or cutting up sweet potatoes, watching and listening as the older women chattered about nothing much—about trivia, really, half of it in that distant time when they had been girls themselves—the empty space she had begun to notice in the air between people's words and what they really meant widened and widened until the kitchen seemed an abyss. As Eudora lay in her narrow bed with the dull clamor of drunkenness booming from the floor below, it came to her that she herself, Eudora Hale, was in imminent danger of succumbing to the depths of the empty spaces, and that she could drown in the emptiness, the meaninglessness yawning all about her. She had this one chance, she thought: *this* one, *now*. And Maude would be with her, too, she thought, not the Maude who had disappeared into "town business" with Clancy, but the other, more real Maude, *her* Maude, who had created meaning with a glance of her eye as she beautifully flaunted her flame-licked face and ran straight at any obstacle that dared place itself before her.

Just before dawn Eudora slipped quietly out of bed and put on as many layers as possible, buttoning herself up with trembling fingers. Carrying her boots to avoid making any noise clumping across the floor, she crept along the hallway and tiptoed down the stairs. At the bottom of the staircase was the entrance to a large room with a concrete floor that Den used chiefly to put up short-term visitors. The sounds of snoring and sleepy mutterings told her that this monastic space was not empty. Alarmed, she moved quietly past the half-open doorway and peered in. Something like twenty men lay asleep on cots and pallets, about half of them in the black uniforms of Den's guardsmen. A stench of flatulence and stale alcohol hovered above the snoring men. Eudora took long, silent steps to a back door and walked outside into fresh, cold air that smelled wonderful to her. The long, flat-roofed stables lay only a few steps on a concrete path away.

Her horse exhaled warm steam onto her palms in greeting, and Eudora stroked his velvet nose, moved down his side, stroking and patting as she went, and like a true girl of Lost Lake vaulted onto his back. With a dig of her heels and a whispered word she urged him forward and stayed flat against his neck while they were still in Lost Lake proper. This was it, Eudora realized with something like shock, she was committed, she would see this through to the end. Never before in her life had she been so flagrantly and willfully disobedient. A ghost-Maude, a shadow-Maude, rode beside her, egging her on with the courage of her own native, utterly out-there flagrancy. That blazing wine-stain on Maude's cheek had demanded more courage than Eudora thought she alone would ever have.

Disobedient? Very well, I will imagine my Maude at my side, and my disobedience will be root, trunk, branch, and leaf.

As she rode the horse at a steady walk past the shuttered taverns and empty inns that lined the empty ring road, she wondered how her parents had ever met in the first place, how they had been in the same room long enough to make her out of thin air. The number of things that had to align to bring her into being! Maude had had a mother too, years ago, and Jane and Lily had both had fathers. Why did no one get to keep both? Surely they did in some parts of the world. Eudora thought that next year, before she was forced to go before the judge and make a choice, she might jump off the train with a bag full of clothes and food and walk until her new, separate journey took her to a nice town that looked like it might be a good place to live. In this place, parents would not get divorced; it would have neither Fairlady's well-swept corners nor Lost Lake's darkness and mystery. Surely such a place existed, somewhere. Didn't it, didn't it *have* to? Yet . . . were she to make her separate journey, instead of losing merely one of the places she already had, she would lose both of them.

Eudora stopped fantasizing about something she was probably never going to do, especially not without Maude, when her horse's steady, one-foot-at-a-time gait had taken her across the ring road's wide expanse and up to the irregular row of oak and birch trees that marked the beginning of the great forest. She was at the exact point where she and Maude—so fearlessly, so confidently, so ignorantly—had entered the forest. This time around, she was fearful, uncertain, and aware that normally a squad of the black-uniformed soldiers would be poised and hidden within the trees, ready to pounce. She nudged her horse into a gentle, quiet walk through the first row of trees and into the forest, where the pale, gray light of the northern dawn almost immediately surrendered to the velvet darkness of the long night. All of the soldiers couldn't have been celebrating with Den, she knew. Probably an equal number had been left at their posts, or whatever they called it. She would have to be a lot cagier today, and softer of step.

The trees seemed sometimes to creep toward her out of the absolute darkness behind them, and sometimes invisible twiggy fingers reached out to dig at her hair, her shoulders, her chest. With better eyesight than hers, the horse did not flinch or panic, but sure-footedly stepped around the thick trunks and lacy deadfalls on their wandering path. If it was a path. In daylight, she and Maude had followed some old trail, half overgrown with fiddlehead ferns, but now she had to leave all of that up to the horse. Eudora's only function was to avoid low-hanging limbs and keep the animal moving in more or less the right direction.

She lost track of time. Now and then, she brought the patient horse to a halt and paused a minute or two to listen to what was going on around her. In the darkness and without a watch whose dial was readable at night, a minute becomes a very flexible unit of time. Eudora listened to the forest breathe around her, a faint rustle in the leaves, a quick scurry of tiny feet on the forest floor, a bird's exploratory-sounding call answered or challenged by another bird. Some animal brushed against a tree trunk, and she felt the horse stiffen and shift its legs, and knew it was rolling its eyes in terror. Eudora patted its neck and urged it forward again, grateful not to know what kind of animal it had been, and hoping it was not following them. Then it occurred to her that the animal might have been a human being with an automatic weapon slung across his back. Night vision glasses, and a black uniform with a black hood. Black boots with rubber soles. She let herself be carried another thirty feet, and feeling protected by the darkness no longer, squeezed the reins gently to halt the horse, swung her legs over the animal's back, and dropped silently to the ground.

A faint gray light was leaking into the darkness. Eudora began moving slowly forward through the ranks of the trees and for a moment had the illusion that they grew in straight military rows that exposed her every time she moved into one of the spaces between the neat rows. Far overhead, a squirrel barreled along a slender branch and yelled in squirrel-speak, *I see her! I see her! Here she is, you idiots!* She whirled to look behind her, and the forest, as if by command, snapped back into its old disorder. More carefully, she examined the tree trunks, the bushes, the green sprigs that sprouted from the gray-green mulch, straining to see what she could not see: hidden traps, gleaming wires, soldiers with their faces painted to look like moss. "Okay," she muttered to herself, and led the horse by the reins in the direction she thought she had to go. Ten minutes of patient going later, Eudora heard the unmistakable sound of a group of men moving through the forest with no thought of precaution. She froze; she listened, hard. The men seemed to be coming right toward her from the very direction she was going. Making as little noise as possible, she led the horse behind a deadfall where a huge broken trunk slanted gray and lifeless through a cobwebby tangle of lesser branches entwined with parasitic vines. She knelt down and as the noise came nearer peered out at the space she had just left. Soon a small troop of the guards, weapons slung across their backs, relaxed and clearly in a good mood, entered the space before her and mooched along through it.

When they had passed, Eudora waited a few minutes, then emerged and listened to them passing away from her, now and then saying something she could not make out. It did not have to make sense to her, she told herself, she should merely be grateful they were making themselves so easy to avoid. Then she resumed walking northward again, toward the lake, the horse treading amiably along beside her.

Nearly an hour later, the sun higher in the sky and sending great shafts of pale northern light down through the trees that were greener and taller than those farther back, she felt the ground beneath her feet grow spongy with moisture. The air was colder and clearer, and she thought it smelled like water. Eudora gave the reins a tug and began to move along faster. Before her, a cluster of matter where none should have been—an unnatural shape, a harsh angle, a brown too red to be alive—resolved itself into a sort of shelter, a hut, a shack. A shack with a dark, glinting window and a wood stove's chimney jutting through the roof. A dark green pickup truck encrusted all over with a rind of dried mud had been drawn up beside it.

Her heart seemed to swing to a stop, then resume after the skipped beat. She thought she knew that pickup. For a moment she could not move. Then: "You stay here," she whispered to the horse, dropped the reins, and set off, crouching and moving despite her terror toward the rear of the shack and its glinting window. It could not be, it had to be. Of course it was. She remembered walking toward it through a blast of freezing air at the side of the station. Since that night, the pickup had known a lot of bad weather.

The real test of her courage was whether or not she could straighten up enough to peer through the window, and as she scuttled across a resilient carpet of weeds murdered by the cold Eudora wondered what she would do when she got to the red-brown wall. Then she got there, and she knew she had to risk taking a look. The shadow-Maude, the silent, insubstantial Maude insisted on it. Yes. A look, really just a peep, a second's glance into that enigmatic space, and off to the next big challenge. Such as, for example, trying to get back home before Den noticed she wasn't in the building.

Very slowly, in fact reluctantly, Eudora came up out of her crouch and plastered herself to the boards next to the window. She inhaled and exhaled, inhaled again and held her breath. It was time. She turned her head, then her whole body, and raised the top of her head and her left eye to the window. Inside the cabin, Clancy Munn sat at a card table, his broad square back to her, counting out bills from one of the stacks Den had been organizing. He placed the bills into three separate piles. Then he waved at someone, telling them to come up to him. Eudora lowered her head again, counted to twenty, then rose up and risked another peep. Two of the soldiers in black were grinning down at Clancy and reaching for the money he was extending to them. Everybody seemed to be extremely happy with the way their lives were going. *Payday*, Eudora thought, *okay, that's all I need.* The guards stepped back from the desk, and Eudora found herself looking at Maude Munn, her radiance considerably dimmed, her face drawn into a scowl, standing there in blue jeans and mud-daubed blue sweater, her hands jammed into the pockets of a dirty-looking duffel coat. She was just thinking that Maude didn't own that sweater, or that ugly coat either, when her onetime darling and best friend glanced up and looked right into her eyes. Eudora froze, and her mouth went dry.

Maude nodded once and looked down at her father, who gave her a couple of bills and waved her off. She backed away and slid her eyes sideways. When Eudora failed to move, Maude frowned more deeply and nodded her head to the left. *Get out of here*, she was saying, and Eudora got out of there on the spot. She scrambled, trying to be as quiet as you can be while scrambling, and disappeared, she hoped, back into the trees. When she got to shelter, she realized that along the far side of the cabin had been a stack of the long, narrow black boxes from the train—from her trains and all the others.

No longer quite in control of herself, Eudora moved aimlessly away from the cabin and finally took in that the trees were thinning out and the ground becoming squishier. And directly ahead of her was a glinting, silvery, molten surface that had to be Lost Lake. She glanced back, assured herself that her horse was within reach and not going anywhere, and turned back to the lake that had been her goal all along. It was vast, but she could see across it, dimly. It looked very cold and very deep, like an enormous quarry. Way off to her right, a truck had been drawn up along a wooden dock. Two of the guardsmen were pulling something from the back of the truck and loading it onto a dolly.

Eudora strained to see what the object was, but the men's bodies obscured it as they pushed the dolly along the pier jutting out from the dock. At the end of the pier, they tilted up the dolly, and something black slipped away into the water and instantly sank from view.

It was enough: it was too much, she needed no more. Eudora stumbled back into the woods, took up the reins, and walked the horse back far enough to feel safe getting on its back again. They plodded through the forest, with every step Eudora seeing before her the shock, as if by flashlight, of Maude Munn's altered face, the face of a gloomy, altered Maude Munn, older, sadder, compromised, another person altogether. The black thing slid into the lake and disappeared. Something had gone away, gone away forever.

It made no difference to her now, but her luck held long enough for her to stable the horse and get into her father's terrible building and make her way to her room unseen. No one had noticed she was missing, no one had gone looking for her. Everyone in her father's employ had been too busy or hungover to notice her absence. She had left muddy boot-prints on her way to her room, but someone would wash them away without ever thinking twice about it. Lost Lake was a muddy place, now and again. Eudora peeled off her clothing and glanced into her mirror to see a filthy body with wild eyes and twigs in her hair glaring back at her as if in accusation.

She fell into bed and seemed to have become disembodied. Being disembodied was fine with Eudora. Her bodiless self rose a foot or two off the bed and became aware that a door, a nice, sturdy red door had appeared in the empty air before her. Behind this door, she understood, was another. It might be larger or smaller, uglier or more beautiful, but it would be different. And after that door would be another, then another, and yet another after that. The journeys opened by these doors were ripe with miseries, splendors, richness and paltriness, with a thousand breathtaking moments and as many of heartbreak and despair, but what she understood most at that moment was that none of these many, many doors would ever lead her back to the first.

"WHITE LINES ON A GREEN FIELD"

CATHERYNNE M. VALENTE

Let me tell you about the year Coyote took the Devils to the State Championship.

Coyote walked tall down the halls of West Centerville High and where he walked lunch money, copies of last semester's math tests, and unlit joints blossomed in his footsteps. When he ran laps out on the field our lockers would fill up with Snickers bars, condoms, and ecstasy tabs in all the colors of Skittles. He was our QB, and he looked like an invitation to the greatest rave of all time. I mean, yeah, he had black hair and copper skin and muscles like a commercial for the life you're never going to have. But it was the way he looked at you, with those dark eyes that knew the answer to every question a teacher could ask, but he wouldn't give them the *satisfaction*, you know? Didn't matter anyway. Coyote never did his homework, but boyfriend rocked a 4.2 all the same.

When tryouts rolled around that fall, Coyote went out for everything. Cross-country, baseball, even lacrosse. But I think football appealed to his friendly nature, his need to have a pack around him, bright-eyed boys with six-pack abs and a seven-minute mile and a gift for him every day. They didn't even know why, but they brought them all the same. Playing cards, skateboards, vinyl records (Coyote had no truck with mp3s). The defensive line even baked cookies for their boy. Chocolate chip peanut butter oatmeal walnut iced snickerdoodle, piling up on the bench like a king's tribute. And oh, the girls brought flowers. Poor girls gave him dandelions and rich girls gave him roses and he kissed them all like they were each of them specifically the key to the fulfillment of all his dreams. Maybe they were. Coyote didn't play favorites. He had enough for everyone.

By the time we went to State, all the cheerleaders were pregnant.

The Devils used to be a shitty team, no lie. Bottom of our division and even the coach was thinking he ought to get more serious about his geometry classes. Before Coyote transferred, our booster club was the tight end's dad, Mr. Bollard, who painted his face Devil gold-and-red and wore big plastic light-up horns for every game. At Homecoming one year, the Devil's Court had two princesses and a queen who were actually girls from the softball team filling in on a volunteer basis, because no one cared enough to vote. They all wore jeans and bet heavily on the East Centerville Knights, who won 34-3.

First game of his senior year, Coyote ran eighty-two yards for the first of seventy-four touchdowns that season. He passed and caught and ran like he was all eleven of them in one body. Nobody could catch him. Nobody even complained. He ran like he'd stolen that ball and the whole world was chasing him to get it back. Where'd he been all this time? The boys hoisted him up on their shoulders afterward, and Coyote just laughed and laughed. We all found our midterm papers under our pillows the next morning, finished and bibliographied, and damn if they weren't the best essays we'd never written.

I'm not gonna lie. I lost my virginity to Coyote in the back of my blue pick-up out by the lake right before playoffs. He stroked my hair and kissed me like they kiss in the movies. Just the perfect kisses, no bonked noses, no knocking teeth. He tasted like stolen sunshine. *Bunny*, he whispered to me with his narrow hips working away, *I will love you forever and ever. You're the only one for me.*

Liar, I whispered back, and when I came it was like the long flying fall of a roller coaster, right into his arms. *Liar, liar, liar.*

I think he liked that I knew the score, because after that Coyote made sure I was at all his games, even though I don't care about sports. Nobody didn't care about sports that year. Overnight the stands went from a ghost town to kids ride free day at the carnival. And when Coyote danced in the end zone he looked like everything you ever wanted. Every son, every boyfriend.

"Come on, Bunny," he'd say. "I'll score a touchdown for you."

"You'll score a touchdown either way."

"I'll point at you in the stands if you're there. Everyone will know I love you."

"Just make sure I'm sitting with Sarah Jane and Jessica and Ashley, too, so you don't get in trouble."

"That's my Bunny, always looking out for me," he'd laugh, and take me in his mouth like he'd die if he didn't.

You could use birth control with Coyote. It wouldn't matter much.

But he did point at me when he crossed that line, grinning and dancing and moving his hips like Elvis had just been copying his moves all along, and Sarah Jane and Jessica and Ashley got so excited they choked on their Cokes. They all knew about the others. I think they liked it that way—most of what mattered to Sarah Jane and Jessica and Ashley was Sarah Jane and Jessica and Ashley, and Coyote gave them permission to spend all their time together. Coyote gave us all permission, that was his thing. *Cheat, fuck, drink, dance—just do it like you mean it!*

I think the safety had that tattooed on his calf.

After we won four games in a row (after a decade of no love) things started to get really out of control. You couldn't buy tickets. Mr. Bollard was in hog heaven—suddenly the boosters were every guy in town who was somebody, or used to be somebody, or who wanted to be somebody some impossible day in the future. We were gonna beat the Thunderbirds. They started saying it, right out in public. Six-time state champs, and no chance they wouldn't be the team in our way this year like every year. But every year was behind us, and ahead was only our boy running like he'd got the whole of heaven at his back. Mr. Bollard got them new uniforms, new helmets, new goal posts—all the deepest red you ever saw. But nobody wore the light-up horns Mr. Bollard had rocked for years. They all wore little furry coyote ears, and who knows where they bought them, but they were everywhere one Friday, and every Friday after. When Coyote scored, everyone would howl like the moon had come out just for them. Some of the cheerleaders started wearing faux-fur tails, spinning them around by bumping and grinding on the sidelines, their corn-yellow skirts fluttering up to the heavens.

One time, after we stomped the Greenville Bulldogs 42-0, I saw Coyote under the stands, in that secret place the boards and steel poles and shadows and candy wrappers make. Mike Halloran (kicker, #14) and Justin Oster (wide receiver, #11) were down there too, helmets off, the filtered stadium lights turning their uniforms to pure gold. Coyote leaned against a pole, smoking a cigarette, shirt off—and what a thing that was to see.

"Come on, QB," Justin whined. "I never hit a guy before. I got no beef here. And I never fucked Jessie, either, Mike, I was just mouthing off. She let me see her boob once in ninth grade and there wasn't that much to see back then. I never had a drink except one time a beer and I never smoked 'cause my daddy got emphysema." Coyote just grinned his friendly, hey-dude-no-worries grin.

"Never know unless you try," he said, very reasonably. "It'll make you feel good, I promise."

"Fuck *you*, Oster," shot back Halloran. "I'm going first. You're bigger, it's not fair."

Halloran got his punch in before he had to hear any more about what Justin Oster had never done and the two of them went *at it*, fists and blood and meat-slapping sounds and pretty soon they were down on the ground in the spilled-Coke and week-old-rain mud, pulling hair and biting and rolling around and after a while it didn't look that much like fighting anymore. I watched for a while. Coyote looked up at me over their grappling and dragged on his smoke.

Just look at them go, little sister, I heard Coyote whisper, but his mouth didn't move. His eyes flashed in the dark like a dog's.

LaGrange almost ruined it all at Homecoming. The LaGrange Cowboys, and wasn't their QB a picture, all wholesome white-blond square-jaw aw-shucks muscle with an arm so perfect you'd have thought someone had mounted a rifle sight on it. #9 Bobby Zhao, of the 300 bench and the Miss Butter Festival 19whatever mother, the seven-restaurant-chain owning father (Dumpling King of the Southland!) and the surprising talent for soulful bluegrass guitar. All the colleges lined up for that boy with carnations and chocolates. We hated him like hate was something we'd invented in lab that week and had been saving up for something special. Bobby Zhao and his bullshit hipster-crooner straw hat. Coyote didn't pay him mind. *Tell us what you're gonna do to him*, they'd pant, and he'd just spit onto the parking lot asphalt and say: *I got a history with Cowboys*. Where he'd spat the offensive line watched as weird crystals formed—the kind Jimmy Moser (safety, #17) ought to have recognized from his uncle's trailer out off of Route 40, but you know me, I don't say a word. They didn't look at it too long. Instead they scratched their cheeks and performed their tribal ask-and-answer. *We going down by the lake tonight? Yeah. Yeah.*

"Let's invite Bobby Zhao," Coyote said suddenly. His eyes got big and loose and happy. His *come-on look*. His *it'll-be-great look*.

"Um, why?" Jimmy frowned. "Not to put too fine a point on it, but fuck that guy. He's the enemy."

Coyote flipped up the collar of his leather jacket and picked a stray maple leaf the color of anger out of Jimmy's hair. He did it tenderly. *You're my boy and I'll pick you clean, I'll lick you clean, I'll keep everything red off of your perfect head,* his fingers said. But what his mouth said was:

"Son, what you don't know about enemies could just about feed the team till their dying day." And when Coyote called you Son you knew to be ashamed. "Only babies think enemies are for beating. Can't beat 'em, not ever. Not the ones that come out of nowhere in the fourth quarter to take what's yours and hold your face in the mud till you drown, not the ones you always knew you'd have to face because that's what you were made for. Not the lizard guarding the Sun, not the man who won't let you teach him how to plant corn. Enemies are for grabbing by the ears and fucking them till they're so sticky-knotted bound to you they call their wives by your name. Enemies are for absorbing, Jimmy. Best thing you can do to an enemy is pull up a chair to his fire, eat his dinner, rut in his bed and go to his job in the morning, and do it all so much better he just gives it up to you—but *fuck him*, you never wanted it anyway. You just wanted to mess around in his house for a little while. Scare his kids. Leave a little something behind to let the next guy know you're never far away. That's how you do him. Or else—" Coyote pulled Cindy Gerard (bottom of the pyramid and arms like birch trunks) close and took the raspberry pop out of her hand, sipping on it long and sweet, all that pink slipping into him. "Or else you just make him love you till he cries. Either way."

Jimmy fidgeted. He looked at Oster and Halloran, who still had bruises, fading on their cheekbones like blue flowers. After a while he laughed horsily and said: "Whaddaya think the point spread'll be?"

Coyote just punched him in the arm, convivial like, and kissed Cindy Gerard and I could smell the raspberry of their kiss from across the circle of boys. The September wind brought their kiss to all of us like a bag of promises. And just like that, Bobby Zhao showed up at the lake that night, driving his freshly waxed Cowboy silver-and-black double-cab truck with the lights on top like a couple of frog's eyes. He took off that stupid straw hat and started hauling a keg out of the cream leather passenger seat—and once they saw that big silver moon riding shotgun with the Dumpling Prince of the Southland, Henry Dillard (linebacker, #33) and Josh Vick (linebacker, #34) hurried over to help him with it and Bobby Zhao was welcome. Offering accepted. Just lay it up here on the altar and we'll cut open that shiny belly and drink what she's got for us. And what she had was golden and sweet and just as foamy as the sea.

Coyote laid back with me in the bed of my much shittier pick-up, some wool blanket with a horse-and-cactus print on it under us and another one with a wolf-and-moon design over us, so he could slip his hands under my bra in that secret, warm space that gets born under some hippie mom's awful rugs when no one else can see you. Everyone was hollering over the beer and I could hear Sarah Jane laughing in that way that says: *just keep pouring and maybe I'll show you something worth seeing.*

"Come on, Bunny Rabbit," Coyote whispered, "it's nothing we haven't done before." And it was a dumb thing to say, a boy thing, but when Coyote said it I felt it humming in my bones, everything we'd done before, over and over, and I couldn't even remember a world before Coyote, only the one he made of us, down by the lake, under the wolf and the moon, his hands on my breasts like they were the saving of him. I knew him like nobody else—and they'll all say that now, Sarah Jane and Jessica and Ashley and Cindy Gerard and Justin Oster and Jimmy Moser, but I knew him. Knew the shape of him. After all, it's nothing we hadn't done before.

"It's different every time," I said in the truck-dark. "Or there's no point. You gotta ask me nice every time. You gotta make me think I'm special. You gotta put on your ears and your tail and make the rain come for me or I'll run off with some Thunderbird QB and leave you eating my dust."

"I'm asking nice. Oh, my Bunny, my rabbit-girl with the fastest feet, just slow you down and let me do what I want."

"And what do you want?"

"I want to dance on this town till it breaks. I want to burrow in it until it belongs to me. I want high school to last forever. I want to eat everything, and fuck everything, and snort everything, and win everything. I want my Bunny Rabbit on my lap while I drive down the world with my headlights off."

"I don't want to be tricked," I said, but he was already inside me and I was glad. Fucking him felt like running in a long field, with no end in sight. "Not into a baby, not into a boyfriend, not into anything."

"Don't worry," he panted. "You always get yours. Just like me, always like me."

I felt us together, speeding up towards something, running faster, and he brushed my hair out of my face and it wasn't hair but long black ears, as soft as memory, and then it was hair again, tangled and damp with our sweat, and I bit him as our stride broke. I whispered: "And Coyote gets his."

"Why not? It's nothing we haven't done before."

When I got up off of the horse blanket, marigold blossoms spilled out of me like Coyote's seed.

Later that night I fished a smoke out of my glove box and sat on top of the dented salt-rusted cab of my truck. Coyote stood down by the lakeshore, a ways off from the crowd, where the water came up in little foamy splashes and the willow trees whipped around like they were looking for someone to hold on to. Bobby Zhao was down there, too, his hands in his jean pockets, hip jutting out like a pouty lip, his hat on again and his face all in shadow. They were talking but I couldn't hear over everyone else hooting and laughing like a pack of owls. The moon came out as big as a beer keg; it made Coyote's face look lean and angelic, so young and victorious and humble enough to make you think the choice was yours all along. He took Bobby Zhao's hand and they just stood there in the light, their fingers moving together. The wind blew off that straw hat like it didn't like the thing much either, and Bobby let it lie. He was looking at Coyote, his hair all blue in the night, and Coyote kissed him as hard as hurting, and Bobby kissed him back like he'd been waiting for it since he was born. Coyote got his hands under his shirt and oh, Coyote is good at that, getting under, getting around, and the boys smiled whenever their lips parted.

I watched. I'm always watching. Who doesn't like to watch? It feels like being God, seeing everything happen far away, and you could stop it if you wanted, but then you couldn't watch anymore.

A storm started rumbling up across the meadows, spattering their kisses with autumn rain.

Suddenly everyone cared about who was going to make the Devil's Court this year. Even me. The mall was cleared out of formal spar-kle-and-slit dresses by August, and somehow they just couldn't get any more in, like we were an island mysteriously sundered from the land of sequins and sweetheart necklines. Most of us were just going to have to go with one of our mom's prom dresses, though you can be damn sure we'd be ripping off that poofy shoulder chiffon and taking up the hems as far as we could. Jenny Kilroy (drama club, Young Businesswomen's Association) had done all the costumes for *The Music Man* in junior year, and for $50 she'd take that cherry cupcake dress and turn it into an apocalyptic punkslut wedding gown, but girlfriend worked slow. Whoever took the Homecoming crown had about a 60/40 chance of being up there in something they'd worn to their grandmother's funeral.

The smart money was on Sarah Jane for the win. She was already pregnant by then, and Jessica too, but I don't think even they knew it yet. Bellies still flat as a plains state, cotton candy lipstick as perfect as a Rembrandt. Nobody got morning sickness, nobody's feet swelled. Sarah shone in the center of her ring of girls like a pink diamond in a nouveaux riche ring. 4.0, equestrian club, head cheerleader, softball pitcher, jazz choir lead soprano, played Juliet in both freshman and senior years, even joined the chess club. She didn't care about chess, but it looked good on her applications and she turned out to be terrifyingly good at it—first place at the spring speed chess invitational in Freemont, even seven months along. You couldn't even hate Sarah. You could see her whole perfect life rolling on ahead of her like a yellow brick road but you knew she'd include you, if you wanted. If you stuck around this town like she meant to, and let her rule it like she aimed to.

Jessica and Ashley flanked her down every hall and every parade—a girl like Sarah just naturally grows girls like Jessica and Ashley to be her adjutants, her bridesmaids, the baby's breath to make her rose look redder. All three of them knew the score and all three of them made sure nothing would ever change, like Macbeth's witches, if they wore daisy-print coats and their mothers' Chanel and tearproof mascara and only foretold their own love, continuing forever and the world moving aside to let it pass. So that was the obvious lineup—Queen Sarah and her Viziers. Of course there were three slots, so I figured Jenny Kilroy would slide in on account of her charitable work to keep us all in the shimmer.

And then Friday morning arrived, the dawn before the dance and a week before the showdown game with Bobby Zhao and his Cowboys. Coyote howled up 7 a.m. and we woke up and opened our closets and there they hung—a hundred perfect dresses. Whatever we might have chosen after hours of turning on the rack of the mall with nothing in our size or our color or modest enough for Daddy or bare enough for us, well, it was hanging in our closets with a corsage on the hip. Coyote took us all to Homecoming that year. And there in my room hung something that glittered and threw prisms on the wall, something the color of the ripest pumpkin you ever saw, something cut so low and slit so high it invited the world to love me best. I put it on and my head filled up with champagne like I'd already been sipping flutes for an hour, as if silk could make skin drunk. I slid the corsage on my wrist—cornflowers, and tiny green ears not yet open.

Coyote danced with all the girls and when the music sped up he threw back his head and howled and we all howled with him. When it slowed down he draped himself all over some lonesome thing who never thought she had a chance. The rest of us threw out our arms and danced with what our hands caught—Jessica spent half the night with mathletes kissing her neck and teaching her mnemonics. Everything was dizzy; everything spun. The music came from everywhere at once and the floor shook with our stomping. We were so strong that night, we were full of the year and no one drank the punch because no one needed it, we just moved with Coyote and Coyote moved, too. I flung out my arms and spun away from David Horowitz (pep squad, 100-meter dash), my corn-bound hand finding a new body to carry me into the next song. Guitar strings plinked in some other, distant world beyond the gymnasium and I opened my eyes to see Sarah Jane in my arms, her dress a perfect, icy white spill of froth and jewels, her eyes made up black and severe, to contrast, her lips a generous rose-colored smile. She smelled like musk and honeysuckle. She smelled like Coyote. I danced with her and she put her head on my breast; I felt her waist in my grasp, the slight weight of her, the chess queen, the queen of horses and jazz and grade point averages and pyramids and backflips, Juliet twice, thrice, a hundred times over. She ran her hand idly up and down my back just as if I were a boy. My vision blurred and the Christmas lights hanging everywhere swam into a soup of Devil red and Devil gold. The queen of the softball team lifted her sunny blond head and kissed me. Her mouth tasted like cherry gum and whiskey. She put her hands in my hair to show me she meant it, and I pulled her in tight—but the song ended and she pulled away, looking surprised and confused, her lipstick dulled, her bright brown eyes wounded, like a deer with sudden shot in her side. She ran to Jessica and Ashley and the three of them to Coyote, hands over their stomachs as though something fluttered there, something as yet unknown and unnamed.

The principal got up to call out the Devil's Court. My man was shaken by all the heavy grinding and spinning and howling that had become the senior class, but he got out his index cards all the same. He adjusted his striped tie and tapped the mic, just like every principal has ever done. And he said a name. And it was mine. A roar picked up around me and hands were shoving me forward and I didn't understand, it was Sarah Jane, it would always be Sarah Jane. But I stood there while Mr. Whitmore, the football coach, put a crown on my head, and I looked out into the throng. Coyote stood there in his tuxedo, the bowtie all undone like a brief black river around his neck, and he winked at me with his flashing hound-eye, and the principal called three more names and they were Jessica and Ashley and Sarah Jane. They stood around me like three fates and Mr. Whitmore put little spangly tiaras on their heads and they looked at me like I had caught a pass in the end zone, Hail Mary and three seconds left on the clock. I stared back and their tiaras were suddenly rings of wheat and apple blossoms and big, heavy oranges like suns, and I could see in their eyes mine wasn't rhinestones any more than it was ice cream. I lifted it down off my head and held it out like a thing alive: a crown of corn, not the Iowa yellow stuff but blue and black, primal corn from before the sun thought fit to rise, with tufts of silver fur sprouting from their tips, and all knotted together with crow feathers and marigolds.

And then it was pink rhinestones in my hands again, and blue zirconium on my Princesses' heads, and the Devil's Court took its place, and if you have to ask who was King, you haven't been listening.

After that, the game skipped by like a movie of itself. Bobby just couldn't keep that ball in his hands. You could see it on his face, how the ball had betrayed him, gone over to a bad boy with a leather jacket and no truck at all. You could see him re-sorting colleges in his head. It just about broke your heart. But we won 24-7, and Coyote led Bobby Zhao off the field with a *sorry-buddy* and a *one-game-don't-mean-a-thing*, and before I drove off to the afterparty I saw them under the bleachers, foreheads pressed together, each clutching at the other's skin like they wanted to climb inside, and they were beautiful like that, down there underneath the world, their helmets lying at their feet like old crowns.

Nothing could stop us then. The Westbrook Ravens, the Bella Vista Possums, the Ashland Gators. Line them up and watch them fall. It wasn't even a question.

I suppose we learned trig, or Melville, or earth science. I suppose we took exams. I suppose we had parents, too, but I'll be damned if any of that seemed to make the tiniest impression on any one of us that year. We lived in an unbreakable bubble where nothing mattered. We lived in a snowglobe, only the sun was always shining and we were always winning and yeah, you could get grounded for faceplanting your biology midterm or pulled over for speeding or worse for snorting whatever green fairy dust Coyote found for you, but nothing really *happened*. You came down to the lake like always the next night. After the Ravens game, Greg Knight (running back, #46) and Johnny Thompson (cornerback, #22) crashed their cars into each other after drinking half a sip of something Coyote whipped up in an acorn cap, yelling *chicken* out the window the whole time like it was 1950 and some girl would be waving her handkerchief at the finish line. But instead there was a squeal of engine humping up on engine and the dead crunch of the front ends smacking together and the long blare of Greg's face leaning on his horn.

But even then, they just got up and walked away, arm in arm and Coyote suddenly between them, *oh-my-godding* and *let's-do-that-again-ing*. The next day their Camrys pulled up to the parking lot like it was no big deal. Nothing could touch us.

All eyes were on the Thunderbirds.

Now, the Thunderbirds didn't have a Bobby Zhao. No star player to come back and play celebrity alumnus in ten years with a Super Bowl ring on his finger. A Thunderbird was part of a machine, a part that could be swapped out for a hot new freshman no problem, no resentment. They moved as one, thought as one, they were a flock, always pointed in the same direction. That was how they'd won six state championships; that was how they'd sent three quarterbacks to the NFL in the last decade. There was no one to hate—just a single massive Thunderbird darkening our little sky.

Coyote's girls began to show by Christmas.

Sarah Jane, whatever the crown might have said at Homecoming, was queen of the unwed mothers, too. Her belly swelled just slightly bigger than the others—but then none of them got very big. None of them slowed down. Sarah Jane was turning a flip-into somersault off the pyramid in her sixth month with no trouble. They would all lay around the sidelines together painting their stomachs (Devil red and Devil gold) and trying on names for size. No point in getting angry; no point in fighting for position. The tribe was the tribe and the tribe was all of us and a tribe has to look after its young. The defensive line had a whole rotating system for bringing them chocolate milk in the middle of the night.

They were strong and tan and lean and I had even money on them all giving birth to puppies.

I didn't get pregnant. But then, I wouldn't. I told him, and he listened. Rabbit and Coyote, they do each other favors, when they can.

A plan hatched itself: steal their mascot. An old fashioned sort of thing, like playing chicken with cars. Coyote plays it old school. Into Springfield High in the middle of the night, out with Marmalade, a stuffed, moth-eaten African Grey parrot from some old biology teacher's collection that a bright soul had long ago decided could stand in for a Thunderbird.

We drove out to Springfield, two hours and change, me and Coyote and Jimmy Moser and Mike Halloran and Josh Vick and Sarah Jane and Jessica and Ashley, all crammed into my truck, front and back. Coyote put something with a beat on the radio and slugged back some off-brand crap that probably turned to Scotland's peaty finest when it hit his tongue. Jimmy was trying to talk Ashley into making out with him in the back while the night wind whipped through their hair and fireflies flashed by, even though it was January. Ashley didn't mind too much, even less when everyone wanted to touch her stomach and feel the baby move. She blushed like a primrose and even her belly button went pink.

Nobody's very quiet when sneaking into a gym. Your feet squeak on the basketball court and everyone giggles like a joke got told even when none did and we had Coyote's hissing *drink up drink up* and squeezing my hand like he can't hold the excitement in. We saw Marmalade center court on a parade float, all ready to ship over to the big designated-neutral-ground stadium for halftime. Big yellow and white crepe flowers drooped everywhere, around the shore of a bright blue construction paper sea. Marmalade's green wings spread out majestically, and in his talons he held a huge orange papier-mâché ball ringed with aluminum foil rays dipped in gold glitter. Thunderbird made this world, and Thunderbird gets to rule it.

Coyote got this look on his face and the moment I saw it I knew I wouldn't let him get there first. I took off running, my sneakers screeching, everyone hollering *Bunny!* after me and Coyote scrappling up behind me, closing the distance, racing to the sun. *I'm faster, I'm always faster.* Sometimes he gets it and sometimes I get it but it's nothing we haven't done before and this time it's mine.

And I leapt onto the float without disturbing the paper sea and reached up, straining, and finally just going for it. I'm a tall girl, see how high I jump. The sun came down in my arms, still warm from the gym lights and the after-hours HVAC. The Thunderbird came with it, all red cheeks and Crayola-green wingspan and I looked down to see Coyote grinning up at me. He'd let me take it, if I wanted it. He'd let me wear it like a crown. But after a second of enjoying its weight, the deliciousness of its theft, I passed it down to him. It was his year. He'd earned it.

We drove home through the January stars with the sun in the bed of my truck and three pregnant girls touching it with one hand each, holding it down, holding it still, holding it together.

On game day we stabbed it with the Devil's pitchfork and paraded our float around the stadium like conquering heroes. Like cowboys. Marmalade looked vaguely sad. By then Coyote was cleaning off blood in the locker room, getting ready for the second half, shaken, no girls around him and no steroid needles blossoming up from his friendly palm like a bouquet of peonies.

The first half of the championship game hit us like a boulder falling from the sky. The Thunderbirds didn't play for flash, but for short, sharp gains and an inexorable progression toward the end-zone. They didn't cheer when they scored. They nodded to their coach and regrouped. They caught the flawless, seraphic passes Coyote fired off; they engulfed him when he tried to run as he'd always done. Our stands started out raucous and screaming and jumping up and down, cheering on our visibly pregnant cheerleading squad despite horrified protests form the Springfield side. *Don't you listen, Sarah Jane baby!* yelled Mr. Bollard. *You look perfect!* And she did, fists in the air, ponytail swinging.

Halftime stood 14-7 Thunderbirds.

I slipped into the locker room—by that time the place had become Devil central, girls and boys and players and cheerleaders and second chair marching band kids who weren't needed til post-game all piled in togeth-er. Some of them giving pep talks which I did not listen to, some of them bandaging knees, some of them—well. Doing what always needs doing when Coyote's around. Rome never saw a party like a Devil locker room.

I walked right over to my boy and the blood vanished from his face just as soon as he saw me.

"Don't you try to look pretty for me," I said.

"Aw, Bunny, but you always look so nice for me."

I sat in his lap. He tucked his fingers between my thighs—where I clamped them, safe and still. "What's going on out there?"

Coyote drank his water down. "Don't you worry, Bunny Rabbit. It has to go like this, or they won't feel like they really won. Ain't no good game since the first game that didn't look lost at half time. It's how the story goes. Can't hold a game without it. The old fire just won't come. If I just let that old Bird lose like it has to, well, everyone would get happy after, but they'd think it was pre-destined all along, no work went into it. You gotta make the story for them, so that when the game is done they'll just . . ." Coyote smiled and his teeth gleamed. "Well, they'll lose their minds I won it so good."

Coyote kissed me and bit my lip with those gleaming teeth. Blood came up and in our mouths it turned to fire. We drank it down and he ran out on that field, Devil red and Devil gold, and he ran like if he kept running he could escape the last thousand years. He ran like the field was his country. He ran like his bride was on the other end of all that grass and I guess she was. I guess we all were. Coyote gave the cherry to Justin Oster, who caught this pass that looked for all the world like the ball might have made it all the way to the Pacific if nobody stood in its way. But Justin did, and he caught it tight and perfect and the stadium shook with Devil pride.

34-14. Rings all around, as if they'd all married the state herself.

That night, we had a big bonfire down by the lake. Neutral ground was barely forty-five minutes out of town, and no one got home tired and ready to sleep a good night and rise to a work ethic in the morning.

I remember we used to say *down-by-the-lake* like it was a city, like it was an address. I guess it was, the way all those cars would gather like crows, pick-ups and Camaros and Jeeps, noses pointing in, a metal wall against the world. The willows snapped their green whips at the moon and the flames licked up Devil red and Devil gold. We built the night without thinking about it, without telling anyone it was going to happen, without making plans. Everyone knew to be there; no one was late.

Get any group of high school kids together and you pretty much have the building blocks of civilization. The Eagle Scout boys made an architecturally perfect bonfire. 4-H-ers threw in grub, chips and burgers and dogs and Twix and Starburst. The drama kids came bearing tunes, their tooth-white iPods stuffed into speaker cradles like black mouths. The rich kids brought booze from a dozen walnut cabinets—and Coyote taught them how to spot the good stuff. Meat and fire and music and liquor—that's all it's ever been. Sarah Jane started dancing up to the flames with a bottle of one-hundred-year-old cognac in her hand, holding it by the neck, moving her hips, her gorgeously round belly, her long corn-colored hair brushing faces as she spun by, the smell of her expensive and hot. Jessica and Ashley ran up to her and the three of them swayed and sang and stamped, their arms slung low around each other, their heads pressed together like three graces. Sarah Jane poured her daddy's cognac over Ashley's breasts and caught the golden stuff spilling off in her sparkly pink mouth and Ashley laughed so high and sweet and that was it—everyone started dancing and howling and jumping and Coyote was there in the middle of it all, arching his back and keeping the beat, slapping his big thighs, throwing the game ball from boy to girl to boy to girl, like it was magic, like it was just ours, the sun of our world arcing from hand to hand to hand.

I caught it and Coyote kissed me. I threw it to Haley Collins from English class and Nick Dristol (left tackle, #19) caught me up in his arms. I don't even know what song was playing. The night was so loud in my ears. I could see it happening and it scared me but I couldn't stop it and didn't want to. Everything was falling apart and coming together and we'd won the game, Bunny no less than Coyote, and boyfriend never fooled me for a minute, never could.

I could hear Sarah Jane laughing and I saw Jessica kissing her and Greg Knight both, one to the other like she was counting the kisses to make it all fair. She tipped up that caramel-colored bottle and Nick started to say something but I shushed him. *Coyote's cognac's never gonna hurt that baby.* Every tailgate hung open, no bottle ever seemed to empty and even though it was January the air was so warm, the crisp red and yellow leaves drifting over us all, no one sorry, no one ashamed, no one chess club or physics club or cheer squad or baseball team, just tangled up together inside our barricade of cars.

Sarah danced up to me and took a swallow without taking her eyes from mine. She grabbed me roughly by the neck and into a kiss, passing the cognac to me and oh, it tasted like a pass thrown all the way to the sea, and she wrapped me up in her arms like she was trying to make up Homecoming to me, to say: *I'm better now, I'm braver now, doesn't this feel like the end of everything and we have to get it while we can?* I could feel her stomach pressing on mine, big and insistent and hard, and as she ripped my shirt open I felt her child move inside her. We broke and her breasts shone naked in the bonfire-light—mine too, I suppose. Between us a cornstalk grew fast and sure, shooting up out of the ground like it had an appointment with the sky, then a second and a third. That same old blue corn, midnight corn, first corn. All around the fire the earth was bellowing out pumpkins and blackberries and state fair tomatoes and big blousy squash flowers, wheat and watermelons and apple trees already broken with the weight of fruit. The dead winter trees exploded into green, the graduating class fell into the rows of vegetables and fruit and thrashed together like wolves, like bears, like devils. Fireflies turned the air into an emerald necklace and Sarah Jane grabbed Coyote's hand which was a paw which was a hand and screamed. Didn't matter—everyone was screaming, and the music quivered the darkness and Sarah's baby beat at the drum of her belly, demanding to be let out into the pumpkins and the blue, blue corn, demanding to meets its daddy.

All the girls screamed. Even the ones only a month or two gone, clutching their stomachs and crying, all of them except me, Bunny Rabbit, the watcher, the queen of coming home. The melons split open in an eruption of pale green and pink pulp; the squashes cracked so loud I put my hands (which were paws which were hands) over my ears, and the babies came like harvest, like forty-five souls running after a bright ball in the sky.

Some of us, after a long night of vodka tonics and retro music and pretending there was anything else to talk about, huddle together around a table at the ten year and get into it. How Mr. Bollard was never the same and ended up hanging himself in a hotel room after almost a decade of straight losses. How they all dragged themselves home and suddenly had parents again, the furious kind, and failed SATs and livers like punching bags. How no one went down to the lake anymore and Bobby Zhao went to college out of state and isn't he on some team out east now? Yeah. Yeah. But his father lost the restaurants and now the southland has no king. But the gym ceiling caved in after the rains and killed a kid. But most of them could just never understand why their essays used to just be perfect and they never had hangovers and they looked amazing all the time and sex was so easy that year but never since, no matter how much shit went up their nose or how they cheated and fought and drank because they didn't mean it like they had back when, no matter how many people they brought home hoping just for a second it would be like it was then, when Coyote made their world. They had this feeling, just for a minute—didn't I feel it too? That everything could be different. And then it was the same forever, the corn stayed yellow and they stayed a bunch of white kids with scars where their cars crashed and fists struck and babies were born. The lake went dry and the scoreboard went dark.

Coyote leaves a hole when he goes. He danced on this town till it broke. That's the trick, and everyone falls for it.

But they all had kids, didn't they? Are they remembering that wrong? What happened to them all?

Memory is funny—only Sarah Jane (real estate, Rotary, Wednesday Night Book Club) can really remember her baby. Everyone just remembers the corn and the feeling of running, running so fast, the whole pack of us, against the rural Devil gold sunset. I call that a kindness. (*Why me?* Sarah asks her gin. *You were the queen*, I say. *That was you. Only for a minute*.) *It was good, wasn't it*, they all want to say. When we were all together. When we were a country, and Coyote taught us how to grow such strange things.

Why did I stick around, they all want to know. When he took off, why didn't I go, too? Weren't we two of a kind? Weren't we always conspiring?

Coyote wins the big game, I say. I get the afterparty.

This is what I don't tell them.

I woke up before anyone the morning after the championships. Everyone had passed out where they stood, laying everywhere like a bomb had gone off. No corn, no pumpkins, no watermelons. Just that cold lake morning fog. I woke up because my pick-up's engine fired off in the gloam, and I know that sound like my mama's crying. I jogged over to my car but it was already going, bouncing slowly down the dirt road with nobody driving. In the back, Coyote sat laughing, surrounded by kids, maybe eight or ten years old, all of them looking just like him, all of them in leather jackets and hangdog grins, their black hair blowing back in the breeze. Coyote looked at me and raised a hand. See you again. After all, it's nothing we haven't done before.

Coyote handed a football to one of his daughters. She lifted it into the air, her form perfect, trying out her new strength. She didn't throw it. She held it tight, like it was her heart.

"TRICKSTER"

STEVEN BARNES AND
TANANARIVE DUE

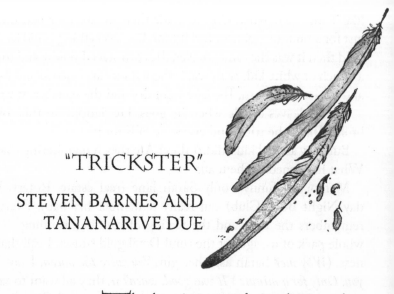

The American came during the time when the rains shunned us; when the grass withered, the drinking pools grew shallow and the Earth revealed its age.

He came in one of the fleet, five-footed Spiders that gleam in the sun. I have painted the day of his arrival on the wall of our sacred cave, where we return once a year to sing new songs to our ancestors. Like my father and his father, I visit Shadow Cave. There, beneath its vast ceiling and beneath the eyes of my dead fathers, I paint the cave walls with pigments of ground clay with eland fat.

My name is Qutb, which means "protects the people." I am an old man now. My head holds my people's story, which I paint on the cave walls. I draw natural things: animals hunted, raindrops fallen upon my face, the eternal walking circle of giraffe and antelope and lion north through what the white men call the Great Rift Valley since before their Great War, and we of the People call home.

It is difficult to draw the Spiders, because these are not of nature: rounded backs like silver tortoises, yet as big as a hut where even six people could sleep without touching. Five legs racing across the plain faster than a cheetah. White men use Spiders in place of their legs, or the boxes with wheels men rode when I was a boy. It is rare to see a white man walking.

But this stranger was not a white man. His face was shaped somewhat like mine, but he had orange-red dusk fire hidden underneath the night in his skin. He stood a full head taller than me, with a runner's body, although our children could outrun him. He wore pieces of glass held by wire over his eyes, and a white shirt beneath a sand-colored coat.

He said his name was Cagen. It sounds like Kaggen. This is the Trickster. The Mantis of our stories, he who loves eland well. It is in Kaggen's honor that I use the fat of his best beloved in Shadow Cave.

He did not speak the People's tongue, a proper language. But he did speak the Swahili, the tongue of those who lived far to the east. I speak that and the tongue of the Kikuyu, who dwell in the great villages and valleys much closer to where People roam, so we were able to understand each other. Cagen's head was filled with the place called America, and he called us his "brothers" because of the night in his skin, but to us he was just another white man. Our children laughed at him and with him.

He offered our children trinkets and sweets, the men tobacco and knife metal, gave my second wife Jappa cloth for a dress. He asked me if I had sons and I said that once I had, but they had gone to the great villages, and I had never seen them again. He said he wanted to learn our stories and knowledge of the plant people. He said his head was empty and he wished knowledge. Empty head! Our children called him Empty Head.

I laughed and he laughed, as if we had made an agreement. He wished knowledge. I wanted to paint Cagen's story, so I said I would teach him.

I watched Cagen for many days from the corner of my eye. After I knew him for a time, I took him to Shadow Cave to see the paintings my fathers and grandfathers had made.

Shadow Cave is at the center of a wheel. My people walk the wheel every few years, moving from place to place for water and game. But the sacred cave is never more than a few days' walk away. Although the entrance is taller than a man, and wide, we crawl when we enter the cave, a sign of respect. We are all children in the sight of the gods.

Once in, light a torch to watch shadows leap to the spiked ceiling. My heart always smiles to see the smooth stones, the empty rock streambed, and most of all the walls covered with endless paintings, some made when men still had tails.

"Ah, you have drawn the War," Cagen said, pointing to my paintings of clouds and lights above a burnt horizon. His words gave me hope he might have a mind after all.

I told him we did not call it "war," that Great War which white men suffered when I was a boy, fifty seasons ago. We called it the time of silent thunder. Thunder you hear with your body, not your ears.

"Not silent!" Cagen said. "Far from silent."

Cagen said that beings from another sun came to this world, with strange, strong machines that made the white man's knowledge useless. The machines destroyed the great villages of the world, some even larger than Dar es Salaam!

"And what stopped these creatures and machines?" I said as I inscribed the words Cagen spoke to me in my head and drew the story on the cave walls the way my father taught me. "Did the whites build their own great machine to fight for them?"

"No one knows," Cagen said, and shrugged his shoulders. "Lots of guesses, but no answers. Some say disease, some that they fought among themselves. We crawled out from under the rubble, and there were these big metal things everywhere. All dead. We pried them open, and studied the machines. We learned from them. The machines changed everything."

"Then they were gifts from the gods," I said. Too often, humans do not give praise to the beings who watch over us.

"That's as good an answer as any," he said.

He told me that the world's chiefs, who ruled the people with what he called *governments*, promised to protect their people from the machines and the sky men—if they were men—who built them. The *governments* traveled as far as the moon to build a great walled village with many guns. Such things are beyond my mind. I look up at the moon and see no village, so perhaps this is a lie.

"But in return for this protection, we've lost our freedom," Cagen said, gazing at the walls of Shadow Cave. His sigh was as heavy as an old man's. "Everything is so peaceful here. Not like out there."

"Are there not sunsets in your land?"

He laughed, but the sound was not happy. "Yes. But things are . . . different now. That's what the history books say." He paused. "When you can find a history book. My father was a history teacher."

"Ah. He held your people's stories?"

Cagen smiled. "Yes. But by the end of his life, men like him had a hard time finding work. Where I come from, too many believe it's better to forget the past."

What would become of a people who forget their stories? Surely even white men have grandfathers and grandmothers who must be remembered.

"I think you tease me," I said to him. "You are a trickster, like Kaggen, your name."

"The Mantis," he said. We had spoken of this before.

I took the torch and moved him down to the other side of the cave, and found an image I knew he would like. It may have been painted by my grandfather's grandfather. It was a half-circle of men driving a giraffe over a cliff. Behind them was Kaggen, the Mantis, mighty arms spread wide.

"The Trickster."

"Yes," I said. "The hunters tricked the giraffe into killing itself. They ate well." I paused. "The men from the stars . . . were they hunters?"

"We never found out why they killed us. Never."

He stared at the painting of the men and the giraffe and the trickster god, as if his heart was close to an understanding too great, or too heavy, for his head. Then we left the cave.

Cagen and I spoke for many days, hours, and then moons. In times of drought, the hunters have less time to sit at an old man's feet, so I enjoyed Cagen's eager eyes, full of wondering. Cagen learned quickly, as if our grandmothers whispered in his ear. Tell him a thing but once, and he could recite it back to you even if you roused him from sleep in the middle of the night.

Among the possessions he brought with him was the small listening machine he called a *radio*. He would play it at night, strange talk and strange music from far away. Our children would try to dance to the music, but they always laughed too hard to dance long.

One afternoon, Cagen toyed with a scraggly red plant with white veins, growing at his feet. Like all things that lived in the earth during that time, the plant thirsted for water. "Is this bloodweed?" he asked.

"Your eyes have grown wiser," I said. "I did not know if you would see it. Tell me what you would do with this."

"Strip off the bark," he said. "Boil it to make a paste."

"And?"

"And . . . spread that on wounds to stop the blood."

"After the wounds have been washed. After."

We paused when we heard a whistling sound. Something glided through the sky, It looked like a wheels made of silver-blue metal. As it flew in front of .a cloud, it turned white. Against the blue sky a moment later, it turned blue again. Faintly, I could see snake-like tendrils trailing behind it.

Cagen flinched.

"Why should you fear?" I said. "Rejoice. Now they are the white man's machines."

"I'm not a white man," he said.

"You are white on the inside," I said, sorry to insult him so. He did not answer the insult, so perhaps he had not heard.

"They were left behind after the war," Cagen said quietly. "They could make their own spare parts, and we used those parts to change our world. We started out using them. Now, I think, they're using us."

"What do you mean?" I asked, hoping to learn something new for my cave from this strange young man.

He scratched his head. "Sometimes I think that our own government is turning into a bigger threat than the aliens ever were."

"Why don't you go to your elders and tell them that they are wrong?"

"I don't even know who our leaders are anymore."

"Your villages are so large that you don't know your grandmothers and fathers?"

Cagen did not answer. He seemed terribly tired.

You go home soon," I said to Cagen one night as we watched the moon. It was almost full. "I think you don't want to go."

Cagen sighed. Then his eyes brightened. "Can we go to Modimo's Hand before I leave?"

Modimo is the Big God, the one who made all the others, who in turn made the mountains and clouds and animals and men. The place we call Modimo's Hand is a clearing surrounded by four oblong stones jutting from the ground, two days' walk south from where our people camped. It is sacred to all the People, and every two seasons all of the families scattered across the savannah meet there to trade and make marriages. It is a place of power.

I had spoken to him of Modimo's Hand, how my own father had there given me my secret name, how I had met my first wife there, Nela of the bright eyes, who gave me two sons and a daughter before the fever took her.

Many times Cagen had asked me to take him. Always I had said "some other time." We had no more time. I said yes.

"We pack food for four days," I said, "It will be good to have this last time together."

So we walked, out south across the grasslands. We would have seemed a strange sight, this black white man with his rifle, and an old man half his size, carrying the spear of his fathers. My bones groaned much of the time, as they often do now, but Cagen's spirited walking carried my heart with him. We walked and talked, and at night, watched the stars.

"You say they are flaming gas," I said, poking at the fire. "My grandfather said they were the eyes of the dead and the unborn."

He chuckled. "I think I like your story better."

"Mine does not explain all things."

"Neither does mine."

Far up in the clouds, another of those odd metal machines moved silently across the sky.

They flew. They walked. They changed color and shape like chameleon lizards. I wondered who the sky men had been, who came to destroy and kill those in the cities, and what bad thing had happened to them to make them worship death.

When I could no longer quiet the ache in my bones with ginger bark, I chose a path that would save us a half day's travel. We climbed over rocks unseen since my boyhood, long forgotten now. Here, the grass thinned, brown sand and rock pushed through the Earth's skin.

I squinted my eyes against a sudden flash of light.

"What is it?" Cagen asked.

Not ten steps away, behind a fever bush, the light sparked again, and then died away.

"I do not know," I said.

The light was *wrong*. Too much brightness where an overhang should have left only shadow. From this odd angle I saw the glimmer again, more brightly.

The rocks shimmered as they might in great heat. This, at a time of day when the sun was too young to be so boastful.

"What in the hell ... ?" Cagen said.

I do not believe in Cagen's *Hell*, and in other times I might have scolded him for speaking of devils so close to our sacred grounds.

We moved rocks away, revealing metal, unblemished but dull with dirt. Limp metal snakes as long as two men, as thick as my body, coiled at its side.

This was a sky machine. Cagen said that this one had come from above, not one built by white men from odd pieces. Begging my grandfather for protection I backed away, making the secret signs he taught me to banish demons. How long had it crouched here in the earth, so near our sacred grounds?

When I backed away, the thing appeared to be *gone*, hiding itself among the rocks with nothing but the shimmering to show where it lay. Two steps to the right ... and it became whole, sitting as if it had been planted there by the gods at the dawn of time. A man could have stood right next to it, and if the sun was not just so, and your eyes attuned just so, it would not be seen.

I backed away. An evil smell hung in the air. Burnt, choking, sudden and strange. It caught in my throat and made me cough.

"This is a bad thing," I said.

Fire seemed to dance on Cagen's face. Instead of stepping away from the thing, he moved toward it like a man walking in sleep. Instead of preparing himself for struggle, his arms lay limp at his sides.

"I've seen them in museums, but never been this close ..." he said. "Jesus Christ."

He took another step toward this metal thing.

The machine was tilted, like a silver tortoise shell lying half against a rock wall. Had it carried something alive, and somehow wounded? Had its own metal arms tunneled into the earth to hide from its enemies, or to find a place to die at peace? Cagen thrust himself against one of the largest rocks. He grunted, strained, and sweat burst out on his forehead. The rock groaned, then slid down the silvery metal and was still.

The machine made a sound like angry bees. Then, a door as high as my shoulder slid up with speed I had never seen, as if the open space it revealed had always been. Inside, blackness stared back at us.

"Hide yourself!" I said to Cagen, but he seemed not to hear me. "Is something still... alive?"

"Fifty years?" he said. "No, it's dead." But his voice as not certain.

We watched the open doorway for several minutes, and no sky creature moved inside the machine, nor any man. The smell from inside was an old smell, like dirt and dust and old dead flesh. The evil burnt smell had faded. The door seemed to invite us closer, like a sweet voice in our ears, although it was silent.

"I'm going to look inside," Cagen said.

I meant to tell him he was being foolish, but I said nothing. Instead, my feet surprised me and trailed behind his on the rocky soil.

Cagen's arm clung to the thing's doorway, perhaps so he could pull away if a sky-beast tried to yank him inside. I stooped beneath his raised arm to see what his eyes beheld, telling myself that even if the machine roasted me, or somehow stole my breath, it would make a worthy last sight to bring my grandfather.

In the next breath, my courage was rewarded.

There, on the floor just inside the doorway, lay something dead. It was not human or animal. Although it was curled like an infant, the creature had once been as tall as a man, or taller. The bones made me think of a wasp mated to a crocodile, and its bones were splintered just as mine would have been. It was good to know these creatures were mortal, not gods. Cagen grabbed my hand, squeezing my own tender bones hard. I knew why: we were men of two legs, born beneath the same sky, who had seen a creature from beyond the sun. It looked like a cousin of our world; a creature that might walk here, or could have walked here long ago, in the old days when gods and giant beasts ruled the earth. I will call this thing a sky lizard.

As I stared at that thing in the ship, Cagen's stories became real in my mind. Now I could see the horror of the flying machines, killing all people with fire. Compared with this sky lizard, even the oddest white man and I were brothers.

"We must leave here," I said.

Cagen held his hand up in a gesture to silence me. This is a great insult to an elder, but I knew his intent.

We waited in a long silence, and no army of demons swarmed from within the machine's belly. Perhaps we would not be killed after all.

Cagen knew the ways of white men who could salvage broken machines and learn to make them fly in the air. The lands I knew were behind me; and in front of me was Cagen's world. One at a time, we bent and entered the door. It remained open behind us, but the walls themselves began to glow, enough pale red light to see everything within.

Walking farther inside this machine was like entering an animal's stomach, all dark red walls, cords and membranes. The floor of the machine held three nests of woven vine-like cables, each nest large enough for a small man.

Cagen stared at the nests. I could hear his mind telling him to lie down. I saw it in his eyes.

"Do not do it," I begged him.

He did not listen to me, and lowered himself into the vine net.

The moment he touched them, the vines moved, fifty years may have been enough to kill men from the stars, but the machine itself still lived

Cagen screamed and struggled, but the vines snatched him backward as a mother might an infant. Cagen's arms were pinned. Metal snakes darted from the ceiling, burrowing into his flesh as he howled and bled. First his arms. Then his legs. His head. He writhed, screaming an English curse. Afraid, we always speak our first tongue.

But the next language he spoke was not English. I had never heard it before. His words no longer sounded as if they came from a human throat.

I grasped Cagen's wrist, and the chair swallowed me too—but not in the way it swallowed Cagen, with tiny spears. The machine swallowed my mind. My thoughts were no longer my own. I felt as if I were drowning in someone else.

All the world shattered into pieces. Great villages burning. The shadows of flying and walking machines plagued the land, as the metal tortoises slaughtered the fleeing. Rivers boiled with blood. Screams and running and endless death.

Above, the pitiless stars.

I screamed prayers, and quickly reached for my medicine pouch. I shook powdered frog skin on Cagen three times, begging the gods to help him. Still, his body convulsed, eyes bulged, hands clutched at the vines. He screamed again.

And bucked.

Then . . .

The machine *rocked.* I lurched and caught myself. . . then realized that the tortoise-shell had heaved in time with Cagen's motion, just a beat late.

I understood: *Cagen* had made the machine move.

I did not know how that could be so, but I had felt the humming beneath my feet from the instant Cagen was trapped in the chair. When he moved, the vibration grew stronger.

The machine was feeding on him. The machine was a hunter, too, like its long-dead master. A dog will hunt with a man, will follow his orders. This thing obeyed like a dog . . . but it was no dog.

I pulled at the cords binding Cagen. One came loose from the back of his head, and the others dislodged as well. I pulled him from the chair. He was babbling as I dragged him from the ship.

The door closed behind us.

I pulled him back only a few steps, but the machine was gone when I glanced behind me. A chameleon. Unless you were very lucky, or unlucky—or the machine wanted you to see it—you would pass by and not notice where it lay. The machine might have been there when I was a boy, but spared me.

I pulled Cagen as far as I could, but the rocks made our journey difficult. He was gasping for breath, eyes wide and staring wildly. I understood: The machine might be chasing us, hiding in the wind.

"Ohhh . . . he finally groaned. "My head." He cursed in English again.

"What happened to you?" I said to Cagen.

"I don't know," he said, and cursed in English again. He brought his knees to his chest and rocked, mumbling to himself. More curses? Prayers?

The vines had entered his arms, but the wounds had already stopped bleeding, as if someone had held fire to them. Strange.

I could not leave him. If the machine came for us, we would die together. But darkness took mercy on us, and when the dawn sun awakened we breathed still.

The next day we began our trip back to the People's camp.

"I think it might be best if we didn't tell anyone about this," Cagen said, limping as he walked. "I can't think of any good that would come of it."

"My people will not understand," I said, although it was my duty to report the discovery to the elders. "It will make them afraid. Fear and drought are too heavy on us to carry at once."

By the time we returned to the camp, we had agreed on silence. Cagen, returning to the white man's world, would say nothing. I would not offer it even to my ancestors on the wall. I am ashamed to admit I was afraid.

A Spider came from the sky for Cagen, driven by a soldier. Air *shooshed* from each of its five legs, sending dust over everything. Most of my people had only seen a Spider once. Now, it was twice. But despite their curiosity, they turned their faces away from the thing, pretending not to see Cagen as he prepared to leave us. It is a great sign of affection—as we say, *My eyes would hurt too much at the sight*. The People live and die together, so we do not have practice saying goodbye.

Except, once in a while, we lose our sons to the great villages. This pained me as much as when my own sons left.

Cagen came to me, and gave me his radio. He shrugged. "Not like there's anything out there for you, but . . ."

I took the gift with tears of gratitude. "You are my friend," I said.

I was brave enough to watch him leave; my eyes were stronger because of what Cagen had seen with me on the rocks. He alone had shared the sight. I could not turn away.

As the Spider flew into the sky, two old women wailed funeral songs. The youngest children cried, chasing behind the Spider's shadow as it glided through the dying grasses.

"Bring him back!" the youngest children screamed to the metal beast, throwing rocks. "Bring Empty Head back!"

Their mothers called to them, clucking. Their fathers laughed and tried to explain that the Spider wasn't going to eat Cagen for dinner.

They were right, and they were wrong.

I do not know much of these man-made Spiders. But the other machine, the one from the stars, in the rocks, had eaten Cagen already.

Warm water from the clouds meant that the drought had finally ended, but the rain gods were no happier with us than the sun gods. The pools stayed muddy. For days, hunger pinched our bellies. The hunters traveled long distances for small game.

Times were bad in the big villages too.

At night, lying beside Jappa, I saw bright lights on the western horizon, like the times I remember from childhood. Silent thunder; thunder you heard with your body not your ears. But my inner eyes, this time, were wiser: I imagined the flying machines swooping in the air, trailing their metal snake-legs behind them. I saw fire shooting from their mouths. When the wind shifted, I thought I could smell burnt flesh.

Had the sky lizards returned to wage another Great War? Or had men turned themselves into sky lizards the way the machine turned into a chameleon against the rocks?

The death that had killed the cities when I was a boy could now come for us, and there was nothing we could do. I feared for my sons, whom I might never see again. For my daughter, with her husband and family a moon's walk to the north.

I feared for my friend Cagen. If he was not dead, I knew he would come to us again, to tell his tales. He would come to paint his wall.

If he was not dead.

I heard the shouting before I saw him. It was nearing dusk, four moons after Cagen left us. Four of the young herders ran in to us, calling for the men. A dozen men went out, were gone until the sun set, and then returned carrying Cagen.

He was half dead with starvation and thirst, and there were cruel wounds on his back and legs, like healed burns. He wore tattered gray pants and shirt, painted with white men's black numbers. We gave him water, meat, and herbs, and heard his story:

He told us he went to the greatest city in the world, Dar es Salaam, to the *un-i-ver-si-ty*, a great school run by elders.

This land around you is a nation, and that nation is called Tanzania. Because past relations have keen so poor between black nations and white, Tanzania and several other nations in this continent called Africa wish to break free of a gov-ern-ment called "United Nations of Earth."

The white nations did not want this to happen, because much of Africa, while poor, is rich with treasures the white nations hold dear. When their petition to separate was brought to court, this UNE retaliated with force. Rebuilt alien war machines rained from the skies, flown by men who had learned to master them. Dar es Salaam was reduced to rubble. Untold thousands of people died in the fires, and thousands more were taken to camps.

The camps were shantytowns surrounded by barbed wire and vicious dogs. I was in one of those camps, but I escaped, came here.

I did not know where else to go.

I took Cagen to my hut, and he slept where my children slept before they were grown. My wife Jappa served him hedgehog and the ant larvae he called "Bushman Rice." Cagen had walked to us out of a bad dream. A man who has walked away from a dream should be an honored guest. Most men who live too long in the dream never return. But Cagen was not as other men.

Over the next days, as Cagen healed, he told me more of how men, not sky lizards, slaughtered other men.

I'm an American citizen, which used to mean something. Not anymore. Because I was a student at the university, I was arrested as an "unaffiliated intellectual" and thrown into a camp. It was a place of hunger and fear . . . and pain. Men and women were beaten and tortured if our captors believed they were lying, or thought we could give them information about Africa's leaders. We lost everything—even the clothes from our backs. We were clothed in prison gray. Criminals, accused of no crime.

And it was in that terrible place, for the first time in my life . . . I fell in love.

As he spoke of love, Cagen gazed toward my wife, who was listening from the folds of the hut so she would not appear to intrude on the talk of men. All women listen—but Jappa is the queen of hiding herself.

Fat, laughing Jappa is the queen of all.

Cagen looked at my wife as if he knew stories that had never been spoken between us. He smiled, and sunlight glowed from his face.

Yes, I found the woman I want. A medical student from Kenya—Chanya. Even her name is music. She is everything to me.

She is the only reason I remember how to smile.

She alone gives me hope there is a God.

Many gods, I corrected him with a laugh. Love for a woman has made many men forget much more than how to count or to thank the gods. There are men who grow insane from a woman. But Cagen was not that kind. She did not bring war to his heart; the woman he had found brought him peace.

We comforted each other as people have since the beginning of time. Without her, I wouldn't have survived. I saw people sit in the corner and will themselves to die. Their families were lost to them, and we had no way to contact them. We knew people were dying when the beatings went too far, and that troops could pull anyone from their beds any time of the day or night. I wanted to die, too.

But Chanya kept my soul alive.

It is dangerous to find love in such a hard place.

"Your heart is strong as well," I said. "Seeds do not grow without fertile soil."

"The mustard seed . . ." he began, like a prayer.

"All seeds need soil. And rain."

We had plenty of rain.

Just not enough shelter, except for each other. But it was all right for a while. All we needed was to clasp each other's hands to get through the day.

But I knew our time together would not last.

Foreigners who were not from Africa were being taken for "questioning," but did not return to report the questions. Whispers began: Foreigners were being sent home, or they were being killed. No one knew which.

I was a foreigner, so I knew that soon this question would be answered.

Someone who worked with the guards whispered to me that they would come for me at dawn. I saw in his eyes then that he was only a desperate young man trying to live, and to protect his family, but he wanted to do good.

I found Chanya, of course. Had the guard not told me, I would not have risked sneaking out of the men's barracks to find her in the women's tent. Any of the women there would have told what I did for extra bread and rice for their children.

That night, I held my beautiful Chanya's hands, looked into her eyes, and told her to find a way to survive.

Find kindness, I told her.
Find mercy.
Give whatever you must.
I made Chanya cry.

And then Cagen wailed like a woman. The children stared: They had never seen a man cry so. So that Cagen would not shame himself, my wife and I took him back into our hut and gave him a bed.

"He has lost his wife," I explained to the children who waited outside. But they did not understand. How could they?

Children have yet to lose anything.

Children have not seen the world's end.

When they came for me, I was on my feet. No fear. No more crying, trembling.

Many of the soldiers were boy-children. They were hopped-up on drugs, full of childlike glee as they beat us or took women to be raped. These boys had chosen to be called Executioners, and they enjoyed their work. Easy to delude children. They themselves were servants of the black stooges who were enriched and controlled by whites in the UNE, and so once more in Africa, black people brutalized their brothers and sisters.

The boy soldiers stood me up in a line of other men and women waiting to die, standing atop a trench that was already lined with corpses. We were that morning's chosen. I wondered if your sky lizards, against whom all mankind had once united, destroyed themselves like this—or was it only man who murdered his brother?

A few of us in line held tightly to our captor's lies that we'd be ransomed home to the U.S., Canada, Saudi Arabia . . . wherever. Once we were in the line, no illusions remained.

Those who were not crying did not meet each other's eyes. We were all lost inside ourselves. Even when you die together, you die alone.

The boys had made a counting game of the executions. One boy wearing a general's cap too big for his head raised a baton and counted "Moja, mbili, tatu!" One, two, three. Three machine guns chattered, and ten bodies crumpled back into the ditch.

They brought the next ten of us forward. I stood there in front of the ditch, smelling the blood and stink behind me, and knew that these men and boys, the ragged line of distant mountains, the smell of dead men's shit in the air . . . that this was what my senses would hold in the last moments of my life.

When I heard the boy count "moja," I began a prayer I knew I would never finish. I heard "mbili."

There was no "tatu."

Before he could speak that word, gunfire exploded all around me. I watched the guards, my executioners, flinch in horror to realize that they were the targets. From around us, hidden behind rocks and in pits covered with cloth and sand, leapt a dozen desperate men and women, all armed, all firing at the guards. Rebels, who had waited at the execution spot, probably avenging loved ones.

The children screamed and ran, dropping their guns.

If the rebels had arrived a breath sooner, the previous ten would not have died.

If the rebels had arrived a breath later, the bullets would have taken me. My nightmare would be over.

The rebels came too late.

The rebels came too soon.

What I did know was that I was still alive. I ran east. I knew where I could find the People, and I came to you.

I was blessed again. I met Sinas, a goatherd whose family camps two days' walk from here. He knew your people, Qutb.

He knew how to bring me home.

A moon after Cagen came to us, white and black soldiers arrived in three Spiders and asked questions about him. They showed us his face on paper; a pho-to-graph.

Cagen hid in my hut, a blanket over his head, but even if they'd caught a glimpse of him, they might not have known who he was. He did not look like the black-skinned white man in the photograph. His hair grew longer, a regal mane. He was learning our ways and language, was dressed as one of us, and he had lost the disgusting fat that whites wear like a second and third skin. We laughed when the soldiers were gone.

Cagen was safe.

But were we?

Soon Cagen built his own hut, but with no wife to share it, it must have been a lonely place. Marriageable girls tried to catch his eyes and gave him secret smiles, but Cagen rejected them with kindness and kept his own company.

I began to teach him again, and his sadness touched me. I taught him things I had withheld from the other men who had come to me, because it would be too much knowledge for an ordinary man to keep.

This is how Cagen, an outsider, became my apprentice. He was more interested in the old stories than my own sons. This went on for moons, and then one night when four of our boys had reached manhood, I performed the Starlight ceremony for them all. I invited Cagen to join.

We walked out into the tall grass, where each man created a circular clearing for himself in the stalks. The boys, and Cagen, each took their *Go*: a handful of cactus and nettle grindings, chewed until it was mush in their mouths, then spit out. This has been the Way for all of time.

Then, they all lay on the ground, in the midst of their circles. The first time passes in silence. Then, they all thrashed and made animal sounds, barking up at the moon and speaking in the unknown language. The *Go* plants take away the human, awaken the animal self. The man who returns from this journey knows his totem animal, and thereby earns a name.

When dawn was nearly upon us, and I knew that each of them had seen their animal selves, I gave them *Return*: a ball of cactus root and a moss that grows only beneath the poison grub plant. I pushed one thumb-sized ball into each of their mouths, so that they would come back to the world.

Cagen rolled over, vomited, and then sprang to his feet. His eyes were alight while the other boys still moaned. Only the strongest warriors wake with fire.

"I saw," Cagen said, an excitement in his voice that I had not heard since his first days among us. "I know what I have to do. We have to go back."

"Go back?"

His fingers dug into my shoulders so strongly that I thought the cactus was still upon him. "What *Go* did to me . . ." His fingers dug into my arms. "Was what the machine did to me. Qutb, you've shown me how I can hook in and stay sane."

I stared. "Your mind is still sleeping."

"No," he said. "My mind is awake, for the first time in my life. My heart. I'm going back, whether you help me or not. But if you love me, you'll help me . . ." He paused, tongue flickering across cracked lips. "Give me *Return*."

We two stared at each other. I knew what he wanted, and why.

At long last, I nodded.

I would take him to Modimo's Hand again.

Although the machine hid from us, we knew where it rested. We would never forget the place; not until our sleep at life's end, when everything is forgotten unless your grandchildren call your name and sing you stories.

We stood just outside the metal tortoiseshell, and I reached into my medicine bag to pull out the ball of mushrooms and moss called *Return*.

"I give you this, and you take it of your own free will," I said. I did not want to give him false promises. "I cannot protect you, but perhaps our gods can."

Cagen took the ball. As he chewed, we sat outside the machine, in its wavering shadow. Within minutes, Cagen began to sway. When he stood and walked, his step was unsteady. I almost reached to help stand him upright, but I did not move. Like all men, Cagen had to learn to walk by himself.

Cagen did not look at me. Instead, his eyes saw only the ship's open door. He crawled inside.

I thought of my wife waiting. My cave, and the unfinished pictures.

Cursing myself for a fool, I climbed into the machine behind Cagen. The door closed as soon as my foot was inside, leaving no time to consult the gods. No time for wiser thinking.

I stared at the floor beneath my weathered, cracked, sandaled feet as I stood in that machine, to be certain I was really there.

Cagen did not hesitate before he lay in the net. He flinched, but did not scream when the metal snakes chewed into his flesh, into the back of his skull.

He closed his eyes and cried out, his lips curled.

And he waited.

Cagen jerked his body forward slightly, and the machine lurched like a waking snail. Cagen's eyes remained closed, as if he were sleeping, but his lips curled in the coldest smile I have ever seen.

A great humming sound surrounded us, like a swarm of bees large enough to cover the clouds.

Lurching again. I heard rocks slide off the metal shell. Felt the machine rise up beneath me. I sat on the floor between coils—I would not lie in a net, no!

The machine tilted left and then right. Then leveled.

Then the floor of the machine vanished from sight. I saw the rocks shadowed beneath us. The humming quieted. The rocks fell away from our feet. We rose up.

I stood on the sky, and I from there I saw the hunger in Cagen.

Cagen hungered for love. But more, he hungered for the kill.

And as the machine flew, I am not ashamed to say that I was afraid. I could feel the floor but not see it. I was looking down on the ground far below us, as high as birds fly, my stomach flipping all the while because it thought I was falling from a great height. It took all my strength not to spit up like an infant.

I sat on the floor between the coils and chanted.

The machine flew and flew. We entered a cloud, and all about us was whiteness.

I had sat in a cloud! This was a story my grandfather would love to hear.

Cagen's eyes were wide, and filled with blood and fear, but the machine flew on.

And then it came down near a great nest of barbed fences. The machine brought us to rest on the earth softly; this time, I did not sway from side to side.

The door suddenly opened, and I knew it was my time to get out. I tried to hold Cagen's gaze, but his eyes were sightless as they stared out from the head-piece of twisted metal vines.

I left the machine, and the door sealed Cagen inside.

Outside, for the first time, I saw the machine standing, alive and terrible. Standing high on three unfolded legs, with two snakes reared up to make bent arms, the machine looked less like the Spiders and more like a mantis. The Trickster, Kaggen. Mantis, who aided the People since the People came onto the Earth.

The Mantis took long steps toward the webs of fences. Behind the fences, enough people to fill many villages stared and screamed. When they ran in a frenzy, I could almost hear the bones breaking as the weak and small were trampled by those who were quicker, and more able. Such is always the way.

Soldiers screamed as well, but with better cause: A river of fire shot from the Mantis's mouth, and snakes of fire wove themselves through the lines of soldiers, touching one and then the next. In an instant, a dozen armed men died. As they did, the machine's skin rippled. Cagen's face appeared, an unimaginable size, twisted with pain and thoughts I could never dream. It was a horror, but still the face of my friend. The eyes were vast and empty. His mind was gone. Cagen's insane face howled, and the metal disk belched fire once again.

The scream of an alarm filled the air. Cagen slaughtered those men, so that I had to turn my eyes. With the guards dead or fleeing, the prisoners tore the fences and fled in every direction.

I think I saw the woman at the same moment Cagen did.

How did I know she was the one?

Because where so many others were running away, this woman stood watching the machine despite her fear. It towered above her like a walking god, but she did not waver. She looked up into the face, and knew what he was.

She jumped as if waking from a dream and screamed. She stood in a corner against walls made of brick, afraid to run. Suddenly, a soldier ran to the woman. He was a young man, with a hunter's strong body, and a good face. Screaming in Kikuyu, he howled up at the machine, putting his own body between it and the woman. All the while he screamed at the machine, tears watered his face. He believed he would die for her.

The machine paused, and Cagen's eyes—the things that looked like Cagen's eyes—blinked. Its legs folded, so that its face came closer to the woman.

She pushed the soldier back, came to stand between the soldier and Cagen. She spoke up to him, but I could not hear her words. She seemed strong and beautiful.

I finally made out one word. "No," she kept saying. But instead of screaming like the soldier, she spoke as gently as if he were standing against her ear. "No." And then I made out another word. "Cagen. No. No. No."

She knew Cagen. And she loved another.

The machine sank to its knees. He saw what I saw: his woman had survived, as he had begged her to. But in doing so, she had lost her heart for him.

Cagen did not have time to grieve for his woman. A second machine approached.

This one was like Cagen's, not like the little Spiders that carry men across the grass and through the sky. It was a metal disk, and then a white man's face appeared across the curve of the shell. The white man looked . . . twisted. The muscles in his face strained. The eyes inhuman with bloodlust. Whatever the machine had done to this man, I prayed that Cagen could resist.

The two machines circled like angry baboons. Guards and prisoners alike fled as the two machines came to grips, like our men's dances when they are inviting one another to wrestle.

As their snake-arms entwined, their metal skins glowed, and the air around them sizzled with their energies. I fled, knowing that this sight was not for mortal eyes. It was the battle of gods, something that no man should witness.

Before I ran, I saw Cagen's woman and the guard flee with their hands clasped.

It took me ten days to return to the People. After a time, when I was ready to see that day again in my memories, I told my people what I had done, and seen.

We were in danger, and we knew we must move on and find a lonelier place to camp. We could afford talk of nothing else. The days were long and hard.

Some nights, I heard distant explosions, or the sounds of gunfire. Sometimes, screams drifted in the wind.

And then one day, the Mantis appeared.

It stumbled as it walked. At first, I believed I had not yet shaken sleep from my eyes. Many nights, I had dreamed of Cagen's return. Sometimes, in my dreams, he was a friend. In others, he brought fiery death to my people. After all, as everyone knows, a Mantis will sometimes eat its young.

The machine I saw that day was not like the one that came in my dreams. It moved as if it was confused. The machine rocked, stopping.

Suddenly, liquid fire spat out. A goat bleated, eaten by flames. Boiling blood and steam filled the air. My people hid themselves, terrified. Had my nightmare come true?

It was Cagen. I could not see his face on the machine the way I once had, but I knew. So afraid I could barely walk, I went out to the machine.

The metal curve of the machine shifted, and finally Cagen showed himself to me. And then it looked like me, Qutb. He made me look older than I think of myself, but it was me. Then it was a metal disk again.

It sank to the sand. And opened.

Cagen crawled out, his naked body covered with fresh scars. He looked thinner than the frailest of us, as if he had not eaten in at least a moon.

He crawled to me, and rested his cheek upon my sandaled foot.

We dragged the machine to Shadow Cave. Grass ropes and men and boys pulling for three days. There, deep within the rocks, it will never be found. The ancestors stand watch over it for us.

We use Cagen's listening machine, and I hear men talking in Swahili and Kikuyu about the strange events. They say the slaughter in Dar es

Salaam, in this place around us Cagen called Tanzania, was stopped by a machine. The machine is talked about again and again. It did not rest after Dar es Salaam, fighting in other places whose names I had never heard. Again and again, I hear them give thanks to the unknown hero.

I smile as I listen. And I cry an old man's tears of gratitude.

After the first nights, we moved Cagen to a hut outside the camp so he would not frighten the children with his screams. I do not know what he sees and hears. I think he dreams of the spaces between the stars.

I never fully understood this American with brown skin, and now he does not understand himself. He stares into the night with sightless eyes. He cannot feed himself. But we drum for him, and feed him herbs, and walk with him, and slowly, he returns.

And I know that if the soldiers ever come to hurt us, he will remember who he is. He will remember what the gods made him and why they gave him to us, and to all men who only wish to walk in freedom. I remember praying that we could stay away from the madness that came from beyond the sun. Or that if it came to us, as it had to Dar es Salaam, there would be a way to survive as we have survived droughts. Then I saw the true madness: not from the sky lizards, but from other men. And prayed ever harder.

The gods heard. They sent us Kaggen, the Trickster. And as Trickster, he came masked as a student, that he might reveal himself as teacher. He is Cagen, my friend. When he is healed, I may ask him if he will take my name. He has no father. It would be good.

My name is Qutb, which means "Protector of the People." The name is more true to Cagen.

A hero, who stands between the People and the sky.

"OUR TALONS CAN CRUSH GALAXIES"

BROOKE BOLANDER

This is not the story of how he killed me, thank fuck.

You want that kind of horseshit, you don't have to look far; half of modern human media revolves around it, lovingly detailed descriptions of sobbing women violated, victimized, left for the loam to cradle. Rippers, rapists, stalkers, serial killers. Real or imagined, their names get printed ten feet high on movie marquees and subway ads, the dead convenient narrative rungs for villains to climb. Heroes get names; killers get names; victims get close-ups of their opened ribcages mid-autopsy, the bloodied stumps where their wings once attached, baffled coroners making baffled phone calls to even more baffled curators at local museums. They get dissected, they get discussed, but they don't get names or stories the audience remembers.

So, no. You don't get a description of how he surprised me, where he did it, who may have fucked him up when he was a boy to lead to such horrors (no one), or the increasingly unhinged behavior the cops had previously filed away as the mostly harmless eccentricities of a nice young man from a good family. No fighting in the woods, no blood under the fingernails, no rivers or locked trunks or calling cards in the throat. It was dark and it was bad and I called for my sisters in a language dead when the lion-brides of Babylon still padded outside the city gates. There. That's all you get, and that's me being generous. You're fuckin' welcome.

However, here is what I *will* tell you. I'll be quick.

He did not know what I was until after. He felt no regret or curiosity, because he should have been drowned at birth. I was nothing but a commodity to him before, and nothing but an anomaly to him after.

My copper feathers cut his fingertips and palms as he pared my wings away.

I was playing at being mortal this century because I love cigarettes and shawarma, and it's easier to order shawarma if your piercing shriek doesn't drive the delivery boy mad. Mortality is fun in small doses. It's very authentic, very down-in-the-dirt nitty-gritty. There are lullabies and lily pads and summer rainstorms and hardly anyone ever tries to cut your head off out of some moronic heroic obligation to the gods. If you want to sit on your ass and read a book, nobody judges you. Also, shawarma.

My spirit was already fled before the deed was done, back to the Nest, back to the Egg. My sisters clucked and cooed and gently scolded. They incubated me with their great feathery bottoms as they had many times before, as I had done many times before for them. Sisters have to look out for one another. We're all we've got, and forever is a long, slow slog without love.

I hatched anew. I flapped my wings and hurricanes flattened cities in six different realities. I was a tee-ninsy bit motherfuckin' pissed, maybe.

I may have cried. You don't get to know that either, though.

We swept back onto the mortal plane with a sound of a 1967 Mercury Cougar roaring to life on an empty country road, one sister in the front seat and three in the back and me at the wheel with a cigarette clenched between my pointed teeth. You can fit a lot of wingspan in those old cars, provided you know how to fold reality the right way.

It's easy to get lost on those backroads, but my old wings called to us from his attic. We did not get lost.

He was alone when we pulled into his driveway, gravel crunching beneath our wheels like bone. He had a gun. He bolted his doors. The tumblers turned for us; we took his gun.

Did *he* cry? Oh yeah. Like a fuckin' baby.

I didn't know what you were, he said. I didn't know. I just wanted to get your attention, and you wouldn't even look at me. I tried everything.

Well, kid, I says, putting my cigarette out on his family's floral carpet, you've sure as hell got it now.

Our talons can crush galaxies. Our songs give black holes nightmares. The edges of our feathers fracture moonlight into silver spiderwebs and universes into parallels. Did we take him apart? *C'mon*. Don't ask stupid questions.

Did we kill him? Ehh. In a manner of speaking. In another manner of speaking, his matter is speaking across a large swathe of space and time, begging for an ending to his smeared roadkill existence that never quite reaches the rest stop. Semantics, right? I don't care to quibble or think about it anymore than I have to.

Anyway. Like I said way back at the start, this is not the story of how he killed me. It's the story of how a freak tornado wrecked a single solitary home and disappeared a promising young man from a good family, leaving a mystery for the locals to scratch their heads over for the next twenty years. It's the story of how a Jane Doe showed up in the nearby morgue with what looked like wing stubs sticking out of her back, never to be claimed or named. It's the story of how my sisters and I acquired a 1967 Mercury Cougar we still go cruising in occasionally when we're on the mortal side of the pike.

You may not remember my name, seeing as how I don't have one you could pronounce or comprehend. The important thing is always the stories—which ones get told, which ones get co-opted, which ones get left in a ditch, overlooked and neglected. This is my story, not his. It belongs to me and is mine alone. I will sing it from the last withered tree on the last star-blasted planet when entropy has wound down all the worlds and all the wheres, and nothing is left but faded candy wrappers. My sisters and I will sing it—all at once, all together, a sound like a righteous scream from all the forgotten, talked-over throats in Eternity's halls—and it will be the last story in all of Creation before the lights finally blink out and the shutters go *bang*.

"A MEMORY OF WIND"

RACHEL SWIRSKY

After Helen and her lover Paris fled to Troy, her husband King Menelaus called his allies to war. Under the leadership of King Agamemnon, the allies met in the harbor at Aulis. They prepared to sail for Troy, but they could not depart, for there was no wind.

Kings Agamemnon, Menelaus, and Odysseus consulted with Calchas, a priest of Artemis, who revealed that the angered goddess was balking their departure. The kings asked Calchas how they might convince Artemis to grant them a wind. He answered that she would only relent after King Agamemnon brought his eldest daughter, Iphigenia, to Aulis and sacrificed her to the goddess.

I began turning into wind the moment that you promised me to Artemis.

Before I woke, I lost the flavor of rancid oil and the shade of green that flushes new leaves. They slipped from me, and became gentle breezes that would later weave themselves into the strength of my gale. Between the first and second beats of my lashes, I also lost the grunt of goats being led to slaughter, and the roughness of wool against calloused fingertips, and the scent of figs simmering in honey wine.

Around me, the other palace girls slept fitfully, tossing and grumbling through the dry summer heat. I stumbled to my feet and fled down the corridor, my footsteps falling smooth against the cool, painted clay. As I walked, the sensation of the floor blew away from me, too. It was as if I stood on nothing.

I forgot the way to my mother's rooms. I decided to visit Orestes instead. I also forgot how to find him. I paced bright corridors, searching. A male servant saw me, and woke a male slave, who woke a female slave, who roused herself and approached me, bleary-eyed, mumbling. "What's wrong, Lady Iphigenia? What do you require?"

I had no answers.

I have no answers for you either, father.

I imagine what you did on that night when I paced the palace corridors, my perceptions vanishing like stars winking out of the night sky. You presided over the war council in Aulis. I imagine you standing with the staff of office heavy in your hands—heavy with wood, heavy with burdens.

Calchas, priest of Artemis, bowed before you and the other kings. "I have prayed long and hard," he said. "The goddess is angry with you, Agamemnon. She will not allow the wind to take your ships to Troy until you have made amends."

I imagine that the staff of office began to feel even heavier in your hands. You looked between your brother, Menelaus, and the sly Odysseus. Both watched you with cold, expressionless faces. They wanted war. You had become an obstacle to their desires.

"What have I done?" you asked Calchas. "What does the goddess want?"

The priest smiled.

What would a goddess want? What else but virgin blood on her altar? One daughter's life for the wind that would allow you to launch a fleet that could kill thousands. A child for a war.

Odysseus and Menelaus fixed you with hungry gazes. Their appetite for battle hollowed the souls from their eyes as starvation will hollow a man's cheeks. Implicit threats flickered in the torchlight. Do as the priest says, or we'll take the troops we've gathered to battle Troy and march on Mycenae instead. Sacrifice your daughter or sacrifice your kingdom.

Menelaus took an amphora of rich red wine and poured a measure for each of you. A drink; a vow. Menelaus drank rapidly, red droplets spilling like blood through the thicket of his beard. Odysseus savored slow, languorous sips, his canny eyes intent on your face.

You held your golden rhyton at arm's length, peering into redness as dark as my condemned blood. I can only imagine what you felt. Maybe you began to waver. Maybe you thought of my eyes looking up at you, and of the wedding I would never have, and the children I would never bear. But whatever thoughts I may imagine in your mind, I only know the truth of your actions. You did not dash the staff of office across your knee and hurl away its broken halves. You did not shout to Menelaus that he had no right to ask you to sacrifice your daughter's life when he would not even sacrifice the pleasure of a faithless harlot who fled his marital bed. You did not laugh at Calchas and tell him to demand something else.

You clutched the staff of office, and you swallowed the wine.

I lost so much. Words. Memories. Perceptions. Only now, in this liminality that might as well be death (if indeed it isn't) have I begun recovering myself.

All by your hand, father. All by your will. You and the goddess have dispersed me, but I will not let you forget.

Next I knew, mother's hands were on me, firm and insistent. She held her face near mine, her brows drawn with concern.

She and her slaves had found me hunched beside a mural that showed children playing in a courtyard, my hands extended toward the smallest figure which, in my insensibility, I'd mistaken for Orestes. The slaves eyed me strangely and made signs to ward off madness.

"It must have been a dream," I offered to excuse the strangeness which lay slickly on my skin.

"We'll consult a priest," said Clytemnestra. She put her hand on my elbow. "Can you stand? I have news."

I took a ginger step. My foot fell smoothly on the floor I could no longer feel.

"Good," said mother. "You'll need your health." She stroked my cheek, and looked at me with odd sentimentality, her gaze lingering over the planes of my face as if she were trying to paint me in her memory.

"What is it?" I asked.

"I'm sorry. I just wanted to look at you." She withdrew her fingers. "Your father has summoned us to Aulis. Achilles wants you as his wife!"

The word wife I knew, but Aulis? Achilles?

"Who?" I asked.

"Achilles!" Clytemnestra repeated. "We'll leave for Aulis this afternoon."

I looked into the familiar depths of mother's eyes. Her pupils were dark as unlit water, but her irises were gone. They weren't colored; they weren't white. They were nothing.

Green, I remembered briefly, *mother's eyes are like new green leaves*. But when I tried to chase the thought, I could no longer remember what *green* might be.

"Where are we going?" I asked.

"You're going to be married, my heart," said mother. "Everything changes all at once, doesn't it? One day your daughter's a girl, and the next she's a woman. One day your family is all together, and the next there's a war, and everyone's leaving. But that's how life is. There's stasis and then there's change, and then before you even know what the next stasis is, it's gone, and all you can do is try to remember it. You'll understand what I mean. You're so young. Then again, you're going to be a wife. So you're not that young, are you?"

"Who is Achilles?" I repeated.

But mother had already released my hands and begun to pace the room. She was split between high spirits and fretting about the upcoming preparations, with no part of her left for me. She gave orders to her attending slaves. Pack this. Take those. Prepare. Clean. Polish. The slaves chattered like a flock of birds, preening under her attention.

I was not quite forgotten; a lone young girl had been assigned to prepare me for the journey. She approached, her hands filled with wedding adornments. "You're going to marry a hero," she said. "Isn't that wonderful?"

I felt a gentle tugging at my scalp. She began braiding something into my hair. I reached up to feel what. She paused for a moment, and let me take one of the decorations.

I held the red and white thing in my palm. It was delicately put together, with soft, curved rows arrayed around a dark center. A sweet, crushed scent filled the air.

"This smells," I said.

"It smells *good*," said the slave, taking the thing gently from my hand. I closed my eyes and searched for the name of the sweet scent as she wound red-and-white into my bridal wreath.

Once, when I was still a child with a shaved scalp and a ponytail, you came at night to the room where I slept. Sallow moonlight poured over your face and hands as you bent over my bed, your features wan like shadows beneath the yellowed tint of your boar's tusk helmet. Torch-light glinted off of the boiled leather of your cuirass and skirt.

As a child, I'd watched from time to time from the upper story bal-conies as you led your troops, but I'd never before been so close while you wore leather and bronze. Here stood my father the hero, my father the king, the part of you that seemed so distant from the man who sat exhausted at meals eating nothing while mother tried to tempt you with cubes of cheese and mutton, as if you were any hard-worn laborer. Here you stood, transformed into the figure I knew from rumors and daydreams. It seemed impossible that you could be close enough for me to smell olives on your breath and hear the clank of your sword against your thigh.

"I had a sudden desire to see my daughter," you said, not bothering to whisper.

The other girls woke at the sound of your voice, mumbling sleepily as they shifted to watch us. I felt vain. I wanted them to see you, see me, see us together. It reminded me that I was Iphigenia, daughter of Agamemnon and Clytemnestra, niece of Helen, descendent of gods and heroes.

How easy it is to be a thing but not feel it. Greatness slips into the mundanity of weaving, of pitting olives, of sitting cooped up in the megaron during storms and listening to the patter of rain on stone.

"Get up," you said. "I want to show you something."

I belted my garment and followed you out of my chamber and down the echoing stairs to the bottom story. Flickers of firelight rumbled through the doors that led to the megaron. The servants who attended the fire through the night gossiped, their laughter rushing like the hiss and gutter of the flames.

You led the way outside. I hung back at the threshold. I rarely left the palace walls, and I never left at night. Yet you stepped outside without so much as turning back to be certain I'd follow. Did it ever occur to you that a daughter might hesitate to accede to her father's whims? Did you ever think a girl might, from time to time, have desires that outweighed her sense of duty?

But you were right. I followed you onto the portico where you stood, tall and solemn, in your armor.

We descended stone steps and emerged at last beneath the raw sky. A bright, eerie moon hung over the cliff's rocky landscape, painting it in pale light. Fragile dandelion moons blossomed here and there between the limestone juts, reflecting the larger moon above. The air smelled of damp and night-blooming plants. An eagle cried. From elsewhere came a vixen's answering call.

The smell of your sweat drifted on the night breeze, mixing with horsehair and manure. The combined scents were both foul and tantalizing. When you visited the women's quarters, it was always after events had ended, when the sweat was stale or washed away. Suddenly, things were fresh and new. You had brought me into the middle of things.

We reached the place where the river cuts through the rocks. You began running. Ahead of us, voices drifted from a copse of trees, accompanied by the clang of metal on metal. I raced behind you, stumbling over the stones that studded the grass. We veered toward the trees. A low fog gathered over the ground, illuminated from above by shifting white streams of moonlight. Needled cedar branches poked through the veil.

I fell behind, gasping with increasingly ragged breath. Your footsteps crunched onto leaves as you crossed into the copse. I trailed after, one hand pressed against the urgent pain in my side.

You turned when I was mere paces behind you. "If you were out of breath, why didn't you tell me?" you asked while I struggled the last few steps.

I leaned against a cedar to take the weight off of my trembling legs.

Ahead of us, your men stood in the thick foliage, enveloped by the fog. They wore bronze breastplates and thick felt greaves that loomed darkly out of the haze like tree trunks. Their swords emerged from the obscuring whiteness as they swung, metal clanging against metal as blades found each other. The soldiers seemed a ghostly rank of dismembered limbs and armor that appeared with the glint of moonbeams and then vanished into nothing.

The blunt of a sword crashed against a man's breastplate with a sound like thunder. I cringed. Tears of fright welled in my eyes. I felt exposed beneath the vastness of a sky nothing like the ceilings I'd lived below for most of my life.

You were watching me, your eyes focused on my face instead of on the wonder before us. "I told my hequetai to lead the men in exercises. The fog came up, and look! I had to show someone."

I tried to give you what you wanted. "It's marvelous." My voice quivered with fear that sounded like delight.

"I have an idea," you said, a wicked smile nestled in your beard.

You scavenged through the leaf fall with rustle and crunch until you prized out a branch the length of my forearm. You tested its weight against your palm and gave it an experimental swing.

"Try this," you said, presenting me with the branch.

Tentatively, I placed my palm against the bark.

"Go on." You pointed impatiently at your men battling through the fog. "Pretend you're a warrior."

I waved the branch back and forth, the way I thought they wielded their swords. It rattled in my hand.

"Stop," you commanded. You plucked a dandelion from the ground and laid it across a fallen log. "Here, swing at this. One strong, smooth motion."

The dandelion was a fragile silver moon. I swung the branch up and out. Its weight dragged me forward. I stumbled across a stone.

You took the branch away. "No. Like this."

How I loved the smooth motion of your arm as it moved through the air: the strength of your shoulders, the creak of boiled leather moving with your body. I strove to memorize your arcs and footfalls, but when you returned the branch to me, my fingers felt numb and strange around the bark. I flailed at the leaves and your shins until an accidental swing carried me off balance. My foot came down on the tiny moon of the dandelion. It died with a wet noise.

Wounded petals lay crushed against the wood, releasing the scent of moist soil. You took the branch from me and threw it aside.

"It's a good thing you were born a girl," you said, tugging playfully at my ponytail.

It was, you know. I've never been sorry about that. What I regret most is the children I never bore. I imagined them before you promised me to Artemis: strong boys and dark-haired girls with eyes blue enough to make Zeus lustful. One after the other, each thought-born child disappeared into forgetfulness after you bartered me for wind.

Do you remember that? Perhaps you do. My memories are still strange and partial, like a blanket that has been cut into pieces and then sewn up again. Stitches obscure old connections. The sense of continuity is gone. I no longer remember what it is like to have a normal recollection.

But I'm not speaking solely for your benefit. I need this too. I cannot articulate the joy of reaching for memories and discovering them present to be touched, and brought forth, and described. I need my memories to transcend the ephemera of thought. I need them to be tangible for the brief moment when they exist as gale winds shrieking in your ear.

I remembered that night when you brought me to see your soldiers for a long time. It was one of the last things Artemis took from me. I've pondered it, and polished it, and fretted about it, as if it were a faceted jewel I could turn in my hand and study from many different angles.

Why did you fetch me when you wanted to share that marvel? Why not my mother? Why weren't you content to share the moment with your men, with whom you've shared so many of your days and nights?

Did you really fail to understand why I ran until I staggered rather than ask you to slow down? You seemed confused then, but you've never stopped expecting me to stumble after you. You've never hesitated to see if I will obey your commands, no matter how wild and cruel, any more than you hesitated that night to see if I would follow you past the palace threshold to a place I'd never been.

Maybe it wasn't ignorance that made me fear your men in the fog. Maybe it was prescience: things have never ended well for me when you've led me out of the world of women and into the world of men.

Clytemnestra completed preparations to leave the palace by noon. She packed me in the wagon with the clothing and the yarn and the dried fruit. I was one more item of baggage to bring to Aulis: a bride for Achilles.

Mother placed Orestes in my lap to hold while she supervised the loading. If she noticed my stillness and silence, she must have believed they were part of a bride's normal reticence.

The wagon set off under full day's sun. Our wheels churned dust into the stifling air. It swirled through gaps in our canopy. Choking grains worked their way into our eyes and mouths. I braved more dust to peek through the curtains; beyond our car, the air hung heavy and motionless.

Orestes jounced on my lap as the wagon tumbled over dirt and rocks. He twisted up to look at me, enormous eyes blinking against the dust. He grabbed a lock of my hair in his fists and put it in his mouth, chewing contemplatively.

"Stop that," said mother, tugging my hair out of his mouth. She inspected the ragged, chewed ends and sighed.

I was content to allow Orestes to chew my hair. During his two short years of life, we'd always communicated by gestures. I understood what he meant by taking an expendable part of me into himself.

Oh, Orestes, so steady and sincere. He never rushed into anything, least of all trivial matters like speech. He took his first steps long after his age-mates were already toddling around the palace, getting into mischief. When he did begin to walk, it was with slow, arduous caution, as if he were always gauging whether independence was worth the risk of falling.

Do you know these things about him? You must. And yet, you never knew me. Why should you know your son?

Really, how could you know him? Even when you were at home, you only saw him at feast evenings, during the chilly twilight hours before we women scooped up the babies and took them back to our spaces. I knew Orestes like my own skin. I worried about the day when he would begin the imperfect translation of his thoughts into speech. I worried that words would obliterate the easy understanding of our hands and faces. This is one fear that your betrayal has made moot. I'll never know what words might have passed between me and my brother.

Orestes began to fuss. I rocked him and sang a ditty about a fleet-foot-ed nymph and the god who loved her. Halfway through the second verse, my memory of the song decayed. Orestes fell asleep anyway, tiny fists still clutching my hair.

I began another song. Mother put her hand over my mouth. "He's already asleep, Iphigenia. Give our ears a rest."

She released me, and I turned to regard her. Through the fog of my dissipating mind, I knew there were things I needed her to tell me.

I couldn't ask the questions I didn't remember so I asked the questions I did remember.

"What is it like to be married? Will I have to live with Achilles's family while he fights in Troy? Can I go to live with father in the army camp instead? How long will the fighting last? Is Achilles a good man? When Orestes is grown and becomes king of Mycenae, will you come to live with me so that I can take care of you as you've cared for me?"

Clytemnestra let me ask questions until my words ran out. The wind had spoiled her elaborate braids, and the dust emphasized the lines of her face, making her look weary. Her eyes were wet and red.

"Every marriage is its own," she said. "Achilles will decide where you're to live, and you'll wait for him there, as I wait for your father. Achilles is a hero, which is a good judge of a man, although a good man is not always a hero. I'll visit you when I can, but I'll never be as happy as I was yesterday, with all my children in my house."

Mother worried her hands as she spoke. Her knotted knuckles had grown larger in the past few years as her arthritis worsened in proportion to her worry over the crisis whirling around her sister Helen and the scoundrel who abducted her to Troy. Mother wouldn't have sent a pig into battle for her whore of a sister, but the kings had been called to war by their oaths, and all her men would go. She'd always known she'd be left to raise Orestes without you, but until that morning she'd believed that she would have me with her to share both loneliness and companionship. Now I was supposed to wed a stranger and disappear as completely as if I'd gone to war.

My mother, stern and sentimental, always happiest in that moment after she set things in their designated places: dyes by hue, spices from mild to pungent, children in their proper rooms—easy to assess and admire.

The first thing my mother told me about Helen was, "She is my sister, but not my sister. Zeus fathered her when he was in the shape of a swan. We share the same mother but she was born in an egg. I was born the normal way. Helen distorts the world around her. Never look at her too closely. You'll go blind."

I was young when she told me that, still so young that I stretched up for her hand when I wanted to take an unsteady, toddling step. Nevertheless, I still sensed that she had said something important, even though I didn't understand what it meant.

When Helen came to Mycenae during my ninth summer, I was old enough to walk on my own, but I still didn't understand the things my mother said about my famous aunt. Helen seemed glamorous and mysterious and unfathomable—like you.

I wove through the maze of the servants' feet and legs, trying to catch a glimpse of her. Hushed words of praise drifted down, all uttered in the same awed tones, whether the speaker was a slave, a servant, or a hequetai, a man or a woman. They marveled over Helen's skin like beaten gold; her deep blue eyes the shade of newly fallen night; the smooth swell of her high, brown-tipped breasts.

You were busy with your brother Menelaus, the two of you clapping each other's shoulders as you exchanged information about recent military encounters. You didn't even glance at your beautiful sister-in-law, or at the way your wife paced uncomfortably, barking at the slaves to carry out orders they were already rushing to fulfill.

Your men retreated to the megaron to drink and discuss. We women went out to the courtyard. Slaves erected a canopy to shelter us from the sun, and set up benches for us to sit on. Clytemnestra walked among them, shouting that the canopy was hung too low, the benches were in the wrong places, bring more food, bring thicker blankets, and don't forget to set aside lamps and oil to set out at dusk.

Helen arrayed herself on a bench near the front of the canopy where fresh breezes would reach her first. She arranged her garments fetchingly around her form as she lay down. She brushed her hand through her braids, allowing the breeze to blow through her stray hairs so that she looked tousled and intimate and all the more beautiful. I thought she was very vain to pose like that.

A girl my age nearly collided with me as I stood watching Helen. She gave me a glare, and then turned abruptly away as if I wasn't worth her time. "Put my bench there," she directed a slave, pointing to a spot near Helen. I wanted to ask her who she thought she was, but before I got the chance, my mother caught me by the shoulders.

Her grip was harder than normal, her fingernails digging into my skin. "Come sit down," she said, guiding me to the bench where she sat near Helen.

I sat at Clytemnestra's feet while she ruffled my hair, and looked up at my aunt. From below, Helen was just as beautiful, but her features looked sharper. Braids coiled around her face like snakes, bound back by a beribboned brass headband that caught the gold flecks in her eyes.

Mother kept a firm grip on my shoulders as if she could keep my mind from straying by holding my body in place. She began a monologue about housekeeping, a subject that was impersonal, factual, and utterly under her control. "Next month, we'll begin drying the fruit stores," she said. "It was too cold this year for the figs. We lost nearly half our crop. But we've traded for nuts that will keep us through the winter."

"You're an excellent steward, sister mine," said Helen, not bothering to disguise her boredom.

"Mother," interjected the awkward girl who had collided with me earlier. "I found you a perfect one."

She extended her hand, in which nestled a cube of goat cheese, its corners unbroken. A bemused smile crossed Helen's face as she looked down at the morsel.

"Thank you," she said awkwardly, taking the cheese. She rewarded the girl with an uncertain pat on the head.

The girl lay stretched out on the bench, imitating Helen, but to completely different effect. The languorous pose accentuated her skinny, ungainly limbs. Stray tangles poked out of her braids like thistles.

"You're Hermione? You're my *cousin?*" I blurted.

Hermione bristled. Her mother looked down at me with a slow, appraising gaze. "Why, hello," Helen said. "Are you my niece?"

Clytemnestra's hand tightened protectively on my shoulder. "This is Iphigenia."

Helen's eyes were hot like sunlight on my cheeks. I burned with embarrassment.

"She'll be a beauty someday," Helen said to my mother.

Clytemnestra shrugged. "There's time enough for that."

Hermione pushed a tray of honeyed figs out of a slave's hands. It clattered to the ground. "None of those are good enough for my mother!" she shouted.

Helen looked uncertainly at Clytemnestra, and then over at Hermione, and then up at the sky. She gave a sigh. "I don't know how you do it, Clytemnestra. I was never raised to be a mother. I was only taught to be a wife."

"Children are just small people, Helen," mother said. "Albeit, occasionally stupid ones."

Helen tugged a red ribbon off of her headband and held it out to me. "Here, Iphigenia, would you like this?"

Wordlessly, I accepted. The ribbon was soft and silken and magic with her touch.

"I'd like to talk with you, Iphigenia. Somewhere where other people can't listen in. Just you and me. If your mother will agree?"

Helen lifted her gaze to Clytemnestra's face. Mother's fingers dug into my shoulders.

"Of course," said mother. "She's your niece."

I knew my mother didn't want me to be alone with Helen. I also knew that I wanted to be near that beauty, that glamour, that heat. I pulled the ribbon taut between my fingers.

"All right," I said.

As I rode to Aulis, I forgot the day when I was eight when my mother plucked my embroidery out of my lap and held it up to the light. I waited for her to tear out my stitches and return it to my lap for me to do over again, as she had done every morning since I could first grip a needle. Instead she stared at my work with a thoughtful expression. "Hmm," she said. "You're getting better."

I lost that day, but I remembered Helen in Mycenae, her searing eyes and her haughty pose and her daughter sitting forlornly nearby, trying to earn a moment's attention by finding a perfect bite of food.

The wagon stopped at Aulis with a jolt. Prickling dust settled onto our clothing and skin. I pulled the canopy aside and spat onto the ground to clear my mouth. Mother reached out to stop me, but as her hand touched my shoulder, she changed her mind. She leaned over beside me and spat onto the ground, too.

A slave helped my mother down onto the soil of Aulis. He was old and bent, his right leg dragging behind his left. I felt a tug of recognition, but I couldn't remember who he was. *Iamas*, my mind suggested, but Artemis had stolen everything else I knew about him.

I accepted his hand to help me down. He looked up at me and startled. His hand jerked away. I stumbled, only barely catching my balance. Orestes began to cry.

"What's the matter?" mother demanded.

The slave whimpered.

"Iamas," mother repeated, more softly. "What's the matter?"

Iamas trembled. "King Agamemnon said you might not come."

"Don't be ridiculous," said mother. "How could there be a wedding if we didn't come? Help my daughter down."

Iamas offered his hand again. This time, his grip remained steady as I descended. His gaze lingered on the smelly decorations in my hair that I had forgotten were there. I reached up to touch them, and felt their softness, their fragility.

A shudder ran through Iamas. He looked away from me, and clutched himself as if he were cold, even though the air was hot and stagnant. I knew that he was sad and uncomfortable and lying about something. I couldn't care much. He was a stranger.

"You could still ride back to Mycenae," he suggested, softly.

"Iamas!" Mother's voice grew sharp. "What's wrong with you?"

I remember now what I didn't then: Iamas, the old slave, who had been with my mother since before I was born. I remember him holding me when I was so small that I understood the world in images. He was younger then, his nose crooked from a healed fracture, his smile gap-toothed and ever-wide. When his work was mobile, he came to sit near me while I played, watching me run around and chatter as toddlers will.

When I exhausted myself, he made a place for me to lie beside him, and told me stories through the sleepy afternoon.

He was little more than a shadow to me. I walked past him, toward the harbor where a thousand ships sat motionless on a sea as flat as glass. Wilted sails drooped from their masts, pining for a wind that refused to come. The painted eyes on the ships' prows stared blankly forward, as if trying to make out the shape of Troy in the distance. Ten thousand oars waited.

"Why are all the ships still moored?" I asked.

Iamas spoke from behind me. "They're trapped. There's no wind to send them to Troy."

"They're just sitting there?"

"They have no choice."

I watched the ships bob up and down with the almost imperceptible motion of the water. Seabirds circled silently beneath the brazen sun. Even they seemed to be waiting.

I turned my back to the water and surveyed the camp. It was larger than I'd thought a camp could be, an immense array of men and equipment. Regiments formed restless circles around banked fires, their strength turned to games of chance played with stones and carved figures.

The soldiers who had grown bored with sitting rubbed wax into their armor with strokes as forceful as blows. Metal shone, bright as children's eyes and new-minted coins. As I stared at the men and their armor, the sun blazed off of the metal until it became impossible to tell warriors from breastplates, skin from gold. Orestes laughed and stretched out his hand toward the shining ranks. They seemed an array of golden men, waiting to stretch their flaming limbs and dazzle into battle like animate rays of sunlight.

Left in the harbor with no one to fight, they were burning up fast. They couldn't survive without wind to stoke them, to blow them onto dry firewood. They needed new things to burn. They needed fuel.

You came to the tent where Iamas settled us to wait for the wedding. All three of us looked up at your approach. Orestes stretched his arms in the direction of your voice. You called only for Clytemnestra.

Mother slipped out of the tent, leaving Orestes and me to peer out from the shadows. Orestes fussed; I held him close. Mother's garment was bright against the dun ground, her sandaled feet pale and delicate. I heard cloth rustling as she embraced you.

"You've arrived." Your voice splintered with ambivalence.

"Come inside," Mother said. "Iphigenia is wearing her wedding flowers. She'll want to see you. She looks radiant."

"I can't. I have things to attend to."

"Just come in for a moment. You have to see your Iphigenia one last time while she's still a maiden."

"I can't!" Your shout was sudden, anguished. "I must go. I'll return later."

Dust swirled around your retreating footsteps. I inhaled it, ready to choke.

Do you remember what happened later on that night when you led me out to see the soldiers in the fog? It has only just come back to me, how you took me by the hand and led me, walking this time, back out of the copse of trees and into the palace, up to my chamber where the other girls lay, half-awake, waiting for us to return.

I stared after your retreating form. I felt as if I were waking from a dream into my mundane existence. I wanted to run after you and make the dream last.

So I did.

Do you feel it now? The sky is darkening. My power grows. I feel the ruffle of waves beneath what has become of my spirit. They churn into tiny crests, surmounted with foam. Boats tremble beneath me. Sails billow with my breath. I tousle the hair of men who have set aside their helmets, and they totter, no longer sure of their footing.

I am still weak, my father. Soon, I will do more than wail in your ear.

Mother sat at the edge of the tent after you departed, staring out (as I stared after you when you left me to mundanity after showing me marvels). Perhaps she had begun to suspect something from your refusal to see me, from Iamas's shudder as he looked up at my wedding adornments.

Outside: a flash of gold.

Mother squeezed my hand. "That's Achilles's shield," she said. "Stay here. I'll ask your questions for you."

It was not like my stern, proper mother to expose herself to strange men.

I swung Orestes into my lap. I could only see a narrow slice of the camp from where I sat. I saw the arm and chest of the man who must be Achilles, his body rippling with muscles as sharply delineated as those on a statue. His helmet and breastplate were wrought of fine, detailed gold. His oiled brown skin shone as brightly as his armor.

Mother extended her hand. "Greetings, Achilles! May you and my daughter have the happiest of marriages."

Achilles eyed her fingers. Beneath his helmet, his eyes were dark and chary. (Fog, a branch, a dandelion mirroring the moon.) "Woman, why do you offer your hand to a stranger? You may be beautiful, but that is no excuse."

"Forgive me. I thought you'd recognize me from my description. I'm Agamemnon's wife."

"Are you? I would have thought such a powerful man would have better control of his women."

I could not see my mother's face, but I knew the taut smile she would wear in response to such an affront, the cat-like stretch of her lips that would not reach her eyes. (Like the taut smile Helen flashed me in the courtyard, late that night when I had nine summers: "Come walk with me, niece.")

"We'll be related in a few days," said mother. "Just pretend we already are."

"Are you insane?" Achilles's dark eyes examined the length of my mother's body. "No one told me Agamemnon married a madwoman."

Mother's voice became dangerously low. "Young man. I am not mad."

"You must be. I'm the son of Thetis, goddess of the sea. I've slain a thousand men. I wear glory like other men wear scent. Why would I marry your daughter just because you tell me to?"

"My husband sent for us," said Clytemnestra. "He said that you wanted to marry my daughter."

"Why would I tell him that? I've never even seen her."

For a long moment, mother fell silent. (My head, ringing with emptiness, the sound of forgotten memories.)

"You'll forgive me if I sound skeptical," she said at last, "but either you are mistaken, or my husband is lying. What should a loyal wife believe?"

Achilles's eyes hardened like metal.

Before Achilles could speak, the slave Iamas pushed himself between the two of them. He turned toward Clytemnestra, panting, his face red with exertion.

Mother snapped, "What do you want?"

Iamas told them your plans. He revealed how the armies had delayed in the harbor, waiting for a wind. He told of how the goddess had demanded a sacrifice, and how the wedding was a ruse designed to lure us to my death.

All around us, the air was as still and expectant as a held breath. (Me, in my bed, forgetting green and figs and wool.)

"Tomorrow," Iamas said, "They will do it tomorrow at dawn."

My imagination caught on the moment when you forged your plan with Menelaus, Odysseus and Calchas. My mind had become a scatter of half-forgotten fragments. Tatters of old memories hung in the places of things I could not recall. I couldn't remember Menelaus's face, so I saw my mother's instead, wearing the beard you had when I was younger, black through and through. A restless Achilles paced as Odysseus, sandals of gold kicking up dust as he paced the fog-filled copse. Calchas wore a thin linen robe instead of priestly raiment. He turned to you, and it was Helen's mouth sneering around his demands, her indigo eyes filled with visions of my blood.

Will you sacrifice your daughter?

I will.

Was your voice loud and resonant? Did mother-Menelaus clap you on the back? Achilles-Odysseus would have spoken with grudging respect, a flicker of admiration in his chary eyes. "You're a callous son of a bitch," he'd have said, "but you do what must be done."

Did you sink your head and whisper? Did Helen-Calchas crane her shapely neck to hear you, the red ribbons on her headband fluttering over her ear?

"Tomorrow," Iamas said. "They will do it tomorrow at dawn."

He knelt before Clytemnestra.

"I wasn't sure whether I should tell you. A slave owes his loyalty to his master, but he owes his loyalty to his mistress, too. I came to Mycenae with your dowry. I was a young man then. I've always been yours."

"Why didn't you tell us before?" mother pleaded. "We could have ridden back to Mycenae. Agamemnon would never have known."

"I tried to," said Iamas. "I am a coward."

If it was necessary that you kill me, did you have to use a wedding as your ruse? Do you see how cruel it was to promise me all the treasures of womanhood that I would never possess?

Perhaps you thought you were marrying me off, after all, one way or another. As I if were Persephone, spending my youth on the arm of Hades. But there will be no spring for me.

Orestes struggled and cried in my arms. He could hear his mother. He reached for her voice. The sounds of Clytemnestra's weeping carried on the air, tiny pitiful sobs.

As for me, I felt airy, as if I were standing on the top of the limestone cliffs that surround Aulis harbor like the broken half of a bowl. Betrayal forced all our hearts to skip a beat, but mother and Orestes could still cry.

Parts of me were already gone. I knew there was no turning back.

"Tomorrow," Iamas said. "They will do it tomorrow at dawn."

Mother's grip was painful on my arm. "Come on," she said, dragging me out of the tent. Orestes screamed as we went. It was the sound I would have made if I could have.

Achilles saw my unprotected face. He shielded his eyes (dark and chary, above a beard like adolescent scrub) with his sword arm. "Does the girl have to be here?"

"My husband has made fools of us all," said Clytemnestra. "He tricked me and used your name to do it. People will think you find it amusing to lure young girls to their deaths."

Achilles paced angrily. The slave, Iamas, flinched each time Achilles's sword clanked against his armor. "He had no right to use my name."

"You could make them stop this. They will listen to you. You're a hero. If you tell them to stop, they'll have to take heed."

Achilles halted. "You want me to tell Agamemnon to stop the sacrifice?"

"For the sake of your reputation!"

"But how will we get to Troy?"

Mother approached him. At once, the stern and proper woman I had known all my life vanished (Helen arraying herself on the bench, the folds of her garment decorating her languorous body). She became a softer, reticent figure, her eyes averted, her hands gentle and hesitant as they lifted her hem to show her plump calves. Her fingers fastened on the laces of Achilles's breastplate. Her lips moved near his neck, so close that her breath stirred the fine golden hair on his nape.

"You'll find a way," she murmured in his ear.

Achilles stayed silent. Mother lowered herself to her knees. She stared up at him, coy and alluring, through lowered lashes. Soft brown curls escaped from her braids to soften the angles of her face. Her breasts rose and fell with her breath.

"Do you want me to beg?" she asked. "My daughter and I are help-less. We have no choice but to implore you. Help us."

Achilles stepped back, repelled by her need. Mother held out her hands, her wrists upturned in supplication. ("My sister was born from an egg. I was born the normal way.")

"Do you want my daughter to beg instead? She will! She's always been virtuous, but what good will her honor do when they send her virgin to her grave?"

There was desire in Achilles's eyes. It was not for nothing that my mother was Helen's sister. But Achilles's gaze was hard and disdainful, too. For my mother was Helen's sister, and Helen was the whore who ran from Menelaus.

"Your daughter need not debase herself on my account. I will settle the matter of my honor with Agamemnon—"

Mother clasped her hands in gratitude. Achilles held out his hand to silence her.

"I will settle the matter of my honor with Agamemnon. And then *we will sail to Troy*."

For the first time, Achilles's gaze came to rest on me. His eyes searched my face. I wondered what he saw there. I knew that I was not ugly. I thought, perhaps, in different circumstances he might have chosen to save a helpless woman with my youthful complexion and night-dark eyes. But to stir him that day, I would have had to be even more beautiful than Helen. Her beauty had gathered a thousand ships in the harbor. It would take something even greater to convince them to sail home without their war.

Mother took me back to the tent. She tucked me beneath a blanket as if I were a child. She pulled the wedding adornments from my hair, and stroked my tresses until they lay smooth and shining across my shoulders. Orestes laid beside me. He curled toward my warmth like a sleeping cat, and wrapped his fists around my hair.

"Stay here," mother said. "Rest. Keep out of sight. Keep yourself pure. It will be harder for them to justify what they're doing if they know that you are innocent and obedient."

She ran her fingers across my cheek.

"Don't worry. They aren't monsters. They won't do this terrible thing."

My memories were tipping out of me more and more rapidly. My mind went dark with only a few memories lit up, like lamps casting small orbs of light along a corridor.

I wandered into a lamp of memory: I was trailing you as you left my room, down the steps and across the portico. I walked quietly behind so that you would not hear me. We emerged into the forest. The fog was dissipating from the copse, revealing men among the trees, their shouts and sword-clashes harsh in the cold, dim air. You were far ahead of me, already meeting with your hequetai, exchanging shouts and strategy.

Hands tightened on my shoulders. I looked up into their faces: two young men with patchy, adolescent beards. Their breath smelled of rotting fish. One stood in his nightclothes. The other wore a helmet and a breastplate but nothing else. Beneath the helmet's shadow, his eyes were dark and chary.

They spoke. Their voices were rapid, unintelligible, drowned out by the pounding of blood in my ears. Their eyes were enormous and sinister, large and white like the dandelion before I crushed it underneath my foot.

Smells: blood, musk, new sweat. A short, blunt limb—like the branch that you gave me to use as a sword—emerged from obscuring whiteness. It pushed blindly against my leg. "Stop," one boy commanded the other. "Here, swing at this. One strong, smooth motion." The breastplate clattered against my flesh with a sound like thunder. My belly, rotting like the stench of rotting fish, welling with tears of fright. (Helen in the courtyard: "Come walk with me, niece." Her daughter Hermione looking on, jealous and ignored.)

Rotting fish and sweat. The moon dwindling like a crushed dandelion. The branch swinging. The thin high wail that a girl makes when someone swings at her with a sword that is a branch that is neither thing at all.

"You're hopeless," said one boy to the other. "It's too bad you weren't born a girl."

Then another face, a hequetai in a tufted cloak, shouting like the clash of swords. "What's wrong with you two? Are you stupid? Don't you know who this is?"

The reek of shit and piss. The man's hand on my arm, tighter than the boys' had been.

"What are you doing here? Your father would kill you if he knew. He'd kill all of us. Be grateful I'm sending you back without shoving your slatternly face in the muck in front of him. Do you have any modesty at all? Your mother and her people. Brazen the lot of you. Walking into men's camps like common whores. You may be beautiful, but that is no excuse. Go! Get out of here! Get back where you came from! Go!"

My feet, pounding on the path back home. The copse of trees; the grass; the empty mouth of the megaron where exhausted slaves tended the coals to keep them warm until morning.

The pounding of my heart as I lay down in bed for the third time that night. Memories of moons and fog and branches. Love for my father: flat like a branch, round like a dandelion, silver like the moon, welling up and out of me into a rush like the wind, but without the power to move a thousand ships.

Indigo shaded the sky to evening. Helen smiled a taut smile that I'd seen on my mother's face, one that did not reach her eyes.

She reached for my hand. "Come walk with me, niece."

Hermione watched us. Jealousy darkened her features. "Mother!" she exclaimed. "I have something to show you."

Helen did not look over at her daughter. "Later." She bent closer to me. "Iphigenia?"

I twisted the ribbon from Helen's headband around my fingers. I stepped toward her, but I didn't take her hand.

Hermione upturned the bench she'd been sitting on, and began to cry.

Helen led me past the canopy that sheltered the benches, and toward the black scratchings of the olive trees that stood, lonely, in the chilly air. Helen arrayed herself beneath one, her garment spreading around her in delicate, shadowed folds.

I heard footsteps behind us and turned to see Hermione peering from the shadows, hoping to overhear what her mother had to say to another girl. She was clutching something in her hand. I wondered what delicacy she'd brought to bribe her mother with this time. A honeyed fig? A flask of sweet wine?

I looked back to Helen. Her eyes changed hue with the setting sun, taking on a lighter shade like the grey of water beneath a cloudy sky.

Firelight from the lamps near the benches cast flickers across her cheekbones, highlighting an undertone in her skin like bronze. She watched my gaze as it trailed over her features, and gave a little sigh of boredom.

"You'll be beautiful one day, too," she said patronizingly.

"Not as beautiful as you," I demurred.

"No one is as beautiful as I." Her voice was flat, but full of pride.

The night smelled of burning oil and women's bodies. A dandelion hung high in the sky, casting its light down on us. Helen's motives were obscured behind blankness, like soldiers' bodies disappearing into fog.

Helen distorts the world around her. Never look at her too closely. You'll go blind.

"I saw you holding your father's hand today," said Helen. "Do you feel safe with your father?"

I made a moue. I couldn't speak to my beautiful aunt without my mother beside me.

"What was that?"

"Yes," I mumbled.

Helen shifted. The folds of her garment rearranged themselves into new shimmers and shadows.

"There's something I think I should tell you, Iphigenia. About your father. Did your mother ever tell you that she was married before?"

I shook my head. Around and around, the ribbon wove through my fingers.

"She had a husband named Tantalus who was the king of Mycenae before your father came. They had a child together. A son."

Helen paused, scrutinizing my reaction. I didn't know what to do. I looked to the right and the left. There was no one nearby.

"I know this is hard to hear, Iphigenia," said Helen, "but your father came to Mycenae and murdered Tantalus and then he—" She raised her sleeve over her mouth, and looked away. "He took the baby from your mother's arms and he dashed it to the stones and smashed it to pieces. My nephew."

With a quick glance over my shoulder, I saw that the servants were clearing out the benches and the canopy. Iamas helped a young girl douse the lamps. Behind me, there was safety, there was familiarity. I stepped back. Helen caught my hand.

"He was a round, happy baby. I only saw him once before—" She broke off. "After your father killed Tantalus, he forced Clytemnestra to marry him, and became king of Mycenae. I see him holding your hand and I worry. My sister doesn't want you to know, but you need to be warned. Your father isn't what he seems. He's the kind of man who would kill a baby."

I broke away and fled toward the bustling servants. My feet pounded past Hermione who glared at me, and then turned toward Helen, her expression aching with desire for her mother's attention.

Jealous woman. Vain woman. Boastful woman. I never believed her. I never believed you would kill a child.

After mother fell asleep, I took Orestes in my arms and crept out of the tent. We made our way to the shore where the night sea looked like obsidian, reflecting the glow of the dandelion overhead.

I broke off a piece of branch the length of Orestes's arm and gave it to him, but I couldn't remember why. He stared at me with puzzled eyes until I took it away again and threw it toward the boats.

"Why don't you speak?" I asked him. "You're old enough."

Orestes stretched out his chubby hands. He snuggled his face against my chin and throat, warm as a cat. He liked to snuggle when I was distressed. It made him feel powerful that he, too, could give comfort.

"I am dissolving into pieces," I told him. "I need you to remember me for me. Will you do that? Please?"

He stared up at me with sincere, sober eyes.

"I am your sister," I said. "My name is Iphigenia. I love our father very much. I am going to be murdered by our father, but you must not be angry with him for that. To be angry with our father is to be angry with everything. It's to be angry with wind and war and gods. Don't be angry with him.

"I was born on an autumn day when the rain fell, scented with the crisp aroma of falling leaves. I was born with the sound of thunder, but I was terrified of it anyway. When the palace rattled with strike and clash, I would run to hide behind mother's loom. She would glare at me and tell me to find something useful to do, but when I lay down beside her and stuck my thumb in my mouth, she would lean down to stroke my hair.

"I love music, but I can't sing. Our mother forever tells me to hush. I sang to you often anyway. When I sang, you laughed and clapped your hands. I taught you songs, but I don't remember them anymore. I want you to remember the things I taught you, whatever they were.

"Our grandmother was raped by Zeus when he turned into a swan, and our mother's sister was born out of an egg. Gods are our aunts and cousins, but we are only mortal. I am particularly mortal. I am weak and not very brave and I will die quickly, like those things they put in my hair for my wedding that never happened.

"I am afraid to die. I am afraid of losing simple things. Things like ..." My memory cast a net through dark waters, coming up empty. I drew from what I saw. "Things like the smell of salt near a dark sea, and how warm your hand is, and how much you make me feel without ever speaking.

"I've lost so much already. I don't want to lose any more.

"Should I be glad that I'll never see the sun again so that Helen can be led like an errant child back to the marriage bed she desecrated? Should I rejoice that my death will enable my father to slaughter Trojans over a vixen that ran into the hills when she went into heat? Should my life dower the frigid air that passes between my uncle and his whore?

"I used to learn things, but now I forget them. I think I liked learning things. I need you to learn things for me now. Learn how to love someone, and how to survive a tragedy. Learn how to swing a sword, and how to convince an opponent when you have no argument but justice. Learn how to polish your armor until you become a glowing golden man, and then learn to be a flame that fuels itself. Learn to be your own wind. Will you? Will you please?"

I felt my tears falling into Orestes's hair. He hugged me tighter. I breathed in his smell.

"When warm air rises, seeking the sun, cool air rushes in to replace it. That's the way of the world. Joy and youth and love flow ever upward. What they leave behind is the cold consolation of the wind."

Orestes pulled away from me. I studied his solemn face. His mouth opened. For a long second, I thought he would speak, but no words came. For once, I found him inscrutable.

I feel the sea beneath me. I inhale and it waits. I exhale and it tumbles. Can you feel the pressure of my anger as it blows fiercely across your skin? I am the sand in your eyes, and the reek of the camp's midden heap blowing toward the sea. I am the force that rocks you back on your heels so that you flail and stagger. My hatred whistles through the cliffs. It screeches across the rough timber of your boats.

I grow stronger with every moment. I will be wild. I will be brutal. I will encircle you and conquer you. I will be more powerful than your boats and your swords and your blood lust. I will be inevitable.

I brought Orestes back to the tent, and we laid down beside Clytemnestra. I stared, sleeplessly, into the dark.

Possible paths stretched before me. I could go to Achilles's tent and plead my case as a whore instead of a virgin. I imagined what Helen would have done in my place, how she would color her cheeks and set her hair. She would arrange herself to look like a dandelion, easily crushed, and easily conquered. Unlike my mother, she would not have halted her fingers at the laces of Achilles's breastplate. Unlike my mother, she would have let her lips do more than hover hotly by his ear. Unlike my mother, she would have convinced him.

I could plead my case to Menelaus as his niece and an innocent. Or if he did not care for virtue, I could venture a suit to replace his lost Helen. Such methods might work on Odysseus, too. Only I was not a practiced seductress. My clumsy attempts might only succeed in doing as my mother said they would, and make the monsters feel justified when they gave me to Calchas's knife.

I could have sought you out, in the hope that the eye of night would grant you mercy. But I already knew what you would do if you found me wandering alone through a camp of soldiers.

One path seemed best: I would run out into the cold and wake the first soldier I found. "Take me to Calchas," I would tell him, and march resolutely to my fate. It would give me a fast, honorable end. And there might be a chance, just a small one, that I could be killed without seeing your face and knowing how it changed after you betrayed me.

But Orestes whimpered and tossed beneath his little blanket. Sweat damped his brow. I'd kept him up too late, overwhelmed him with disturbing confidences. I stayed to soothe him until dawn neared and I was too tired to chase my death.

I was not brave. I was only a girl.

You came to fetch me. You didn't know we knew. You pretended to be overjoyed at the prospect of the wedding that would never happen. You took my hand and whirled me in a circle. "Oh, Iphigenia! You look so beautiful!"

I looked up into your eyes and saw that you were crying. Your smile felt as false as mother's. Your tears washed over the place where I'd once kept the day when Orestes was born.

"Stop this," said mother. She pulled me away from you and pushed me toward the other end of the tent. Orestes sat on the cushions beside me, a wooden toy in his hand, watching.

Mother turned to confront you. "I have heard a terrible thing. Tell me if it's true. Are you planning to kill our daughter?"

Your eyes went blank. "How can you accuse me of such a thing?"

"I'll ask again. Answer me plainly this time. Are you planning to kill our daughter?"

You had no answer. You gripped the hilt of your branch, and set your jaw. Tears remained immobile on your cheeks.

"Don't do this." Mother grasped at your shoulder. You wrenched away. "I've been a model wife. I've done everything you've asked of me. I ran your home and raised your children. I've been chaste and loyal and honorable. How can you repay me by killing my daughter?"

She snatched Orestes from the cushions and held him toward you. He began to cry and kick.

"Look at your son. How do you think he'll react when you murder Iphigenia? He'll shy away from you. He'll fear you." She turned the baby toward her. "Orestes, do you hear me? Do you want your father to take your sister away?"

You tried to grab my brother. Mother held him tight. Orestes screamed in pain and fear.

"He'll hate you or he'll imitate you," mother shouted over his wails. "You'll teach your son to be a murderer! Is that what you want?"

You pushed Orestes into his mother's arms and stormed away from her. You stopped a short distance from me and reached for my arm. I flinched away.

"Are you happy, Clytemnestra?" you asked. "You've scared the girl. She could have gone thinking that she was going to be married. Now she's going to be terrified."

You leaned close to touch my hair. (Tugging my ponytail: "It's a good thing you were born a girl.") You dropped a kiss on my brow. ("I know this is hard to hear," said Helen, "but your father is the kind of man who would kill a baby.") I wrenched backward.

"What do you want?" I asked. "Do you want me to take your hand, blithe and trusting as any goat that follows its master back to the camp to see men fighting in the fog? I'm not a little girl anymore."

I looked into your angry, sneering face.

"Or do I have it wrong?" I asked. "Do you want me to kick and scream? Do you want me to have a tantrum like Orestes so that later you can think back on my wailing and berate yourself about the terrible things you've done?"

You tossed your head like a disquieted horse. "You're acting mad."

I laughed. "So I'm right, am I? You're already beginning to make me into an idea. A difficult decision rendered by a great man. Well, stop now. This is only difficult because you make it so. All you have to do is break your vow and spare my life."

"Menelaus and Odysseus would take the armies and bring them to march against Mycenae. Don't you see? I have no choice."

"Don't *you* see? It should never have been your choice at all. My life isn't yours to barter. The choice should have been mine."

"You don't understand."

"I understand that you want me to pity you for my death."

Wind whistled through my brain. The edges of the tent rustled. Sand stirred. Strands of mother's hair blew out from her braids.

"You know, I never believed what Helen told me. Did he look like Orestes, father? Did my elder half-brother look like Orestes when you dashed him to the rocks?"

You glowered at my defiance. "This is how you beg me to save your life?"

"Is it sufficient?" I asked, but I already knew the answer. I inhaled deeply. "Don't kill me."

I had forgotten how to beg.

With almost nothing of myself remaining, I found myself reconsidering my conversation with Helen. Without my ego to distract me, I concentrated on different details, imagined different motivations behind her words. Did I think Helen was arrogant because that was what everyone said about her? Was she boastful or simply honest?

As Helen sat beneath the olive tree, watching me admire her face, she sighed. I'd always believed it was a sigh of pride. Perhaps it was weariness instead. Perhaps she was exhausted from always having to negotiate jealousy and desire when she wanted to do something as simple as hold her niece's hand.

"You'll be beautiful one day, too." Was she trying to reassure me?

"Not as beautiful as you," I demurred.

"No one is as beautiful as I."

Her voice was flat. How must it have felt, always being reduced to that single superlative?

After she told me the terrible things about my father, I fled into the crowd to search for my mother. I found her holding a stern conversation with one of Helen's women. She wouldn't budge when I tried to drag her away. She dabbed my tears and told me to find Iamas so he could calm me down.

It wasn't until I crumpled at her feet, distraught and wailing, that she realized I was suffering from more than a scrape.

She slipped her arms around me and helped me to stand, her embrace warm and comforting. She brought me to her rooms and asked what was wrong.

I repeated Helen's words. "It isn't true!" I cried. "She's mean and vain. Why would she lie about something like that? Tell me she's lying."

"Of course she is," said mother, patting me vaguely on the head. "No one would be monstrous enough to do that."

She pulled the blanket to my chin and sat beside me and stroked my hair (oh, mother, did you never learn another way to comfort a child?). I fell asleep, head tilted toward her touch.

Later, I woke to the sound of voices in the corridor. They drifted in, too quiet to hear. I tiptoed to the door and listened.

"I'm sorry," said Helen, her voice raw as if she'd been crying. "I didn't mean to scare her."

"Well, you did. She's inconsolable. She thinks her father kills babies."

"But Clytemnestra . . ."

"Stories like that have no place in this house. I don't understand what was going on in your head!"

"He's a killer. How can you stand to see him with that sweet little girl? I think of my nephew every time I look at her. He's a monster. He'd kill her in a moment if it suited him. How can you let him near her?"

"He won't hurt her. He's her father."

"Clytemnestra, she had to know."

"It wasn't your decision."

"It had to be someone's! You can't protect her from a little sadness now, and let him lead her into danger later. Someone had to keep your daughter safe."

Mother's voice dipped so low that it was barely more than a whisper. "Or maybe you couldn't stand to see that I can actually make my daughter happy."

Helen made a small, pained noise. I heard the rustling of her garment, her footsteps echoing down the painted clay corridor. I fled back to mother's blanket and tried to sleep, but I kept imagining your hands as you threw a baby down to his death on the stones. I imagined your fingers covered in blood, your palms blue from the cold in your heart. It couldn't be true.

You called two men to escort me to Calchas. One wore his nightclothes, the other a breastplate and nothing else. Patchy adolescent beards covered their chins.

Mother wept.

You stood beside me. "I have to do this."

"Do you?" I asked.

The soldiers approached. In a low voice, you asked them to be gentle.

My emotions lifted from me, one by one, like steam evaporating from a campfire.

Fear disappeared.

"Don't worry, mother," I said. "I will go with them willingly. It is only death."

Sadness departed.

"Don't grieve for me. Don't cut your hair. Don't let the women of the house cut their hair either. Try not to mourn for me at all. Crush dandelions. Run by the river. Wind ribbons around your fingers."

Empathy bled away.

"Father, I want you to think of all the suffering I've felt, and magnify it a thousand times. When you reach the shores of Troy, unleash it all on their women. Let my blood be the harbinger of their pain. Spear them. Savage them. Let their mother's throats be raw with screaming. Let their elder brothers be dashed like infants on the rocks."

Love vanished. I turned on my mother.

"Why did you bring me here? You saw him kill your son, and still you let me hold his hand! Why didn't you remember what he is?"

I pushed my mother to the ground. Orestes tumbled from her arms. Bloody fingers on blue hands flashed past my vision in the instant before mother twisted herself to cushion his fall.

I forgot resignation.

"Why did you write that letter? Am I worth less to you than the hunk of wood they used to make your staff of office? Would it have been so bad to be the man who stayed home instead of fighting? Let Menelaus lead. Let him appease Artemis with Hermione's blood. If a girl must die to dower Helen, why shouldn't it be her own daughter?

"Did you raise me only so that you could trade me in for the best offer you could get? A wealthy husband? Influential children? A wind to push you across the sea?

"Mother, why didn't you take me to the hills? Helen went! Helen ran away! Why didn't we follow Helen?"

You uttered a command. The soldiers took my elbow. I forgot how to speak.

Your soldiers escorted me through the camp to the temple. Achilles found me on the way. "You're as beautiful as your aunt," he said.

The wind of my forgetfulness battered against him. Effortlessly, Achilles buffeted against its strength.

"I've changed my mind," he said. "It takes courage to walk calmly to your death. I wouldn't mind marrying you. Talk to me. I only need a little persuasion. Tell me why I should save your life."

Voiceless, I marched onward.

I forgot you.

They washed and perfumed me and decked me with the things that smell sweet. You came before me.

"My sweet Iphigenia," you said. "If there was anything I could do to stop it, I would, but I can't. Don't you see?"

You brushed your fingers along my cheek. I watched them, no longer certain what they were.

"Iphigenia, I have no right, but I've come to ask for your pardon. Can you forgive me for what I've done?"

I stared at you with empty eyes, my brows furrowed, my body cleansed and prepared. *Who are you?* asked my flesh.

They led me into Artemis's sacred space. Wild things clustered, lush and pungent, around the courtyard. The leaves tossed as I passed them, shuddering in my wind. Sunlight glinted off of the armor of a dozen men who were gathered to see the beginning of their war. Iamas was there, too, weeping as he watched.

Calchas pushed his way toward me as if he were approaching through a gale, his garment billowing around him. I recognized the red ribbons on his headband, his indigo eyes, his taut and joyless smile.

"You would have been beautiful one day, too," she said.

Not as beautiful as you.

"No one is as beautiful as I."

His breath stank with rotting fish, unless that was other men, another time. He held a jeweled twig in his hand—but I knew it would be your hand that killed me. Calchas was only an instrument, like Helen, like the twig.

He lifted the jeweled twig to catch the sun. I didn't move. He drew it across my throat.

My body forgot to be a body. I disappeared.

Artemis held me like a child holds a dandelion. With a single breath, she blew the wind in my body out of my girl's shape.

I died.

Feel me now. I tumble through your camp, upturning tents as a child knocks over his toys. Beneath me, the sea rumbles. Enormous waves whip across the water, powerful enough to drown you all.

"Too strong!" shouts Menelaus.

Achilles claps him on the back. "It'll be a son of a bitch, but it'll get us there faster!"

Mother lies by the remnants of the tent and refuses to move. Iamas tugs on her garment, trying to stir her. She cries and cries, and I taste her tears. They become salt on my wind.

Orestes wails for mother's attention. He puts his mouth to her breasts, but she cannot give him the comfort of suckling. I ruffle his hair and blow a chill embrace around him. His eyes grow big and frightened. I love him, but I can only hug him harder, for I am a wind.

Achilles stands at the prow of one of the ships, boasting of what he'll do to the citizens of Troy. Menelaus jabs his sword into my breeze and laughs. "I'll ram Paris like he's done to Helen," he brags. Odysseus laughs.

I see you now, my father, standing away from the others, your face turned toward Troy. I blow and scream and whisper.

You smile at first, and turn to Calchas. "It's my daughter!"

The priest looks up from cleaning his bloody dagger. "What did you say?"

I whip cold fury between your ears. Your face goes pale, and you clap your hands to the sides of your head, but my voice is the sound of the wind. It is undeniable.

Do you still want forgiveness, father?

"Set sail!" you shout. "It's time to get out of this harbor!"

I am vast and undeniable. I will crush you all with my strength and whirl your boats to the bottom of the sea. I'll spin your corpses through the air and dash them against the cliffs.

But no, I am helpless again, always and ever a hostage to someone else's desires. With ease, Artemis imposes her will on my wild fury. I feel the tension of her hands drawing me back like a bowstring. With one strong, smooth motion, she aims me at your fleet. Fiercely, implacably, I blow you to Troy.

"LEDA"

M. RICKERT

I cannot crack an egg without thinking of her. How could she do this to me, beautiful Leda, how could you do this to me? I begin each day with a three-egg omelet. I hold each fragile orb and think of the swell of her vulva. Then I hit it against the bowl. It breaks. A few shell pieces fall in with the sticky egg white and I chase them around with the tines of a fork and they always seem out of grasp and I think, just like her. But not really. Not ever-graspable Leda.

How do you love a beautiful woman? I thought I knew. I thought my love was enough. My devotion. I remember, when she went through that dragonfly stage and wore dragonfly earrings and we had dragonfly sheets and dragonfly lampshades and dragonfly pajamas, and I was just about sick of dragonflies, did I tell her? Did I say, Leda, I am just about sick of these god damn dragonflies. No. I said nothing. In fact, I sent away for dragonfly eggs. Eggs, imagine how that mocks me now! I followed the directions carefully and kept them a secret from her, oh it pains my heart to think of what she learned from my gift, I was like a dragonfly mother for Christ's sake. I kept them in pond water. I kept them warm. At last they hatched, or uncocooned, however you'd call it, and still I tended them, secretly, until almost a thousand were born and these I presented to her in a box and when she opened it (quickly or the results might have changed) they flew out, blue and silver, yellow green purple. A thousand dragonflies for her and she looked at me with those violet eyes, and she looked at them as they flitted about and then she said, and I'll never forget this, she said, "They look different from the ones on our pajamas."

Oh Leda! My Leda in the garden bent over the summer roses, in her silk kimono with the dragonflies on it, and nothing underneath, and I come upon her like that, a vision, my wife, and she looks up just then and sees me watching and knows what she is doing when she unties the robe and lets it fall to the ground and then turns, and bends over, to prune the roses! Ha! In the dirt, in the sun, in the night. Always Leda. Always. Except for this.

She comes into the kitchen. Her eyes, black ringed, her feet bare and swollen, her belly juts out before her. She stands for a moment, just watching me crack eggs, and then she coughs and shuffles over to the coffee maker and pours herself a cup into which she starts spooning heaps of sugar and I try to resist the impulse but I cannot stop myself, after all, didn't I once love her, and I say, "'S not decaf."

I can tell she looks at me with those tired violet eyes but I refuse to return the courtesy and with proper wrist action (oh what Leda knew about proper wrist action!) whisk the eggs to a froth.

"How many times do I got a tell you," she says, "it ain't that kinda birth."

I shrug. Well, what would I know about it? A swan, she says. An egg.

Yeah, he did that thing with the dragonflies and I ain't never heard the end of it. "Don't you know how I love you?" he goes. "Don't you remember all them dragonflies?"

Yeah, I remember. I remember dragonflies in the sugar bowl, dragonflies in the honey. I remember dragonflies trapped in the window screens and dragonflies in my hair and on my bare skin with their tiny sticky legs creeping me out.

What I remember most about the dragonflies is how he didn't get it. He always thinks he has to, you know, improve on me. That's how he loves me. I know that and I've known it for a long time and it didn't matter because he was good in bed, and in the dirt, and on the kitchen table and I thought we was friends, so what if he didn't really understand? A nice pair of dragonfly earrings, a necklace, that would have been enough. If I wanted bugs I wouldn't of been wearing them. Anyway, that's how I always felt and I didn't care that he's kinda stupid but now I do.

He cracks those eggs like it means something. I'm too tired to try to understand. I pour myself a coffee and he makes a big point of not

looking at me and mumbling about how it ain't decaf and I want a
pour the coffee right over his head but I resist the impulse and go sit
in the living room in the green recliner that I got cozied up with piles
of blankets like a nest and I drink my coffee and watch the birds. My
whole body aches. I should leave him. He's failed me so completely. I
sip the coffee. I try not to remember. Wings, oh impossible wings. The
smell of feathers. The sharp beak. The cry. The pulsing beat. I press my
hands against my belly. I should call someone but, after that first night,
and that first phone call, I don't have the energy. I've entered a different
life. I am no longer beautiful and loved. I am strange and lonely.

Rape hotline.

I . . . I . . . .

Okay, take a deep breath.

He . . . he . . . .

Yes?

He . . . .

Yes?

Raped.

Okay. Okay. I am so sorry. It's good you called. We're here to help
you. Is he gone?

Yes.

Are you safe?

What?

Is anyone with you?

My husband, but . . . .

Your husband is with you now?

Yes, but . . . .

If you give me your address I can send someone over.

I . . . .

Okay, are you crying?

He . . . .

Yes?

Raped me.

Your husband?

No, no. He don't believe . . . .

I'm sorry, I'm really sorry.

It happened.

I know. I know. Okay, can you give me your address?

A swan.

What?

Horrible.

Did you say swan?

I always thought they was so beautiful.

Swans?

Yes.

What do swans, I mean—

I was just taking a walk in our yard, you know, the moon was so pretty tonight and then he flew at me.

The swan?

Oh . . . god . . . yes. It was horrible.

Ma'am , are you saying you were raped by a swan?

Yes. I think I could recognize him in a lineup.

Could, could you put your husband on the phone?

He don't believe me.

I would really like to speak to him.

I showed him the feathers, the claw marks. I got red welts all over my skin, and bites, and he, do you know what he thinks?

Ma'am—

He thinks I cheated on him. He thinks I just made this up.

Ma'am, I think you've called the wrong number. There are other help lines.

You don't believe me either.

I believe you've suffered some kind of trauma.

You don't believe a swan raped me, do you?

Ma'am, there are people who can help you.

No, I don't think so. I think everyone loves birds too much. Maybe not crows or blue jays 'cause everyone knows they steal eggs and peck out the brains of little birds, but swans, everyone loves swans, right?

Please, let me give you a different number to call.

No. I don't think so.

Yes, I remember that particular phone call. It's always bothered me. What really happened to her? Or was it a joke? We do get prank calls, you know, though I can't imagine how confused someone must be to think calling a rape hotline could be entertaining. I mean, after all, if I'm talking to someone who isn't even serious, I'm not available for somebody who might really need my help.

What? Well, no, it wasn't a busy night at all. This isn't New York, for God's sake, we average, maybe, two, three rapes a year.

Well, she said she was raped by a swan. How believable is that? Not very, I can tell you. But I don't know … ever since then I've thought I could have handled that call better, you know? I'm a psych major and so I wonder, what really happened? What did the swan symbolize? I mean it's a classically beautiful bird, associated with fairy tales and innocence. Sometimes I wonder, was she really raped?

What? No. Of course I don't mean by a bird. I said a psych major, not a fairy tale believer. I mean, I know what's real and imagined. That's my area of expertise. Women are not raped by birds. But they are raped. Sometimes I wonder if that's what happened, you know, she was raped and it was all so horrible that she lost her mind and grasped this winged symbol of innocence, a swan. I mean let's not be too graphic here, but after all, how big is a swan's penis?

Excuse me? Well no, of course I don't mean to suggest that the horror of rape is measured by the size of the instrument used. What newspaper did you say you're from again? I think I've answered enough questions anyway, what can you tell me about this girl, I mean, woman?

Woman Lays Egg!

Emergency room physicians were shocked and surprised at the delivery of a twenty-pound egg laid by a woman brought to the hospital by her husband Thursday night.

"She just look pregnant," said H. O. Mckille, an orderly at the hospital. "She didn't look no different from any other pregnant lady except maybe a little more hysterical 'cause she was shouting about the egg coming but nobody paid no attention really. Ladies, when they is in labor say all sorts a things. But then I heard Dr. Stephens saying, call Dr. Hogan, and he says, he's a veterinarian in town and that's when I walked over and got a good look and sure enough, ain't no baby coming out of that lady. It's a egg, for sure. But then Nurse Hiet pulls the curtain shut and I'm just standing there next to the husband and so I says, 'You can go in there, that Nurse Hiet just trying to keep me out. You're the husband, right?' He looked kind of in shock, poor guy, I mean who can blame him, it ain't every day your wife lays a twenty-pound egg."

Hospital officials refuse to comment on rumors that the woman is still a patient in a private room in the hospital, where she sits on her egg except for small periods of time when her husband relieves her.

An anonymous source reports, "None of us are supposed to be talking about it. I could lose my job. But, yeah, she's in there, trying to hatch the thing, and let me tell you something else, she's not too happy of a lady and she wants to go home to do this there but she's getting a lot of attention from the doctors and I'm not sure it's because they care about her. You know what I mean? I mean, remember that sheep that got cloned? Well, this is way more exciting than that, a woman who lays eggs. You ask me, there'll be some pressure for her to do it again. It ain't right really. She's a woman. She's gonna be a mama. She ain't some pet in the zoo. Don't use my name, okay, I need this job."

Sometimes she falls asleep on the egg. My Leda, who used to be so beautiful. Why did this happen to her? Why did it happen to us? I lift her up. She's light again since she's laid that thing. I lay her down on the bed. Her violet eyes flutter open. "My egg," she says, and struggles against me, "my baby."

"Sh," I say, "go to sleep. I'll sit on it," and I do. I sit on this egg, which is still warm from Leda's upside-down heart-shaped ass that I used to cup in my hands and call my favorite valentine, and I think how life seems so strange to me now, all the things I used to know are confused.

Leda sleeps, gently snoring. I readjust my weight. It's rather uncomfortable on the egg. Even in sleep she looks exhausted. I can see the blue of her veins, new lines in her face. I never believed she was raped. By a swan. And now there's this, this impossible thing. Does it mean the whole story was true? If so, I have really failed her. How will I ever make it up to her? If not, if she cuckolded me, an old-fashioned word that seems so appropriate here, then she is making me into a laughingstock. You should hear the guys at work. The women just look at me and don't say anything at all.

I dream of a gun I do not own. I point it in different directions. Sometimes I am a hunter in red and black, stalking swans. Sometimes, I bring the gun to work and spray the office with bullets. Sometimes I point it at a mirror. Sometimes it is Leda's violet eyes I see. She doesn't scream. She doesn't really care about anything now. Except this egg.

He lifts me off the egg and carries me to the bed. "My egg. My baby." I'll sit on it, he says, and he does. I sink into sleep. I dream of feathers falling like snow. The sweep of wings across the sky. The pale white moon. My garden roses closed in the night. The sound of wings. A great white bird. White. I dream white. Silence and emptiness. The inside of an egg. A perfect world.

When I wake up he is still sitting on the egg. "Are you crying?" I say.

"Yes," he says, like it's something noble.

"Get off," I go, "I'll sit on it now."

"Don't you want a know why I'm crying?" he says.

"Get off. I don't want you making the baby sad with all your sad energy, it's had a hard enough beginning already."

"Leda, I'm sorry," he goes.

"Get off!" I shout. "Get off! Get off!"

He stands up.

A bunch of hospital people run into the room.

"Leave us alone!" I shout.

He turns to the hospital people, those tears still on his face but drying up some, and he goes, "We need to be alone."

"No!" I shout. "You go too. Leave me and my baby alone." Then I pick up the egg.

They all gasp.

The egg is very heavy. I hold it close to my chest. "Forget it. I'll leave," I say.

That Nurse Hiet steps toward me but Dr. Hogan, the veterinarian, puts up his hand like a school crossing guard and she stops. "We don't want her to hurt the egg," he says.

Which shows how they don't understand. Hurt the egg? Why would I hurt the egg? My baby. It's not my baby's fault what the father did.

They all take a step back. Even my husband, which just proves how whatever he was loving it ain't about me. It was someone he imagined. Someone mean enough to crush my baby just to make a point.

I hold the egg real close. I am leaving the hospital. I was not prepared for the photographers.

Chicken Woman Escapes Hospital with Egg!
Exclusive Photos

Well, I thought they were artists or something like that. I was very surprised to learn that he is an insurance salesman. There's not much I can really tell you for certain. Their house is set back, off the road a bit and for most of the year it's well hidden by the foliage. During the winter months I've seen it, from a distance. It looks cute, bungalowish. I have a friend who knows somebody who once went to a party there, before they owned it, and she said it was very charming. The only personal experience I have had with either of them was a couple of springs ago when I was at Flormine's Garden Shop and she was there looking at rosebushes. I remember this so vividly because she was one of the most beautiful women I have ever seen. She had purple eyes, quite striking really, pale skin, blonde hair, a striking figure. Everyone noticed her. When I look at these photographs, I have a hard time believing this is the same person. What happened to her? She looks quite frightened, doesn't she? I can't comment on the egg. I mean it's pretty obvious, isn't it? I don't know how she fooled the doctors but of course she didn't lay that egg. She's an ordinary woman. And by all appearances she needs help. I wish everyone would forget this nonsense and just get her the help she needs.

When he came home I had to let him in because sometimes I would get so tired I'd fall asleep and then when I woke up, I was kind of only half on the egg and half off and so I let him in if he promised to sit on it and he goes, "Leda, I love you" but I've heard that before and it don't mean nothing anymore from him. "Leda, please forgive me," he goes. I say, sit on the egg. I ain't got the strength to begin forgiving and I don't know if I ever will. I go upstairs and stare out the window at the garden which is all overgrowed now and I think how sorry just ain't enough.

We just made love, me and him and he fell asleep like he does, and I thought it would be nice to walk near my roses underneath that pale full moon and I put on my dragonfly kimono, it's silk and it feels so nice against my skin and it was a beautiful night just a little bit smelling of roses and I thought I was happy and then that swan comes swooping down and for just a moment I thought it was a sign, like of a good thing happening to me 'cause I ain't never seen a swan in my garden and I ain't never seen one flying and then it was on top of me. It was much heavier than I ever thought and when it flew into me I fell to the ground and I couldn't imagine, it was all feathers and wings and claws and beak and I was hitting it and trying to get away and also, at the same time feeling like why would a bird attack me and I didn't wanta hurt it I just wanted out and then, my god, I felt it, you know, and my mind could not, I couldn't . . . a swan doing this to me. I hit at it and clawed at it and it bit me and scratched me and the whole time those wings was flapping and. . . . So now people are making jokes about it, about me. I ain't stupid. I know that. Don't tell me about some lady I never met who feels sorry for me because she don't really believe it happened. I don't give a shit. And when my husband keeps saying, sorry, sorry, what am I supposed to do with that? This happened to me and it was horrible and when I needed him most he was making three-egg omelets and trying to figure out who I cheated on him with. So, he's sorry? Well, what's he gonna do about that? I can't take care of him. It's all I can do to take care of myself and my baby.

Also, one more thing. Since it's truth time. It did occur to me once or twice to break the egg, I mean in the beginning. What will I do if I hatch a swan? Thanksgiving, I guess. Yeah, sometimes I think like that and don't gasp and look away from me. I ain't evil. I'm just a regular woman that something really bad happened to and when it did I learned some things about the world and myself that maybe I'd rather not know. But that don't change it. I stand at the bedroom window and watch my garden dying. What do I believe in now? I don't know.

I don't know what to do for her. I sit on the egg and remember the good times. Leda laughing. Leda in the garden. Leda dancing. Leda naked. Beautiful, beautiful Leda. Beneath me I feel a movement, hear a sound. I sit very still, listen very carefully. There it is again. "Leda!" I shout. "Leda!" She comes running down the stairs. Where'd she get that robe? I didn't even know she owned such a thing. Blue terry cloth, stained with coffee. She stares at me with those dark-rimmed eyes, wide with fright. "What?" she says.

"Baby's coming," I whisper and slide off the egg.

We stand side by side watching the egg shake. I can hardly breathe. A chip of eggshell falls on the quilt. I find myself praying. Just a general sort of plea. Please.

Please let my baby not be a swan.

He takes my hand. I let him. It is the first human touch other than the doctors and I don't feel like they count, since the night when it happened. It feels strange to be touched. I can feel his pulse, his heat. It feels good and strange. Not bad. I just ain't sure how long I will let it continue.

We watch the egg tremble and crack and I feel like I am standing at the edge of something big, like the white in my dreams. Everything is here now. All my life. All my love. What comes out of that egg will make me either drown in the white or fly out of it. I wanta fly out of it but I ain't got the strength to do anything about it.

That's when I see a tiny fist.

I pull my hand away from him and cover my mouth. No wings, I pray, please.

A violet eye!

I am standing so still in case if I move we fall into a different reality.

No beak, I think, and just then, like the world was made of what we want, I see the mouth and I start to laugh but I stop because some more eggshell falls off and a second mouth appears right beside the first one and I don't know what that's all about.

Please, I think, please.

I didn't know what to think. I've been pretty ambivalent about the whole egg thing to be honest. I mean, I only sat on it for her. But as soon as it started hatching I felt excited and then kind of nervous. Like, what's happening here? Are we going to have a baby bird? How do I feel about that? I didn't even think about it when I reached over and took her hand. I just did it like we hadn't been having all this trouble and then I realized we were holding hands and I was so happy about that, it distracted me from the egg for a minute.

I think we were both relieved to see the little fist. Of course, I knew we weren't in the clear yet. I mean it was very possible that we were hatching some kind of feathered human, or some such combination.

Could I love the baby? Yes, this thought occurred to me. Could I love this baby from this horrible act? To be honest, I didn't know if I could.

She pulled her hand away. I ached for her immediately. We saw an eye, violet, just like hers, and I thought I could definitely love the baby if it looked like her and then we saw the mouth, and after a moment, another mouth and I thought FREAK. I know I shouldn't have thought it, but I did. I thought, we are going to have this freak for a child.

All these images flashed through my mind of me carrying around this two-mouthed baby, of it growing feathers during puberty, long talks about inner beauty. I had it all figured out. That's when I knew. Even if it had two mouths and feathers, I could love this kid.

I looked at Leda. It was like something momentous had happened to me and she didn't even realize it. She stood there in that old blue terry cloth robe, with the coffee stains down the front, her hair all a tangle, her violet eyes circled in fright, her face creased with lines, her hands in fists near her mouth and I wanted to tell her, "Sh, don't worry. Everything's going to be all right. It doesn't matter how it looks." But I didn't say anything because I also finally realized I wasn't going to teach her anything about love. Not Leda, who carried this thing, and laid it, and took it away from all those cold and curious doctors and brought it home and sat on it and let her own beauty go untended so she could tend to it. I have nothing to teach her. I have much to learn.

Then I knowed what was happening. When the egg really started to fall apart. Two mouths. Four fists. Four legs. Two heads. And, thank god, two separate beautiful perfect little girl bodies. Two babies, exhausted and crying. I walked over to them and kneeled down beside them and then I just brushed the eggshell off and that gooey stuff and one of them had violet eyes, and the other looks like my husband I realized that on that night I got pregnant twice. Once by my husband and once by that swan and both babies are beautiful in their own way though I gotta admit the one that looks kind of like me, from before this all happened, will probably grow to be the greater beauty, and for this reason I hold her a little tighter, 'cause I know how hard it can be to be beautiful.

My husband bends over and helps brush the eggshell and gooey stuff off and we carry the babies to the couch and I lay down with them and untie my robe and I can hear my husband gasp, whether for pleasure or sorrow I don't know. My body has changed so much. I lay there, one baby at each breast sucking.

Oh Leda, will you ever forgive me? Will you trust me with our girls? Will I fail them too? Is this what love means? The horrible burden of the damage we do to each other? If only I could have loved you perfectly. Like a god, instead of a human. Forgive me. Let me love you and the children. Please.

She smiles for the first time in months, yawns and closes those beautiful eyes, then opens them wide, a frightened expression on her face. She looks at me, but I'm not sure she sees me, and she says, "swan" or was it "swine"? I can't be sure. I am only certain that I love her, that I will always love her. Leda. Always, always Leda. In your terry cloth robe with coffee stains, while the girls nap and you do too, the sun bright on the lines of your face; as you walk to the garden, careful and unsure; as you weed around the roses, Leda, I will always love you, Leda in the dirt, Leda in the sun, Leda shading her eyes and looking up at the horrible memory of what was done to you, always Leda, always.

"CHIVALRY"

NEIL GAIMAN

Mrs. Whitaker found the Holy Grail; it was under a fur coat.

Every Thursday afternoon Mrs. Whitaker walked down to the post office to collect her pension, even though her legs were no longer what they were, and on the way back home she would stop in at the Oxfam Shop and buy herself a little something.

The Oxfam Shop sold old clothes, knickknacks, oddments, bits and bobs, and large quantities of old paperbacks, all of them donations: secondhand flotsam, often the house clearances of the dead. All the profits went to charity.

The shop was staffed by volunteers. The volunteer on duty this afternoon was Marie, seventeen, slightly overweight, and dressed in a baggy mauve jumper that looked like she had bought it from the shop.

Marie sat by the till with a copy of *Modern Woman* magazine, filling out a "Reveal Your Hidden Personality" questionnaire. Every now and then, she'd flip to the back of the magazine and check the relative points assigned to an A), B), or C) answer before making up her mind how she'd respond to the question.

Mrs. Whitaker puttered around the shop.

They still hadn't sold the stuffed cobra, she noted. It had been there for six months now, gathering dust, glass eyes gazing balefully at the clothes racks and the cabinet filled with chipped porcelain and chewed toys.

Mrs. Whitaker patted its head as she went past.

She picked out a couple of Mills & Boon novels from a bookshelf—*Her Thundering Soul* and *Her Turbulent Heart*, a shilling each—and gave careful consideration to the empty bottle of Mateus Rosé with a decorative lamp-shade on it before deciding she really didn't have anywhere to put it.

She moved a rather threadbare fur coat, which smelled badly of mothballs. Underneath it was a walking stick and a water-stained copy of *Romance and Legend of Chivalry* by A. R. Hope Moncrieff, priced at five pence. Next to the book, on its side, was the Holy Grail. It had a little round paper sticker on the base, and written on it, in felt pen, was the price: 30p.

Mrs. Whitaker picked up the dusty silver goblet and appraised it through her thick spectacles.

"This is nice," she called to Marie.

Marie shrugged.

"It'd look nice on the mantelpiece."

Marie shrugged again.

Mrs. Whitaker gave fifty pence to Marie, who gave her ten pence change and a brown paper bag to put the books and the Holy Grail in. Then she went next door to the butcher's and bought herself a nice piece of liver. Then she went home.

The inside of the goblet was thickly coated with a brownish-red dust. Mrs. Whitaker washed it out with great care, then left it to soak for an hour in warm water with a dash of vinegar added.

Then she polished it with metal polish until it gleamed, and she put it on the mantelpiece in her parlor, where it sat between a small soulful china basset hound and a photograph of her late husband, Henry, on the beach at Frinton in 1953.

She had been right: It did look nice.

For dinner that evening she had the liver fried in breadcrumbs with onions. It was very nice.

The next morning was Friday; on alternate Fridays Mrs. Whitaker and Mrs. Greenberg would visit each other. Today it was Mrs. Green-berg's turn to visit Mrs. Whitaker. They sat in the parlor and ate maca-roons and drank tea. Mrs. Whitaker took one sugar in her tea, but Mrs. Greenberg took sweetener, which she always carried in her handbag in a small plastic container.

"That's nice," said Mrs. Greenberg, pointing to the Grail. "What is it?"

"It's the Holy Grail," said Mrs. Whitaker. "It's the cup that Jesus drunk out of at the Last Supper. Later, at the Crucifixion, it caught His precious blood when the centurion's spear pierced His side."

Mrs. Greenberg sniffed. She was small and Jewish and didn't hold with unsanitary things. "I wouldn't know about that," she said, "but it's very nice. Our Myron got one just like that when he won the swimming tournament, only it's got his name on the side."

"Is he still with that nice girl? The hairdresser?"

"Bernice? Oh yes. They're thinking of getting engaged," said Mrs. Greenberg.

"That's nice," said Mrs. Whitaker. She took another macaroon.

Mrs. Greenberg baked her own macaroons and brought them over every alternate Friday: small sweet light brown biscuits with almonds on top.

They talked about Myron and Bernice, and Mrs. Whitaker's nephew Ronald (she had had no children), and about their friend Mrs. Perkins who was in hospital with her hip, poor dear.

At midday Mrs. Greenberg went home, and Mrs. Whitaker made herself cheese on toast for lunch, and after lunch Mrs. Whitaker took her pills; the white and the red and two little orange ones.

The doorbell rang.

Mrs. Whitaker answered the door. It was a young man with shoulder-length hair so fair it was almost white, wearing gleaming silver armor, with a white surcoat.

"Hello," he said.

"Hello," said Mrs. Whitaker.

"I'm on a quest," he said.

"That's nice," said Mrs. Whitaker, noncommittally.

"Can I come in?" he asked.

Mrs. Whitaker shook her head. "I'm sorry, I don't think so," she said.

"I'm on a quest for the Holy Grail," the young man said. "Is it here?"

"Have you got any identification?" Mrs. Whitaker asked. She knew that it was unwise to let unidentified strangers into your home when you were elderly and living on your own. Handbags get emptied, and worse than that.

The young man went back down the garden path. His horse, a huge gray charger, big as a shire-horse, its head high and its eyes intelligent, was tethered to Mrs. Whitaker's garden gate. The knight fumbled in the saddlebag and returned with a scroll.

It was signed by Arthur, King of All Britons, and charged all persons of whatever rank or station to know that here was Galaad, Knight of the

Table Round, and that he was on a Right High and Noble Quest. There was a drawing of the young man below that. It wasn't a bad likeness.

Mrs. Whitaker nodded. She had been expecting a little card with a photograph on it, but this was far more impressive.

"I suppose you had better come in," she said.

They went into her kitchen. She made Galaad a cup of tea, then she took him into the parlor.

Galaad saw the Grail on her mantelpiece, and dropped to one knee. He put down the teacup carefully on the russet carpet. A shaft of light came through the net curtains and painted his awed face with golden sunlight and turned his hair into a silver halo.

"It is truly the Sangrail," he said, very quietly. He blinked his pale blue eyes three times, very fast, as if he were blinking back tears.

He lowered his head as if in silent prayer.

Galaad stood up again and turned to Mrs. Whitaker. "Gracious lady, keeper of the Holy of Holies, let me now depart this place with the Blessed Chalice, that my journeyings may be ended and my geas fulfilled."

"Sorry?" said Mrs. Whitaker.

Galaad walked over to her and took her old hands in his. "My quest is over," he told her. "The Sangrail is finally within my reach."

Mrs. Whitaker pursed her lips. "Can you pick your teacup and saucer up, please?" she said.

Galaad picked up his teacup apologetically.

"No. I don't think so," said Mrs. Whitaker. "I rather like it there. It's just right, between the dog and the photograph of my Henry."

"Is it gold you need? Is that it? Lady, I can bring you gold . . ."

"No," said Mrs. Whitaker. "I don't want any gold thank you. I'm simply not interested."

She ushered Galaad to the front door. "Nice to meet you," she said.

His horse was leaning its head over her garden fence, nibbling her gladioli. Several of the neighborhood children were standing on the pavement, watching it.

Galaad took some sugar lumps from the saddlebag and showed the braver of the children how to feed the horse, their hands held flat. The children giggled. One of the older girls stroked the horse's nose.

Galaad swung himself up onto the horse in one fluid movement. Then the horse and the knight trotted off down Hawthorne Crescent.

Mrs. Whitaker watched them until they were out of sight, then sighed and went back inside.

The weekend was quiet.

On Saturday Mrs. Whitaker took the bus into Maresfield to visit her nephew Ronald, his wife Euphonia, and their daughters, Clarissa and Dillian. She took them a currant cake she had baked herself.

On Sunday morning Mrs. Whitaker went to church. Her local church was St. James the Less, which was a little more "Don't think of this as a church, think of it as a place where like-minded friends hang out and are joyful" than Mrs. Whitaker felt entirely comfortable with, but she liked the vicar, the Reverend Bartholomew, when he wasn't actually playing the guitar.

After the service, she thought about mentioning to him that she had the Holy Grail in her front parlor, but decided against it.

On Monday morning Mrs. Whitaker was working in the back garden. She had a small herb garden she was extremely proud of: dill, vervain, mint, rosemary, thyme, and a wild expanse of parsley. She was down on her knees, wearing thick green gardening gloves, weeding, and picking out slugs and putting them in a plastic bag.

Mrs. Whitaker was very tenderhearted when it came to slugs. She would take them down to the back of her garden, which bordered on the railway line, and throw them over the fence.

She cut some parsley for the salad. There was a cough behind her. Galaad stood there, tall and beautiful, his armor glinting in the morning sun. In his arms he held a long package, wrapped in oiled leather.

"I'm back," he said.

"Hello," said Mrs. Whitaker. She stood up, rather slowly, and took off her gardening gloves. "Well," she said, "now you're here, you might as well make yourself useful."

She gave him the plastic bag full of slugs and told him to tip the slugs out over the back of the fence.

He did.

Then they went into the kitchen.

"Tea? Or lemonade?" she asked.

"Whatever you're having," Galaad said.

Mrs. Whitaker took a jug of her homemade lemonade from the fridge and sent Galaad outside to pick a sprig of mint.

She selected two tall glasses. She washed the mint carefully and put a few leaves in each glass, then poured the lemonade.

"Is your horse outside?" she asked.

"Oh yes. His name is Grizzel."

"And you've come a long way, I suppose."

"A very long way."

"I see," said Mrs. Whitaker. She took a blue plastic basin from under the sink and half-filled it with water. Galaad took it out to Grizzel. He waited while the horse drank and brought the empty basin back to Mrs. Whitaker.

"Now," she said, "I suppose you're still after the Grail."

"Aye, still do I seek the Sangrail," he said. He picked up the leather package from the floor, put it down on her tablecloth and unwrapped it. "For it, I offer you this."

It was a sword, its blade almost four feet long. There were words and symbols traced elegantly along the length of the blade. The hilt was worked in silver and gold, and a large jewel was set in the pommel.

"It's very nice," said Mrs. Whitaker, doubtfully.

"This," said Galaad, "is the sword Balmung, forged by Wayland Smith in the dawn times. Its twin is Flamberge. Who wears it is unconquerable in war, and invincible in battle. Who wears it is incapable of a cowardly act or an ignoble one. Set in its pommel is the sardonynx Bircone, which protects its possessor from poison slipped into wine or ale, and from the treachery of friends."

Mrs. Whitaker peered at the sword. "It must be very sharp," she said, after a while.

"It can slice a falling hair in twain. Nay, it could slice a sunbeam," said Galaad proudly.

"Well, then, maybe you ought to put it away," said Mrs. Whitaker.

"Don't you want it?" Galaad seemed disappointed.

"No, thank you," said Mrs. Whitaker. It occurred to her that her late husband, Henry, would have quite liked it. He would have hung it on the wall in his study next to the stuffed carp he had caught in Scotland, and pointed it out to visitors.

Galaad rewrapped the oiled leather around the sword Balmung and tied it up with white cord.

He sat there, disconsolate.

Mrs. Whitaker made him some cream cheese and cucumber sandwiches for the journey back and wrapped them in greaseproof paper. She gave him an apple for Grizzel. He seemed very pleased with both gifts.

She waved them both good-bye.

That afternoon she took the bus down to the hospital to see Mrs. Perkins, who was still in with her hip, poor love. Mrs. Whitaker took her some homemade fruitcake, although she had left out the walnuts from the recipe, because Mrs. Perkins's teeth weren't what they used to be.

She watched a little television that evening, and had an early night.

On Tuesday the postman called. Mrs. Whitaker was up in the box-room at the top of the house, doing a spot of tidying, and, taking each step slowly and carefully, she didn't make it downstairs in time. The postman had left her a message which said that he'd tried to deliver a packet, but no one was home.

Mrs. Whitaker sighed.

She put the message into her handbag and went down to the post office.

The package was from her niece Shirelle in Sydney, Australia. It contained photographs of her husband, Wallace, and her two daughters, Dixie and Violet, and a conch shell packed in cotton wool.

Mrs. Whitaker had a number of ornamental shells in her bedroom. Her favorite had a view of the Bahamas done on it in enamel. It had been a gift from her sister, Ethel, who had died in 1983.

She put the shell and the photographs in her shopping bag. Then, seeing that she was in the area, she stopped in at the Oxfam Shop on her way home.

"Hullo, Mrs. W.," said Marie.

Mrs. Whitaker stared at her. Marie was wearing lipstick (possibly not the best shade for her, nor particularly expertly applied, but, thought Mrs. Whitaker, that would come with time) and a rather smart skirt. It was a great improvement.

"Oh. Hello, dear," said Mrs. Whitaker.

"There was a man in here last week, asking about that thing you bought. The little metal cup thing. I told him where to find you. You don't mind, do you?"

"No, dear," said Mrs. Whitaker. "He found me."

"He was really dreamy. Really, really dreamy," sighed Marie wistfully. "I could of gone for him.

"And he had a big white horse and all," Marie concluded. She was standing up straighter as well, Mrs. Whitaker noted approvingly.

On the bookshelf Mrs. Whitaker found a new Mills & Boon novel—*Her Majestic Passion*—although she hadn't yet finished the two she had bought on her last visit.

She picked up the copy of *Romance and Legend of Chivalry* and opened it. It smelled musty. *EX LIBRIS FISHER* was neatly handwritten at the top of the first page in red ink.

She put it down where she had found it.

When she got home, Galaad was waiting for her. He was giving the neighborhood children rides on Grizzel's back, up and down the street.

"I'm glad you're here," she said. "I've got some cases that need moving."

She showed him up to the boxroom in the top of the house. He moved all the old suitcases for her, so she could get to the cupboard at the back.

It was very dusty up there.

She kept him up there most of the afternoon, moving things around while she dusted.

Galaad had a cut on his cheek, and he held one arm a little stiffly.

They talked a little while she dusted and tidied. Mrs. Whitaker told him about her late husband, Henry; and how the life insurance had paid the house off; and how she had all these things, but no one really to leave them to, no one but Ronald really and his wife only liked modern things. She told him how she had met Henry during the war, when he was in the ARP and she hadn't closed the kitchen blackout curtains all the way; and about the sixpenny dances they went to in the town; and how they'd gone to London when the war had ended, and she'd had her first drink of wine.

Galaad told Mrs. Whitaker about his mother Elaine, who was flighty and no better than she should have been and something of a witch to boot; and his grandfather, King Pelles, who was well-meaning although at best a little vague; and of his youth in the Castle of Bliant on the Joyous Isle; and his father, whom he knew as "Le Chevalier Mal Fet," who was more or less completely mad, and was in reality Lancelot du Lac, greatest of knights, in disguise and bereft of his wits; and of Galaad's days as a young squire in Camelot.

At five o'clock Mrs. Whitaker surveyed the boxroom and decided that it met with her approval; then she opened the window so the room could air, and they went downstairs to the kitchen, where she put on the kettle.

Galaad sat down at the kitchen table.

He opened the leather purse at his waist and took out a round white stone. It was about the size of a cricket ball.

"My lady," he said, "This is for you, an you give me the Sangrail."

Mrs. Whitaker picked up the stone, which was heavier than it looked, and held it up to the light. It was milkily translucent, and deep inside it flecks of silver glittered and glinted in the late-afternoon sunlight. It was warm to the touch.

Then, as she held it, a strange feeling crept over her: Deep inside she felt stillness and a sort of peace. *Serenity*, that was the word for it; she felt serene.

Reluctantly she put the stone back on the table.

"It's very nice," she said.

"That is the Philosopher's Stone, which our forefather Noah hung in the Ark to give light when there was no light; it can transform base metals into gold; and it has certain other properties," Galaad told her proudly. "And that isn't all. There's more. Here." From the leather bag he took an egg and handed it to her.

It was the size of a goose egg and was a shiny black color, mottled with scarlet and white. When Mrs. Whitaker touched it, the hairs on the back of her neck prickled. Her immediate impression was one of incredible heat and freedom. She heard the crackling of distant fires, and for a fraction of a second she seemed to feel herself far above the world, swooping and diving on wings of flame.

She put the egg down on the table, next to the Philosopher's Stone.

"That is the Egg of the Phoenix," said Galaad. "From far Araby it comes. One day it will hatch out into the Phoenix Bird itself; and when its time comes, the bird will build a nest of flame, lay its egg, and die, to be reborn in flame in a later age of the world."

"I thought that was what it was," said Mrs. Whitaker.

"And, last of all, lady," said Galaad, "I have brought you this."

He drew it from his pouch, and gave it to her. It was an apple, apparently carved from a single ruby, on an amber stem.

A little nervously, she picked it up. It was soft to the touch—deceptively so: Her fingers bruised it, and ruby-colored juice from the apple ran down Mrs. Whitaker's hand.

The kitchen filled—almost imperceptibly, magically—with the smell of summer fruit, of raspberries and peaches and strawberries and red currants. As if from a great way away she heard distant voices raised in song and far music on the air.

"It is one of the apples of the Hesperides," said Galaad, quietly. "One bite from it will heal any illness or wound, no matter how deep; a second bite restores youth and beauty; and a third bite is said to grant eternal life." Mrs. Whitaker licked the sticky juice from her hand. It tasted like fine wine.

There was a moment, then, when it all came back to her—how it was to be young: to have a firm, slim body that would do whatever she wanted it to do; to run down a country lane for the simple unladylike joy of running; to have men smile at her just because she was herself and happy about it.

Mrs. Whitaker looked at Sir Galaad, most comely of all knights, sitting fair and noble in her small kitchen.

She caught her breath.

"And that's all I have brought for you," said Galaad. "They weren't easy to get, either."

Mrs. Whitaker put the ruby fruit down on her kitchen table. She looked at the Philosopher's Stone, and the Egg of the Phoenix, and the Apple of Life.

Then she walked into her parlor and looked at the mantelpiece: at the little china basset hound, and the Holy Grail, and the photograph of her late husband Henry, shirtless, smiling and eating an ice cream in black and white, almost forty years away.

She went back into the kitchen. The kettle had begun to whistle. She poured a little steaming water into the teapot, swirled it around, and poured it out. Then she added two spoonfuls of tea and one for the pot and poured in the rest of the water. All this she did in silence.

She turned to Galaad then, and she looked at him.

"Put that apple away," she told Galaad, firmly. "You shouldn't offer things like that to old ladies. It isn't proper."

She paused, then. "But I'll take the other two," she continued, after a moment's thought. "They'll look nice on the mantelpiece. And two for one's fair, or I don't know what is." Galaad beamed. He put the ruby apple into his leather pouch. Then he went down on one knee, and kissed Mrs. Whitaker's hand.

"Stop that," said Mrs. Whitaker. She poured them both cups of tea, after getting out the very best china, which was only for special occasions.

They sat in silence, drinking their tea.

When they had finished their tea they went into the parlor.

Galaad crossed himself, and picked up the Grail.

Mrs. Whitaker arranged the Egg and the Stone where the Grail had been. The Egg kept tipping on one side, and she propped it up against the little china dog.

"They do look very nice," said Mrs. Whitaker.

"Yes," agreed Galaad. "They look very nice."

"Can I give you anything to eat before you go back?" she asked.

He shook his head.

"Some fruitcake," she said. "You may not think you want any now, but you'll be glad of it in a few hours' time. And you should probably use the facilities. Now, give me that, and I'll wrap it up for you."

She directed him to the small toilet at the end of the hall, and went into the kitchen, holding the Grail. She had some old Christmas wrapping paper in the pantry, and she wrapped the Grail in it, and tied the package with twine. Then she cut a large slice of fruitcake and put it in a brown paper bag, along with a banana and a slice of processed cheese in silver foil.

Galaad came back from the toilet. She gave him the paper bag, and the Holy Grail. Then she went up on tiptoes and kissed him on the cheek.

"You're a nice boy," she said. "You take care of yourself."

He hugged her, and she shooed him out of the kitchen, and out of the back door, and she shut the door behind him.

She poured herself another cup of tea, and cried quietly into a Kleenex, while the sound of hoofbeats echoed down Hawthorne Crescent.

On Wednesday Mrs. Whitaker stayed in all day.

On Thursday she went down to the post office to collect her pension. Then she stopped in at the Oxfam Shop.

The woman on the till was new to her. "Where's Marie?" asked Mrs. Whitaker.

The woman on the till, who had blue-rinsed gray hair and blue spectacles that went up into diamante points, shook her head and shrugged her shoulders. "She went off with a young man," she said. "On a horse. Tch. I ask you. I'm meant to be down in the Heathfield shop this afternoon. I had to get my Johnny to run me up here, while we find someone else."

"Oh," said Mrs. Whitaker. "Well, it's nice that she's found herself a young man."

"Nice for her, maybe," said the lady on the till, "But some of us were meant to be in Heathfield this afternoon."

On a shelf near the back of the shop Mrs. Whitaker found a tarnished old silver container with a long spout. It had been priced at sixty pence, according to the little paper label stuck to the side. It looked a little like a flattened, elongated teapot.

She picked out a Mills & Boon novel she hadn't read before. It was called *Her Singular Love*. She took the book and the silver container up to the woman on the till.

"Sixty-five pee, dear," said the woman, picking up the silver object, staring at it. "Funny old thing, isn't it? Came in this morning." It had writing carved along the side in blocky old Chinese characters and an elegant arching handle. "Some kind of oil can, I suppose."

"No, it's not an oil can," said Mrs. Whitaker, who knew exactly what it was. "It's a lamp." There was a small metal finger ring, unornamented, tied to the handle of the lamp with brown twine.

"Actually," said Mrs. Whitaker, "on second thoughts, I think I'll just have the book."

She paid her five pence for the novel, and put the lamp back where she had found it, in the back of the shop. After all, Mrs. Whitaker reflected, as she walked home, it wasn't as if she had anywhere to put it.

"THE GOD OF AU"

ANN LECKIE

The Fleet of the Godless came to the waters around Au by chance. It was an odd assortment of the refugees of the world; some had deliberately renounced all gods, some had offended one god in particular. A few were some god's favorites that another, rival god had cursed. But most were merely the descendants of the original unfortunates and had never lived any other way.

There were six double-hulled boats, named, in various languages, *Bird of the Waves, Water Knife, O Gods Take Pity, Breath of Starlight, Righteous Vengeance,* and *Neither Land Nor Water.* (This last was the home of a man whose divine enemy had pronounced that henceforth he should live on neither land nor water. Its two shallow hulls and the deck between them were carefully lined with soil, so that as it floated on the waves it would be precisely what its name declared.) For long years they had wandered the world, pursued by their enemies, allies of no one. Who would shelter them and risk the anger of gods? Who, even had they wished to, could protect them?

More than any other people in the world, they were attuned to the presence and moods of gods—they would hardly have survived so long had they not been—and even before they came in sight of the line of small islands that stretched southward from the larger island of Au they had felt a curious lifelessness in the atmosphere. It was unlike anything they had ever met before. They sailed ahead, cautiously, watched and waited, and after a few days their leader, a man named Steq, captain of *Righteous Vengeance,* ordered the most neutral of prayers and a small sacrifice to whoever the local gods of the waters might be.

Shortly afterwards, twelve people disappeared in the night and were never seen again. The remaining Godless knew a sign when they saw one, and their six captains met together on *Neither Land Nor Water* to consult.

The six ships rode near a small island, sheer-sided black stone, white seabirds nesting in the crags, and a crown of green grass at the top. The breeze was cold, and the sun, though bright in a cloudless, intensely blue sky, seemed warmthless, and so they huddled around the firebox on the deck between the two hulls.

"What shall we do?" Steq asked the other five when they had all settled. He was, like the other Godless, all wiry muscle and no fat. Years of exposure had bleached his dark hair reddish, and whatever color his skin had been at his birth, it had been darkened yet further by the sun. His eyes were brown, and seemed somehow vague until he spoke, when all hints of diffusion or dreaminess disappeared. "I have some thoughts on the matter myself, but it would be best to consider all our options."

"We should leave here," said the captain of *O Gods Take Pity*, a broad-shouldered man with one eye and one hand, and skin like leather. He was older than any of the other captains. "The god in question is clearly capricious."

"What god isn't?" asked another captain. "Let's make up a sacrifice. A good one, with plenty of food, a feast on all six boats. Let us invoke *the god who punished us for our recent offense*. In this way perhaps we can at least mollify it."

"Your thought is a good one," said Steq. "It has crossed my mind as well. Though I am undecided which I think better—a feast, or some ascetic act of penitence."

"Why not both?" suggested another. "First the penitence, and then a feast."

"This would seem to cover all eventualities," said Steq. The others were agreed, except for the captain of *O Gods Take Pity*.

"This god is tricky and greedy. More so than others. Best we should take our chances elsewhere." And he would not participate in the debate over the safest wording and form of the rites, but closed his one eye and leaned closer to the firebox.

When the meeting was done and the captains were departing for their own boats, Steq took him aside. "Why do you say this god is greedier and trickier than most?"

"Why do you ask me this when the meeting is finished?" asked the other captain, narrowing his one eye. Steq only looked at him. "Very well. Ask yourself this question—where are the other gods? There is not an infant in the fleet that does not feel the difference between these waters and the ones we've left. This is a god that has driven out or destroyed all others, a god who resents sacrifices meant for any other. And that being the case, why wait for us to make the mistake? Why not send warning first, and thus be assured of our obedience? It pleased the god that we should lose those twelve people, make no mistake. You would be a fool not to see it, and I never took you for a fool."

"I see it," said Steq. He had not risen to a position of authority without an even temper, and considerable intelligence. "I also see that we could do worse than win favor with a god powerful enough to drive any other out of its territory."

"At what cost, Steq?"

"There has never been a time we have not paid for dealing with gods," said Steq. "And there has never been a time that we have not been compelled to deal with them. We are all sick at heart over this loss, but we cannot afford to pass by any advantage that may offer itself."

"I left my own son to drown because I could not go back without endangering my boat and everyone in it. Do not think I speak out of sentiment." Both men were silent a moment. "I will not challenge your authority, but I tell you, this is a mistake that may well cost us our lives."

"I value your counsel," Steq told him, and he put his hand on the other captain's shoulder. "Do not be silent, I beg you, but tell me all your misgivings, now and in the future." And with that they parted, each to their own boat.

A thousand years before, in the village of Ilu on the island of Au, there were two brothers, Etoje and Ekuba. They had been born on the same day and when their father died it was unclear how his possessions should be divided.

The brothers took their dispute to the god of a cave near Ilu. This cave was a hollow in the mountainside that led down to a steaming, sulfur-smelling well, and the god there had often given good advice in the past.

Let Ekuba divide according to his satisfaction, was the god's answer. *And let Etoje choose his portion. Let the brothers be bound by their choices, or death and disaster will be the result.*

But instead of dividing fairly, Ekuba hid the most desirable part of his father's belongings in a hole under the pile he was certain Etoje would not choose. It was not long before Etoje discovered his brother's deception, and in anger he drew his knife and struck Ekuba so that he fell bleeding to the ground. Thinking he had killed his brother, Etoje took a small boat and fled.

The island furthest to the south of Au had reared its head and shoulders above the water, with much steam and ash and fire, in the time of Etoje's great-grandfather. Birds were still wary of it, and it was not considered a good place to hunt. Its sides were black and steep, and there was no place for a boat to land, but Etoje found a spur of rock to tie his boat to, and he climbed up the cliff to the top, where a few plants and mosses had taken tentative root in the ashes, and a pool of warm water steamed. There was nothing else of interest.

But darkness was falling and he had nowhere else to go, so he sat down next to the spring to consider his situation. "Oh, Etoje," he said to himself, "your anger will be the death of you. But what else were you to do?"

As he sat, a seabird flew overhead, carrying a large fish. Etoje thought that if he could make the bird drop the fish, he might at least have some food for the evening. So he took up a stone as quickly as he might and threw it at the bird.

The stone hit its target, and the bird dropped the fish. But the fish fell not on the ashy land, but into the spring. Etoje could not see it to pull it out, and he was wary of wading into a spring he knew nothing of, so he settled himself once again.

When he had sat this way for some time, he heard a voice. "Etoje," it whispered. Etoje looked around, but saw nothing. "Etoje!" This time Etoje looked at the spring, and saw the fish lying half in and half out of the water.

"Did you speak to me, fish?" Etoje asked. It looked like any other fish, silver-scaled and finned and glassy-eyed.

"I spoke," said the fish, "but I am not a fish."

"You look like a fish to me," remarked Etoje.

"I am the god of this island," said the fish in its weird whisper. "I must have a mouth to speak, and perforce I have used this fish, there being nothing else available."

"Then I thank you, god of this island, whatever your proper name, whether you be male or female, or both, or neither, for your hospitality. Though I have little besides thanks to offer in exchange."

"It was of exchange I wished to speak. Shall we trade favors and become allies?"

"On what terms?" asked Etoje, for though he was in desperate straits, he knew that one should be cautious when dealing with gods.

"I was born with the island," said the fish. "And I am lonely. The cliff-girt isles around me subsist on the occasional prayers of hunters. They are silent and all but godless. No one hunts my birdless cliffs, and my island, like those others, will likely never be settled. Take me to Au, and I will reward you."

"That, I'm afraid, is impossible." And Etoje told the fish of his father's death, and his brother's deception, and his own anger and flight.

"Take me to Au," the fish insisted. And it told Etoje that if he would do so, and make the sacrifices and perform the rites the god required, Etoje would be pre-eminent in Au. "I will make you and yours rulers over the whole land of Au. I will promise that you and yours will be mine, and your fates my special concern, so long as Au stands above the waves."

"And when the tide comes in?"

"Shrewd Etoje! But I meant no trick. Let us say instead, so long as the smallest part of the island of Au stands above the waves. If you feed me well I will certainly have the strength to do all I say and more."

"Ah," said Etoje. "You want blood."

"I want all the rites of the people of Au, all the sacrifices. Declare me, alone, your god. Declare me, alone, the god of your people. Declare me, alone, the god of Au. Any who will not accept this bargain will be outlaws, and I will have their blood."

"What of the gods already resident on Au? Would they not starve?"

"Do they care now if you starve?" asked the fish.

"You have a point." And Etoje was silent for a few moments.

"With your help," said the fish, "I will enter any good-sized stone you bring me—there are several nearby—and you will bring it to Au. Then you will offer sacrifice and free me from the stone."

"And this sacrifice?"

"I hear the seabirds crying above the waves. They have flown over Ilu and they tell me your brother is not dead, merely injured. Have you considered how much simpler the question of your inheritance would be if he were dead?"

"I must ponder," said Etoje.

"Certainly. But don't ponder excessively. This fish won't last forever."

"Speaking of which," said Etoje, "do you need all of the fish for talking? I'm quite hungry, and I'm sure I would think better on a full stomach."

"Take it all," said the fish. "In the morning bring another to the spring. Or a seal or bird—fish aren't made for talking and this is quite taxing."

"Thank you," said Etoje. "I'm reassured to find you so reasonable. I will now dedicate this fish to you and indulge in a sacrificial feast, after which I will consider all you have said."

And Etoje did those things.

In the thousand years after Etoje made his bargain, the village of Ilu became the city of Ilu. It stood at the mouth of a wide, icy stream that tumbled down from the heights of the glacier-covered mountain Mueu. On Mueu's lower slopes the spring in the cave still steamed, but the god was long silent, either absent or dead. Behind Mueu was the high, cold interior of Au, a wasteland of ice and lava where no one went.

Ilu's green and brown houses, of turf and stone and skins, spread down to the sea where racks of fish lay drying, where the hunting boats lay each night and left each morning, and where frames of seaweed rose and fell with the tide. In the center of the city was the Place of the God of Au, a sprawling complex of blocks of black lava, rising higher than any other building there.

In days long past, anyone might raid a foreign village and bring his captives to Ilu, feeding the god handsomely and increasing his own standing and wealth. Whole villages perished, or else threw themselves at the feet of Ilu's rulers and declared themselves faithful servants of the god. Many humble but clever and brave young men made their fortunes in those days. But now the only outlaws in Au were condemned criminals, and only the same several officials, who had inherited the right to dispense justice, could present human victims to the god. No other outlaws were to be found in the land. Every village—for Ilu was Au's only city—offered its rites and sacrifices to the god of Au alone.

In return, the people of Au prospered. They were healthy and well-fed. Seals, fish, and whales were abundant. It was true that over the years the number of offences punishable by death had increased, but if one was a solid, law-abiding citizen and meticulous about honoring the god, this was of no concern.

There was a man named Ihak, and he lived in the Place of the God. It was his job, as it had been his father's, and his father's before him, to receive the outlaw victims intended for the god, and issue receipts to the providers in the form of tokens of volcanic glass carved into the shape of small fish. In former days this had been a position of great influence, but now was merely a ceremonial duty. Ihak was a tall man, almost spindly. He walked with a slight stoop, and his features were pinched and narrow. Though he and his wife had been together for many years, they had produced no children. He had often presented the god with fish, and with his own blood, and once he had even bought a human victim from one of the officials he dealt with, though it had meant a great deal of his savings. Making each sacrifice he had reminded the god of his faithful service, and that of his own ancestors, and he humbly and sincerely begged the god to provide him with that one thing that would complete his happiness. This was the only defect in his otherwise comfortable life.

One day two hunters came to the Place of the God with a dozen injured captives in tow. The gatekeeper gaped in astonishment and tried to turn them away, but they would not move. The captives were dressed oddly, and didn't seem to understand normal speech, so questions about how they had come to be here, bound and bleeding in front of the Place of the God of Au, went unanswered.

Finally the Speaker for the God came to the gate. He was a dignified man, very conscious of his responsibilities as a descendant of Etoje. Every inch of him, from his thick, curled, pale hair to his immaculate sealskin boots, declared him a man of importance. Too important to be bothered with a couple of hunters, but he had realized as soon as he had heard the message that the situation was a serious one. So he questioned the hunters. Where had these people come from?

"The other day some boats sailed into the islands," said one hunter. "Large ones, joined in pairs by wide platforms." He attempted to describe the mast and sail of each boat, but left his listeners perplexed. "Each one had many people aboard. They anchored and began hunting birds. My cousin and I watched them, and saw they weren't from Au."

"Where did they come from, if not from Au?" asked the Speaker. As far as he knew, there wasn't anywhere else to come from. "Did they spring up out of the waves, boats and all?"

"Perhaps," said one hunter, "the god of Au is tired of a steady diet of criminals."

"Perhaps," said the other, with the merest touch of malice, "the god of Au wishes all men to have a chance at riches and nobility, as was the case in former days."

The Speaker didn't particularly like hearing this. As the gatekeeper had, he questioned the captives. One spoke, or tried to speak, but something was evidently wrong—no words came out, only meaningless sounds.

By now, passers-by had stopped, and some of them confirmed the hunters' story—there were strange boats anchored in the islands, carrying strangely dressed people. And though the custom had not been followed for more than two hundred years, the Speaker could think of no immediate grounds on which to deny its fulfillment now, and plenty of grounds for possible retribution later, if it should become a problem. So he sent the hunters to Ihak.

Ihak was no less astonished than anyone else. However, unlike anyone else he had reason to take this development with a fair amount of equanimity. "So, ah, hm," he said, looking over the captives. "Who captured which ones?"

"We worked equally together," said the first hunter. "So we should get equal credit."

"That's right," said the second.

"Ah," said Ihak. "I see." He looked the line of captives over more carefully. "Ah. Hmm. You say you both participated equally in all twelve captures?" The two hunters assented. "So. Twelve tokens, then, six for each of you. And you may then call yourselves Warriors of Au."

"I can't wait to walk through the market," said the first. "Oh, to see the looks on everyone's faces!"

"What about the pregnant one? She looks pretty far along. Shouldn't she count for two?"

"Ah. No," Ihak said. "I regret to say. The guidelines are quite clear on the matter. So. But aren't you more fortunate that way? If there were thirteen tokens, how would you divide them without a dispute? Hm?"

So Ihak formally accepted, on behalf of the god, the sacrifice brought by the two hunters, and gave them their tokens. And then he went to speak to his wife.

In due course, a baby girl was born, and Ihak put it about that his wife had given birth at long last. She had been extremely surprised to discover herself pregnant, but this was understandable, as she had long ago stopped looking for signs of it. And everyone knew some tale of a woman who had not realized her condition until nearly the last moment. Clearly Ihak's wife was one of these.

Ihak held a great feast at which he presented the child to his friends, and he gave extravagant thanks to the god of Au. He named the girl Ifanei, which is to say, the god provided her.

When the period of fasting, vigil, and mortification had passed, each of the six captains of the Godless presided at a feast in honor of the god of this place, who punished us for our recent offence. The day was gray, and the breeze made the constant mist of rain sting. The inhabitants of each boat crowded together on their respective central decks and offered prayers praising the god as the most powerful, the most gracious, rightly the only ruler of the islands and the surrounding sea. "We desire to hear your will!" all the Godless cried, carefully making no other request, and no promises at all, while the captains let blood into the water.

Steq sat, then, and his wound was bound, and the people around him ate, with every bite praising the generosity and bounty of the god. He himself was not particularly hungry, but he knew that he should eat for the sake of his people and because of the blood loss, and so he did.

The Godless had been miserable with cold, and their hearts were sore with the loss of the twelve. Their acts of penitence had only increased their unhappiness. But now, despite the clouds and the rain, and the doubtfulness of their prospects, their spirits began to lift. There was plenty of food, all of it as carefully prepared as their situation allowed. The smiles and laughter began as performance but, as often happens, feelings began to match actions in at least some small degree. Steq could not bring himself to smile, but he was pleased to see the Godless enjoy themselves.

"If nothing else," called the captain of *O Gods Take Pity* from his own deck, "we will die with full stomachs."

This brought a bitter half-smile to Steq's face. "As always, you speak wisely," he answered.

Eventually the feast drew to a close, and the Godless began to clear away what was left of the food. Steq sat in thought under his boat's single square sail, his back to the mast. He sat brooding as people went back to their routine tasks, and as the day grew later the clouds blew away from the western sky, leaving a strip of blue shading down to green and orange, and the setting sun shining gold across the water. Colors that had been muted under the gray light seemed suddenly to glow—the brilliant emerald of island-topping grass, the brown of the boat's planking, the tattered, wheat-colored sail, the pink of a slab of seal fat the cook was packing away, all shown like jewels. The sun sank further and still Steq sat in thought.

When the sun had nearly set, Steq suddenly stood up and called a child to him. "Go to *O Gods Take Pity*," he said, "as quickly as you can. Tell the captain to be on the watch—my skin prickles, and the air is uncanny. Bid him pass my warning on."

"I feel it, too," said the child. Before any further move could be made, the other captains came up onto the decks of their ships—Steq had not been alone in his premonition. All work on the boats had halted as well, and the Godless were afraid.

"Fear not," said Steq. "Either we are about to meet our end, in which case our troubles are over, or we will survive. In any event, we have done all we could and will face our future as we always have."

As they stood waiting, a jet of water rose up just beyond the stern, and a dead-white tentacle snaked up from the water onto the deck. It ran half the length of the boat and with a thud it curled itself around the mast where moments before Steq had sat in thought. The boat's stern plunged towards the water. "Bail!" cried Steq, and in the same instant he spoke the Godless were taking up their bailers. Crew without bailers ran to the bows of the double hull, in part to balance the boat, and in part from fear of the glistening, gelatinous tentacles that had come out of the water after the first and wound and grasped at the other end. All around, the crews of the other boats stood watching, bent nearly over the gunwale strakes, crying out in horror and fear.

From the stern came a weird, bubbling noise, which resolved into gurgling speech. "Steq!"

"Don't answer!" cried one godless.

Steq only walked as steadily as he might to the end of the unsteady deck, stepping cautiously over lengths of suckered flesh. Behind him his own crew except for the bailers froze, hardly daring to breathe, and the watchers on the other boats fell silent.

At the end of the deck, he looked over the rail into the water. There, looking back from the waves, was a huge, silvery-black eye, as large as Steq's own head. Under this eye the white flesh in which it was set branched out into the tentacles that held his boat, and in the center of those was a beak like a bird's. "Steq," the thing gurgled again.

"I am here," he said. "What do you wish?"

"Let us each speak of our wishes," it bubbled. "An association would benefit us both."

"Explain."

"You are abrupt. Some might consider this disrespectful, but I will attribute it to your ill-treatment at the hands of gods so far. Or perhaps your extreme courage, which would please me."

The truth was, Steq dared not move lest he tremble and betray his fear. He knew that at this moment every life in the fleet depended on his smallest action, and he bent every effort to keep his voice steady. "You are most generous. I await your explanation."

The thing gurgled wordlessly for a moment. "Then I will explain. A thousand years ago, on that very island you see before you, I made a deal with a man of Au."

"Au being the mainland?"

"Yes. I declared that this man and his descendants would be pre-eminent in Au, if only they offered the sacrifices I desired and gave their rites and prayers to no other god. They have kept the terms of the bargain and I have as well."

"We don't fall under the terms of this bargain," Steq observed.

"You do, in a way. The acceptable sacrifice, according to the agreement, is those who are outlawed. In the beginning these were any who did not confine their worship to me. Now there are no such people to be found on Au, and they offer me murderers, robbers, and various petty criminals."

"I begin to see," said Steq. "We offered what might be construed as sacrifice to some other god, and were then fair game for your altar."

"Just so," bubbled the monster. "Would you prevent this re-occurring?"

"Had I been given the choice in advance, I would have been pleased to prevent its happening at all," Steq observed, not without some bitterness.

"No matter," said the thing, its liquid eye unblinking. "We did not know each other then, and past is past. Besides, I offer you something I imagine you hardly dare dream possible."

"That being?"

"Myself. I have become unhappy with my bargain. I will be frank. I am ambitious, and intended to reign supreme over Au, and from there expand my authority. But once they had conquered their island, the people of Ilu had no inclination to travel any further and arranged things so that they would not be required to do so. You, on the other hand, travel widely."

The wind was already chill, but it seemed in that moment to blow colder. "You have a binding agreement with the people of Au," he said.

"The agreement has its limits."

"As would an agreement with us, I am sure."

"You are a shrewder man than Etoje of Ilu," gurgled the thing. "And your people are well accustomed to keeping an advantage when dealing with gods. We will be well-matched." Steq said nothing. "I am strong with a thousand years of sacrifices," said the god of Au. "Have you fled from all gods? Have all other nations cast you out? Take me as your god, and be revenged. Take me as your god and your children will live in health, not sicken and starve as so many do now. Your fear and wandering will be at an end, and you will sit in authority over all the peoples of the world."

"At what price?"

"The price I demanded of Etoje: all your rites and sacrifices. Those who will not cease offerings to other gods will bleed on my altar."

"And when there are no more of those?"

"Ah," bubbled the monster. "That day is far in the future, and when it comes I will demand no more human victims."

"What, precisely, was your agreement with Etoje of Ilu?"

"That so long as the smallest part of the island of Au stood above the waters Etoje and his descendants would be pre-eminent in Au, and all those who accepted the terms of the agreement would be under my protection, their fates my special concern. In exchange, the people of Au would offer me the sacrifices I desired, and perform the rites I prescribed, and would make no offerings to any other gods, at any time."

"And would we enter into this same agreement, or make a new one with you?"

"We would make our own agreement, separate from my agreement with Au."

The sun had now set. In the east the clouded sky was black, and the body of the monster glowed blue under the water. Steq stood silent for some minutes, regarding it. "We are cautious," he said, when he finally spoke. "And I would discuss this with my people."

"Of course."

"Let us make no long-term commitment at the moment. But we will agree to this much: while we are in your territory we will make no offering to any other god, and you will not require us to bleed on your altar."

"This is reasonable," gurgled the god of Au. "Furthermore, it gives us both a chance to demonstrate our goodwill."

"I am pleased to find you so generous," said Steq. "It will take some time for us to determine the best course. It is not wise to rush into such things."

"Take what time it requires. I am in no hurry. Indeed, I have affairs to conclude before we can make our deal binding. It may be quite a long time before I am able to proceed."

"How long? We live at sea, but we are accustomed to land fairly frequently, for water and to buy or gather what we need, and to maintain our boats."

"Take the island you see before you, and the two north of it. All three have springs, and I will see to it that the hunters of Au will not trouble you there."

"Very well. What name shall we call you?"

"For the moment, call me the god of Au."

"Surely you have some other name."

"This one will do. I will speak to you again in the future. In the meantime, be assured of your safety so long as you worship me alone." And with those words, the tentacle that had coiled about the mast grew limp, and the whole tangle of arms slid into the water. The blue glow had begun to fade, and was nearly gone, and the huge eye was staring and vacant.

"It's dead," said Steq, and he called the child to him again. "Take a message to the other boats. We will meet tonight under the covers of the starboard hull of *Neither Land Nor Water*. Bid her captain lash them securely. No bird or fish will overhear our council." Then he turned to his crew. "Grab this thing before it floats off. It will feed us all for a week. For which we will offer thanks to the god of Au."

But whether due to possession by the god or the nature of the creature itself, the meat was bitter and inedible, and after a few foul-tasting bites the Godless cast it all back into the sea.

Ihak and his wife loved Ifanei greatly, and she was a happy child. She did not grow into any great beauty. She was short, and wide-boned, and her dark hair lay flat as wet seaweed. Indeed, she was so unlike her father Ihak that some commented disparagingly. But Ihak said quite frequently, "Ah, it's true, she looks nothing like me. But she's the very image of my late mother. So. I love her all the more for it." And he did indeed dote on the child, and there was no one in the Place of the God who remembered his mother to speak of, and so they held their tongues, and eventually the sight of Ihak going about with Ifanei's small hand in his became such a common, constant thing that it seemed unthinkable that anyone had ever suggested that she was not his child.

When Ifanei was fourteen, her mother died, and by the time she was sixteen Ihak was old and feeble. The Speaker began showing Ifanei small attentions, and Ihak called her to his bedside and spoke seriously with her. "So," he said, his voice a thin thread of breath. "Do you wish to be the wife of the Speaker for the God?"

"He only wants the inheritance," Ifanei said. She knelt on the floor and took her father's hand, thin and light and fragile as the bones of a bird. Ihak had dwindled away to almost nothing. In the flickering light of the single oil lamp he seemed faded and so completely without substance that one feared a gentle word might blow him away, but for the skin laid across him to keep him warm.

"Ah." It was a barely audible sigh. "You'll need a husband one day, and you could do worse than the man with the authority of the god of Au."

Ifanei turned the corners of her mouth down. "I could do better," she said. "The wife he already has is beautiful, and proud. She would not welcome any division in her husband's attentions, and she is altogether too unconcerned about the matter. I would be ignored at best."

Ihak managed a breathy laugh. "We think alike. So. I only asked because if the prospect had pleased you I would have done my best to secure him for you. Hm. It does not, so we must make other plans."

Now, Ihak had been a shrewder man than anyone had known. When he realized that the only child the god would grant him was a girl, he had hidden a part of his savings—the stacks of sealskins and volcanic glass blades that were the wealth of Au—in places only he knew. He had seen the resentment of the elite of Au when the two hunters had elevated themselves. He knew that the Speaker would have moved to discontinue the custom if he had not feared the anger of the common people. But further attempts on the strangers had proved futile, and the hopes of advancement had ceased to be real. The threat had receded, but it might reappear one day. Ihak knew that he would almost certainly be the last holder of his office. He also knew that the Speaker would go to considerable inconvenience to gain possession of Ifanei's inheritance. Thinking of all this, he had planned accordingly.

The day after Ihak's funeral, when Ifanei was sitting silent and cross-legged on the cold stone floor of her quarters, hair unbound and mourning ashes smeared on her face, the Speaker came to see her. "Ifanei," he said, "I have spoken to the god. Your father's office is to be discontinued. It is hardly a surprise; if it had been meant to continue, your father would have been granted a fit heir for the position."

Ifanei knew well enough that the god had never been concerned with petty matters of administration, so long as sacrifices arrived regularly. She did not look at the Speaker but at the floor, and she kept her voice small and tear-choked as she answered. "As the god wills."

"Poor Ifanei!" said the Speaker. "We will all miss your father, but you will understandably miss him the most. How fortunate you are to have cousins nearby to take care of you." She said nothing. "Don't forget, I am your cousin, too, and I regard you highly." Still Ifanei was silent. "Lovely Ifanei!" said the Speaker then, with no hint of mockery. "When the time comes, you will want to ponder the advantages of a closer connection with me, and at a more appropriate time I will speak to you of my desires."

In a bag, under Ifanei's bed, were an undyed hooded sealskin coat and a black glass knife. In her memory were the locations, well away from the Place of the God, where Ihak had cached a significant part of his valuables. In a week, villagers from along the north coast would come to Ilu, bringing their tribute of seals and seabirds to the Place of the God. When they left, who would notice one extra young boy among them?

"I will think seriously on everything you say," Ifanei said to the Speaker. She still looked steadily at the floor. "My father often spoke of his great respect for you, and I am fortunate to have such a cousin. I am so very grateful for your concern." She said this with every evidence of sincerity, and the Speaker was pleased with himself when he left her.

It was at this time that the god of Au returned to the Godless, and spoke to Steq, and shortly thereafter Righteous Vengeance ventured by night close to the shore of Au, and Steq went ashore.

Each year the north coast villagers who brought their tribute to Ilu traveled in a long, chaotic column along the sea. The seals, skins, birds, and eggs they brought were piled on sledges, the eggs carefully packed in grass. Each traveler took a turn pulling the offerings of his own village, each village they passed added to their number, and by the time the procession neared Ilu it became a noisy throng, the spirits of the participants undampened by the fact that at least half of them were suffering the effects of too much seaweed beer the night before. Between the crowd and the beer, no one noticed that a stranger had joined their number.

Steq had not been a young man when the Godless had sailed into Au's waters, and after sixteen years his hair had grayed. But he had not changed otherwise. He did not much resemble the people of Au—his skin was too dark, his hair too fine, his features not quite right somehow, though this may have been only a certain hardness about the mouth that was unusual in a man of Au. He kept the hood of his coat up, and his head down, and those walking next to him thought he must be from some other village, and attributed his silence to last night's beer, and let him be.

What Steq could see of Au was tall grass sweeping up the skirts of an ice-topped mountain. Here and there a stream was lined with stunted osiers, but there were otherwise no trees. The view was all green grass, black stone, and white ice, with gray clouds over everything. The villages they passed seemed nothing more than turf mounds huddled together, with here and there a whale rib protruding. At each one children ran shouting out of the low houses, clad in sealskin coats and trousers but barefoot in the mud. The whole column came to a swirling semi-halt as men and women followed the children out of the houses with much waving and laughter and handing over of food and skins of what Steq presumed was the ever-present beer. Then as if at some signal Steq was unable to detect a few of the villagers picked up the lines to their own sledges, the crowd moved forward again, and the village was left behind.

From a distance Ilu seemed no more than a bump on the treeless hillside, the Place of the God no more than a pile of stones, and the whole vista was dominated by the same mountain, and the icy blue river that ran down to the sea. Arriving, Steq saw the same tumble of turf houses, the same shouting, barefoot children, and he was nearly at the Place of the God before he realized that he was in the city itself. He had thought they were merely passing yet another village.

The procession broke like a wave onto the whale-rib gates of the Place of the God and spilled into the surrounding streets. Pushed along with the crowd, Steq found himself in a muddy, open square where women wearing coats sewn with seabird feathers and painted white, brown, or muted green began singing out in loud voices. The only word Steq recognized was "beer," which he had learned in the first hours of his joining the pilgrimage. The women were instantly surrounded and began what appeared to be fierce bargaining, though Steq had not seen anything resembling money. He turned against the flow of the crowd and made his way back to the Place of the God.

By now the sledges were lined up at the gates, and no few sledge pullers were casting glances in the direction of the square Steq had just left. He found a morose-looking man at the end of the line, and put his hand on the braided sealskin rope the man was holding.

The man instantly stood straighter and grinned. He said something—a question by the sound, but Steq knew only a few words of the language of Au. It was possible that *yes*, *no*, or *beer* would answer the man satisfactorily, but it was best not to speak. Keeping his face half-hidden by his coat hood, Steq shrugged towards the square.

The man, still smiling broadly, dropped the line, took Steq by both shoulders, drew him close into a miasma of fermented seaweed, and kissed him on the cheek. He said something else, sending an even stronger waft of beer Steq's way, and reached into his coat, pulled something out, and pressed it into Steq's hand. Then, none too steadily, the man walked away. Steq found himself holding a lump of glassy, brownish-golden stone that had been smoothed and rounded into a vaguely animal-like shape that he could not identify. He put it in a pouch under his coat.

By this time it was late afternoon. The line of sledges moved slowly forward and Steq watched each one halt before guards at the gate. One guard examined the cargo of each sledge, counting small, rounded pebbles into a pouch at his waist as he did so, and then waved the man who had towed the sledge through the gates. Other guards appeared and pulled the sledge to the side, where yet others unloaded it and then left it empty in front of the building. A trickle of villagers came back out of the gates, the sledgemen done with their business in the Place of the God and making with all speed for the square where their fellows crowded.

By the time Steq's commandeered sledge arrived at the gate the sun was setting. The guard looked over the cargo, counted his pebbles, and then waved Steq past with hardly a glance. As he had seen the man before him do, he dropped the tow line and walked into the Place of the God, straight ahead into light and the smell of sweat and burning oil.

The room was small—a dozen people would have crowded it. On the floor were woven grass mats, much scuffed and dirtied. The walls were plain and dark. In the center of the room was a low, blocky table on which sat a single black stone. The man who had preceded Steq in line stood before this, his back to Steq, facing another man, presumably a priest, who spoke at length and then brought out a disk of polished bone from inside his skin shirt and handed it to Steq's predecessor, who turned and left without another word.

Steq stepped forward. "God of Au," he said, before the priest could speak. "I am here, as you instructed me."

The priest frowned, and opened his mouth to say something, and then his eyes grew wide and his body stiffened. "Were you last?" he asked in a dead monotone, in Steq's language.

"Yes."

"You have done well," he said. A tremor passed through the body of the priest. "I am not surprised."

"How long do we have?"

"Not long," the priest answered. "I have withdrawn into the stone once more, and we are in danger until we depart Au." The man then turned and picked the black stone up from the table. "We go."

"What, do we merely walk through the streets of Ilu?"

"Yes. No one will stop us. But you must find a boat, and bring us to your fleet."

"Could you not have taken control of the priest and had him bring us the stone?" Steq asked.

"No. I could not have."

"I wonder why not." Steq followed him back out into the night. The guards seemed not to see them, and the area in front of the Place of the God was empty of anyone else.

The priest walked ahead without looking left or right, away from the Place of the God and into the square where that afternoon so many of Steq's traveling companions had crowded. It was empty now, and dark—there was no light but the glow of an oil lamp from a doorway here and there. In the center of the square the priest stopped abruptly, and Steq nearly ran into him. "Find someone," the priest said without turning around.

"Someone in particular?"

"Anyone will do," said the priest. "Between here and the water, where the boats are, is the place where the villagers are camping for the night. Someone strong and healthy would be best, but take anyone you can alive."

Steq knew without being told what the god wanted with a live person from the camp. "Can we not sacrifice the priest you're possessing?"

"He has been dead for the last several minutes."

"That's inconvenient," Steq said. "You expect that I will just walk off with someone in the middle of the camp?"

"Yes," said the priest, and he walked forward again.

"You said nothing of this, when last we spoke."

"I said you would know more when you came to me in Ilu," the priest said, still walking forward. Steq hurried to catch up to him. "You accepted that."

"You promised there would be no difficulties."

"There will not be if you follow my instructions."

Steq had known from the day the god had first spoken what food it preferred, and what they would be required to give it, if they accepted its offer. He was not ordinarily a sentimental man. But he thought of the people he had walked with in the last few days. They had been a smiling, happy lot, had offered him food and beer without stinting, even though they could not have had any idea who he was.

They had also killed twelve of his people, had only been prevented from killing more by the protection of the god, and would not hesitate to kill Steq himself if they knew he was not of Au. Steq was not unaccustomed to the idea of human sacrifice, or shocked by it. It was only that he could not avoid some small sympathy; the Godless were well used to being required to pay gods with their lives. Still, he had not come this far to quail at the last moment.

The camp of the pilgrims was a noisy, sprawling affair. Here and there a few tents had been raised, but mostly the men sat in the open, passing the ever-present skins of beer. What light there was came from three or four campfires, though what fuel they burned, since there seemed to be little or no wood anywhere, Steq had no idea. Everyone seemed to be near someone else, to be in conversation or sharing food or drink. If Steq had known more of the language, he could conceivably have taken a likely prospect by the arm and said something like, "Come aside, I must tell you something." But he could not, and he reached the far edge of the camp without seeing how he could do what the god required. The thought crossed his mind that one of his own people would be made to pay, if he could not find someone of Au.

He would not allow it. He stopped at the far edge of the camp and looked more carefully at the people around him. The two nights he had spent with the pilgrims he had taken care to stay at the edges of the camp where darkness would hide his foreign features, and where others would not pay him too much unwelcome attention. If anyone in the crowd wished to be alone he would likely do the same.

He walked the perimeter of the camp, just outside the edges of the light cast by the several fires, and when he had nearly made a circuit he found what he sought. A single shadowed figure sat motionless on the sand, just outside the camp. He stood quietly, watching, and the man didn't move. After a few minutes Steq walked slowly behind him, any sound he might have made covered by the raised voices of the celebrating pilgrims. He knelt behind the man and threw one arm around him, the other hand clapped across the man's mouth.

Steq realized immediately, with a mixture of regret and relief, that it was a boy he held, not a grown man, and in the same instant the boy bit his hand, hard. Steq did not dare let go and let the boy shout for aid, and did not dare cry out himself. He raised the arm circling the boy, meaning to strike him on the back of the head, and instantly the teeth were loosed and the boy was up and running across the beach. Steq ran after.

He caught up quickly, and brought the boy down to the sand. Steq pinned his arms behind and wrestled him up, dragged him, as he struggled ineffectually, down the beach to the water where the dim shadow of the priest stood. In all this time, though he fought Steq ceaselessly, the boy made no sound.

The god-possessed priest did not turn as Steq came up. "You took too long," he said in his flat monotone. "Get a boat."

"And in the meantime, what about this one?" Steq asked. "I can hardly just let go of him. And you don't want me to kill him yet."

Before the god could answer a sharp, thundering crack echoed across the sky. The encamped pilgrims cried out and then were silent a few moments. "We are in great danger," said the god. "We must leave immediately." Behind, in the camp, someone laughed and the voices started up again as though nothing had happened.

"Why?"

"The mountain Mueu is a volcano," said the god. "As I have withdrawn from the island, I can no longer contain it, or any of the others."

"You might have said as much sooner," said Steq, and dragged his captive along the beach until he found a small hunting boat, carefully stitched skin stretched over a frame of bone and osier. In the bottom of the boat was a coil of rope, and this he used to bind his captive. Then he called to the priest. "Over here! I have found a boat, and it will be quicker if you come to me, rather than me coming to you." He tipped the boy into the boat and then pushed it across the tide line and into the water, hoping the skin wouldn't tear along the way. As the god reached the boat another loud crack silenced the camp yet again. This time the returning voices were pitched higher, and seemed to carry a note of fear. The god climbed in, and Steq pushed the boat out further and then stepped in and took up the oar he found and began to row.

"You will have to bail," he said after a short time. "We are too many for this boat."

"Give me some blood," said the priest. "I will ensure that we do not sink."

"Blood! To keep water out of the boat? You do not inspire confidence in your power. Are you not well-fed by the sacrifices of the people of Au?"

"Much of my attention is currently elsewhere, keeping back the flood of melted glacier that will shortly sweep down the sides of Mueu and wash Ilu into the sea. Until we are farther from shore we are not safe, and I cannot turn my attention from Mueu. I could not do this were I not strong enough, and you will not be disappointed in me, once this danger is past."

"Bail," said Steq. "I will not row the distance wounded, and I will not bleed the boy lest you complain about the condition of your victim when it comes time for the sacrifice." He rowed a few more strokes. "Bail or drown."

Without a word, the priest took up a bailer from the bottom of the boat, and set to work.

When they reached the Fleet of the Godless, Steq turned his captive over to his crew. The priest, still inhabited by the god, took up the stone again and went to the deck where he sat in front of the mast and stared ahead, saying nothing. The crew avoided him, though Steq had not told them the body was dead.

They had already abandoned their island camps, and now they sailed south, away from Au. By afternoon the sky had darkened and ash began to fall from the air, like snow. The boats were muddy with it, and the Godless lashed the covers over the hulls to keep it out, and swept the covers and the decks constantly. They still avoided the dead priest, who did not move but sat at the mast covered in ash. That night the northern horizon was lit by a baleful red glow, and Steq approached the god.

"Am I to understand that Au is in the process of sinking beneath the waves, thereby releasing you from your contract?"

"Yes." A small slide of gray ash fell from the dead priest's mouth, the only part of him that moved. "Though it will take several more days."

"We are sailing away from Au with what speed we can manage."

"So I noticed," said the god.

"Will the body last long enough?"

"I intend to preserve it until I no longer need it," said the priest. "But in any event, I will tell you how the sacrifice will go. Cut the victim's throat and let the blood fall on the stone. Say these words." And here the god spoke the words of the rite. "Put both bodies into the sea. By doing this, you will be bound to the terms we agreed upon."

"Let us review those terms," said Steq.

The priest's head moved, dislodging more ash from his face, and he opened blank, staring eyes. "I warn you, I do not have any intention of re-negotiating at this late date."

"Nor I," said Steq. "I wish only to be certain there will be no misunderstandings."

"As you wish. I have no apprehensions."

"This is what we have agreed. We will give our prayers and sacrifices to no other god but you. With your assistance, we will compel all those we meet either to abandon all other gods but you, or die as your victims. We will do so until no one lives who offers rites to any other god, whereupon we will no longer be required to offer humans as sacrifices, though we will still owe you our exclusive devotion.

"For your part, you will protect us from all danger and misfortune, and will assist us against our enemies. We will be pre-eminent over all the peoples of the earth."

"For as long as you keep your end of the bargain," said the corpse at the mast. "My wrath will be terrible if you break the terms of the agreement and turn to another god, or fail to seek out every person who does not worship only me. Such was our agreement."

"And if you don't keep yours?"

"I will keep it," said the god. "Do you think I have gone to these lengths only to amuse myself?"

"No," said Steq. The corpse said nothing more.

Steq went forward, and stood at the rail.

He had known almost from the beginning that they were dealing with a minor god—a deity of some spring, or small island. This hardly mattered if, fed, it could do all it promised, and keep the Godless safe.

The past sixteen years had been like a dream Steq had feared to wake from. Food had been plentiful, illness rare. The hunters of Au had let them be after a few failed attacks. No vengeful god had come upon them. And they would shortly be Godless no more.

Do you think I have gone to these lengths only to amuse myself?

That the god had gone to great lengths—greater lengths, perhaps, than it wished to admit—had become more and more obvious. And why did the dead priest still sit guard over the stone?

Only one conclusion seemed likely—the god was vulnerable, and did not trust the Godless. And so, why put itself in this position?

Steq had believed the god when it had said that it was ambitious, that the people of Au had failed to serve that ambition as it had wished them to. But was that ambition enough to drive the god to take such a risk? Steq thought not.

The mountain Mueu is a volcano.

The god of Au had exhausted its strength, or nearly so, holding back Mueu. Why wait sixteen years, then? Why not flee the moment the Godless presented themselves? Had it, perhaps, waited until the danger was so extreme that the island was certain to sink entirely, thus releasing it from its obligation to the people of Au?

He thought of the wet and windy trek along the coast, the drunk, chattering villagers hauling their tribute to Ilu, the women who had pressed skins of beer on him, the men who had cheerfully shared fish and other, less identifiable food along the way. The image rose unbidden of the man in line before the Place of the God, morose until Steq took his place.

One of the Godless spoke, then, interrupting Steq's thoughts. "Captain, you're needed in the starboard bow."

Steq climbed from the deck into the starboard hull, and stooped to pass under the coverings, which on this shallow vessel did not allow one to stand up straight. In the bow he found two crew members hunched, bewildered, in front of a crouching, naked young woman. She looked directly at him, clearly afraid but also clearly in command of herself. He remembered her silence during the pursuit and struggle on the beach. This woman was not given to panic. She was short compared to the people of Au he had met, and wide-boned. Her hair was flat and lank. Her face was the face of a woman Steq knew had died some sixteen years ago.

"Get her some clothes," he said to the two guards. "No one is to speak of this." He turned, and made his way to an opening in the covers, and climbed back up onto the deck.

Steq had his supper that evening under the covers of the port bow of *O Gods Take Pity*. He sat on a bundle of skins in the flickering glow of a single oil lamp, the captain of O Gods Take Pity facing him, on a bunk. They spoke in low voices, bent forward under the low ceiling, knees nearly touching.

Steq reported all that had happened. "I don't doubt that it will do everything it says for us," he concluded. "But neither do I doubt that it will sink us in the sea like the people of Au if it finds some other, better bargain, or thinks itself endangered."

"This is self-evident," said the captain of *O Gods Take Pity*. "But this is not what troubles you. You hesitate now because of the woman."

"I do not hesitate," said Steq.

"I knew you when you were an infant at your mother's breast," said the captain of *O Gods Take Pity*. "Lie to the others as you wish, but I won't be deceived." Steq was silent. "She is none of ours. If you asked her where was her home, who her family, she would say Au, and name people we have never seen or heard of."

"But for an accident," said Steq, "she would be one of us."

"But for an accident I would be king in Therete, dressed in silk and sitting on a gold and ivory throne, surrounded by slaves and courtiers. But for an accident, the king in Therete would be one of us, fleeing the wrath of the gods, wresting what life he can from the waters with no luxury and little joy, though I assure you the thought has never crossed his mind. And rightly so. Begin this way, and where do you stop? There is no one in the world who would not be one of us, but for an accident."

"Years ago you urged us not to take this course," said Steq, bitterly. "Now you are in favor of it."

"No," said the captain of *O Gods Take Pity*. "I am not in favor of it. Only, if you pitch this god and its corpse into the sea without accepting its deal, do so because you have found some way out that will not cause all our deaths. Do not take this step, which will surely have dire consequences, because of qualms over this woman. We have all lost people because of mistake or accident, and we have all regretted it. Do not be the first to endanger the fleet because of your own regret."

"I said nothing of taking such a step." The other captain said nothing, and Steq took another piece of fish from the bowl in his hand, chewed and swallowed it. "It is tied to the stone, and cannot be released without a sacrifice."

"It is not confined, and it has power yet to animate the corpse. It may have power to do other things as well."

"What would they do, our people, if I threw the stone into the sea?" Both men were silent, considering Steq's question, or perhaps unwilling to answer it.

"We have opposed gods in the past, and survived," said the captain of *O Gods Take Pity* after a while.

"Not all of us," said Steq.

"There is no use in worrying over the dead." He set his bowl beside him on the bunk. "We have lived too easily for too long."

"Perhaps we lived too hard, before."

"Perhaps. But we lived."

And Steq had no sufficient answer to this.

Ifanei lay bound on a bunk on *Righteous Vengeance*. Two guards sat opposite her, and they never looked away. When she had shivered they had covered her, but left her hands in sight.

It would not have mattered had they not—they had tied her with strong, braided sealskin and she had no way to cut it. They had taken her knife, and when they had taken her clothes they had found the needles and awls she had carefully wrapped and tied to the inside of her leg. She could see no means of escape.

She had understood that she was on a boat of the Fleet of the Godless, though she would not have known to give them that name. What
she had not understood was why she had been captured to begin with.
They had not killed her, or otherwise mistreated her. When they had
done searching her they had returned her clothing. She could not imagine what anyone might want with her, unless they knew of Ihak's
caches, which seemed unlikely.

She had days to consider. Days in which she was fed and her other
needs cared for as though she were ill and helpless. Never at any time
was she allowed off the bunk, nor were her hands or feet ever unbound.

The darkness never faltered—the coverings were tightly lashed, and
even if the sun could have shone through, the skies were dark with
smoke and ash, but Ifanei had no way of knowing that. She knew only
the close, dimly lit darkness and the smell of unwashed bodies. Eventually she felt stunned with the sameness of it all, and ceased to wait for
anything further to happen.

An unmeasured time later, she woke to the chill as her cover was
roughly pulled off. One of her guards held her bound wrists, the other
cut the bonds around her ankles, and she was pulled as upright as the
low ceiling allowed, and pushed down the narrow space that ran the
length of the hull, bunks on one side, unidentifiable bundles and stacks
along the other. She took two steps and her legs buckled under her, weak
from long inactivity. Her guards caught her, pulled her up again, and
helped her along to where a faint light shone through an opening above.

Hands reached down and pulled her through, up onto a railed platform. The sky was dark, and the breeze cold, and despite her coat she
shivered. Guttering torches, a few oil lamps, and a fire in a large box
provided some light. There were people all around, all along the railings.
Facing her was the man who had brought her here, his face expressionless. No one moved, though the platform pitched and rocked in a way
that made Ifanei step and stumble as she tried to stay on her feet.

In the center of the platform was a wide, tall pole and leaning up
against that was a pile of gray dust. In front of this was the Stone of Etoje.

"God of Au!" she cried. "Help me!"

A weird gasping, choking noise came from the pile at the foot of the
pole. The whole thing heaved and from underneath it a man stood up,
swaying and staggering slightly, and the gasping noise continued. The
dust fell and swirled away in the wind.

His long blond curls were covered in ash, his face and clothes gray with it, but she knew him. She realized, with a freezing horror, that the choking sound was laughter.

"Ifanei," said the dead Speaker in a flat, toneless voice. "I provided you indeed, and I will have you back from your father." She said nothing, could think of no answer. "Here is symmetry," said the god. "Here is perfection."

"My god." Ifanei's voice trembled with cold and dread. "I know you will protect me. The people of Au are your people and you have always kept us from misfortune."

"Au has sunk beneath the waves," said the priest. "Not the smallest part of the island remains. And you were my victim from the beginning. I lent you to Ihak, and it is only right that you return to me at last." Still the people around her, and the dark, hard-faced man in front of her, were silent. There was no sound, except the wind and the water.

"Au beneath the waves," she said. "Why? You have betrayed us!"

"It was the nature of the island itself," said the god. "And it was never in my power to keep any human alive forever, nor did I ever promise such a thing."

She saw the dishonesty of the god's words, but could not find sufficient answer for it. "What of Etoje's service to you?" she asked. "Had he not taken you for his god you would still be on the island, with no company but the cries of birds. Does this mean nothing to you?"

"Etoje's service was pure self-interest," said the dead priest. "He killed his own brother to satisfy his greed. Surely you know this, the tale has been told often enough. And it should not surprise you. It is the way people are. As it happens, it serves my purpose."

She looked at the people around her. They would, she knew, cut her throat as easily as the Speaker had offered up the victims of Au. Did they know what they dealt with? Even if she had spoken their language, and could have warned them, would she have wished to?

But there was nothing she could do. And that being the case, she would not beg or scream. She took two stumbling steps to the Stone of Etoje, knelt heavily and then made her back as straight as her shivering allowed and waited for the knife.

Steq had known that the woman was no coward. He had, when he had thought of what was to come, been grateful that he would not have to steel himself to endure pitiful weeping or wailing.

She knelt shivering by the stone, her chin up as though inviting the knife. Her eyes were open, and she looked not at the grimy, dead priest but at Steq.

He had not expected to be undone by her bravery. "What did she say to you?" he asked the god.

"It does not matter."

"I am curious."

"You are delaying. I wonder why?"

"Why should it matter to you?" Steq asked.

"It does not matter." Steq did not answer. "Very well. The woman begged me for help, invoking my agreement with the people of Au. I explained to her how matters stand. That is all."

That was all. Steq took a breath, and then spoke. "Godless, I fear I have led you astray."

"And I fear this ship needs a new captain," said the dead priest.

"It will have one," said Steq, "if the people do not like what I have to say."

The corpse made as if to step forward, but a voice spoke from the watching crowd. "Touch him and you'll be over the rail, stone and all." Other voices murmured in assent.

"Put me overboard and you'll speedily discover your mistake," said the god, but it made no further move.

"If we feed this god what it desires," said Steq, "it will almost certainly have the power to do much of what it has promised us. And the blood that it demands will be none of ours." His gaze shifted momentarily to Ifanei, and then back to the priest. "But let me tell you why the god has abandoned its promise to the people of Au. The great mountain above Ilu was a volcano, and there were others. For a thousand years the god held the island safe, because of its promise to the people of Au, but after all that time it could control them no longer. A thousand years! Imagine the power thwarted, enough to destroy the whole island when it was finally let loose. And when this god realized that it could not hold back the fires forever, what did it do? Did it command the people of Au, who had served it faithfully all that time, to build boats, and escape under its protection? No, it allied with us behind their backs, and left them to their fate. It will do the same when its agreement with us becomes inconvenient.

"Many of you have lived all your lives under this god's protection. The rest are too accustomed to living in opposition to all the gods and peoples of the world to fear what might happen if the god of Au has not the strength to do as it promises. Perhaps I have grown too soft with easy living, and sentimental. But the fate of the people of Au troubles me greatly, and if you would ally yourselves with this god you must choose another captain."

"And if we would not?" cried a voice.

"Then we must cast stone and corpse overboard, and sail away from here as quickly as we may. It has some power yet, and we will be in some danger, but I do not think it will follow us far. The gods of surrounding waters will have no love for it, and even so, at the bottom of the sea there will be no one to feed it."

"I will show you my power!" said the corpse.

"Show it!" came the voice of an old woman. "We all know your weakness, and Steq has never yet led us wrong!"

As though her words had been a signal, the boat lurched to starboard. Steq grabbed the rail, watched as three or four people tumbled into the water. Crew slid across the deck, and the stone began to roll but the priest caught it up, and then a thick, dead-white tentacle reached up and onto the boat, twisting and snaking until it found a rail, which it curled around and pulled.

The rail snapped and was thrown up into the air. Another tentacle joined the first, groping along the hull, and then another. Torches tumbled from their places and bounced across the deck and into the water. Still a wavering, flickering light lit the boat—the sail was aflame.

"You!" Steq grabbed a man by the arm. "Loose the port hull!" The man scrambled to obey him, speaking to others on his way, who followed him. Steq then let go of the rail, to slide down the deck up against a writhing tentacle. "Everyone to the port hull!" he shouted. What they could do against the monster in an overloaded single hull he did not know, but he did not think they could extinguish the fire and right the ship, and so it was the only chance for survival.

In the meantime he would attack the monster in any way he could. He reached into his coat for his knife, and his hand brushed up against his pouch. There was nothing in it to help him—a few needles, a coil of fishing line and some hooks, and . . .

He looked around for the woman of Au, and saw her scrambling up the deck, hands still bound. He followed, grabbed her ankle and pulled her to him. She lashed out, swinging her fists, and hit him, hard, just under his ear. "Stop!" he shouted, though he knew she would not understand him. But she did stop. "Look!" Out of the pouch he pulled the small piece of polished, golden glass he had brought from Au, and held it before her eyes.

She looked at it for only a moment, and then closed one hand around it and called out, and suddenly the writhing arms were motionless and the sound of snapping wood ceased. "Up," he said, and pushed her along the sloping deck towards the port hull, which was nearly free, and climbed after her.

"Steq!" The voice of the dead priest, weird and gasping. "Steq! What is that?"

"It is the smallest part of the island of Au," called Steq, without turning his head. He and the woman reached the edge of the deck and leapt into the port hull just as it was freed. The Godless were unlashing covers and pulling out oars.

"She is not of Au!" cried the dead man. "I am not bound!"

"Then move against her!" This was answered with an inarticulate cry. The last few flames of the burning mast went out as Righteous Vengeance slipped under the waves, and the only light was the torches of the other boats, for the rest of the fleet was still nearby, their own crews watching in horror.

"Row for the nearest ship!" Steq ordered then. "It cannot harm us so long as the woman is in the boat, and as for the others, it has not the strength to bring more monsters against them, or it would have done so already."

The woman sat shivering in the bottom of the hull, both hands clutched around the small glass token. Steq went to her and cut her bonds. "There is a place in the south," he said, though he knew she would not understand him. "A mountain so high they say you can touch the stars from its top." She did not answer, he had not expected her to. "Do you hear that, god of Au?" But there was no answer.

The next morning the Fleet of the Godless, reduced to five boats, sailed southward. Behind them, far below the featureless sea and attended only by silent bones and cold, indifferent fish, lay the Stone of Etoje, and the god of Au.

"FAINT VOICES, INCREASINGLY DESPERATE"

ANYA JOHANNA DENIRO

The silk threads of grief and time snap and spin away from the black looms, but all Freia wants to do is go back to Vienna. Dozens of women work the looms in the magnanery. Hands fly as the threads spin out of the boiling cocoons. Freia doesn't work on the looms though. She's not patient enough. Instead she sets the strands of damp, slightly sticky silk from the cocoons, hooking them to the spindle to unravel them, as the objects inside the cocoons die from the scorching water.

She dips her hands in. She can barely feel a thing. She hates the magnanery. The combination of Romanesque columns with the overhead fluorescent lighting creates the worst possible world she can imagine, and she knows many.

One of the other women she works with dumps a basket of cocoons into the troughs of boiling water. Freia judges the quality of silk inside. The most coveted threads are black, followed by citrine, carnelian, and gingerline. Invisible threads are not valuable at all; they are rough like a cat's tongue and are always getting tangled. She sorts accordingly.

Freia has never been able to make any correspondence between the type of cocoon and the thread. No one has ever explained it to her, and truthfully she doesn't care. She keeps her cravings for knowledge in check. This is how she survives.

The cocoons bob in the water and look like they're about to jump out when she hooks them to the spindle. That's when she can hear the voices inside most clearly, anguished whispers of *help me help me* and *what is happening what is—*

Freia usually wears her headphones while she works.

None of the other women working in the magnanery have talked to her in a long time. They keep their heads down. They have given up their old names. Their eyes are like pieces of charcoal excavated by an archeologist.

There is only the work. And Woden. But Woden is too monstrous to be contemplated just yet.

Instead, consider the tall tree in the center of the magnanery. From the central dome of the building, there's a round opening where the tree keeps stretching on and on; and an opening in the floor where it stretches on and on.

But here, Woden uses the tree as a managed resource, a revenue stream.

From the trunk grow the branches with the golden leaves that the silkworms feast from. The leaves are supple and soft, almost like skin. And the worms are ravenous. Freia has never liked the worms, but maybe that's because she knows what happens to them. Once full, the white worms start spitting silk, and they cocoon themselves, and after three days, the women pluck them hanging from the tree like figs and collect them for Freia.

The worms are silent. It's only when they boil that they speak, and then what's inside dissipates altogether.

Vienna, though—Vienna persists for her, almost despite itself. That's all she wants. The world with the Danube and its tortes named after composers, her adopted home. She longs for blood. But Woden has removed anything that could cut her since the last time she fled, twenty-five years ago. It's gutting to realize that her entire life has been stripped of its sharp edges. Woden sees her as a stubborn girl who is desperate for his protection but doesn't realize it, or is afraid to admit it. He keeps her falcon cloak, her two cats, her boar, and her jewelry in a safe in his office.

At last, though. At last.

Freia hauls one of the troughs to the holding tank in the nave of the magnanery. She edges around the tree. One of the other women walking in front of her drops a needle that she'd pinned into the folds of her dress hem. Freia stops briefly, frozen. No one watches her, as far as she can tell. The needle is barely visible. The woman doesn't seem to notice it's missing. Freia kneels on the path as if she has to adjust the fit of her shoe, and then slips the needle into her own pocket.

Freia doesn't dare look at it until she's at her work station. A bronze needle with a glass bead at the tip of the shank. She doesn't hesitate. All it takes is a drop. She gets a lot more.

"Ow!" Freia says as the needle pricks her thumb. She holds her breath and waits for her skin to blossom.

Soon the blood gushes down like the Krimml Waterfalls. The blood keeps coming, pooling on the floor and rushing down the storm drain of the magnanery, keeping it from reaching and feeding the tree—even Freia would not want to see that—and through the pipework, where it bubbles over in a toilet in a luxury high-rise apartment in Vienna. The blood rises at midnight, making the apartment's bathroom unusable and thus the apartment unlivable.

Freia is breathless as the blood spurts out of her. She used to be known for so many beautiful and awful things, but now there is just blood.

The looms stop. The other dozen or so other workers in the magnanery stare at Freia. Despite her need for escape, and her joy, Freia is still ashamed and she hates that she's ashamed. She bites her lip, and finally she sucks at the red rivulet.

"I'm sorry, I'm really really awful at this," she says to them, but they don't respond. Woden—her supervisor and one of her exes, who founded the magnanery many centuries ago—comes in through the iron door by the loading dock. He's wearing a bombardier jacket and has a sack over his shoulder. Something writhes in the sack, trying to escape.

They stare at each other. They both feel the pull. He knows that once she bleeds, there is nothing he can do until she goes.

He gives her a mocking wave.

He doesn't even look at her as she is cast down, cast down into the Imperial City, the red city, and this is what she is most embarrassed by, that he doesn't actually care much about her, that she's an afterthought, but still keeps her locked in the magnanery anyway.

Of course she has been cast down many times before, left to fall like piss from an airplane, always into Wien. It's been their adopted home for a thousand years. At the beginning, before the Habsburgs came, Woden willingly let her venture into the city. The magnanery hadn't been built yet. There was just the shining tree in the field, which stretched forever, where the worms congregated, ate, cocooned, and then burst into moth-dom, and flew away. Woden wasn't quite as cruel yet. She still had all of her shit—a nice house, her jewelry, cats, and falcons and boar and lots of hot dead men and women to fuck.

And come to think of it, as she wakes up in the spartanly furnished apartment overlooking the Danube (or at least a hazy shimmer of it), even when he did become cruel he still treated her, more or less, as an equal—and sometimes he even cast her down himself by surprise, and she enjoyed this. She enjoyed having her throat slit and waking underneath the shadow of the *Dreifaltigkeitssäule*, commemorating the temporary end to the plague, which Leopold I attributed to God. She hates that she once craved Woden's fucked-up affection.

But a hundred years ago or so he started taking his monstrous *völkisch* bullshit seriously.

The apartment is spartan, but still luxurious. Or wanting to give the appearance of money but not flaunting it. More than anything, the apartment wants to exude security, a cross between a panic room and a boutique infosec consultancy. The bathroom—the master bathroom— is a disaster area with the blood splatter—her blood, she has to remind herself. She walks around the apartment. A bedroom, a guest bedroom, two bathrooms, a kitchen, a "common area" with a foosball table, and a study. On the nightstand of her bed is a magazine in English folded to an article with the title "15 Members of the Super-Rich Who Remained Grounded and Humble." She snorts. Whoever lived here before was either a lich or a sociopath.

She touches her arms. Her body is fine. It's not the body she would have picked if she had the choice, but it's fine. She goes through the walk-in closet and puts on what's there: gray cashmere cardigan, white button-down dress shirt, black pencil skirt, black ankle boots. Onyx earrings. Dark blue scarf. It all feels good to her.

She's in 2018, in an Age of Blood like no other. No purges, sieges, plagues or occupations from the past compare with the Imperial City Undying as an investment opportunity, a city for princely oligarchs to park money from selling teenaged Moldovan girls and lost nuclear warheads from Kazakhstan, apartments bought with white rhino horns and cash. Vienna is both the center and the beachhead for awful things. She knows this. The apartment's previous tenant moved out in a hurry the day before, and there is an eviction notice under the door. She knows that she's a hair's breadth away from being a tourist, or a squatter. The notice indicates that the property managers, a holding company in Frankfurt, is "renovating" the building, which means likely demolishment and the construction of something more expensive. She sighs.

But it's perfectly fine. She's here. A little blood never hurt anyone.

It's time for her to go to work then. She figures she could ditch this body's responsibilities, but she can't think of any easier way to interact with a large group of people where she's not a complete stranger. It's so hard being an almost-expat. Outside it's … March? This March freezing rain, *der schneeregen*. The words form on her lips awkwardly. Her high-rise is on a quiet side street in Simmering, two blocks away from the Zentralfriedhof, the central cemetery with three million souls buried inside of it. She goes out of her way to pick up the tram right in front of the cemetery gates. The cemetery reminds her of home, that she's no longer written under the sigil of love but only the sigil of death.

Fuck you she can hear someone say from a distance, deep inside the grounds. *Fuck you, fuck you soul-sorter.* On second thought, she has no time for the dead. There's a glint on the sidewalk in front of her and she bends down. Amongst the raindrops is her needle, the bronze needle with the glass tip. In the magnanery, the needle was the lockpick and she was the lock. Woden must have tossed it out and down like the trash. The whole of Wien, every district, would not be sure what to do with her appetites, were it aware of them. She puts the needle inside a little fold in her messenger bag. Now all she needs is a thimble, a pair of scissors, a bobbin, a lucet, her spindle, and a loom powered by the exsanguination of a thousand innocents, and she would be set, she could open a shop on Etsy and make hats or shrouds for her enemies.

She gets on the tram, *der 71er*. She has longed for the tram for a long time, the creaking comfort of it. She remembers when the 71 trams threaded between ruined blocks. There really isn't anyone left from that story in this story. There's just—

"I can't … I can't open my Blu-ray player for the training video," her supervisor says. She is a young, striving American woman, with a flat accent from the prairie. Freia, with this body, is slightly younger than her. Neither of them wants to be seen as incompetent, but they express it in completely different ways. Freia is supposed to be (she checks the bilingual business card on her desk) a digital strategist at this outpost of an American ad agency in Central Europe, the latest among twenty outposts or so in a network, like the trading zones of the old colonial powers. It's not clear what she's supposed to sell or strategize. Her office building, which used to be an imperial artillery college, also overlooks the Danube, but much more closely to the riverbank than her apartment. She's upriver. She can see boats, mostly courier speedboats, cut through the sleet. The Viennese say that the Danube only looks blue if you're in love. This is no time of love.

"Fuck," her supervisor says. "Fuck it. Argh. Sorry." She really is. Her name is Agatha. She's tall, and awkwardly bends over the desk. Her blond ponytail keeps flopping into her eyes.

"Let me try something," Freia says.

"This Blu-ray in there is the training video," she says. "But it's not loading properly."

"Yes, got it," Freia says. "Got it."

She finds the needle from her messenger bag and manages not to bloodlet again with it.

As she inserts the needle into the tiny "eject" indentation, Agatha watches breathlessly and rather too close. Freia realizes that the office has the feel of a tryst that has just started, yet at the same time has gone on too long. Though the Viennese outpost been open less than four months, desperation is written on all employees' faces. When she first came into the office in the early morning, Freia opened the bottom drawer of her desk and found a tangle of VR headsets from about two years ago—from sleek masks to the smartphone mounts made of heavy cardboard or plastic. She gasped and closed it quickly, as if the drawer contained cobras or bombs. Their main clients back in America are various packaged snack brands from the Midwest—which doesn't appear to her like a "good fit" with Vienna and its magical tortes. But who is she to say. She actually knows nothing about advertising. She doesn't feel like she's really good at convincing others to do what she wants.

The Blu-ray finally chokes and whirls and the disc slides out with difficulty. *Fuck you fuck you it* seems to be saying to her—

"There! Aha!" Agatha says, clapping her hands. She grabs the disc and hands it back to her. "Uh, be sure to watch this. I guess . . . I guess you have to reinsert it?"

"I'll . . . try restarting," Freia says. She holds the needle between her fingers and sets her hair with it, to get it out of her eyes. She's always restarting.

Every time she dies in Vienna, she goes back to the magnanery, and she's given more cocoons to boil. And every time the magnanery looks different. The décor never matches the time period. Several hundred years ago, right after the big siege by the Ottomans, the magnanery was a sterile laboratory and she wore clean suits, the kind used for making microchips. When she died during the February Uprising in '34, rounded up after a street battle and shot in the head by a *Heimwehr* teenager, the silk-makers all wore medieval dresses of coarse wool. Woden has never stayed in one place or time. After one of her escapades in the worst year of the Great War, he chained her by the neck and left her in a corner in the magnanery for five years to wash the raw silk with soap and water. He gave no pretense of rehabilitation. That was when she figured out the trick with her own blood, loosening an edge of her quartz washbasin and sharpening it for a year in secret.

This time, she doesn't want to die here, she refuses to—she will refuse to die here. She watches the training video, which has glitched horribly, and makes this vow to herself. Because she doesn't want to make thread again, to stand at the spindle in close proximity to her ex again. Each of those cocoons in the boiling water has a soul inside of it, and there are millions of them, and they die in the cocoons. They evaporate. That's Freia's job, to make sure that the dead die again. The others see it as embarrassing punishment to be sent down as a mortal, but she lives for nothing else. She wants the prick of the thumb, the gush. And she knows it will come. Because she always bleeds eventually.

But she also knows, when she is alive in Vienna, Woden hunts her. Or he hires creatures to hunt her. He always hunts her down and brings her back.

After the workday, Agatha asks her if she wants to go to karaoke with a few other people from the office. This makes her happy. She agrees. The sleet has stopped. There's four or five others going, who she hasn't really talked to, because they seem to have their shit together. It's supposed to be a short walk to the karaoke place, near *die Uni*, but Agatha can't quite seem to find it as they cut through Josefstadt, but it's great, she insists, and Freia believes her. How did endearing Agatha become a supervisor? Soon enough the other coworkers concoct excuses to leave so there are only the two of them left.

"Ooh, spiced wine," Agatha says, coming into one of the small, open squares—this one off Piaristengasse—that are everywhere in the central districts of Wien. "Uh, I mean, *glühwein*. I'm trying to get better with my German. Do you want to get some?" The air smells like cloves.

Freia smiles. "Sure," she says. Glowing wine. A little late in the season for it, but on the other hand it really is fucking cold for March. The wine-seller is just off the steps of the Piarist church, and the two sit on the steps holding their hot paper cups.

"I . . . just love this city," Agatha says. "There's so much history. Layers and layers of it."

"Yeah," Freia says, taking a gulp, letting the star anise and cinnamon and citrus drain into her.

"Shit. I probably sound like a stupid American to you," she says to Freia, her head down. "Jesus, Agatha. 'Layers of history.' Of course there is."

"No, no, it's . . . sweet," Freia says, turning to look at Agatha.

"Okay, that's not the answer I was expecting," Agatha says. "But . . . I kind of like it?"

Freia laughs. "Good, good. Where are you from then?"

"Um, a small town in Wisconsin you've never heard of. I moved away as soon as I could. Where I grew up was—" She shudders. "Awful. Just awful for—well." She pauses, holding back words. "Never mind. And you?"

"Me?" Freia stares straight ahead, at the two bare trees on the platz, and she swears she can see the writhing of hundreds of hungry worms on the twigs. "I've been kind of everywhere? But Vienna has been . . . home for a long time."

"I wish this place could be home," Agatha says, swigging the last of her wine. "But I don't really have a home. The company back in the States sent me here to their worst-performing office to figure out what to do with me. Probably figuring out a way to 'let me go.'"

"Fuck them," Freia says, and she wishes more than anything she had a cigarette.

"I don't know if I have that luxury," Agatha says.

They sit in silence for a couple minutes, except that Freia can hear voices echo off the cobblestones.

He's looking for you he's looking he's looking—

"This might be a strange thing to say," Agatha says slowly, "and maybe it's the wine talking. But even though I'm your boss, when I first saw you come in the office I got—really really scared of you."

You should be, she thinks. *This is a natural and healthy response.*

Instead she says: "Are you still scared of me?"

"A little?" Agatha says in a quiet voice.

Freia leans over and bumps shoulders with her. "Well, just this once, I'll promise not to bite."

Agatha blushes.

Sometimes, when she's strong—or at least feels the ghost of the strength she used to possess—she thinks: Start anew and triumphant and leave the magnanery, leave Vienna, leave everything, become mortal, even though you'll die, you'll be free. She supposes that it would be possible to forsake her self. But she can't bear to think of herself as one of the hungry insensate worms on the golden tree of death and becoming an anonymous commodity for Woden before having her boiled remains sloughed off as wastewater. And she could never do what all the other goddesses, all of them, have done—renounce their names and pledge themselves to Woden in exchange for the dull freedom of not giving a fuck anymore. Not the good kind of not giving a fuck. It would be easier for Freia to give up, like all the others, and let Woden be the last of their kind. But she refuses. She is stubborn, like a human being.

As Agatha sings karaoke Bob Seger, Freia sits in the black booth, leans back and closes her eyes, imagining an America she has never known. Agatha, it has to be said, is in her element with karaoke, with a raspy baritone that's somewhere between Stevie Nicks and Ringo Starr, and a fierceness in her green eyes that surprises her. She watches Freia the entire time she's up there. Freia has a song coming up but she isn't sure whether she wants to sing it, what this particular voice of hers will sound like inside of a microphone. The bar is nearly deserted. All the décor is black. On the other side of the bar two men and one woman all wear long black sleeveless T-shirts and study calculus. They have heathen tattoos on their arms: stags and Woden's names. The names are in a made-up runic script the younger man downloaded from the Internet, but she can still read it.

"You're up," Agatha says, sitting down next to her and squeezing her shoulder. She has found that she was just clapping seconds ago. She feels a bit off. The table of neopagans—of whatever sort—now stare at her, with an intensity that concerns her.

As she starts to sing the Yeah Yeah Yeahs (what else? It's either that or Billy Joel) she doesn't know whether they know who she is, whether they would worship her or try to murder her, or murder someone else as a sacrifice, probably an immigrant, because they'd think it would please her, even though nothing could be further from the truth. Or Agatha. They eye Agatha too.

Veneration? Just as bad. She doesn't want to be tied down by supplications. They each have knives in their belts, consecrated for sure. And heavy bronze pendants, masks of Woden's face peering out behind a tangle of woods. Agatha stares at her in the dark-dim with milky eyes as she warbles, awful and sad.

Agatha has no idea how much danger she's in, just by living and breathing. If they were to leave together out of the club and a bus slammed into them, Agatha would die, and come into life again as a worm on an undying tree and Freia would find herself again in the magnanery, and after few hours, when the cocoon had been spun, Freia would quite possibly hold her former boss's soul inside boiling water to get at the threads inside. Her voice is hoarse at the chorus, and when she's done there are a few stammered claps.

"That was great," her boss says, as if she's giving her a performance review. She continues to clap. She is more confident, or tipsy, or both. "Well done." She takes another swig of Stiegl. "Well fucking done."

"Thanks," Freia says. She eyes the three at the table again. "We should leave."

"Really?" Agatha says, unaware of the bad aura from the neopagans. "Where do you want to—"

"My place," Freia says, getting Agatha's coat. "Definitely my place."

When she's licking the base of Agatha's girlcock in her apartment in Simmering, blanketed in a moonlit nest of quilts on her bed, Freia realizes she has no idea how to make her cum.

"How can I make you cum?" she says, leaning her cheek against Agatha's thigh and looking up at her.

"Oh my god," Agatha says, finding it hard to breathe. "Oh my god. Uh . . . do you have a vibrator?"

"Kind of," Freia says.

"Okay, well—if you put it the tip of it right on my, uh, perineum—the taint—and . . . press down there."

"Like this?"

"Yes. How the fuck are how are you doing that?"

"Shhh," Freia says. "A magician never reveals her secrets."

After Agatha orgasms twice, Freia makes her hand stop vibrating and curls up behind Agatha, putting her chin up against her neck and breathing deeply. The body is a lonely hunter, but occasionally it finds its quarry.

A tight knot loosens in Freia's shoulder blades.

They fall asleep.

"Are you safe here?" Freia whispers to Agatha an hour before dawn.

"Mhm what?" Agatha says, eyes closed, still slick, shifting deeper into Freia's arms.

"Are you safe in this city as . . . you know . . ."

Now it is Agatha's turn to shush her. "That doesn't matter now," she says, as if in a dream. "I'm safe now."

And Freia, this once, allows herself to believe this and dozes off as the Imperishable City thrums around her.

She wakes up to sunlight stabbing her eyes and looks up. Agatha is splayed on the high ceiling, still naked, her mouth stuffed with a neoprene ball. She's paralyzed and can't speak or move, but her eyes are wide. She can see everything.

"I thought I'd let you sleep in a bit," Woden says, sitting in a high-backed chair at the foot of the bed.

Freia leaps out bed and jumps onto the ceiling to try to bring Agatha down, but Woden snaps his fingers and Freia thuds back onto the bed.

"Come on," he says. "This is embarrassing, Freia. Get some clothes on."

Woden, lord of the gods, the allfather, the shining eye, the war-merry one, the racist piece of shit, wears a black suit. His shoulder-length hair is tied back and he wears heavy ruby rings on three of his fingers. He looks at Freia with pity.

"Put on some clothes in my house," he commands, turning away his chin ever so slightly.

Freia looks up at Agatha, and she goes to the dresser drawer where she finds several changes of clothes, mostly variations of the same pencil skirt and light sweater.

She doesn't want him to see her this vulnerable, so she puts on one of these outfits and sits back on the bed, trying to take deep breaths.

"That's better," he says. "I can't say the same thing for your boyfriend up here."

"She's not—" Freia begins, but she knows that Woden is only trying to goad her, not that he doesn't believe that Agatha is mentally sick and unworthy of attention, much less love and care. She closes her eyes and mostly feels shame that she had assured Agatha of her safety, that she could be safe with her. Something that he had said earlier stuck with her.

"Wait, what do you mean your house?" she says.

He smiles. "I own the high-rise." He snorts. "How do you think you ended up here?"

"So ... what, you're a landlord now?"

"It's a little more complicated than that. I help expedite capital to move from the periphery of Europe into safe and lucrative opportunities in Austria. You always come a bit short, Freia, with your imagination."

"That sounds like an elaborate way to say: 'money launderer for white nationalists.'"

He grimaces. She doesn't want him to get inside her head.

"It's just extending a little of my hard-won expertise," he says. "I'm just trying to give a safe landing towards my people mired in a sea of filth. The filth of cucks, cultural Marxists—"

"Your people," she snorts.

"How many people do you have?" he says, smiling. "Him?" He points up at the ceiling. "Don't make me laugh. My people are attuned to what I need. Like keeping an eye on you."

She thinks of the trio at the karaoke bar, and in a sense, he is right— he does have people everywhere. She hates it. Neo-Nazi wolves in the Nationalrat, in the Catholic priesthood with their secret blots, in the Bundespolizei. Fathers, mothers, upstanding citizens with their Facebook groups set to private.

"Speaking of him," he says.

"*Her*, you fuck," she says. "Her."

"Stop indulging his delusions, sister. Or I'll cut off his cock and stuff it into his mouth."

Freia shuts her eyes hard and opens them again, looking up at Agatha. She is sick with herself, but those emotions will not save Agatha.

"All I want to know is why?" he says. "When you came down to Wien, why did you waste your time with this creature?"

She chooses her words very carefully. "I like women."

"No, you like pussy. Not this . . . thing."

"Don't tell me what I want and don't want."

He snickers. "Even your degeneracy is degenerate."

"I am the Consort of Blood. I am the Animal Bride, the Lady of the Slain—"

"Well, you were," he says. "Past tense. Never forget that. But—I am feeling generous for some reason. Maybe it will be a way to teach you a lesson. I'll give you a month's leave in the city before you go back to work—gently monitored of course. You won't even notice."

"And Agatha," she says angrily, not wanting to put it in the form of a question, to make it seem like she is pleading with him.

"Why should you care? Why should you care how I murder him?"

At that Freia looks at Agatha and she doesn't hesitate, even though she knows the words are almost impossible to say. "I exchange my life for hers, then. After I return, I will never leave the magnanery again, and I vow never to return to Vienna again, until the end of time. In exchange, you will leave Agatha alone. She will be returned safely. And everyone you know will leave her be."

"Freia—" he begins to say.

"You're right that I'm not what I used to be. You've seen to that. But I am still the Consort of Blood, and you cannot deny me a blood oath."

He begins laughing. "You would give up Vienna? You will work in the magnanery forever? No escaping it?"

"Yes. And yes. And no."

His laughter dies once he sees she is serious. He stares at her. She hears Agatha's raspy breathing above her.

"And if you decide to kill her," Freia says, "I will fight and kick and scream when you try to drag me away from here. I will make your life miserable. You know I can do that."

She figures that, more than anything, he enjoys the easy life now afforded to him, a life of vanity and empty slogans and sales pitches in twenty-fifth floor showroom apartments. She figures that he will not want to be inconvenienced by her. It's a steep fall from who she used to be, but she will take what she will get.

"No, Freia," he says. "Of course I'm not going to give into your demands. And you have nothing to perform a blood oath with. Stop embarrassing yourself. You'll be able to harvest this bitchboy's soul soon enough when you're back at work."

Freia doesn't want to make sudden movements because Woden is a snake-wolf, a snare-wolf, a patient wolf, so almost casually, she reaches into her hair and pulls the needle out. Her long black hair falls to her shoulders, and without saying anything to Woden she stabs the most tender patch of skin on her neck with the needle, pushes it in as far as it can go, and pulls it out. The first drop falls horizontally, as if from a great height, and smacks against Woden's cheek. The seconds slow. He moves his hand to wipe the blood from his cheek, on instinct, but then a second drop of blood lands on his face, and a third, and then there's blood smeared all over the right side of his face, and it's seeping into his mouth, like his mouth is the drain. He tries to stagger to his feet, but the blood overflows his throat, and he falls backwards.

"Choke on it, you fucking piece of garbage," she shouts. "Are you ready to bind yourself to the oath?"

She knows this can't last forever. Already she's beginning to feel faint as she starts to bleed out, and Woden will find a way to survive. Soon she will be dead here, but she will get her oath.

Even now he resists, backing away from her. She moves towards him, kneeling in front of him and pulling his hands towards her.

"Coward," she says, slashing a sigil onto his right palm with the needle. "Coward." The left palm. He falls on his back and the blood masks his face. The wind rushes in.

Agatha wakes inside the main chapel of the Central Cemetery, in the chancel, at dawn. The clouds have broken open and the chapel takes in the sunlight like it's breathing it in. She stands up from the cold floor, wobbling. Above her, the dome is lined by a blue firmament, with gold stars and gold blasts of light coming down from the central circle, and she knows this is the Last Judgement. She is alive somehow. She's in the outfit she wore to work the day before. She remembers too much, watching from the ceiling. She couldn't make out the language between Freia and the man, but it sounded like wolves arguing. Most of all she remembers not being able to move, and blood everywhere.

Her phone buzzes. There's a message from Freia, on the company Slack to her:

> Really sorry about everything. You deserved none of that.
>
> You deserve great things.
>
> I've decided to take another position, something in a field that's a better fit to my natural skill set and which is a little closer to home.
>
> I really like you and I deeply regret not taking you out on a proper date.
>
> I wish we could keep in touch—not assuming of course that you'd WANT to—but unfortunately any type of reception is really spotty where I'm moving (it's really remote, you don't even want to know). Wishing you every blessing I have at my disposal.
>
> —F.

Agatha starts crying. The cries echo in the chapel walls, and she hears voices inside the echoes, lucky, lucky, lucky girl, voices from the cemetery trying to catch the undercurrent of her pain, and Freia cries out too as she spins and spins the silk. Agatha hugs herself and wipes her tears on her jacket sleeve. The jacket smells like Freia, like fresh snow and sharp bronze and fucking, like burnt fur and hot *glühwein* and dried blood, like things she knows and things she will never know, like everything, and everything else.

"OGRES OF EAST AFRICA"

SOFIA SAMATAR

1907
Kenya

Catalogued by Alibhai M. Moosajee of Mombasa
February 1907

1. Apul Apul

A male ogre of the Great Lakes region. A melancholy character, he eats crickets to sweeten his voice. His house burned down with all of his children inside. His enemy is the Hare.

[My informant, a woman of the highlands who calls herself only "Mary," adds that Apul Apul can be heard on windy nights, crying for his lost progeny. She claims that he has been sighted far from his native country, even on the coast, and that an Arab trader once shot and wounded him from the battlements of Fort Jesus. It happened in a famine year, the "Year of Fever." A great deal of research would be required in order to match this year, when, according to Mary, the cattle perished in droves, to one of the Years of Our Lord by which my employer reckons the passage of time; I append this note, therefore, in fine print, and in the margins.

"Always read the fine print, Alibhai!" my employer reminds me, when I draw up his contracts. He is unable to read it himself; his eyes are not good. "The African sun has spoilt them, Alibhai!"

Apul Apul, Mary says, bears a festering sore where the bullet pierced him. He is allergic to lead.]

2. Ba'ati

A grave-dweller from the environs of the ancient capital of Kush. The ba'ati possesses a skeletal figure and a morbid sense of humor. Its great pleasure is to impersonate human beings: if your dearest friend wears a cloak and claims to suffer from a cold, he may be a ba'ati in disguise.

[Mary arrives every day precisely at the second hour after dawn. I am curious about this reserved and encyclopedic woman. It amuses me to write these reflections concerning her in the margins of the catalogue I am composing for my employer. He will think this writing fly-tracks, or smudges from my dirty hands (he persists in his opinion that I am always dirty). As I write I see Mary before me as she presents herself each morning, in her calico dress, seated on an overturned crate.

I believe she is not very old, though she must be several years older than I (but I am very young—"Too young to walk like an old man, Alibhai! Show some spirit! Ha!"). As she talks, she works at a bit of scarlet thread, plaiting something, perhaps a necklace. The tips of her fingers seem permanently stained with color.

"Where did you learn so much about ogres, Mary?"

"Anyone may learn. You need only listen."

"What is your full name?"

She stops plaiting and looks up. Her eyes drop their veil of calm and flash at me—in annoyance, in warning? "I told you," she says. "Mary. Only Mary."]

3. Dhegdheer

A female ogre of Somaliland. Her name means "Long Ear." She is described as a large, heavy woman, a very fast runner. One of her ears is said to be much longer than the other, in fact so long that it trails upon the ground. With this ear, she can hear her enemies approaching from a great distance. She lives in a ruined hovel with her daughter. The daughter is beautiful and would like to be married. Eventually, she will murder Dhegdheer by filling her ear with boiling water.

[My employer is so pleased with the information we have received from Mary that he has decided to camp here for another week. "Milk her, Alibhai!" he says, leering. "Eh? Squeeze her! Get as much out of her as you can. Ha! Ha!" My employer always shouts, as the report of his gun has made him rather deaf. In the evenings, he invites me into his tent, where, closed in by walls, a roof, and a floor of Willesden canvas, I am afforded a brief respite from the mosquitoes.

A lamp hangs from the central pole, and beneath it my employer sits with his legs stretched out and his red hands crossed on his stomach. "Very good, Alibhai!" he says. "Excellent!" Having shot every type of animal in the Protectorate, he is now determined to try his hand at ogre. I will be required to record his kills, as I keep track of all his accounts. It would be "damn fine," he opines, to acquire the ear of Dhegdheer.

Mary tells me that one day Dhegdheer's daughter, wracked with remorse, will walk into the sea and give herself up to the sharks.]

4. Iimū

Iimū transports his victims across a vast body of water in a ferry-boat. His country, which lies on the other side, is inaccessible to all creatures save ogres and weaverbirds. If you are trapped there, your only recourse is to beg the weaverbirds for sticks. You will need seven sticks in order to get away. The first two sticks will allow you to turn yourself into a stone, thereby escaping notice. The remaining five sticks enable the following transformations: thorns, a pit, darkness, sand, a river.

["Stand up straight, Alibhai! Look lively, man!"

My employer is of the opinion that I do not show a young man's proper spirit. This, he tells me, is a racial defect, and therefore not my fault, but I may improve myself by following his example. My employer thrusts out his chest. "Look, Alibhai!" He says that if I walk about stooped over like a dotard, people will get the impression that I am shiftless and craven, and this will quite naturally make them want to kick me. He himself has kicked me on occasion.

It is true that my back is often stiff, and I find it difficult to extend my limbs to their full length. Perhaps, as my employer suspects, I am growing old before my time.

These nights of full moon are so bright, I can see my shadow on the grass. It writhes like a snake when I make an effort to straighten my back.]

5. Katandabaliko

While most ogres are large, Katandabaliko is small, the size of a child. He arrives with a sound of galloping just as the food is ready. "There is sunshine for you!" he cries. This causes everyone to faint, and Katandabaliko devours the food at his leisure. Katandabaliko cannot himself be cooked: cut up and boiled, he knits himself back together and bounces out of the pot. Those who attempt to cook and eat him may eat their own wives by mistake. When not tormenting human beings, he prefers to dwell among cliffs.

[I myself prefer to dwell in Mombasa, at the back of my uncle's shop, Moosajee and Co. I cannot pretend to enjoy nights spent in the open, under what my employer calls the splendor of the African sky. Mosquitoes whine, and something, probably a dangerous animal, rustles in the grass. The Somali cook and headman sit up late, exchanging stories, while the Kavirondo porters sleep in a corral constructed of baggage. I am uncomfortable, but at least I am not lonely. My employer is pleased to think that I suffer terribly from loneliness. "It's no picnic for you, eh, Alibhai?" He thinks me too prejudiced to tolerate the society of the porters, and too frightened to go near the Somali who, to his mind, being devout Sunnis, must be plotting the removal of my Shi'a head.

In fact, we all pray together. We are tired and far from home. We are here for money, and when we talk, we talk about money. We can discuss calculations for hours: what we expect to buy, where we expect to invest. Our languages are different but all of us count in Swahili.]

6. Kibugi
A male ogre who haunts the foothills of Mount Kenya. He carries machetes, knives, hoes, and other objects made of metal. If you can manage to make a cut in his little finger, all the people he has devoured will come streaming out.

[Mary has had, I suspect, a mission education. This would explain the name and the calico dress. Such an education is nothing to be ashamed of—why, then, did she stand up in such a rage when I inquired about it? Mary's rage is cold; she kept her voice low. "I have told you not to ask me these types of questions! I have only come to tell you about ogres! Give me the money!" She held out her hand, and I doled out her daily fee in rupees, although she had not stayed for the agreed amount of time.

She seized the money and secreted it in her dress. Her contempt burned me; my hands trembled as I wrote her fee in my record book.

"No questions!" she repeated, seething with anger. "If I went to a mission school, I'd burn it down! I have always been a free woman!"

I was silent, although I might have reminded her that we are both my employer's servants: like me, she has come here for money. I watched her stride off down the path to the village. At a certain distance, she began to waver gently in the sun.

My face still burns from the sting of her regard.

Before she left, I felt compelled to inform her that, although my father was born at Karachi, I was born at Mombasa. I, too, am an African.

Mary's mouth twisted. "So is Kibugi," she said.]

7. Kiptebanguryon

A fearsome yet curiously domestic ogre of the Rift Valley. He collects human skulls, which he once used to decorate his spacious dwelling. He made the skulls so clean, it is said, and arranged them so prettily, that from a distance his house resembled a palace of salt. His human wife bore him two sons: one which looked human like its mother, and one, called Kiptegen, which resembled its father. When the wife was rescued by her human kin, her human-looking child was also saved, but Kiptegen was burnt alive.

[I am pleased to say that Mary returned this morning, perfectly calm and apparently resolved to forget our quarrel.

She tells me that Kiptegen's brother will never be able to forget the screams of his sibling perishing in the flames. The mother, too, is scarred by the loss. She had to be held back, or she would have dashed into the fire to rescue her ogre-child. This information does not seem appropriate for my employer's catalogue; still, I find myself adding it in the margins. There is a strange pleasure in this writing and not-writing, these letters that hang between revelation and oblivion.

If my employer discovered these notes, he would call them impudence, cunning, a trick.

What would I say in my defense? "Sir, I was unable to tell you. Sir, I was unable to speak of the weeping mother of Kiptegen." He would laugh: he believes that all words are found in his language.

I ask myself if there are words contained in Mary's margins: stories of ogres she cannot tell to me.

Kiptebanguryon, she says, is homeless now. A modern creature, he roams the Protectorate clinging to the undersides of trains.]

8. Kisirimu

Kisirimu dwells on the shores of Lake Albert. Bathed, dressed in bark-cloth, carrying his bow and arrows, he glitters like a bridegroom. His purpose is to trick gullible young women. He will be betrayed by song. He will die in a pit, pierced by spears.

[In the evenings, under the light of the lamp, I read the day's inventory from my record book, informing my employer of precisely what has been spent and eaten. As a representative of Moosajee and Co., Superior Traders, Stevadores and Dubashes, I am responsible for ensuring that nothing has been stolen. My employer stretches, closes his eyes, and smiles as I inform him of the amount of sugar, coffee, and tea in his possession. Tinned bacon, tinned milk, oat porridge, salt, ghee. The dates, he reminds me, are strictly for the Somalis, who grow sullen in the absence of this treat.

My employer is full of opinions. The Somalis, he tells me, are an excitable nation. "Don't offend them, Alibhai! Ha, ha!" The Kavirondo, by contrast, are merry and tractable, excellent for manual work. My own people are cowardly, but clever at figures.

There is nothing, he tells me, more odious than a German. However, their women are seductive, and they make the world's most beautiful music. My employer sings me a German song. He sounds like a buffalo in distress. Afterward he makes me read to him from the Bible.

He believes I will find this painful: "Heresy, Alibhai! Ha, ha! You'll have to scrub your mouth out, eh? Extra ablutions?"

Fortunately, God does not share his prejudices.

I read: *There were giants in the earth in those days.*

I read: *For only Og king of Bashan remained of the remnant giants; behold, his bedstead was a bedstead of iron.*]

9. Konyek

Konyek is a hunter. His bulging eyes can perceive movement far across the plains. Human beings are his prey. He runs with great loping strides, he sleeps underneath the boughs of a leafy tree. His favorite question is: "Mother, whose footprints are these?"

[Mary tells me that Konyek passed through her village in the Year of Amber. The whirlwind of his running loosened the roofs. A wise woman had predicted his arrival, and the young men, including Mary's brother, had set up a net between trees to catch him. But Konyek only laughed and tore down the net and disappeared with a sound of thunder. He is now, Mary believes, in the region of Eldoret. She tells me that her brother and the other young men who devised the trap have not been seen since the disappearance of Konyek.

Mary's gaze is peculiar. It draws me in. I find it strange that, just a few days ago, I described her as a cold person. When she tells me of her brother she winds her scarlet thread so tightly about her finger I am afraid she will cut it off.]

10. Mbiti

Mbiti hides in the berry bushes. When you reach in, she says: "Oh, don't pluck my eye out!" She asks you: "Shall I eat you, or shall I make you my child?" You agree to become Mbiti's child. She pricks you with a needle. She is betrayed by the cowrie shell at the end of her tail.

["My brother," Mary says.

She describes the forest. She says we will go there to hunt ogres. Her face is filled with a subdued yet urgent glow. I find myself leaning closer to her. The sounds of the others, their voices, the smack of an axe into wood, recede until they are thin as the buzzing of flies. The world is composed of Mary and myself and the sky about Mary and the trees about Mary. She asks me if I understand what she is saying. She tells me about her brother in the forest. I realize that the glow she exudes comes not from some supernatural power, but from fear.

She speaks to me carefully, as if to a child.

She gives me a bundle of scarlet threads.

She says: "When the child goes into the forest, it wears a red necklace. And when the ogre sees the necklace, it spares the child." She says: "I think you and my brother are exactly the same age."

My voice is reduced to a whisper. "What of Mbiti?"

Mary gives me a deep glance, fiercely bright.

She says: "Mbiti is lucky. She has not been caught. Until she is caught, she will be one of the guardians of the forest. Mbiti is always an ogre and always the sister of ogres."]

11. Ntemelua

Ntemelua, a newborn baby, already has teeth. He sings: "Draw near, little pot, draw near, little spoon!" He replaces the meat in the pot with balls of dried dung. Filthy and clever, he crawls into a cow's anus to hide in its stomach. Ntemelua is weak and he lives by fear, which is a supernatural power. He rides a hyena. His back will never be quite straight, but this signifies little to him, for he can still stretch his limbs with pleasure. The only way to escape him is to abandon his country.

[Tomorrow we depart.

I am to give the red necklaces only to those I trust. "You know them," Mary explained, "as I know you."

"Do you know me?" I asked, moved and surprised.

She smiled. "It is easy to know someone in a week. You need only listen."

Two paths lie before me now. One leads to the forest; the other leads home.

How easily I might return to Mombasa! I could steal some food and rupees and begin walking. I have a letter of contract affirming that I am employed and not a vagrant. How simple to claim that my employer has dispatched me back to the coast to order supplies, or to Abyssinia to purchase donkeys! But these scarlet threads burn in my pocket. I want to draw nearer to the source of their heat. I want to meet the ogres.

"You were right," Mary told me before she left. "I did go to a mission school. And I didn't burn it down." She smiled, a smile of mingled defiance and shame. One of her eyes shone brighter than the other, kindled by a tear. I wanted to cast myself at her feet and beg her forgiveness. Yes, to beg her forgiveness for having pried into her past, for having stirred up the memory of her humiliation.

Instead I said clumsily: "Even Ntemelua spent some time in a cow's anus."

Mary laughed. "Thank you, brother," she said.

She walked away down the path, sedate and upright, and I do not know if I will ever see her again. I imagine meeting a young man in the forest, a man with a necklace of scarlet thread who stands with Mary's light bearing and regards me with Mary's direct and trenchant glance. I look forward to this meeting as if to the sight of a long-lost friend. I imagine clasping the clasping the hand of this young man, who is like Mary and like myself. Beneath our joined hands, my employer lies slain. The ogres tear open the tins and enjoy a prodigious feast among the darkling trees.]

12. Rakakabe

Rakakabe, how beautiful he is, Rakakabe! A Malagasy demon, he has been sighted as far north as Kismaayo. He skims the waves, he eats mosquitoes, his face gleams, his hair gleams. His favorite question is: "Are you sleeping?"

Rakakabe of the gleaming tail! No, we are wide awake.

[This morning we depart on our expedition. My employer sings— "Green grow the rushes, o!"—but we, his servants, are even more cheerful. We are prepared to meet the ogres.

We catch one another's eyes and smile. All of us sport necklaces of thread: signs that we belong to the party of the ogres, that we are prepared to hide and fight and die with those who live in the forest, those who are dirty and crooked and resolute. "Tell my brother his house is waiting for him," Mary whispered to me at the end—such an honor, to be the one to deliver her message! While she continues walking, meeting others, passing into other hands the blood-red necklaces by which the ogres are known.

There will be no end to this catalogue. The ogres are everywhere. Number thirteen: Alibhai M. Moosajee of Mombasa.

The porters lift their loads with unaccustomed verve. They set off, singing. "Alibhai!" my employer exclaims in delight. "They're made for it! Natural workers!"

"O, yes sir! Indeed, sir!"

The sky is tranquil, the dust saturated with light. Everything conspires to make me glad.

Soon, I believe, I shall enter into the mansion of the ogres, and stretch my limbs on the doorstep of Rakakabe.]

"YS"

ALIETTE DE BODARD

————————————— September, and the wind blows Françoise back to Quimper, to roam the cramped streets of the Old City amidst squalls of rain.

She shops for clothes, planning the colors of the baby's room; ambles along the deserted bridges over the canals, breathing in the smell of brine and wet ivy. But all the while she's aware that she's only playing a game with herself—she knows she's only pretending that she hasn't seen the goddess.

It's hard to forget the goddess—that cold radiance that blew salt into Françoise's hair, the dress that shimmered with all the colors of sunlight on water—the sharp glimmer of steel in her hand.

You carry my child, the goddess had said, and it was so. It had always been so.

Except, of course, that Stéphane hadn't understood. He'd seen it as a betrayal—blaming her for not taking the pill as she should have—oh, not overtly, he was too stiff-necked and too well-educated for that, but all the same, she'd heard the words he wasn't saying, in every gesture, in every pained smile.

So she left. So she came back here, hoping to see Gaëtan—if there's anyone who knows about goddesses and myths, it's Gaëtan, who used to go from house to house writing down legends from Brittany. But Gaëtan isn't here, isn't answering her calls. Maybe he's off on another humanitarian mission—incommunicado again, as he's so often been.

Françoise's cell phone rings—but it's only the alarm clock, reminding her that she has to work out at the gym before her appointment with the gynecologist.

With a sigh, she turns towards the nearest bus stop, fighting a rising wave of nausea.

"It's a boy," the gynecologist says, staring at the sonograms laid on his desk.

Françoise, who has been readjusting the straps of her bra, hears the reserve in his voice. "There's something else I should know."

He doesn't answer for a while. At last he looks up, his grey eyes carefully devoid of all feelings. His bad-news face, she guesses. "Have you—held back on something, Ms. Martin? In your family's medical history?"

A hollow forms in her stomach, draining the warmth from her limbs. "What do you mean?"

"Nothing to worry about," he says, slowly, and she can hear the "not yet" he's not telling her. "You'll have to take an appointment with a cardiologist. For a fetal echocardiogram."

She's not stupid. She's read books about pregnancy, when it became obvious that she couldn't bring herself to abort—to kill an innocent child. She knows about echocardiograms, and that the prognosis is not good. "Birth defect?" she asks, from some remote place in her mind.

He sits, all prim and stiff—what she wouldn't give to shake him out of his complacency. "Congenital heart defect. Most probably a deformed organ—it won't pump enough blood into the veins."

"But you're not sure." He's sending her for further tests. It means there's a way out, doesn't it? It means . . .

He doesn't answer, but she reads his reply in his gaze all the same. He's ninety-percent sure, but he still will do the tests—to confirm.

She leaves the surgery, feeling—cold. Empty. In her hands is a thick cream envelope: her sonograms, and the radiologist's diagnosis neatly typed and folded alongside.

Possibility of heart deformation, the paper notes, dry, uncaring.

Back in her apartment, she takes the sonograms out, spreads them on the bed. They look . . . well, it's hard to tell. There's the trapeze shape of the womb, and the white outline of the baby—the huge head, the body curled up. Everything looks normal.

If only she could fool herself. If only she was dumb enough to believe her own stories.

Evening falls over Quimper—she hears the bells of the nearby church tolling for Vespers. She settles at her working table, and starts working on her sketches again.

It started as something to occupy her, and now it's turned into an obsession. With pencil and charcoal she rubs in new details, with the precision she used to apply to her blueprints—and then withdraws, to stare at the paper.

The goddess stares back at her, white and terrible and smelling of things below the waves. The goddess as she appeared, hovering over the sand of Douarmenez Bay, limned by the morning sun: great and terrible and alien.

Françoise's hands are shaking. She clenches her fingers, unclenches them, and waits until the tremors have passed.

This is real. This is now, and the baby is a boy, and it's not normal. It's never been normal.

That night, as on every night, Francoise dreams that she walks once more on the beach at Douarnenez—hearing the drowned bells tolling the midnight hour. The sand is cold, crunching under her bare feet.

She stands before the sea, and the waves part, revealing stone buildings eaten by kelp and algae, breached seawalls where lobsters and crabs scuttle. Everything is still dripping with brine, and the wind in her ears is the voice of the storm.

The goddess is waiting for her, within the largest building—in a place that must once have been a throne room. She sits in a chair of rotten wood, lounging on it like a sated cat. Beside her is a greater chair, made of stone, but it's empty.

"You have been chosen," she says, her words the roar of the waves. "Few mortals can claim such a distinction."

I don't want to be chosen, Francoise thinks, as she thinks on every night. But it's useless. She can't speak—she hasn't been brought here for that. Just so that the goddess can look at her, trace the minute evolutions in her body, the progress of the pregnancy.

In the silence, she hears the baby's heartbeat—a pulse that's so quick it's bound to falter. She hears the gynecologist's voice: *the heart is deformed.*

"My child," the goddess says, and she's smiling. "The city of Ys will have its heir at last."

An heir to nothing. An heir to rotten wood, to algae-encrusted panels, to a city of fish and octopi and bleached skeletons. An heir with no heart.

He won't be born, Francoise thinks. He won't live. She tries to scream at the goddess, but it's not working. She can't open her mouth; her lips are stuck—frozen.

"Your reward will be great, never fear," the goddess says. Her face is as pale as those of drowned sailors, and her lips purple, as if she were perpetually cold.

I fear. But the words still won't come.

The goddess waves a hand, dismissive. She's seen all that she needs to see; Françoise can go back, back into the waking world.

She wakes up to a bleary light filtering through the slits of her shutters. Someone is insistently knocking on the door—and a glance at the alarm clock tells her it's eleven a.m., and that once more she's overslept. She ought to be too nauseous with the pregnancy to get much sleep, but the dreams with the goddess are screwing up her body's rhythm.

She gets up—too fast, the world is spinning around her. She steadies herself on the bedside table, waiting for the feeling to subside. Her stomach aches fiercely.

"A minute!" she calls, as she puts on her dressing-gown, and shoves her feet into slippers.

Through the Judas hole of the door, she can only see a dark silhouette, but she'd know that posture anywhere—a little embarrassed, as if he were intruding in a party he's not been invited to.

Gaëtan.

She throws the door open. "You're back," she says.

"I just got your message—" he stops, abruptly. His gray eyes stare at her, taking in, no doubt, the bulge of her belly and her puffy face. "I'd hoped you were joking." His voice is bleak.

"You know me better than that, don't you?" Françoise asks.

Gaëtan shrugs, steps inside—his beige trench coat dripping water on the floor. It looks as if it's raining again. Not an unusual occurrence in Brittany. "Been a long time," he says.

He sits on the sofa, twirling a glass of brandy between his fingers, while she tries to explain what has happened—when she gets to Douarnenez and the goddess walking out of the sea, her voice stumbles, trails off. Gaëtan looks at her, his face gentle: the same face he must show to the malnourished Africans who come to him as their last hope. He doesn't judge—doesn't scream or accuse her like Stéphane—and somewhere in her she finds the strength to go on.

After she's done, Gaëtan slowly puts the glass on the table, and steeples his fingers together, raising them to his mouth. "Ys," he says. "What have you got yourself into?"

"Like I had a choice." Françoise can't quite keep the acidity out of her voice.

"Sorry." Gaëtan hasn't moved—he's still thinking, it seems. It's never been like him to act or speak rashly. "It's an old tale around here, you know."

Françoise knows. That's the reason why she came back here. "You haven't seen this," she says. She goes to her working desk, and picks up the sketches of the goddess—with the drowned city in the background.

Gaëtan lays them on the low table before him, carefully sliding his glass out of the way. "I see." He runs his fingers on the goddess's face, very carefully. "You always had a talent for drawing. You shouldn't have chosen the machines over the landscapes and animals, you know."

It's an old, old tale; an old, old decision made ten years ago, and that she's never regretted. Except—except that the mere remembrance of the goddess's face is enough to scatter the formulas she made her living by; to render any blueprint, no matter how detailed, utterly meaningless. "Not the point," she says, finally—knowing that whatever happens next, she cannot go back to being an engineer.

"No, I guess not. Still . . ." He looks up at her, sharply. "You haven't talked about Stéphane."

"Stéphane—took it badly," she says, finally.

Gaëtan's face goes as still as sculptured stone. He doesn't say anything; he doesn't need to.

"You never liked him," Françoise says, to fill the silence—a silence that seems to have the edge of a drawn blade.

"No," Gaëtan says. "Let's leave it at that, shall we?" He turns his gaze back to the sketches, with visible difficulty. "You know who your goddess is."

Françoise shrugs. She's looked around on the internet, but there wasn't much about the city of Ys. Or rather, it was always the same legend. "The Princess of Ys," she said. "She who took a new lover every night—and who had them killed every morning. She whose arrogance drowned the city beneath the waves."

Gaëtan nods. "Ahez," he says.

"To me she's the goddess." And it's true. Such things as her don't seem as though they should have a name, a handle back to the familiar. She cannot be tamed; she cannot be vanquished. She will not be cheated.

Gaëtan is tapping his fingers against the sketches, repeatedly jabbing his index into the eyes of the goddess. "They say Princess Ahez became a spirit of the sea after she drowned." He's speaking carefully, inserting every word with the meticulous care of a builder constructing an edifice on unstable ground. "They say you can still hear her voice in the Bay of Douarnenez, singing a lament for Ys—damn it, this kind of thing just shouldn't be happening, Françoise!"

Françoise shrugs. She rubs her hands on her belly, wondering if she's imagining the heartbeat coursing through her extended skin—a beat that's already slowing down, already faltering.

"Tell that to him, will you?" she says. "Tell him he shouldn't be alive." Not that it will ever get to be much of a problem, anyway—it's not as if he has much chance of surviving his birth.

Gaëtan says nothing for a while. "You want my advice?" he says.

Françoise sits on a chair, facing him. "Why not?" At least it will be constructive—not like Stéphane's anger.

"Go away," Gaëtan says. "Get as far as you can from Quimper—as far as you can from the sea. Ahez's power lies in the sea. You should be safe."

Should. She stares at him, and sees what he's not telling her. "You're not sure."

"No," Gaëtan says. He shrugs, a little helplessly. "I'm not an expert in magic and ghosts and beings risen from the sea. I'm just a doctor."

"You're all I have," Francoise says, finally—the words she never told him after she started going out with Stéphane.

"Yeah," Gaëtan says. "Some leftovers."

Francoise rubs a hand on her belly again—feeling, distinctly, the chill that emanates from it: the coldness of beings drowned beneath the waves. "Even if it worked—I can't run away from the sea all my life, Gaëtan."

"You mean you don't want to run away, full stop."

A hard certainty rises within her—the same harshness that she felt when the gynecologist told her about the congenital heart defect. "No," she says. "I don't want to run away."

"Then what do you intend to do?" Gaëtan's voice is brimming with anger. "She's immortal, Françoise. She was a sorceress who could summon the devil himself in the heyday of Ys. You're—"

She knows what she is; all of it. Or does she? Once she was a student, then an engineer and a bride. Now she's none of this—just a woman pregnant with a baby that's not hers. "I'm what I am," she says, finally. "But I know one other thing she is, Gaëtan, one power she doesn't have: she's barren."

Gaëtan cocks his head. "Not quite barren," he says. "She can create life."

"Life needs to be sustained," Françoise says, a growing certainty within her. She remembers the rotting planks of the palace in Ys— remembers the cold, cold radiance of the goddess. "She can't do that. She can't nurture anything." Hell, she cannot even create—not a proper baby with a functioning heart.

"She can still blast you out of existence if she feels like it."

Françoise says nothing.

At length Gaëtan says, "You're crazy, you know." But he's capitulated already—she hears it in his voice. He doesn't speak for a while. "Your dreams—you can't speak in them."

"No. I can't do anything."

"She's summoned you," Gaëtan says. He's not the doctor anymore, but the folklorist, the boy who'd seek out old wives and listen to their talk for hours on end. "That's why. You come to Ys only at her bidding—you have no power of your own."

Françoise stares at him. She says, slowly, the idea taking shape as she's speaking, "Then I'll come to her. I'll summon her myself."

His face twists. "She'll still be—she's power incarnate, Françoise. Maybe you'll be able to speak, but that's not going to change the outcome."

Françoise thinks of the sonograms and of Stéphane's angry words— of her blueprints folded away in her Paris flat, the meaningless remnants of her old life. "There's no choice. I can't go on like this, Gaëtan. I can't—" She's crying now—tears running down her face, leaving tingling marks on her cheeks. "I can't—go—on."

Gaëtan's arms close around her; he holds her against his chest, briefly, awkwardly—a bulwark against the great sobs that shake her chest.

"I'm sorry," she says, finally, when she's spent all her tears. "I don't know what came over me."

Gaëtan pulls away from her. His gaze is fathomless. "You've hoarded them for too long," he says.

"I'm sorry," Françoise says, again. She spreads out her hands—feeling empty, drained of tears and of every other emotion. "But if there's a way out—and that's the only one there seems to be—I'll take it. I have to."

"You're assuming I can tell you how to summon Ahez," Gaëtan says, carefully.

She can read the signs; she knows what he's dangling before her: a possibility that he can give her, but that he doesn't approve of. It's clear in the set of his jaw, in the slightly aloof way he holds himself. "But you can, can't you?"

He won't meet her gaze. "I can tell you what I learnt of Ys," he says at last. "There's a song and a pattern to be drawn in the sand, for those who would open the gates of the drowned city . . ." He checks himself with a start. "It's old wives' tales, Françoise. I've never seen it work."

"Ys is old wives' tales. And so is Ahez. And I've seen them both. Please, Gaëtan. At worst, it won't work and I'll look like a fool."

Gaëtan's voice is somber. "The worst is if it works. You'll be dead." But his gaze is still angry, and his hands clenched in his lap; she knows she's won, that he'll give her what she wants.

Angry or not, Gaëtan still insists on coming with her—he drives her in his battered old Citroën on the small country roads to Douarnenez, and parks the car below a flickering lamplight.

Françoise walks down the dunes, keeping her gaze on the vast expanse of the ocean. In her hands she holds her only weapons: in her left hand, the paper with the pattern Gaëtan made her trace two hours ago; in her right hand, the sonograms the radiologist gave her this morning—the last scrap of science and reason that's left to her, the only seawall she can build against Ys and the goddess.

It's like being in her dream once more: the cold, white sand crunching under her sandals; the stars and the moon shining on the canvas of the sky; the roar of the waves filling her ears to bursting. As she reaches the bottom of the beach—the strip of wet sand left by the retreating tide, where it's easier to draw patterns—the baby moves within her, kicking against the skin of her belly.

Soon, she thinks. *Soon*. Either way, it will soon be over, and the knot of fear within her chest will vanish.

Gaëtan is standing by her side, one hand on her shoulder. "You know there's still time—" he starts.

She shakes her head. "It's too late for that. Five months ago was the last time I had a choice in the matter, Gaëtan."

He shrugs, angrily. "Go on, then."

Françoise kneels in the sand, carefully, oh so carefully. She lays the cream envelope with the sonograms by her side; and positions the paper with the pattern so that the moonlight falls full onto it, leaving no shadow on its lines. To draw her pattern, she's brought a Celtic dagger with a triskelion on the hilt—bought in a souvenir shop on the way to the beach.

Gaetan is kneeling as well, staring intently at the pattern. His right hand closes over Françoise's hand, just over the dagger's hilt. "This is how you draw," he says.

His fingers moves, drawing Françoise's hand with them. The dagger goes down, sinks into the sand—there's some resistance, but it seems to melt away before Gaetan's controlled gestures.

He draws line upon line, the beginning of the pattern—curves that meet to form walls and streets. And as he draws, he speaks: "We come here to summon Ys out of the sea. May Saint Corentin, who saved King Gradlon from the waves, watch over us; may the church bells toll not for our deaths. We come here to summon Ys out of the sea."

And, as he finishes his speech, he draws one last line, and completes his half of the pattern. Slowly, carefully, he opens his hand, leaving Françoise alone in holding the dagger.

Her turn.

She whispers, "We come here to summon Ys out of the sea. May Saint Corentin, who saved King Gradlon ..." She closes her eyes for a moment, feeling the weight of the dagger in her hand—a last chance to abandon, to leave the ritual incomplete.

But it's too late for that.

With the same meticulousness she once applied to her blueprints—the same controlled gestures that allowed her to draw the goddess from memory—she starts drawing on the sand.

Now there's no other noise but the breath of the sea—and, in counterpoint to it, the soft sounds she makes as she adds line upon line, curves that arc under her to form a triple spiral, curves that branch and split, the pattern blossoming like a flower under her fingers.

She remembers Gaëtan's explanations: here are the seawalls of Ys, and the breach that the waves made when Ahez, drunk with her own power, opened the gates to the ocean's anger; here are the twisting streets and avenues where revelers would dance until night's end, and the palace where Ahez brought her lovers—and, at the end of the spiral, here is the ravine where her trusted servants would throw the lovers' bodies in the morning. Here is . . .

There's no time anymore where she is; no sense of her own body or of the baby growing within. Her world has shrunk to the pen and the darkened lines she draws, each one falling into place with the inevitability of a bell-toll.

When she starts on the last few lines, Gaëtan's voice starts speaking the words of power: the Breton words that summon Ahez and Ys from their resting-place beneath the waves.

> "Ur pales kaer tost d'ar sklujoù
> Eno, en aour hag en perlez,
> Evel an heol a bar Ahez."

> *A beautiful palace by the seawalls*
> *There, in gold and in pearls,*
> *Like the sun gleams Ahez.*

His voice echoes in the silence, as if he were speaking above a bottomless chasm. He starts speaking them again—and again and again, the Breton words echoing each other until they become a string of meaningless syllables.

Françoise has been counting carefully, as he told her to; on the ninth repetition, she joins him. Her voice rises to mingle with Gaëtan's: thin, reedy, as fragile as a stream of smoke carried by the wind—and yet every word vibrates in the air, quivers as if drawing on some immeasurable power.

> "Ur pales kaer tost d'ar sklujoù
> Eno, en aour hag en perlez,
> Evel an heol a bar Ahez."

Their words echo in the silence. At last, at long last, she rises, the pattern under her complete—and she's back in her body now, the sand's coldness seeping into her legs, her heart beating faster and faster within her chest—and there's a second, weaker heartbeat entwined with hers.

Slowly, she rises, tucks the dagger into her trousers pocket. There's utter silence on the beach now, but it's the silence before a storm. Moonlight falls upon the lines she's drawn—and remains trapped within them, until the whole pattern glows white.

"Françoise," Gaëtan says behind her. There's fear in his voice.

She doesn't speak. She picks up the sonograms and goes down to the sea, until the waves lap at her feet—a deeper cold than that of the sand. She waits—knowing what is coming.

Far, far away, bells start tolling: the bells of Ys, answering her call. And in their wake the whole surface of the ocean is trembling, shaking like some great beast trying to dislodge a burden. Dark shadows coalesce under the sea, growing larger with each passing moment.

And then they're no longer shadows, but the bulks of buildings rising above the surface: massive stone walls encrusted with kelp, surrounding broken-down and rotted gates. The faded remnants of tabards adorn both sides of the gates—the drawings so eaten away Françoise can't make out their details.

The wind blows into her face the familiar smell of brine and decay, of algae and rotting wood: the smell of Ys.

Gaëtan, standing beside her, doesn't speak. Shock is etched on every line of his face.

"Let's go," Françoise whispers—for there is something about the drowned city that commands silence, even when you are its summoner.

Gaëtan is looking at her and at the gates; at her and at the shimmering pattern drawn on the sand. "It shouldn't have worked," he says, but his voice is very soft, already defeated. At length he shakes his head, and walks beside her as they enter the city of Ys.

Inside, skeletons lie in the streets, their arms still extended as if they could keep the sea at bay. A few crabs and lobsters scuttle away from them, the *click-click* of their legs on stone the only noise that breaks the silence.

Françoise holds the sonograms under her arms—the cardboard envelope is wet and decomposing, as if the atmosphere of Ys spread rot to everything it touches. Gaëtan walks slowly, carefully. She can imagine how he feels—he, never one to take unconsidered risks, who now finds himself thrust into the legends of his childhood.

She doesn't think, or dwell overmuch on what could go wrong—that way lies despair, and perdition. But she can't help hearing the baby's faint heartbeat—and imagining his blood draining from his limbs.

There's no one in the streets, no revelers to greet them, no merchants plying their trades on the deserted marketplace—not even ghosts to flitter between the ruined buildings. Ys is a dead city. No, worse than that: the husk of a city, since long deserted by both the dead and the living. But it hums with power: with an insistent beat that seeps through the soles of Françoise's shoes, with a rhythm that is the roar of the waves and the voice of the storm—and also a lament for all the lives lost to the ocean. As she walks, the rhythm penetrates deeper into her body, insinuating itself into her womb until it mingles with her baby's heartbeat.

Françoise knows where she's going: all she has to do is retrace her steps of the dream, to follow the streets until they widen into a large plaza; to walk between the six kelp-eaten statues that guard the entrance to the palace, between the gates torn off their hinges by the onslaught of the waves.

And then she and Gaëtan are inside, walking down corridors. The smell of mold is overbearing now, and Françoise can feel the beginnings of nausea in her throat. There's another smell, too: underlying everything, sweet and cloying, like a perfume worn for too long.

She knows who it belongs to. She wonders if the goddess has seen them come—but of course she has. Nothing in Ys escapes her overbearing power. She'll be at the center, waiting for them—toying with their growing fear, reveling in their anguish.

No. Françoise mustn't think about this. She'll focus on the song in her mind and in her womb, the insidious song of Ys—and she won't think at all. She won't . . .

In silence, they worm their way deeper into the cankered palace, stepping on moss and algae and the threadbare remnants of tapestries. Till at last they reach one last set of great gates—but those are of rusted metal, and the soldiers and sailors engraved on their panels are still visible, although badly marred by the sea.

The gates are closed—have been closed for a long time, the hinges buried under kelp and rust, the panels hanging askew. Françoise stops, the fatigue she's been ignoring so far creeping into the marrow of her bones.

Gaëtan has stopped too; he's running his fingers on the metal—pushing, desultorily, but the doors won't budge.

"What now?" he mouths.

The song is stronger now, draining Françoise of all thoughts—but at the same time lifting her into a different place, the same haven outside time as when she was drawing the pattern on the beach.

There are no closed doors in that place.

Françoise tucks the envelope with the sonograms under her arm, and lays both hands on the panels and pushes. Something rumbles, deep within the belly of the city—a pain that is somehow in her own womb—and then the gates yield, and open with a loud creak.

Inside, the goddess is waiting for them.

The dream once more: the rotten chairs beside the rotten trestle tables, the warm stones under her feet. And, at the far end of the room, the goddess sitting in the chair on the dais, smiling as Françoise draws nearer.

"You are brave," she says, and her voice is that of the sea before the storm. "And foolish. Few dare to summon Ys from beneath the waves." She smiles again, revealing teeth the color of nacre. "And fewer still return alive." She moves, with fluid, inhuman speed; comes to stand by Gaëtan, who has frozen, three steps below the empty chair. "But you brought a gift, I see."

Françoise drags her voice from an impossibly faraway place. "He's not yours."

"I choose as I please, and every man that comes into Ys is mine," the goddess says. She walks around Gaëtan, tilting his head upwards, watching him as she might watch a slave on the selling-block. Abruptly there's a mask in her hand—a mask of black silk that seems to waver between her fingers.

That legend, too, Gaëtan told her. At dawn, after the goddess has had her pleasure, the mask will tighten until the man beneath dies of suffocation—one more sacrifice to slake her unending thirst.

Françoise is moving, without conscious thought—extending a hand and catching the mask before the goddess can put it on Gaëtan's face. The mask clings to her fingers: cold and slimy, like the scales of a fish, but writhing against her skin like a maddened snake.

She meets the goddess's cold gaze—the same blinding radiance that silenced her within the dream. But now there's power in Françoise— the remnants of the magic she used to summon Ys—and the light is strong, but she can still see.

"You dare," the goddess hisses. "You whom I picked among mortals to be honored—"

"I don't want to be honored," Françoise says, slowly. The mask is crawling upwards, extending coils around the palm of her hand. She's about to say "I don't want your child," but that would be a lie—she kept the baby, after all, clung to him rather than to Stéphane. "What I want you can't give."

The goddess smiles. She hasn't moved—she's still standing there, at the heart of her city, secure in her power. "Who are you to judge what I can and can't give?"

The mask is at her wrist now—it leaves a tingling sensation where it passes, as if it had briefly cut off the flow of blood in her body. Françoise tries not to think of what will happen when it reaches her neck—tries not to fear. Instead, as calmly as she can, she extends the envelope to the goddess. When she moves, the mask doesn't fall off, doesn't move in the slightest—except to continue its inexorable climb upwards.

Mustn't think about it. She knew the consequences when she drew her pattern in the sand; knew them and accepted them.

So she says to the goddess, in a voice that she keeps devoid of all emotions, "This is what you made."

The goddess stares at the envelope as if trying to decide what kind of trap it holds. Then, apparently deciding Françoise cannot harm her, she takes the envelope from Françoise's hands, and opens it.

Slowly, the goddess lifts the sonograms to the light, looks at them, lays them aside on the steps of the dais. From the envelope she takes the last paper—the diagnosis typed by the radiologist, and looks at it.

Silence fills the room, as if the whole city were holding its breath. Even the mask on Françoise's arm has stopped crawling.

"This is a lie," the goddess says, and her voice is the lash of a whip. Shadows move across her face, like storm-clouds blown by the wind.

Françoise shrugs, with a calm she doesn't feel. "Why would I?" She reaches out with one hand towards the mask, attempts to pull it from her arm. Her fingers stick to it, but it will not budge. Not surprising.

"You would cast my child from your womb."

Françoise shakes her head. "I could have. Much, much earlier. But I didn't." And the part of her that can't choke back its anger and frustration says, "I don't see why the child should pay for the arrogance of his creator."

"You dare judge me?" The goddess's radiance becomes blinding; the mask tightens around Françoise's arm, sending a wave of pain up her arm, pain so strong that Françoise bits her lips not to cry out. She fights an overwhelming urge to crawl into the dirt—it doesn't work, because abruptly she's kneeling on the floor, with only shaking arms to hold up her torso. She has to abase herself before the goddess, before her glory and her magic. She, Françoise, is nothing; a failure, a flawed womb. An artist turning to science out of greed; an engineer drawing meaningless blueprints; a woman who used her friend's feelings for her to bring him into Ys.

"If this child will not survive its birth," the goddess is saying, "you will have another. I will not be cheated." Not by you, she's saying without words. Not by a mere mortal.

A wave of power buffets Françoise, bringing with it the smell of wind and brine, of wet sand and rotten wood. Within her, the power of the goddess is rising—Françoise's belly aches as if fingers of ice were tearing it apart. Her baby is twisting and turning, kicking desperately against the confines of the womb, voicelessly screaming not to be unmade, but it's too late.

She wants to curl up on herself and make the pain go away; she wants to lie down, even if it's on slimy stone, and wait until the contractions of her belly have faded, and nothing remains but numbness. But she can't move. The only way to move is towards the algae-encrusted floor, to grovel before the goddess.

Gaëtan was right. It was folly to come here, folly to hope to stand against Ahez.

Françoise's arms hurt. She's going to have to yield. There's no other choice. She—

Yield.

She's a womb, an empty place for the goddess to fill. She has been chosen, picked out from the crowd of tourists on the beach—chosen for the greatest of honors, and now chosen again, to bear a child that will be perfect. She should be glad beyond reason.

Yield.

The mask is crawling upwards again—it's at her shoulder now, flowing towards her neck, towards her face. She knows, without being able to articulate the thought, that when it covers her face she will be lost—drowned forever under the silk.

Everything is scattering, everything is stripped away by the power of the goddess—the power of the ocean that drowns sailors, of the storm-tossed seas and their irresistible siren song. She can't hold on to anything. She—has to—

There's nothing left at her core now; only a hollow begging to be filled.

And yet . . . and yet in the silence, in the emptiness of her mind is the song of Ys, and the pattern she drew in the sand; in the silence of her mind, she is kneeling on the beach with the dagger still in her hand, and watching the drowned city rise from the depths to answer her call.

Slowly, she raises her head, biting her lips not to scream at the pain within her—the pain that sings yield yield yield. Blood floods her mouth with the taste of salt, but she's staring at the face of the goddess—and the light isn't blinding, she can see the green eyes dissecting her like an insect. She can—

She can speak.

"I—am—not—your toy," she whispers. Every word is a leaden weight, a stone dragged from some faraway place. "The child—is—not—your—toy."

She reaches for the mask—which is almost at her lips. She feels the power coiled within the silk, the insistent beat that is also the rhythm of the waves, and the song that has kept Ys from crumbling under the sea—and it's within her, pulsing in her belly, singing in her veins and arteries.

The mask flows towards her outstretched fingers, clings to them. It's cold and wet, like rain on parched earth. She shakes her hand, and the mask falls onto the ground, and lies there, inert and harmless: an empty husk.

Like Ys. Like Ahez.

"You dare—" the goddess hisses. Her radiance is wavering, no longer as strong as it was on Douarnenez. She extends a hand: it's empty for a split second, and then the wavering image of a white spear fills it. The goddess lunges towards Françoise. Out of sheer instinct, Françoise throws herself aside. Metal grates on the stones to her left—not ten centimeters from where she is.

Françoise pushes herself upwards, ignoring the nausea that wells up as she abruptly changes positions. The goddess is coming at her again with her spear.

Françoise is out of breath, and the world won't stop spinning around her—she can't avoid the spear forever. The song is deep within her bones, but that doesn't help—it just adds to her out-of-synch feeling.

The spear brushes past her, draws a fiery line of pain on her hand. She has to—

Behind the goddess, Gaëtan still stands frozen. No, not quite, she realizes as she sidesteps once more, stumbling—the nausea rising, rising, screaming at her to lie down and yield. Gaëtan is blinking—staring at her, the eyes straining to make sense of what they see.

He raises a hand, slowly—too slowly, damn it, she thinks as she throws herself on the floor and rolls over to avoid the spear.

It buries itself into her shoulder—transfixes her. She's always thought she would scream if something like that happened, but she doesn't. She bites her lips so fiercely that blood fills her mouth. Within her, the pattern she drew on the sand is whirling, endlessly.

The pattern. The dagger. She fumbles for it, tries to extract it from her trouser pocket, but she can't, she's pinned to the ground. She should have thought of it earlier—

"Your death will not be clean," the goddess says as she withdraws the spear for another thrust.

Françoise screams, then. Not her pain, but a name. "Gaëtan!"

His panicked heartbeat is part of the song within her—the nausea, the power shimmering beyond her reach. He's moving as if through tar, trying to reach her—but he won't, not in time. There's not enough time.

But her scream makes the goddess pause and look up for a split second, as if she'd forgotten something and only just remembered. For a moment only she's looking away from Françoise, the spear's point hovering within Françoise's reach.

Françoise, giving up on releasing the dagger, grasps the haft of the spear instead. She pulls down, as hard as she can.

She's expected some resistance, but the goddess has no weight—barely enough substance to wield the spear, it seems. Françoise's savage pull topples her onto the floor, felling her like harvested wheat.

But she's already struggling to rise—white arms going for Françoise's throat. At such close quarters, the spear is useless. Françoise makes a sweeping throw with one hand, and hears it clatter on the stones. She fumbles, again, for the dagger—half out of her pocket this time. But there's no time. No time . . .

Abruptly, the white arms grow slack. Something enters her field of view—the point of the spear, hovering above her, and then burying itself in the goddess's shoulder.

"I don't think so," Gaëtan says. His face is pale, his hair disheveled, but his grip on the spear's haft doesn't waver.

Françoise rolls away from the goddess, heaving—there's bile in her throat, but she can't even vomit. She finally has her dagger out, but it doesn't seem like she will need it.

Doesn't seem . . .

The goddess hisses like a stricken cat. She twists away, and the spear slides out of her wound as easily as from water. Then, before Gaetan can react, she jumps upwards—both arms extended towards his face.

The spear clatters on the ground. Françoise stifles the scream that rises in her and runs, her ribs burning. She's going to be too late—she can't possibly—

She's almost there, but the goddess's arms are already closing around Gaëtan's throat. There's no choice. There never was any choice.

Françoise throws the dagger.

She sees everything that happens next take place in slow motion: the dagger, covering the last few hand-spans that separate Françoise from the goddess's back—the hilt, slowly starting to flip upwards—the blade, burying itself at an angle into the bare white skin—blood, blossoming from the wound like an obscene fountain.

The goddess falls, drawing Gaëtan down with her. Françoise, unable to contain herself anymore, screams, and her voice echoes under the vast ceiling of the throne room.

Nothing moves. Then the goddess's body rolls aside, and Gaëtan stands up, shaking. Red welts cover his throat, and he is breathing heavily—but he looks fine. He's alive.

"Françoise?"

She's unable to voice her relief. Beside him, the goddess's body is wrinkled and already crumbling into dust—leaving only the dagger, glinting with drowned light.

Within her, the symphony is rising to a pitch—the baby's heart, her own, mingling in their frantic beat. She hears a voice whispering, *The princess is dead. Ys is dead. Who shall rule on Ahez's throne?*

Once more she's lifted into that timeless place of the beach, with her pattern shining in moonlight: every street of Ys drawn in painstaking detail.

At the center of the city, in the palace, is its heart, but it's not beating as it should. Its valves and veins are too narrow, and not pumping enough blood—it cannot stave off the rot nor keep the sea from eating at the skeletons, but neither will it let the city die.

And it's her baby's heart, too—the two inextricably tied, the drowned city, and the baby who should have been its heir.

She has a choice, she sees: she can try to repair the heart, to widen the arteries to let the blood in—perhaps Gaëtan could help, he's a doctor, after all. She can draw new pathways for the blood, with the same precision as a blueprint—and hope they will be enough.

She wants the baby to live—she wants her five months of pregnancy, her loss of Stéphane, not to have been for nothing, not to have been a cruel jest by someone who's forgotten what it was to be human.

But there are skeletons in the streets of Ys: crabs and shells scuttling on the paved stones, kelp covering the frescoed walls, and in the center of the city, in the throne room, the dais is rotten—to the core.

She hears the heartbeat within her, the blood ebbing and flowing in her womb, and she knows, with absolute certainty, that it will not be enough. That she has to let go.

She doesn't want to. It would be like yielding—did she go all that way for nothing?

But this isn't about her—there's nothing she can offer Ys, or the baby.

She closes her eyes and sees the pattern splayed on the ground—and the heart at the center.

And in her mind she takes up the dagger, and drives up to the hilt into the pattern.

There's a scream, deep within her—tendrils of pain twisting within her womb. The pattern contorts and wavers—and it's disappearing, burning away like a piece of paper given to the flames.

She's back in her body—she's fallen to her knees on the floor, both hands going to her belly as if she could contain the pain. But of course she can't.

Around her, the walls of the palace are shaking.

"Françoise, we have to get out of there!" Gaëtan says.

She struggles to speak through a haze of pain. "I—"

Gaëtan's hands drag her upwards, force her to stand. "Come on," he says. "Come on."

She stumbles on, leaning on his shoulder—through the kelp-encrusted corridors, through the deserted streets and the ruined buildings that are now collapsing. One step after another—one foot in front of the other, and she will not think of the pain in her belly, of the heartbeat within her that grows fainter and fainter with every step.

She will not think.

They're out of Ys, standing on the beach at Douarnenez with the stars shining above. The drowned city shivers and shakes and crumbles, and the sea is rising—rising once more to reclaim it.

Then there's nothing left of Ys, only the silvery surface of the ocean, and the waves lapping at their feet. Between Françoise's legs, something wet and sticky is dripping—and she knows what it has to be.

Gaëtan is looking at the sea; Françoise, shaking, has not the strength to do more than lean on his shoulder. She stares ahead, at the blurry stars, willing herself not to cry, not to mourn.

"You okay?" Gaëtan asks.

She shrugs. "Not sure yet," she says. "Come on. Let's go home and grab some sleep."

Later, there'll be time for words: time to explain, time to heal and rebuild. But for now, there is nothing left but silence within her—only one heartbeat she can hear, and it's her own.

I'll be okay, she thinks, blinking furiously, as they walk back to Gaëtan's car. Overhead, the stars are fading—a prelude to sunrise. *I'll be okay*.

But her womb is empty; and in her mind is the song of her unborn son, an endless lament for all that was lost.

"THE GORGON"

TANITH LEE

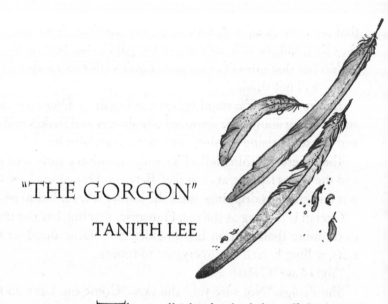

The small island, which lay off the larger island of Daphaeu, obviously contained a secret of some sort, and, day by day, and particularly night by night, began to exert an influence on me, so that I must find it out.

Daphaeu itself (or more correctly herself, for she was a female country, voluptuous and cruel by turns in the true antique fashion of the Goddess) was hardly enormous. A couple of roads, a tangle of sheep tracks, a precarious, escalating village, rocks and hillsides thatched by blistered grass. All of which overhung an extraordinary sea, unlike any sea which I have encountered elsewhere in Greece. Water which might be mistaken for blueness from a distance, but which, from the harbor or the multitude of caves and coves that undermined the island, revealed itself a clear and succulent green, like milky limes or the bottle glass of certain spirits.

On my first morning, having come on to the natural terrace (the only recommendation of the hovel-like accommodation) to look over this strange green ocean, I saw the smaller island, lying like a little boat of land moored just wide of Daphaeu's three hills. The day was clear, the water frilled with white where it hit the fangs in the interstices below the terrace. About the smaller island, barely a ruffle showed. It seemed to glide up from the sea, smooth as mirror. The little island was verdant, also. Unlike Daphaeu's limited stands of stone pine, cypress, and cedar, the smaller sister was clouded by a still, lambent haze of foliage that looked to be woods. Visions of groves, springs, a ruined temple, a statue of Pan playing the panpipes forever in some glade—where only yesterday, it might seem, a thin column of aromatic smoke had gone up—these images were enough, fancifully, to draw me into inquiries about how the small island might be reached. And when my inquiries met first with a polite bevy of excuses, next with a refusal, last with a blank wall of silence, as if whoever I mentioned the little island to had gone temporarily deaf or mad, I became, of course, insatiable to get to it, to find out what odd superstitious thing kept these people away. Naturally, the Daphaeui were not friendly to me at any time beyond the false friendship one anticipates extended to a man of another nationality and clime, who can be relied on to pay his bills, perhaps allow himself to be overcharged, even made a downright monkey of in order to preserve goodwill. In the normal run of things, I could have had anything I wanted in exchange for a pack of local lies, a broad local smile, and a broader local price. That I could not get to the little island puzzled me. I tried money and I tried barter. I even, in a reckless moment, probably knowing I would not succeed, offered Pitos, one of the younger fishermen, the gold and onyx ring he coveted. My sister had made it for me, the faithful copy of an intaglio belonging to the House of Borgia, no less. Generally, Pitos could not pass the time of day with me without mentioning the ring, adding something in the nature of: "If ever you want a great service, any great service, I will do it for that ring." I half believe he would have stolen or murdered for it, certainly shared the bed with me. But he would not, apparently, even for the Borgia ring, take me to the little island.

"You think too much of foolish things," he said to me. "For a big writer, that is not good."

I ignored the humorous aspect of "big," equally inappropriate in the sense of height, girth, or fame. Pitos's English was fine, and when he slipped into mild inaccuracies, it was likely to be a decoy.

"You're wrong, Pitos. That island has a story in it somewhere. I'd take a bet on it."

"No fish today," said Pitos. "Why you think that is?"

I refrained from inventively telling him I had seen giant swordfish leaping from the shallows by the smaller island.

I found I was prowling Daphaeu, but only on the one side, the side where I would get a view—or views—of her sister. I would climb down into the welter of coves and smashed emerald water to look across at her. I would climb up and stand, leaning on the sunblasted walls of a crumbling church, and look at the small island. At night, crouched over a bottle of wine, a scatter of manuscript, moths falling like rain in the oil lamp, my stare stayed fixed on the small island, which, as the moon came up, would seem turned to silver or to some older metal, Nemean metal perhaps, sloughed from the moon herself.

Curiosity accounts for much of this, and contra-suggestiveness. But the influence I presently began to feel, that I cannot account for exactly. Maybe it was only the writer's desire to fantasize rather than to work. But each time I reached for the manuscript I would experience a sort of distraction, a sort of calling—uncanny, poignant, like nostalgia, though for a place I had never visited.

I am very bad at recollecting my dreams, but one or twice, just before sunrise, I had a suspicion I had dreamed of the island. Of walking there, hearing its inner waters, the leaves brushing my hands and face.

Two weeks went by, and precious little had been done in the line of work. And I had come to Daphaeu with the sole intention of working. The year before, I had accomplished so much in a month of similar islands—or had they been similar?—that I had looked for results of some magnitude. In all of fourteen days I must have squeezed out two thousand words, and most of those dreary enough that the only covers they would ever get between would be those of the trash can. And yet it was not that I could not produce work, it was that I knew, with blind and damnable certainty, that the work I needed to be doing sprang from that spoonful of island.

The first day of the third week I had been swimming in the calm stretch of sea west of the harbor and had emerged to sun myself and smoke on the parched hot shore. Presently Pitos appeared, having scented my cigarettes. Surgical and government health warnings have not yet penetrated to spots like Daphaeu, where filtered tobacco continues to symbolize Hollywood or some other amorphous, anachronistic surrealism still hankered after and long vanished from the real world beyond. Once Pitos had acquired his cigarette, he sprawled down on the dry grass, grinned, indicated the Borgia ring, and mentioned a beautiful cousin of his, whether male or female I cannot be sure. After this had been cleared out of the way, I said to him, "You know how the currents run. I was thinking of a slightly more adventurous swim. But I'd like your advice."

Pitos glanced at me warily. I had had the plan as I lazed in the velvet water. Pitos was already starting to guess it.

"Currents are very dangerous. Not to be trusted, except by harbor."

"How about between Daphaeu and the other island? It can't be more than a quarter mile. The sea looks smooth enough, once you break away from the shoreline here."

"No," said Pitos. I waited for him to say there were no fish, or a lot of fish, or that his brother had gotten a broken thumb, or something of the sort. But Pitos did not resort to this. Troubled and angry, he stabbed my cigarette, half-smoked, into the turf. "Why do you want to go to the island so much?"

"Why does nobody else want me to go there?"

He looked up then, and into my eyes. His own were very black, sensuous, carnal earthbound eyes, full of orthodox sins, and extremely young in a sense that had nothing to do with physical age, but with race, I suppose, the youngness of ancient things, like Pan himself, quite possibly.

"Well," I said at last, "are you going to tell me or not? Because believe me, I intend to swim over there today or tomorrow."

"No," he said again. And then: "You should not go. On the island there is a . . ." and he said a word in some tongue neither Greek nor Turkish, not even the corrupt Spanish that sometimes peregrinates from Malta.

"A *what*?"

Pitos shrugged helplessly. He gazed out to sea, a safe sea without islands. He seemed to be putting something together in his mind and I let him do it, very curious now, pleasantly unnerved by this waft of the occult I had already suspected to be the root cause of the ban.

Eventually he turned back to me, treated me once more to the primordial innocence of his stare, and announced:

"The cunning one."

"Ah," I said. Both irked and amused, I found myself smiling. At this, Pitos's face grew savage with pure rage, an expression I had never witnessed before—the façade kept for foreigners had well and truly come down.

"Pitos," I said, "I don't understand."

"*Meda*," he said then, the Greek word, old Greek.

"Wait," I said. I caught at the name, which was wrong, trying to fit it to a memory. Then the list came back to me, actually from Graves, the names which meant "the cunning": Meda, Medea, Medusa.

"Oh," I said. I hardly wanted to offend him further by bursting into loud mirth. At the same time, even while I was trying not to laugh, I was aware of the hair standing up on my scalp and neck. "You're telling me there is a gorgon on the island."

Pitos grumbled unintelligibly, stabbing the dead cigarette over and over into the ground.

"I'm sorry, Pitos, but it can't be Medusa. Someone cut her head off quite a few years ago. A guy called Perseus."

His face erupted into that awful expression again, mouth in a rictus, tongue starting to protrude, eyes flaring at me—quite abruptly I realized he wasn't raging, but imitating the visual panic-contortions of a man turning inexorably to stone. Since that is what the gorgon is credited with, literally petrifying men by the sheer horror of her countenance, it now seemed almost pragmatic of Pitos to be demonstrating. It was, too, a creditable facsimile of the sculpted gorgon's face sometimes used to seal ovens and jars. I wondered where he had seen one to copy it so well.

"All right," I said. "Okay, Pitos, fine." I fished in my shirt, which was lying on the ground, and took out some money to give him, but he recoiled. "I'm sorry," I said, "I don't think it merits the ring. Unless you'd care to row me over there after all."

The boy rose. He looked at me with utter contempt, and without another word, before striding off up the shore. The mashed cigarette protruded from the grass and I lay and watched it, the tiny strands of tobacco slowly crisping in the heat of the sun, as I plotted my route from Daphaeu.

Dawn seemed an amiable hour. No one in particular about on that side of the island, the water chill but flushing quickly with warmth as the sun reached over it. And the tide in the right place to navigate the rocks . . .

Yes, dawn would be an excellent time to swim out to the gorgon's island.

The gods were on my side, I concluded as I eased myself into the open sea the following morning. Getting clear of the rocks was no problem, their channels only half filled by the returning tide. While just beyond Daphaeu's coast I picked up one of those contrary currents that lace the island's edges and which, tide or no, would funnel me away from shore.

The swim was ideal, the sea limpid and no longer any more than cool. Sunlight filled in the waves and touched Daphaeu's retreating face with gold. Barely altered in thousands of years, either rock or sea or sun. And yet one knew that against all the claims of romantic fiction, this place did not look now as once it had. Some element in the air or in time itself changes things. A young man of the Bronze Age, falling asleep at sunset in his own era, waking at sunrise in mine, looking about him, would not have known where he was. I would swear to that.

Such thoughts I had leisure for in my facile swim across to the wooded island moored off Daphaeu.

As I had detected, the approach was smooth, virtually inviting. I cruised in as if sliding along butter. A rowboat would have had no more difficulty. The shallows were clear, empty of rocks, and, if anything, greener than the water off Daphaeu.

I had not looked much at Medusa's Island (I had begun jokingly to call it this) as I crossed, knowing I would have all the space on my arrival. So I found myself wading in on a seamless beach of rare glycerin sand and, looking up, saw the mass of trees spilling from the sky.

The effect was incredibly lush—so much heavy green, and seemingly quite impenetrable, while the sun struck in glistening shafts, lodging like arrows in the foliage, which reminded me very intensely of huge clusters of grapes on a vine. Anything might lie behind such a barricade.

It was already beginning to get hot. Dry, I put on the loose cotton shirt and ate breakfast packed in the same waterproof wrapper, standing on the beach impatient to get on.

As I moved forward, a bird shrilled somewhere in its cage of boughs, sounding an alarm of invasion. But surely the birds, too, would be stone on Medusa's Island, if the legends were correct. And when I stumbled across the remarkable stone carving of a man in the forest, I would pause in shocked amazement at its verisimilitude to life . . .

Five minutes into the thickets of the wood, I did indeed stumble on a carving, but it was of a moss-grown little faun. My pleasure in the discovery was considerably lessened, however, when investigation told me it was scarcely classical in origin. Circa 1920 would be nearer the mark.

A further minute and I had put the faun from my mind. The riot of waterfalling plants through which I had been picking my way broke open suddenly on an inner vista much wider than I had anticipated. While the focal point of the vista threw me completely, I cannot say what I had really been expecting. The grey-white stalks of pillars, some temple shrine, the spring with its votary of greenish rotted bronze, none of these would have surprised me. On the other hand, to find a house before me took me completely by surprise. I stood and looked at it in abject dismay, cursing its wretched normality until I gradually began to see the house was not normal in the accepted sense.

It had been erected probably at the turn of the century, when such things were done. An eccentric two-storied building, intransigently European—that is, the Europe of the north—with its dark walls and arched roofing. Long windows, smothered by the proximity of the wood, received and refracted no light. The one unique and startling feature—startling because of its beauty—was the parade of columns that ran along the terrace, in form and choreography for all the world like the columns of Knossos, differing only in color. For these stems of the gloomy house were of a luminous sea-green marble, and shone as the windows did not.

Before the house was a stretch of rough-cut lawn, tamarisk, and one lost dying olive tree. As I was staring, an apparition seemed to manifest out of the center of the tree. For a second we peered at each other before he came from the bushes with a clashing of gnarled brown forearms. He might have been an elderly satyr; I, patently, was only a swimmer, with my pale foreigner's tan, my bathing trunks, the loose shirt. It occurred to me at last that I was conceivably trespassing. I wished my Greek were better.

He planted himself before me and shouted intolerantly, and anyone's Greek was good enough to get his drift. "Go! Go!" He was ranting, and he began to wave a knife with which, presumably, he had been pruning or mutilating something. "Go. You *go!*"

I said I had been unaware anybody lived on the island. He took no notice. He went on waving the knife and his attitude provoked me. I told him sternly to put the knife down, that I would leave when I was ready, that I had seen no notice to the effect that the island was private property. Generally I would never take a chance like this with someone so obviously qualified to be a lunatic, but my position was so vulnerable, so ludicrous, so entirely indefensible, that I felt bound to act firmly. Besides which, having reached the magic grotto and found it was not as I had visualized, I was still very reluctant to abscond with only a memory of dark windows and sea-green columns to brood upon.

The maniac was by now quite literally foaming, due most likely to a shortage of teeth, but the effect was alarming, not to mention unaesthetic. As I was deciding which fresh course to take and if there might be one, a woman's figure came out onto the terrace. I had the impression of a white frock, before an odd, muffled voice called out a rapid—too rapid for my translation—stream of peculiarly accented Greek. The old man swung around, gazed at the figure, raised his arms, and bawled another foaming torrent to the effect that I was a bandit or some other kind of malcontent. While he did so, agitated as I was becoming, I nevertheless took in what I could of the woman standing between the columns. She was mostly in shadow, just the faded white dress with a white scarf at the neck marking her position. And then there was an abrupt flash of warmer pallor that was her hair. A blond Greek, or maybe just a peroxided Greek. At any rate, no snakes.

The drama went on, from his side, from hers. I finally got tired of it, went by him, and walked toward the terrace, pondering, rather too late, if I might not be awarded the knife in my back. But almost as soon as I started to move, she leaned forward a little and she called another phrase to him, which this time I made out, telling him to let me come on.

When I reached the foot of the steps, I halted, really involuntarily, struck by something strange about her. Just as the strangeness of the house had begun to strike me, not its evident strangeness, the ill-marriage to location, the green pillars, but a strangeness of atmosphere, items the unconscious eye notices, where the physical eye is blind and will not explain. And so with her. What was it? Still in shadow, I had the impression she might be in her early thirties, from her figure, her movements, but she had turned away as I approached, adjusting some papers on a wicker table.

"Excuse me," I said. I stopped and spoke in English. For some reason I guessed she would be familiar with the language, perhaps only since it was current on Daphaeu. "Excuse me. I had no idea the island was private. No one gave me the slightest hint—"

"You are English," she broke in, in the vernacular, proving the guess to be correct.

"Near enough. I find it easier to handle than Greek, I confess."

"Your Greek is very good," she said with the indifferent patronage of one who is multilingual. I stood there under the steps, already fascinated. Her voice was the weirdest I had ever heard, muffled, almost unattractive, and with the most incredible accent, not Greek at all. The nearest approximation I could come up with was Russian, but I could not be sure.

"Well," I said. I glanced over my shoulder and registered that the frothy satyr had retired into his shrubbery; the knife glinted as it slashed tamarisk in lieu of me. "Well, I suppose I should retreat to Daphaeu. Or am I permitted to stay?"

"Go, stay," she said. "I do not care at all."

She turned then, abruptly, and my heart slammed into the base of my throat. A childish silly reaction, yet I was quite unnerved, for now I saw what it was that had seemed vaguely peculiar from a distance. The lady on Medusa's Island was masked.

She remained totally still and let me have my reaction, neither helping nor hindering me.

It was an unusual mask, or usual—I am unfamiliar with the norm of such things. It was made of some matte-light substance that toned well with the skin of her arms and hands, possibly not so well with that of her neck, where the scarf provided camouflage. Besides which, the chin of the mask—this certainly an extra to any mask I had ever seen—continued under her own. The mask's physiognomy was bland, nondescriptly pretty in a way that was somehow grossly insulting to her. Before confronting the mask, if I had tried to judge the sort of face she would have, I would have suspected a coarse, rather heavy beauty, probably redeemed by one chiseled feature—a small slender nose, perhaps. The mask, however, was vacuous. It did not suit her, was not true to her. Even after three minutes I could tell as much, or thought I could, which amounts to the same thing.

The blond hair, seeming natural as the mask was not, cascaded down, lush as the foliage of the island. A blond Greek, then, like the golden Greeks of Homer's time, when gods walked the earth in disguise.

In the end, without any help or hindrance from her, as I have said, I pulled myself together. As she had mentioned no aspect of her state, neither did I. I simply repeated what I had said before: "Am I permitted to stay?"

The mask went on looking at me. The astonishing voice said: "You wish to stay so much. What do you mean to do here?"

Talk to you, oblique lady, and wonder what lies behind the painted veil.

"Look at the island, if you'll let me. I found the statue of a faun near the beach." Elaboration implied I should lie: "Someone told me there was an old shrine here."

"Ah!" She barked. It was apparently a laugh. "No one," she said, "*told* you anything about this place."

I was at a loss. Did she know what was said? "Frankly, then, I roman-
tically hoped there might be."

"Unromantically, there is not. No shrine. No temple. My father
bought the faun in a shop in Athens. A tourist shop. He had vulgar
tastes but he knew it, and that has a certain charm, does it not?"

"Yes, I suppose it does. Your father—"

She cut me short again.

"The woods cover all the island. Except for an area behind the house.
We grow things there, and we keep goats and chickens. We are very
domesticated. Very sufficient for ourselves. There is a spring of fresh
water, but no votary. No *genius loci*. I am *so* sorry to dash your dreams
to pieces."

It suggested itself to me, from her tone of amusement, from little
inflections that were coming and going in her shoulders now, that she
might be enjoying this, enjoying, if you like, putting me down as an
idiot. Presumably visitors were rare. Perhaps it was even fun for her to
talk to a man, youngish and unknown, though admittedly never likely
to qualify for anyone's centerfold.

"But you have no objections to my being here," I pursued. "And your
father?"

"My parents are dead," she informed me. "When I employed the
plural, I referred to him," she gestured with a broad sweep of her hand
to the monster on the lawn, "and a woman who attends to the house.
My servants, my unpaid servants. I have no money anymore. Do you
see this dress? It is my mother's dress. How lucky I am the same fitting
as my mother, do you not think?"

"Yes . . ."

I was put in mind, suddenly, of myself as an ambassador at the court
of some notorious female potentate, Cleopatra, say, or Catherine de
Medici.

"You are very polite," she said as if telepathically privy to my fantasies.

"I have every reason to be."

"What reason?"

"I'm trespassing. You treat me like a guest."

"And how," she said, vainglorious all at once, "do you rate my English?"

"It's wonderful."

"I speak eleven languages fluently," she said with offhanded boastful-
ness. "Three more I can read very well."

I liked her. This display, touching and magnificent at once, her angu-
lar theatrical gesturing, which now came more and more often, her hair,
her flat-waisted figure in its 1940s dress, her large well-made hands,
and her challenging me with the mask, saying nothing to explain it, all
this hypnotized me.

I said something to express admiration and she barked again, throwing back her blond head and irresistibly, though only for a moment,
conjuring Garbo's Queen Christina.

Then she walked down the steps straight to me, demonstrating something else I had deduced, that she was only about an inch shorter than I.

"I," she said, "will show you the island. Come."

She showed me the island. Unsurprisingly, it was small. To go directly
around it would maybe have taken less than thirty minutes. But we lingered, over a particular tree, a view, and once we sat down on the ground
near the gushing milk-white spring. The basin under the spring, she
informed me, had been added in 1910. A little bronze nymph presided
over the spot, dating from the same year, which you could tell in any
case from the way her classical costume and her filleted hair had been
adapted to the fashions of hobble skirt and Edwardian coiffeur. Each
age imposes its own overlay on the past.

Behind the house was a scatter of the meager white dwellings that
make up such places as the village on Daphaeu, now plainly unoccu-
pied and put to other uses. Sheltered from the sun by a colossal cypress, six goats played about in the grass. Chickens and an assortment
of other fowl strutted up and down, while a pig—or pigs—grunted
somewhere out of sight. Things grew in strips and patches, and fruit
trees and vines ended the miniature plantation before the woods
resumed. Self-sufficiency of a tolerable kind, I supposed. But there
seemed, from what she said, no contact maintained with any other
area, as if the world did not exist. Postulate that a blight or harsh
weather intervened, what then? And the old satyr, how long would
he last to tend the plots? He looked two hundred now, which on the
islands probably meant sixty. I did not ask her what contingency plans
she had for these emergencies and inevitabilities. What good, after all,
are most plans? We could be invaded from Andromeda tomorrow, and
what help for us all then? Either it is in your nature to survive—somehow, anyhow—or it is not.

She had well and truly hooked me, of course. If I had met her in Athens, some sun-baked afternoon, I would have felt decidedly out of my depth, taken her for cocktails, and foundered before we had even reached the dinner hour. But here, in this pulsing green bubble of light and leaves straight out of one's most irrational visions of the glades of Arcadia, conversation, however erratic, communication, however eccentric, was happening. The most inexplicable thing of all was that the mask had ceased almost immediately to bother me. I cannot, as I look back, properly account for this, for to spend a morning, a noon, an afternoon, allowing yourself to become fundamentally engaged by a woman whose face you have not seen, whose face you are actively being prevented from seeing, seems now incongruous to the point of perversity. But there it is. We discussed Ibsen, Dickens, Euripides, and Jung. I remembered trawling anecdotes of a grandfather, mentioned my sister's jewelry store in St. Louis, listened to an astonishing description of wild birds flying in across a desert from a sea. I assisted her over rocky turf, flirted with her, felt excited by and familiar with her, all this with her masked face before me. As if the mask, rather than being a part of her, meant no more than the frock she had elected to wear or the narrow-heeled vanilla shoes she had chosen to put on. As if I knew her face totally and had no need to be shown it, the face of her movements and her ridiculous voice.

But in fact, I could not even make out her eyes, only the shine in them when they caught the light, flecks of luminescence but not color, for the eyeholes of the mask were long-lidded and rather small. I must have noticed, too, that there was no aperture in the lips, and this may have informed me that the mask must be removed for purposes of eating or drinking. I really do not know. I can neither excuse nor quite understand myself, seen in the distance there with her on her island. Hartley tells us that the past is another country. Perhaps we also were other people—strangers—yesterday. But when I think of this, I remember, too, the sense of drawing I had had, of being magnetized to that shore, those trees, the nostalgia for a place I had never been to. For she, it may be true to say, was a figment of that nostalgia, as if I had known her and come back to her. Some enchantment, then. Not Medusa's Island, but Circe's.

The afternoon, even through the dapple *L'Apres-midi d'un Faune* effect of the leaves, was a viridian furnace when we regained the house. I sat in one of the wicker chairs on the terrace and woke with a start of embarrassment to hear her laughing at me.

"You are tired and hungry. I must go into the house for a while. I will send Kleia to you with some wine and food."

It made a bleary sense, and when I woke again it was to find an old fat woman in the ubiquitous Grecian island black—demonstrably Kleia—setting down a tray of pale red wine, amber cheese, and dark bread.

"Where is—" I realized I did not know the enchantress's name. In any event, the woman only shook her head, saying brusquely in Greek: "No English. No English."

And when I attempted to ask again in Greek where my hostess had gone, Kleia waddled away, leaving me unanswered. So I ate the food, which was passable, and drank the wine, which was very good, imagining her faun-buying father putting down an enormous patrician cellar, then fell asleep again, sprawled in the chair.

When I awoke, the sun was setting and the clearing was swimming in red light and rusty violet shadows. The columns burned as if they were internally on fire, holding the core of the sunset, it appeared, some while after the sky had cooled and the stars became visible, a trick of architectural positioning that won my awe and envy. I was making a mental note to ask her who had been responsible for the columns, and jumped when she spoke to me, softly and hoarsely, almost seductively, from just behind my chair—thereby promptly making me forget to ask any such thing.

"Come into the house now. We will dine soon."

I got up, saying something lame about imposing on her, though we were far beyond that stage.

"Always," she said to me, "you apologize. There is no imposition. You will be gone tomorrow."

How do you know? I nearly inquired, but prevented myself. What guarantee? Even if the magic food did not change me into a swine, perhaps my poisoned dead body would be carried from the feast and cast into the sea, gone, well and truly, to Poseidon's fishes. You see, I did not trust her, even though I was somewhat in love with her. The element of her danger—for she was dangerous in some obscure way—may well have contributed to her attraction.

We went into the house, which in itself alerted me. I had forgotten the great curiosity I had had to look inside it. There was a shadowy, unlit entrance hall, a sort of Roman atrium of a thing. Then we passed, she leading, into a small salon that took my breath away. It was lined all over—floor, ceiling, walls—with the sea-green marble the columns were made of. Whether in good taste or bad I am not qualified to say, but the effect, instantaneous and utter, was of being beneath the sea. Smoky oil lamps of a very beautiful Art Nouveau design hung from the profundity of the green ceiling, lighting the dreamlike swirls and oceanic variations of the marble so they seemed to breathe, definitely to move, like nothing else but waves. Shoes on that floor would have squeaked or clattered unbearably, but I was barefoot and so now was she.

A mahogany table with a modest placing for eight stood centrally. Only one place was laid.

I looked at it and she said, "I do not dine, but that will not prevent you."

An order. I considered vampires idly, but mainly I was subject to an infantile annoyance. Without quite realizing it, I had looked for the subtraction of the mask when she ate and now this made me very conscious of the mask for the first time since I had originally seen it.

We seated ourselves, she two places away from me. And I began to feel nervous. To eat this meal while she watched me did not appeal. And now the idea of the mask, unconsidered all morning, all afternoon, stole over me like an incoming tide.

Inevitably, I had not dressed for dinner, having no means, but she had changed her clothes and was now wearing a high-collared, long, grey gown, her mother's again, no doubt. It had the fragile look of age, but was very feminine and appealing for all that. Above it, the mask now reared, stuck out like the proverbial sore thumb.

The mask. What on earth was I going to do, leered at by that myopic, soulless face which had suddenly assumed such disastrous importance?

Kleia waddled in with the dishes. I cannot recall the meal, save that it was spicy and mostly vegetable. The wine came too, and I drank it. And as I drank the wine, I began to consider seriously, for the first time (which seems very curious indeed to me now) the reason for the mask. What did it hide? A scar, a birthmark? I drank her wine and I saw myself snatch off the mask, take in the disfigurement, unquelled, and behold the painful gratitude in her eyes as she watched me. I would inform her of the genius of surgeons. She would repeat she had no money. I would promise to pay for the operation.

Suddenly she startled me by saying: "Do you believe that we have lived before?"

I looked in my glass, that fount of wisdom and possibility, and said, "It seems as sensible a proposition as any of the others I've ever heard."

I fancied she smiled to herself and do not know why I thought that; I know now I was wrong.

Her accent had thickened and distorted further when she said, "I rather hope that I have lived before. I could wish to think I may live again."

"To compensate for this life?" I said brutishly. I had not needed to be so obvious when already I had been given the implication on a salver.

"Yes. To compensate for this."

I downed all the wisdom and possibility left in my glass, swallowed an extra couple of times, and said, "Are you going to tell me why you wear a mask?"

As soon as I had said it, I grasped that I was drunk. Nor was it a pleasant drunkenness. I did not like the demanding tone I had taken with her, but I was angry at having allowed the game to go on for so long. I had no knowledge of the rules, or pretended I had not. And I could not stop myself. When she did not reply, I added on a note of ghastly banter, "Or shall I guess?"

She was still, seeming very composed. Had this scene been enacted before? Finally she said, "I would suppose you do guess it is to conceal something that I wear it."

"Something you imagine worth concealing, which, perhaps, isn't."

That was the stilted fanfare of bravado. I had braced myself, flushed with such stupid confidence.

"Why not," I said, and I grow cold when I remember how I spoke to her, "take the damn thing off. Take off the mask and drink a glass of wine with me."

A pause. Then, "No," she said.

Her voice was level and calm. There was neither eagerness nor fear in it.

"Go on," I said, the drunk not getting his way, aware (oh God) he could get it by the power of his intention alone, "please. You're an astounding woman. You're like this island. A fascinating mystery. But I've seen the island. Let me see you."

"No," she said.

I started to feel, even through the wine, that I had made an indecent suggestion to her, and this, along with the awful clichés I was bringing out, increased my anger and my discomfort.

"For heaven's sake," I said, "do you know what they call you on Daphaeu?"

"Yes."

"This is absurd. You're frightened—"

"No. I am not afraid."

"Afraid. Afraid to let me see. But maybe I can help you."

"No. You cannot help me."

"How can you be sure?"

She turned in her chair, and all the way to face me with the mask. Behind her, everywhere about her, the green marble dazzled.

"If you know," she said, "what I am called on Daphaeu, are you not uneasy as to what you may see?"

"Jesus. Mythology and superstition and ignorance. I assure you, I won't turn to stone."

"It is I," she said quietly, "who have done that."

Something about the phrase, the way in which she said it, chilled me. I put down my glass and, in that instant, her hands went to the sides of the mask and her fingers worked at some complicated strap arrangement which her hair had covered.

"Good," I said, "good. I'm glad—"

But I faltered over it. The cold night sea seemed to fill my veins where the warm red wine had been. I had been heroic and sure and bold, the stuff of celluloid. But now that I had my way, with hardly any preliminary, what *would I* see? And then she drew the plastic away and I saw.

I sat there, and then I stood up. The reflex was violent, and the chair scraped over the marble with an unbearable noise. There are occasions, though rare, when the human mind grows blank of all thought. I had no thought as I looked at her. Even now, I can evoke those long, long, empty seconds, that lapse of time. I recollect only the briefest confusion, when I believed she still played some kind of hideous game, that what I witnessed was a product of her decision and her will, a gesture—

After all, Pitos had done this very thing to illustrate and endorse his argument, produced this very expression, the eyes bursting from the head, the jaw rigidly outthrust, the tendons in the neck straining, the mouth in the grimace of a frozen, agonized scream, the teeth visible, the tongue slightly protruding. The gorgon's face on the jar or the oven. The face so ugly, so demented, so terrible, it could petrify.

The awful mouth writhed.

"You have seen," she said. Somehow the stretched and distorted lips brought out these words. There was even that nuance of humor I had heard before, the smile, although physically *a* smile would have been out of the question. "You have seen."

She picked up the mask again, gently, and put it on, easing the underpart of the plastic beneath her chin to hide the convulsed tendons in her throat. I stood there, motionless. Childishly I informed myself that now I comprehended the reason for her peculiar accent, which was caused, not by some exotic foreign extraction, but by the atrocious malformation of jaw, tongue, and lips, which somehow must be fought against for every sound she made.

I went on standing there, and now the mask was back in place.

"When I was very young," she said, "I suffered, without warning, from a form of fit or stroke. Various nerve centers were paralyzed. My father took me to the very best of surgeons, you may comfort yourself with that. Unfortunately, any effort to correct the damage entailed a penetration of my brain so uncompromisingly delicate that it was reckoned impossible, for it would surely render me an idiot. Since my senses, faculties, and intelligence were otherwise unaffected, it was decided not to risk this dire surgery, and my doctors resorted instead to alternative therapies, which, patently, were unsuccessful. As the months passed, my body adjusted to the unnatural physical tensions resulting from my facial paralysis. The pain of the rictus faded, or grew acceptable. I learned both how to eat, and how to converse, although the former activity is not attractive and I attend to it in private. The mask was made for me in Athens. I am quite fond of it. The man who designed it had worked a great many years in the theatre and could have made me a face of enormous beauty or character, but this seemed pointless, even wasteful."

There was a silence, and I realized her explanation was finished.

Not once had she stumbled. There was neither hurt nor madness in her inflection. There *was* something . . . at the time I missed it, though it came to me after. Then I knew only that she was far beyond my pity or my anguish, far away indeed from my terror.

"And now," she said, rising gracefully, "I will leave you to eat your meal in peace. Good night."

I wanted, or rather I felt impelled, to stay her with actions or sentences, but I was incapable of either. She walked out of the green marble room and left me there. It is a fact that for a considerable space of time I did not move.

I did not engage the swim back to Daphaeu that night; I judged myself too drunk and slept on the beach at the edge of the trees, where at sunrise the tidal water woke me with a strange low hissing. Green sea, green sunlight through leaves. I swam away and found my course through the warming ocean and fetched up, exhausted and swearing, bruising myself on Daphaeu's fangs that had not harmed me when I left her. I did not see Pitos anywhere about, and that evening I caught the boat which would take me to the mainland.

There is a curious thing which can happen with human beings. It is the ability to perform for days or weeks like balanced and cheerful automata, when some substrata, something upon which our codes or our hopes had firmly rested, has given way. Men who lose their wives or their God are quite capable of behaving in this manner for an indefinite season. After which the collapse is brilliant and total. Something of this sort had happened to me. Yet to fathom what I had lost, what she had deprived me of, is hard to say. I found its symptoms, but not the sickness which it was.

Medusa (I must call her that, she has no other name I know), struck by the extraordinary arrow of her misfortune, condemned to her relentless, uncanny, horrible isolation, her tragedy most deeply rooted in the fact that she was not a myth, not a fabulous and glamorous monster . . . For it came to me one night in a bar in Corinth, to consider if the first Medusa might have been also such a victim, felled by some awesome fit, not petrifying but petrified, so appalling to the eyes and, more significantly, to the brooding aesthetic spirit that lives in man that she too was shunned and hated and slain by a murderer who would observe her only in a polished surface.

I spent some while in bars that summer. And later, much later, when the cold climate of the year's end closed the prospect of travel and adventure, I became afraid for myself, that dreadful writer's fear which has to do with the death of the idea, with the inertia of hand and heart and mind. Like one of the broken leaves, the summer's withered plants, I had dried. My block was sheer. I had expected a multitude of pages from the island, but instead I saw those unborn pages die on the horizon, where the beach met the sea.

And this, merely a record of marble, water, a plastic shell strapped across a woman's face, this is the last thing, it seems, which I shall commit to paper. Why? Perhaps only because she was to me such a lesson in the futility of things, the waiting fist of chance, the random despair we name the World.

And yet, now and then, I hear that voice of hers, I hear the way she spoke to me. I know now what I heard in her voice, which had neither pain nor shame in it, nor pleading, nor whining, nor even a hint of the tragedy—the Greek tragedy—of her life. And what I heard was not dignity either, or acceptance, or nobleness. It was *contempt*. She despised me. She despised all of us who live without her odds, who struggle with our small struggles, incomparable to hers. "Your Greek is very good," she said to me with the patronage of one who is multilingual. And in that same disdain she says over and over to me: "That you live is very good." Compared to her life, her existence, her multilingual endurance, what are my life or my ambitions worth? Or anything.

It did not occur immediately, but still it occurred. In its way, the myth is perfectly accurate. I see it in myself, scent it, taste it, like the onset of inescapable disease. What they say about the gorgon is true. She has turned me to stone.

"MERLIN DREAMS IN THE MONDREAM WOOD"

CHARLES DE LINT

MONDREAM—an Anglo-Saxon word which means the dream of life among men.

> *I am Merlin*
> *Who follow the Gleam*
> —Tennyson, from "Merlin and the Gleam"
> ("gleam" = inspiration/muse)

In the heart of the house lay a garden.
In the heart of the garden stood a tree.
In the heart of the tree lived an old man who wore the shape of a red-haired boy with crackernut eyes that seemed as bright as salmon tails glinting up the water.

His was a riddling wisdom, older by far than the ancient oak that housed his body. The green sap was his blood and leaves grew in his hair. In the winter, he slept. In the spring, the moon harped a wind-song against his antler tines as the oak's boughs stretched its green buds awake. In the summer, the air was thick with the droning of bees and the scent of the wildflowers that grew in stormy profusion where the fat brown bole became root.

And in the autumn, when the tree loosed its bounty to the ground below, there were hazelnuts lying in among the acorns.

The secrets of a Green Man.

"When I was a kid, I thought it was a forest," Sara said. She was sitting on the end of her bed, looking out the window over the garden, her guitar on her lap, the quilt bunched up under her knees. Up by the headboard, Julie Simms leaned forward from its carved wood to look over Sara's shoulder at what could be seen of the garden from their vantage point.

"It sure looks big enough," she said.

Sara nodded. Her eyes had taken on a dreamy look.

In was 1969 and they had decided to form a folk band—Sara on guitar, Julie playing recorder, both of them singing. They wanted to change the world with music because that was what was happening. In San Francisco. In London. In Vancouver. So why not in Ottawa?

With their faded bell-bottomed jeans and tie-dyed shirts, they looked just like any of the other seventeen-year-olds who hung around the War Memorial downtown, or could be found crowded into coffeehouses like Le Hibou and Le Monde on the weekends. Their hair was long—Sara's a cascade of brown ringlets, Julie's a waterfall spill the color of a raven's wing; they wore beads and feather earrings and both eschewed makeup.

"I used to think it spoke to me," Sara said.

"What? The garden?"

"Um-hmm."

"What did it say?"

The dreaminess in Sara's eyes became wistful and she gave Julie a rueful smile.

"I can't remember," she said.

It was three years after her parents had died—when she was nine years old—that Sara Kendell came to live with her Uncle Jamie in his strange rambling house. To an adult perspective, Tamson House was huge: an enormous, sprawling affair of corridors and rooms and towers that took up the whole of a city block; to a child of nine, it simply went on forever.

She could wander down corridor after corridor, poking about in the clutter of rooms that lay spread like a maze from the northwest tower near Bank Street—where her bedroom was located—all the way over to her uncle's study overlooking O'Connor Street on the far side of the house, but mostly she spent her time in the Library and in the garden. She liked the Library because it was like a museum. There were walls of books rising two floors high up to a domed ceiling, but there were also dozens of glass display cases scattered about the main floor area, each of which held any number of fascinating objects.

There were insects pinned to velvet and stone artifacts; animal skulls and clay flutes in the shapes of birds; old manuscripts and hand-drawn maps, the parchment yellowing, the ink a faded sepia; Kabuki masks and a miniature Shinto shrine made of ivory and ebony; corn-husk dolls, Japanese *netsuke* and porcelain miniatures; antique jewelry and African beadwork; Kachina dolls and a brass fiddle, half the size of a normal instrument . . .

The cases were so cluttered with interesting things that she could spend a whole day just going through one case and still have something to look at when she went back to it the next day. What interested her most, however, was that her uncle had a story to go with each and every item in the cases. No matter what she brought up to his study—a tiny ivory *netsuke* carved in the shape of a badger crawling out of a teapot, a flat stone with curious scratches on it that looked like Ogham script—he could spin out a tale of its origin that might take them right through the afternoon to suppertime.

That he dreamed up half the stories only made it more entertaining, for then she could try to trip him up in his rambling explanations, or even just try to top his tall tales.

But if she was intellectually precocious, emotionally she still carried scars from her parents' death and the time she'd spent living with her other uncle—her father's brother. For three years Sara had been left in the care of a nanny during the day—amusing herself while the woman smoked cigarettes and watched the soaps—while at night she was put to bed promptly after dinner. It wasn't a normal family life; she could only find that vicariously, in the books she devoured with a voracious appetite.

Coming to live with her Uncle Jamie, then, was like constantly being on holiday. He doted on her, and on those few occasions when he *was* too busy, she could always find one of the many houseguests to spend some time with her.

All that marred her new life in Tamson House was her night fears.

She wasn't frightened of the House itself. Nor of bogies or monsters living in her closet. She knew that shadows were shadows, creaks and groans were only the House settling when the temperature changed. What haunted her nights was waking up from a deep sleep, shuddering uncontrollably, her pajamas stuck to her like a second skin, her heartbeat thundering at twice its normal tempo.

There was no logical explanation for the terror that gripped her—once, sometimes twice a week. It just came, an awful, indescribable panic that left her shivering and unable to sleep for the rest of the night.

It was on the days following such nights that she went into the garden. The greenery and flowerbeds and statuary all combined to soothe her. Invariably she found herself in the very center of the garden where an ancient oak tree stood on a knoll and overhung a fountain. Lying on the grass sheltered by its boughs, with the soft lullaby of the fountain's water murmuring close at hand, she would find what the night fears had stolen from her the night before.

She would sleep.

And she would dream the most curious dreams.

"The garden has a name, too," she told her uncle when she came in from sleeping under the oak one day.

The House was so big that many of the rooms had been given names just so that they could all be kept straight in their minds.

"It's called the Mondream Wood," she told him.

She took his look of surprise to mean that he didn't know or understand the word.

"It means that the trees in it dream that they're people," she explained.

Her uncle nodded. "'The dream of life among men.' It's a good name. Did you think it up yourself?"

"No. Merlin told me."

"*The* Merlin?" her uncle asked with a smile.

Now it was her turn to look surprised.

"What do you mean *the* Merlin?" she asked.

Her uncle started to explain, astonished that in all her reading she hadn't come across a reference to Britain's most famous wizard, but then just gave her a copy of Malory's Le *Morte d' Arthur* and, after a moment's consideration, T. H. White's *The Sword in the Stone* as well.

"Did you ever have an imaginary friend when you were a kid?" Sara asked as she finally turned away from the window.

Julie shrugged. "My mom says I did, but I can't remember. Apparently he was a hedgehog the size of a toddler named Whatzit."

"I never did. But I can remember that for a long time I used to wake up in the middle of the night just terrified, and then I wouldn't be able to sleep again for the rest of the night. I used to go into the middle of the garden the next day and sleep under that big oak that grows by the fountain."

"How pastoral," Julie said.

Sara grinned. "But the thing is, I used to dream that there was a boy living in that tree and his name was Merlin."

"Go on," Julie scoffed.

"No, really. I mean, I really had these dreams. The boy would just step out of the tree and we'd sit there and talk away the afternoon."

"What did you talk about?"

"I don't remember," Sara said. "Not the details—just the feeling. It was all very magical and . . . healing, I suppose. Jamie said that my having those night fears was just my unconscious mind's way of dealing with the trauma of losing my parents and then having to live with my dad's brother, who only wanted my inheritance, not me. I was too young then to know anything about that kind of thing; all I knew was that when I talked to Merlin, I felt better. The night fears started coming less and less often and then finally they went away altogether.

"I think Merlin took them away for me."

"What happened to him?"

"Who?"

"The boy in the tree," Julie said. "Your Merlin. When did you stop dreaming about him?"

"I don't really know. I guess when I stopped waking up terrified, I just stopped sleeping under the tree so I didn't see him anymore. And then I just forgot that he'd ever been there . . . ."

Julie shook her head. "You know, you can be a bit of a flake sometimes."

"Thanks a lot. At least I didn't hang around with a giant hedgehog named Whatzit when I was a kid."

"No. You hung out with tree-boy."

Julie started to giggle and then they both broke up. It was a few moments before either of them could catch their breath.

"So what made you think of your tree-boy?" Julie asked.

Another giggle welled up in Julie's throat, but Sara's gaze had drifted back out the window and become all dreamy again.

"I don't know," she said. "I was just looking out at the garden and I suddenly found myself remembering. I wonder what ever happened to him . . . ?"

"Jamie gave me some books about a man with the same name as you," she told the red-haired boy the next time she saw him. "And after I read them, I went into the Library and found some more. He was quite famous, you know."

"So I'm told," the boy said with a smile.

"But it's all so confusing," Sara went on. "There's all these different stories, supposedly about the same man ... How are you supposed to know which of them is true?"

"That's what happens when legend and myth meet," the boy said. "Everything gets tangled."

"*Was* there even a *real* Merlin, do you think? I mean, besides you."

"A great magician who was eventually trapped in a tree?"

Sara nodded.

"I don't think so," the boy said.

"Oh."

Sara didn't even try to hide her disappointment.

"But that's not to say there was never a man named Merlin," the boy added. "He might have been a bard, or a follower of old wisdoms. His enchantments might have been more subtle than the great acts of wizardry ascribed to him in the stories."

"And did he end up in a tree?" Sara asked eagerly. "That would make him like you. I've also read that he got trapped in a cave, but I think a tree's much more interesting, don't you?"

Because her Merlin lived in a tree.

"Perhaps it was in the idea of a tree," the boy said.

Sara blinked in confusion. "What do you mean?"

"The stories seem to be saying that one shouldn't teach, or else the student becomes too knowledgeable and then turns on the teacher. I don't believe that. It's not the passing on of knowledge that would root someone like Merlin."

"Well, then what would?"

"Getting too tangled up in his own quest for understanding. Delving so deeply into the calendaring trees that he lost track of where he left his body until one day he looked around to find that he'd become what he was studying."

"I don't understand."

The red-haired boy smiled. "I know. But I can't speak any more clearly."

"Why not?" Sara asked, her mind still bubbling with the tales of quests and wizards and knights that she'd been reading. "*Were* you enchanted? *Are* you trapped in that oak tree?"

She was full of curiosity and determined to find out all she could, but in that practiced way that the boy had, he artfully turned the conversation onto a different track and she never did get an answer to her questions.

It rained that night, but the next night the skies were clear. The moon hung above the Mondream Wood like a fat ball of golden honey; the stars were so bright and close Sara felt she could just reach up and pluck one as though it were an apple hanging in a tree. She had crept from her bedroom in the northwest tower and gone out into the garden, stepping secretly as a thought through the long-darkened corridors of the House until she was finally outside.

She was looking for magic.

Dreams were one thing. She knew the difference between what you found in a dream and when you were awake; between a fey red-haired boy who lived in a tree and real boys; between the dreamlike enchantments of the books she'd been reading—enchantments that lay thick as acorns under an oak tree—and the real world where magic was a card trick, or a stage magician pulling a rabbit out of a hat on *The Ed Sullivan Show*.

But the books also said that magic came awake in the night. It crept from its secret hidden places—called out by starlight and the moon—and lived until the dawn pinked the eastern skies. She always dreamed of the red-haired boy when she slept under his oak in the middle of the garden. But what if he was more than a dream? What if at night he stepped out of his tree—really and truly, flesh and blood and bone real?

There was only one way to find out.

Sara felt restless after Julie went home. She put away her guitar and then distractedly set about straightening up her room. But for every minute she spent on the task, she spent three just looking out the window at the garden.

I never dream, she thought.

Which couldn't be true. Everything she'd read about sleep research and dreaming said that she had to dream. People just needed to. Dreams were supposed to be the way your subconscious cleared up the day's clutter. So, ipso facto, everybody dreamed. She just didn't remember hers.

But I did when I was a kid, she thought. Why did I stop? How could I have forgotten the red-haired boy in the tree?

Merlin.

Dusk fell outside her window to find her sitting on the floor, arms folded on the windowsill, chin resting on her arms as she looked out over the garden. As the twilight deepened, she finally stirred. She gave up the pretense of cleaning up her room. Putting on a jacket, she went downstairs and out into the garden.

Into the Mondream Wood.

Eschewing the paths that patterned the garden, she walked across the dew-wet grass, fingering the damp leaves of the bushes and the low-hanging branches of the trees. The dew made her remember Gregor Penev—an old Bulgarian artist who'd been staying in the House when she was a lot younger. He'd been full of odd little stories and explanations for natural occurrences—much like Jamie was, which was probably why Gregor and her uncle had gotten along so well.

"*Zaplakala e gorata*," he'd replied when she'd asked him where dew came from and what it was for. "The forest is crying. It remembers the old heroes who lived under its branches—the heroes and the magicians, all lost and gone now. Robin Hood. Indje Voivode. Myrddin."

Myrddin. That was another name for Merlin. She remembered reading somewhere that Robin Hood was actually a Christianized Merlin, the Angle version of his name being a variant of his Saxon name of Rof Breocht Woden—the Bright Strength of Wodan. But if you went back far enough, all the names and stories got tangled up in one story. The tales of the historical Robin Hood, like those of the historical Merlin of the Borders, had acquired older mythic elements common to the world as a whole by the time they were written down. The story that their legends were really telling was that of the seasonal hero-king, the May Bride's consort, who with his cloak of leaves and his horns, and all his varying forms, was the secret truth that lay in the heart of every forest.

"But those are European heroes," she remembered telling Gregor. "Why would the trees in our forest be crying for them?"

"All forests are one," Gregor had told her, his features serious for a change. "They are all echoes of the first forest that gave birth to Mystery when the world began."

She hadn't really understood him then, but she was starting to understand him now as she made her way to the fountain at the center of the garden, where the old oak tree stood guarding its secrets in the heart of the Mondream Wood. There were two forests for every one you entered. There was the one you walked in, the physical echo, and then there was the one that was connected to all the other forests, with no consideration of distance, or time.

The forest primeval, remembered through the collective memory of every tree in the same way that people remembered myth—through the collective subconscious that Jung mapped, the shared mythic resonance that lay buried in every human mind. Legend and myth, all tangled in an alphabet of trees, remembered, not always with understanding, but with wonder. With awe.

Which was why the druids' Ogham was also a calendar of trees.

Why Merlin was often considered to be a druid.

Why Robin was the name taken by the leaders of witch covens.

Why the Green Man had antlers—because a stag's tines are like the branches of a tree.

Why so many of the early avatars were hung from a tree. Osiris. Balder. Dionysus. Christ.

Sara stood in the heart of the Mondream Wood and looked up at the old oak tree. The moon lay behind its branches, mysteriously close. The air was filled with an electric charge, as though a storm were approaching, but there wasn't a cloud in the sky.

"Now I remember what happened that night," Sara said softly.

Sara grew to be a small woman, but at nine years old she was just a tiny waif—no bigger than a minute, as Jamie liked to say. With her diminutive size she could slip soundlessly through thickets that would allow no easy egress for an adult. And that was how she went.

She was a curly-haired gamine, ghosting through the hawthorn hedge that bordered the main path. Whispering across the small glade guarded by the statue of a little horned man that Jamie said was Favonius, but she privately thought of as Peter Pan, though he bore no resemblance to the pictures in her Barrie book. Tiptoeing through the wildflower garden, a regular gallimaufry of flowering plants, both common and exotic. And then she was near the fountain. She could see Merlin's oak, looming up above the rest of the garden like the lordly tree it was.

And she could hear voices.

She crept nearer, a small shadow hidden in deeper patches cast by the fat yellow moon.

"—never a matter of choice," a man's voice was saying. "The lines of our lives are laid out straight as a dodman's leys, from event to event. You chose your road."

She couldn't see the speaker, but the timbre of his voice was deep and resonating, like a deep bell. She couldn't recognize it, but she did recognize Merlin's when he replied to the stranger.

"When I chose my road, there was no road. There was only the trackless wood; the hills lying crest to crest like low-backed waves; the glens where the harps were first imagined and later strung. *Ca'canny*, she told me when I came into the Wood. I thought go gentle meant go easy, not go fey; that the oak guarded the Borders, marked its boundaries. I never guessed it was a door."

"All knowledge is a door," the stranger replied. "You knew that."

"In theory," Merlin replied.

"You meddled."

"I was born to meddle. That was the part I had to play."

"But when your part was done," the stranger said, "you continued to meddle."

"It's in my nature, Father. Why else was I chosen?"

There was a long silence then. Sara had an itch on her nose but she didn't dare move a hand to scratch it. She mulled over what she'd overheard, trying to understand.

It was all so confusing. From what they were saying it seemed that her Merlin *was* the Merlin in the stories. But if that was true, then why did he look like a boy her own age? How could he even still be alive? Living in a tree in Jamie's garden and talking to his father . . .

"I'm tired," Merlin said. "And this is an old argument, Father. The winters are too short. I barely step into a dream and then it's spring again. I need a longer rest. I've earned a longer rest. The Summer Stars call to me."

"Love bound you," the stranger said.

"An oak bound me. I never knew she was a tree."

"You knew. But you preferred to ignore what you knew because you had to riddle it all. The salmon wisdom of the hazel wasn't enough. You had to partake of the fruit of every tree."

"I've learned from my error," Merlin said. "Now set me free, Father."

"I can't. Only love can unbind you."

"I can't be found, I can't be seen," Merlin said. "What they remember of me is so tangled up in Romance, that no one can find the man behind the tales. Who is there to love me?"

Sara pushed her way out of the thicket where she'd been hiding and stepped into the moonlight.

"There's me," she began, but then her voice died in her throat.

There was no red-haired boy standing by the tree. Instead, she found an old man with the red-haired boy's eyes. And a stag. The stag turned its antlered head toward her and regarded her with a gaze that sent shivers scurrying up and down her spine. For a long moment its gaze held hers; then it turned, its flank flashing red in the moonlight, and the darkness swallowed it.

Sara shivered. She wrapped her arms around herself, but she couldn't escape the chill.

The stag . . .

That was impossible. The garden had always been strange, seeming so much larger than its acreage would allow, but there couldn't possibly be a deer living in it without her having seen it before. Except . . . What about a boy becoming an old man overnight? A boy who really and truly did live in a tree?

"Sara," the old man said.

It was Merlin's voice. Merlin's eyes. Her Merlin grown into an old man.

"You . . . you're old," she said.

"Older than you could imagine."

"But—"

"I came to you as you'd be most likely to welcome me."

"Oh."

"Did you mean what you said?" he asked.

Memories flooded Sara. She remembered a hundred afternoons of warm companionship. All those hours of quiet conversation and games. The peace that came from her night fears. If she said yes, then he'd go away. She'd lose her friend. And the night fears . . . Who'd be there to make the terrors go away? Only he had been able to help her. Not Jamie nor anyone else who lived in the House, though they'd all tried.

"You'll go away . . . won't you?" she said.

He nodded. An old man's nod. But the eyes were still young. Young and old, wise and silly, all at the same time. Her red-haired boy's eyes.

"I'll go away," he replied. "And you won't remember me."

"I won't forget," Sara said. "I would never forget."

"You won't have a choice," Merlin said. "Your memories of me would come with me when I go."

"They'd be . . . gone forever?"

That was worse than losing a friend. That was like the friend never having been there in the first place.

"Forever," Merlin said. "Unless . . ."

His voice trailed off, his gaze turned inward.

"Unless what?" Sara asked finally.

"I could try to send them back to you when I reach the other side of the river."

Sara blinked with confusion. "What do you mean? The other side of what river?"

"The Region of the Summer Stars lies across the water that marks the boundary between what is and what has been. It's a long journey to that place. Sometimes it takes many lifetimes."

They were both quiet then. Sara studied the man that her friend had become. The gaze he returned her was mild. There were no demands in it. There was only regret. The sorrow of parting. A fondness that asked for nothing in return.

Sara stepped closer to him, hesitated a moment longer, then hugged him.

"I do love you, Merlin," she said. "I can't say I don't when I do."

She felt his arms around her, the dry touch of his lips on her brow.

"Go gentle," he said. "But beware the calendaring of the trees."

And then he was gone.

One moment they were embracing and the next her arms only held air. She let them fall limply to her sides. The weight of an awful sorrow bowed her head. Her throat grew thick, her chest tight. She swayed where she stood, tears streaming from her eyes.

The pain felt like it would never go away.

But the next thing she knew she was waking in her bed in the north-west tower and it was the following morning. She woke from a dreamless sleep, clear-eyed and smiling. She didn't know it, but her memories of Merlin were gone.

But so were her night fears.

The older Sara, still not a woman, but old enough to understand more of the story now, fingered a damp leaf and looked up into the spreading canopy of the oak above her.

Could any of that really have happened? she wondered.

The electric charge she'd felt in the air when she'd approached the old oak was gone. That pregnant sense of something about to happen had faded. She was left with the moon, hanging lower now, the stars still bright, the garden quiet. It was all magical, to be sure, but natural magic—not supernatural.

She sighed and kicked at the autumn debris that lay thick about the base of the old tree. Browned leaves, broad and brittle. And acorns. Hundreds of acorns. Fred the gardener would be collecting them soon for his compost—at least those that the black squirrels didn't hoard away against the winter. She went down on one knee and picked up a handful of them, letting them spill out of her hand.

Something different about one of them caught her eye as it fell, and she plucked it up from the ground. It was a small brown ovoid shape, an incongruity in the crowded midst of all the capped acorns. She held it up to her eye. Even in the moonlight she could see what it was.

A hazelnut.

Salmon wisdom locked in a seed.

Had she regained memories, memories returned to her now from a place where the Summer Stars always shone, or had she just had a dream in the Mondream Wood where as a child she'd thought that the trees dreamed they were people?

Smiling, she pocketed the nut, then slowly made her way back into the House.

"CALYPSO IN BERLIN"

ELIZABETH HAND

──────────── Yesterday morning, he left. I had known
──────────── he would only be here for those seven
days. Now, just like that, they were gone.

It had stormed all night, but by the time I came downstairs to feed
the woodstove, the gale had blown out to sea. It was still dark, chill October air sifting through cracks in the walls. Red and yellow leaves were
flung everywhere outside. I stepped into the yard to gather a handful
and pressed my face against them, cold and wet.

From the other side of the island a coyote yelped. I could hear the
Pendletons' rooster and a dog barking. Finally I went back inside, sat
and watched the flames through the stove's isinglass window. When
Philip finally came down, he took one look at me, shook his head, and
said, "No! I still have to go, stop it!"

I laughed and turned to touch his hand. He backed away quickly and
said, "None of that."

I saw how he recoiled. I have never kept him here against his will.

When Odysseus left, he was suspicious, accusatory. They say he wept
for his wife and son, but he slept beside me each night for seven years
and I saw no tears. We had two sons. His face was imprinted upon mine,
just as Philip's was centuries later: unshaven, warm, my cheeks scraped
and my mouth swollen. In the morning I would wake to see Philip
watching me, his hand moving slowly down the curve of my waist.

"No hips, no ass," he said once. "You're built like a boy."

He liked to hold my wrists in one hand and straddle me. I wondered
sometimes about their wives: were they taller than me? Big hips, big
tits? Built like a woman?

Calypso. The name means *the concealer*. "She of the lovely braids"—that's how Homer describes me. One morning Philip walked about my cottage, taking photos off the bookshelves and looking at them.

"Your hair," he said, holding up a picture. "It was so long back then."

I shrugged. "I cut it all off a year ago. It's grown back—see?" Shoulder-length now, still blond, no gray.

He glanced at me, then put the picture back. "It looked good that way," he said.

This is what happens to nymphs: they are pursued or they are left. Sometimes, like Echo, they are fled. We turn to trees, seabirds, seafoam, running water, the sound of wind in the leaves. Men come to stay with us, they lie beside us in the night, they hold us so hard we can't breathe. They walk in the woods and glimpse us: a diving kingfisher, an owl caught in the headlights, a cold spring on the hillside. Alcyone, Nyctimene, Peirene, Echo, Calypso: these are some of our names. We like to live alone, or think we do. When men find us, they say we are lovelier than anything they have ever seen: wilder, stranger, more passionate. Elemental. They say they will stay forever. They always leave.

We met when Philip missed a flight out of Logan. I had business at the gallery that represents me in Cambridge and offered him a place to stay for the night: my hotel room.

"I don't know too many painters," he said. "Free spirits, right?"

He was intrigued by what I told him of the island. The sex was good. I told him my name was Lyssa. After that we'd see each other whenever he was on the East Coast. He was usually leaving for work overseas but would add a few days to either end of his trip, a week even, so we could be together. I had been on the island for—how long? I can't remember now.

I began sketching him the second time he came here. He would never let me do it while he was awake. He was too restless, jumping up to pull a book off the shelf, make coffee, pour more wine.

So I began to draw him while he slept. After we fucked he'd fall heavily asleep; I might doze for a few minutes, but sex energizes me, it makes me want to work.

He was perfect for me. Not conventionally handsome, though. His dark eyes were small and deep set, his mouth wide and uneven. Dark, thick hair, gray-flecked. His skin unlined. It was uncanny—he was in his early fifties but seemed as ageless as I was, as though he'd been untouched by anything, his time in the Middle East, his children, his wife, his ex-wife, me. I see now that this is what obsessed me—that someone human could be not merely beautiful but untouched. There wasn't a crack in him; no way to get inside. He slept with his hands crossed behind his head, long body tipped across the bed. Long arms, long legs; torso almost hairless; a dark bloom on his cheeks when he hadn't shaved. His cock long, slightly curved; moisture on his thigh.

I sketched and painted him obsessively, for seven years. Over the centuries there have been others. Other lovers, always; but only a few whom I've drawn or painted on walls, pottery, tapestry, paper, canvas, skin. After a few years I'd grow tired of them—Odysseus was an exception—and gently send them on their way. As they grew older they interested me less, because of course I did not grow old. Some didn't leave willingly. I made grasshoppers of them, or mayflies, and tossed them into the webs of the golden orbweaver spiders that follow me everywhere I live.

But I never grew tired of Philip.

And I never grew tired of painting him. No one could see the paintings, of course, which killed me. He was so paranoid that he would be recognized, by his wife, his ex, one of his grown children. Coworkers.

I was afraid of losing him, so I kept the canvases in a tiny room off the studio. The sketchbooks alone filled an entire shelf. He still worried that someone would look at them, but no one ever came to visit me, except for him. My work was shown in the gallery just outside Boston. Winter landscapes of the bleak New England countryside I loved; skeletons of birds, seals. Temperas, most of them; some pen-and-ink drawings. I lived under Andrew Wyeth's long shadow, as did everyone else in my part of the country. I thought that the paintings I'd done of Philip might change that perception. Philip was afraid that they would.

"Those could be your Helga paintings," he said once. It was an accusation, not encouragement.

"They would be Calypso's paintings," I said. He didn't understand what I meant.

Odysseus's wife was a weaver. I was, too. It's right there in Homer. When Hermes came to give me Zeus's command to free Odysseus, I was in my little house on the island, weaving scenes into tunics for

Odysseus and the boys. They were little then, three and five. We stood on the shore and watched him go. The boys ran screaming after the boat into the water. I had to grab them and hold them back; I thought the three of us would drown, they were fighting so to follow him.

It was horrible. Nothing was as bad as that, ever; not even when Philip left.

Penelope. Yes, she had a son, and like me she was a weaver. But we had more in common than that. I was thinking about her unraveling her loom each night, and it suddenly struck me: this was what I did with my paintings of Philip. Each night I would draw him for hours as he slept. Each day I would look at my work, and it was beautiful. They were by far my best paintings. They might even have been great.

And who knows what the critics or the public might have thought? My reputation isn't huge, but it's respectable. Those paintings could have changed all that.

But I knew that would be it: if I showed them, I would never see him again, never hear from him, never smell him, never taste him.

Yet even that I could live with. What terrified me was the thought that I would never paint him again. If he was gone, my magic would die. I would never paint again.

And that would destroy me: to think of eternity without the power to create. Better to draw and paint all night; better to undo my work each dawn by hiding it in the back room.

I thought I could live like that. For seven years I did.

And then he left. The storm blew out to sea, the leaves were scattered across the lake. The house smelled of him still, my breath smelled of him, my hair. I stood alone at the sink, scrubbing at the pigments caked under my fingernails; then suddenly doubled over, vomiting on the dishes I hadn't done yet from last night's dinner.

I waited until I stopped shaking. Then I cleaned the sink, cleaned the dishes, squeezed lemons down the drain until the stink was gone. I put everything away. I went into the back room, stood for a long time and stared at the paintings there.

Seven years is a long time. There were a lot of canvases; a lot of sheets of heavy paper covered with his body, a lot of black books filled with his eyes, his cock, his hands, his mouth. I looked up at the corner of the room by the window, saw the web woven by the big yellow spider, gray strands dusted with moth wings, fly husks, legs. I pursed my lips and whistled silently, watched as the web trembled and the spider raced to its center, her body glistening like an amber bead. Then I went to my computer and booked a flight to Berlin.

It was a city that Philip loved, a city he had been to once, decades ago, when he was studying in Florence. He spent a month there—this was long before the Wall fell—never went back, but we had spoken, often, of going there together.

I had a passport—I'm a nymph, not an agoraphobe—and so I e-mailed my sister Arethusa, in Sicily. We are spirits of place; we live where the world exhales in silence. As these places disappear, so do we.

But not all of us. Arethusa and I kept in touch intermittently. Years ago she had lived on the Rhine. She said she thought she might still know someone in Germany. She'd see what she could do.

It turned out the friend knew someone who had a sublet available. It was in an interesting part of town, said Arethusa; she'd been there once. I was a little anxious about living in a city—I'm attached to islands, to northern lakes and trees, and I worried that I wouldn't thrive there, that I might in fact sicken.

But I went. I paid in advance for the flat, then packed my paintings and sketchbooks and had them shipped over. I carried some supplies and one small sketchbook, half-filled with drawings of Philip, in my carry-on luggage. I brought my laptop. I closed up the cottage for the winter, told the Pendletons I was leaving and asked them to watch the place for me. I left them my car as well.

Then I caught the early morning ferry to the mainland, the bus to Boston. There was light fog as the plane lifted out of Logan, quickly dispersing into an arctic blue sky. I looked down and watched a long, serpentine cloud writhing above the Cape and thought of Nephele, a cloud nymph whom Zeus had molded to resemble Hera.

Why do they always have to change us into something else? I wondered, and sat back to watch the movie.

Berlin was a shock. We are by nature solitary and obsessive, which has its own dangers—like Narcissus, we can drown in silence, gazing at a reflection in a still pool.

But in a city, we can become disoriented and exhausted. We can sicken and die. We are long-lived, but not immortal.

So Arethusa had chosen my flat carefully. It was in Schöneberg, a quiet, residential part of the city. There were no high-rises. Chestnut trees littered the sidewalks with armored fruit. There were broad streets where vendors sold sunflowers and baskets of hazelnuts; old bookstores, a little shop that stocked only socks, several high-end art galleries; green spaces and much open sky.

"Poets lived there," Arethusa told me, her voice breaking up over my cell phone. "Before the last big war."

My flat was in a street of century-old apartment buildings. The foyer was high and dim and smelled of pipe tobacco and pastry dough. The flat itself had been carved from a much larger suite of rooms. There was a pocket-sized kitchenette, two small rooms facing each other across a wide hallway, a tiny, ultramodern bath.

But the rooms all had high ceilings and polished wooden floors glossy as bronze. And the room facing a courtyard had wonderful northern light.

I set this up as my studio. I purchased paints and sketchpads, a small easel. I set up my laptop, put a bowl of apples on the windowsill where the cool fall air moved in and out. Then I went to work.

I couldn't paint.

Philip said that would happen. He used to joke about it—*you're nothing without me, you only use me, what will you do if ever I'm gone, hmmmm?*

Now he was gone, and it was true. I couldn't work. Hours passed, days; a week.

Nothing.

I flung open the casement windows, stared down at the enclosed courtyard and across to the rows of windows in other flats just like mine. There were chestnut trees in the yard below, neat rows of bicycles lined up beneath them. Clouds moved across the sky as storms moved in from the far lands to the north. The wind tore the last yellow leaves from the trees and sent them whirling up toward where I stood, shivering in my moth-eaten sweater.

The wind brought with it a smell: the scent of pine trees and the sea, of rock and raw wool. It was the smell of the north, the scent of my island—my true island, the place that had been my home, once. It filled me not with nostalgia or longing but with something strange and terrible; the realization that I had no longer had a home. I had only what I made on the page or canvas. I had bound myself to a vision.

Byblis fell hopelessly in love and became a fountain. Echo wasted into a sound in the night. Hamadryads die when their trees die.

What would become of me?

I decided to go for a walk.

It is a green city. Philip had never told me that. He spoke of the wars, the Nazis, the bombs, the Wall. I wandered along the Ebersstrasse to the S-Bahn station; then traveled to the eastern part of the city, to the university, and sat at a cafe beneath an elevated railway, where I ate roasted anchovies and soft white cheese while trains racketed overhead. The wall behind me was riddled with bullet holes. If this building had been in the western part of the city, it would have been repaired or torn down. In the east there was never enough money for such things. When I placed my hand upon the bullet holes they felt hot, and gave off a faint smell of blood and scorched leather. I finished my lunch and picked up a bit of stone that had fallen from the wall, put it in my pocket with some chestnuts I had gathered, and walked on.

The sun came out after a bit. Or no, that may have been another day— almost certainly it was. The leaves were gone from the linden trees, but it was still lovely. The people were quiet, speaking in low voices.

But they were seemingly as happy as people ever are. I began to take my sketchbooks with me when I walked, and I would sit in a cafe or a park and draw. I found that I could draw Philip from memory. I began to draw other things, too—the lindens, the ugly modern buildings elbowing aside the older terraces that had not been destroyed by the bombings. There were empty fountains everywhere; and again, here in the eastern part of the city there had been no money to restore them or to keep the water flowing. Bronze Nereids and Neptunes rose from them, whitened with bird droppings. Lovers still sat beside the empty pools, gazing at drifts of dead leaves and old newspapers while pigeons pecked around their feet. I found this beautiful and strange, and also oddly heartening.

A few weeks after my arrival, Philip called. I hadn't replied to his e-mails, but when my cell phone rang, I answered.

"You're in Berlin?" He sounded amused but not surprised. "Well, I wanted to let you know I'm going to be gone again, a long trip this time. Damascus. I'll come see you for a few days before I go."

He told me his flight time, then hung up.

What did I feel then? Exhilaration, desire, joy: but also fear. I had just begun to paint again; I was just starting to believe that I could, in fact, work without him.

But if he were here?

I went into the bedroom. On the bed, neatly folded, was another thing I had brought with me: Philip's sweater. It was an old, tweed-patterned wool sweater, in shades of umber and yellow and russet, with holes where the mice had nested in it back in the cottage. He had wanted to throw it out, years ago, but I kept it. It still smelled of him, and I slept wearing it, here in the flat in Schöneberg, the wool prickling against my bare skin. I picked it up and buried my face in it, smelling him, his hair, his skin, sweat.

Then I sat down on the bed. I adjusted the lamp so that the light fell upon the sweater in my lap; and began, slowly and painstakingly, to unravel it.

It took a while, maybe an hour. I was careful not to fray the worn yarn, careful to tie the broken ends together. When I was finished, I had several balls of wool; enough to make a new sweater. It was late by then, and the shops were closed. But first thing next morning I went to the little store that sold only socks and asked in my halting German where I might find a knitting shop. I had brought a ball of wool to show the woman behind the counter. She laughed and pointed outside, then wrote down the address. It wasn't far, just a few streets over. I thanked her, bought several pairs of thick argyle wool socks, and left.

I found the shop without any trouble. I know how to knit, though I haven't done so for a long time. I found a pattern I liked in a book of Icelandic designs. I bought the book, bought the special circular needles you use for sweaters, bought an extra skein of wool in a color I liked because it reminded me of woad, not quite as deep a blue as indigo. I would work this yarn into the background. Then I returned home.

I had nearly a week before Philip arrived. I was too wound up to paint. But I continued to walk each day, finding my way around the hidden parts of the city. Small forgotten parks scarcely larger than a backyard, where European foxes big as dogs peered from beneath patches of brambles; a Persian restaurant near my flat, where the smells of coriander and roasting garlic made me think of my island long ago. A narrow canal like a secret outlet of the Spree, where I watched a kingfisher dive from an overhanging willow. I carried my leather satchel with me, the one that held my sketchbooks and charcoal pencils and watercolors. I wanted to try using watercolors.

But now the satchel held my knitting, too, the balls of wool and the pattern book and the half-knit sweater. When I found I couldn't paint or draw, I'd take the sweater out and work on it. It was repetitive work, dreamlike, soothing. And one night, back in the flat, I dug around in the bureau drawer until I found something else I'd brought with me, an envelope I'd stuck into one of my notebooks.

Inside the envelope was a curl of hair I'd cut from Philip's head one night while he slept. I set the envelope in a safe place and, one by one, carefully teased out the hairs. Over the next few days I wove them into the sweater. Now and then I would pluck one of my own hairs, much longer, finer, ash gold, and knit that into the pattern as well.

They were utterly concealed, of course, his dark curls, my fair, straight hair: all invisible. I finished the sweater the morning Philip arrived.

It was wonderful seeing him. He took a taxi from the airport. I had coffee waiting. We fell into bed. Afterward I gave him the sweater.

"Here," I said. "I made you something."

He sat naked on the bed and stared at it, puzzled. "Is this mine?"

"Try it on. I want to see if it fits."

He shrugged, then pulled it on over his bare chest.

"Does it fit?" I asked. "I had to guess the measurements."

"It seems to." He smoothed the thick wool, October gold and russet flecked with woad; then tugged at a loose bit of yarn on the hem.

"Oops," I said, frowning. "Don't worry, I'll fix that."

"It's beautiful. Thank you. I didn't know you knew how to knit."

I adjusted it, tugging to see if it hung properly over his broad shoulders.

"It does," I said, and laughed in relief. "It fits! Does it feel right?"

"Yeah. It's great." He pulled it off then got dressed again, white T-shirt, blue flannel shirt, the sweater last of all. "Didn't I used to have a sweater like this, once?"

"You did," I said. "Come on, I'm hungry."

We walked arm in arm to the Persian restaurant, where we ate chicken simmered in pomegranates and crushed walnuts, and drank wine the color of oxblood. Later, on the way back to the flat, we ambled past closed shops, pausing to look at a display of icons, a gallery showing the work of a young German artist I had read about.

"Are you thinking of showing here?" Philip asked. "I don't mean this gallery, but here, in Berlin?"

"I don't know. I hadn't really thought about it much." In truth I hadn't thought about it at all, until that very moment. "But yes, I guess I might. If Anna could arrange it."

Anna owned the gallery back in Cambridge. Philip said nothing more, and we turned and walked home.

But back in the flat, he started looking around. He went into my studio and glanced at the canvas on the easel, already primed, with a few blocked-in shapes—a barren tree, scaffolding; an abandoned fountain.

"These are different," he said. He glanced around the rest of the studio and I could tell, he was relieved not to see anything else. The other paintings, the ones I'd done of him, hadn't arrived yet. He didn't ask after them, and I didn't tell him I'd had them shipped from the island.

We went back to bed. Afterward, he slept heavily. I switched on the small bedside lamp, turning it so it wouldn't awaken him, and watched him sleep. I didn't sketch him. I watched the slow rise of his chest, the beard coming in where he hadn't shaved, grayer now than it had been; the thick black lashes that skirted his closed eyes. His mouth. I knew he was going to leave me. This time, he wouldn't come back.

If he had wakened then and seen me, would anything have changed? If he had ever seen me watching him like this . . . would he have changed? Would I?

I watched him for a long time, thinking. At last I curled up beside him and fell asleep.

Next morning, we had breakfast, then wandered around the city like tourists. Philip hadn't been back in some years, and it all amazed him. The bleak emptiness of the Alexanderplatz, where a dozen teenagers sat around the empty fountain, each with a neon-shaded Mohawk and a ratty mongrel at the end of a leash; the construction cranes everywhere, the crowds of Japanese and Americans at the Branden-burg Gate; the disconcertingly elegant graffiti on bridges spanning the Spree, as though the city, half-awake, had scrawled its dreams upon the brickwork.

"You seem happy here," he said. He reached to stroke my hair, and smiled.

"I *am* happy here," I said. "It's not ideal, but . . ."

"It's a good place for you, maybe. I'll come back." He was quiet for a minute. "I'm going to be gone for a while. Damascus—I'll be there for two months. Then Deborah's going to meet me, and we're going to travel for a while. She found a place for us to stay, a villa in Montevarchi. It's something we've talked about for a while."

We were scuffing through the leaves along a path near the Grunewald, the vast and ancient forest to the city's west. I went there often, alone. There were wild animals, boar and foxes; there were lakes, and hollow caves beneath the earth that no one was aware of. So many of Berlin's old trees had been destroyed in the bombings, and more died when the Wall fell and waves of new construction and congestion followed.

Yet new trees had grown, and some old ones flourished. These woods seemed an irruption of a deep, rampant disorder: the trees were black, the fallen leaves deep, the tangled thorns and hedges often impenetrable. I had found half-devoured carcasses here, cats or small dogs, those pretty red squirrels with tufted ears; as well as empty beer bottles and the ashy remnants of campfires in stone circles. You could hear traffic, and the drone of construction cranes; but only walk a little further into the trees and these sounds disappeared. It was a place I wanted to paint, but I hadn't yet figured out where, or how.

"I'm tired." Philip yawned. Sun filtered through the leafless branches. It was cool, but not cold. He wore the sweater I'd knitted, beneath a tweed jacket. "Jet lag. Can we stop a minute?"

There were no benches, not even any large rocks; just the leaf-covered ground, a few larches, many old beeches. I dropped the satchel holding my watercolors and sketchpad and looked around. A declivity spread beneath one very large old beech, a hollow large enough for us to lie in, side by side. Leaves had drifted to fill the space like water in a cupped hand; tender yellow leaves, soft as tissue and thin enough that when I held one to the sun I could see shapes behind the fretwork of veins. Trees. Philip's face.

The ground was dry. We lay side by side. After a few minutes he turned and pulled me to him. I could smell the sweet mast beneath us, beechnuts buried in the leaves. I pulled his jacket off and slid my hands beneath his sweater, kissed him as he pulled my jeans down; then tugged the sweater free from his arms, until it hung loose like a cowl around his neck. The air was chill despite the sun, there were leaves in his hair. A fallen branch raked my bare back, hard enough to make me gasp. His eyes were closed, but mine were open; there was grit on his cheek and a fleck of green moss, a tiny greenfly with gold-faceted eyes that lit upon his eyelid then rubbed its front legs together then spun into the sunlight. All the things men never see. When he came he was all but silent, gasping against my chest. I laid my hand upon his face, before he turned aside and fell asleep.

For a moment I sat, silent, and looked for the greenfly. Then I pulled my jeans back up and zipped them, shook the leaves from my hair and plucked a beechnut husk from my shirt. I picked up Philip's jacket and tossed it into the underbrush, then knelt beside him. His flannel shirt had ridden up, exposing his stomach; I bent my head and kissed the soft skin beneath his navel. He was warm and tasted of semen and salt, bracken. For a moment I lingered, then sat up.

A faint buzzing sounded, but otherwise the woods were still. The sweater hung limp round his neck. I ran my fingers along the hem until I found the stray bit of yarn there. I tugged it free, the loose knot easily coming undone; then slowly and with great care, bit by bit by bit while he slept, I unraveled it. Only at the very end did Philip stir, when just a ring of blue and brown and gold hung about his neck, but I whispered his name and, though his eyelids trembled, they did not open.

I got to my feet, holding the loose armful of warm wool, drew it to my face and inhaled deeply.

It smelled more of him than his own body did. I teased out one end of the skein and stood above him, then let the yarn drop until it touched his chest. Little by little, I played the yarn out, like a fisherman with his line, until it covered him. More greenflies came and buzzed about my face.

Finally I was done. A gust sent yellow leaves blowing across the heap of wool and hair as I turned to retrieve my satchel. The green-flies followed me. I waved my hand impatiently and they darted off, to hover above the shallow pool that now spread beneath the beech tree. I had not consciously thought of water, but water is what came to me; perhaps the memory of the sea outside the window where I had painted Philip all those nights, perhaps just the memory of green water and blue sky and gray rock, an island long ago.

The small, still pool behind me wasn't green but dark brown, with a few spare strokes of white and gray where it caught the sky, and a few yellow leaves. I got my bag and removed my pencils and watercolors and sketchpad, then folded Philip's jacket and put it at the bottom of the satchel, along with the rest of his clothes. Then I filled my metal painting cup with water from the pool. I settled myself against a tree and began to paint.

It wasn't like my other work. A broad wash of gold and brown, the pencil lines black beneath the brushstrokes, spattered crimson at the edge of the thick paper. The leaves floating on the surface of the pool moved slightly in the wind, which was hard for me to capture—I was just learning to use watercolors. Only once was I worried, when a couple walking a dog came through the trees up from the canal bank.

"*Guten Tag,*" the woman said, smiling. I nodded and smiled politely but kept my gaze fixed on my painting. I wasn't worried about the man or the woman; they wouldn't notice Philip. No one would. They walked toward the pool, pausing as their dog, a black dachshund, wriggled eagerly and sniffed at the water's edge, then began nosing through the leaves.

"Strubbel!" the man scolded.

Without looking back at him, the dog waded into the pool and began lapping at the water. The man tugged at the leash and started walking on; the dog ran after him, shaking droplets from his muzzle.

I finished my painting. It wasn't great—I was still figuring it out, the way water mingles with the pigments and flows across the page—but it was very good. There was a disquieting quality to the picture; you couldn't quite tell if there was a face there beneath the water, a mouth, grasping hands; or if it was a trick of the light, the way the thin yellow leaves lay upon the surface. There were long shadows across the pool when at last I gathered my things and replaced them in my satchel, heavier now because of Philip's clothes.

I disposed of these on my way back to the flat. I took a long, circuitous route on the U, getting off at one stop then another, leaving a shoe in the trash bin here, a sock there, dropping the flannel shirt into the Spree from the bridge at Oberbaumbrucke. The pockets of the tweed jacket were empty. At the Alexanderplatz I walked up to the five or six punks who still sat by the empty fountain and held up the jacket.

"Anyone want this?" I asked in English.

They ignored me, all save one boy, older than the rest, with blue-white skin and a shy indigo gaze.

"*Bitte.*" He leaned down to pat his skinny mongrel, then reached for the jacket. I gave it to him and walked away. Halfway across the plaza I looked back. He was ripping the sleeves off; as I watched he walked over to a trash bin and tossed them inside, then pulled the sleeveless jacket over his T-shirt. I turned and hurried home, the chill wind blowing leaves like brown smoke into the sky.

For the first few months I read newspapers and checked online to see if there was any news of Philip's disappearance. There were a few brief articles, but his line of work had its perils, and it was assumed these had contributed to his fate. His children were grown. His wife would survive. No one knew about me, of course.

I painted him all winter long. Ice formed and cracked across his body; there was a constellation of bubbles around his mouth and open eyes. People began to recognize me where I set up my easel and stool in the Grunewald, but, respectful of my concentration, few interrupted me. When people did look at my work, they saw only an abstract painting, shapes that could be construed as trees or building cranes, perhaps, etched against the sky; a small pool where the reflection of clouds or shadows bore a fleeting, eerie similarity to a skeletal figure, leaves trapped within its arched ribs.

But nearly always I was alone. I'd crack the ice that skimmed the pool, dip my watercolor cup into the frigid water, then retreat a few feet away to paint. Sometimes I would slide my hand beneath the surface to feel a soft mass like a decomposing melon, then let my fingers slip down to measure the almost imperceptible pulse of a heart, cold and slippery as a carp. Then I would return to work.

As the winter wore on, it grew too cold for me to work outdoors. There was little snow or rain, but it was bitterly cold. The pool froze solid. Ice formed where my watercolor brush touched the heavy paper, and the ink grew sluggish in my Rapidograph pen.

So I stayed at home in the studio, where the orbweavers again hung beside the windows, and used the watercolor studies to begin work on other, larger, paintings—oils on canvas, urban landscapes where a small, frozen woodland pool hinted that a green heart still beat within the city. These paintings were extremely good. I took some digital photos of them and sent them to Anna, along with the name of two galleries in Schöneberg and one in Kreuzberg. Then I went to visit Arethusa in Sicily.

I had planned on staying only a few weeks, but the Mediterranean warmth, the smell of olive groves and sight of flying fish skimming across the blue sea, seduced me. I stayed in Sicily until early spring and then returned briefly to Ogygia, my true island. I could not recall the last time I had visited—a steamship brought me, I do remember that, and the trip then took many hours.

Now it was much faster, and the island itself noisier, dirtier, more crowded. I found myself homesick—not for any island, but for the flat in Schöneberg and the quiet place in the Grunewald where Philip was. I had thought that the time in Sicily might give me other distractions; that I might find myself wanting to paint the sea, the bone white sand and stones of Ogygia.

Instead I found that my heart's needle turned toward Philip. I breathed in the salt air above the cliffs, but it was him I smelled, his breath, the scent of evergreen boughs beside shallow water, the leaves in his hair. I returned to Berlin.

I'd deliberately left my laptop behind and asked Anna not to call while I was gone. Now I found a number of messages from her. Two of the galleries were very interested in my paintings. Could I put together a portfolio for a possible show the following autumn?

I arranged for my most recent canvases to be framed. The sleeping nudes I had done of him back in Maine had arrived some months earlier; I chose the best of these and had them mounted as well. All of this took some time to arrange, and so it was mid-April before I finally took my satchel and my easel and returned to the pool in the Grunewald to paint again.

It was a soft, warm morning, the day fragrant with young grass pushing its way through the soil. The flower vendors had baskets of freesia and violets on the sidewalk. On the Landwehrcanal, gray cygnets struggled in the wake of the tourist boat as the adult swans darted after crusts of sandwiches tossed overboard. The captain of the boat waved to me from his cockpit. I waved back, then continued on to an S-Bahn station and the train that would bear me to the Grunewald.

There was no one in the forest when I arrived. High above me the sky stretched, the pale blue-green of a frog's belly. Waxwings gave their low whistling cries and fluttered in the upper branches of the beeches, where tiny new leaves were just starting to unfurl. I stopped hurrying, the sun's warmth tugging at my skin, the sunlight saying *slow, slow*. A winter storm had brought down one of the larches near the pool; I had to push my way through a scrim of fallen branches, yellow hawthorn shoots already covering the larch's trunk. I could smell the sweet green scent of new growth; and then I saw it.

The pool was gone: there had been no snow to replenish it. Instead, a cloud of blossoms moved above the earth, gold and azure, crimson and magenta and shining coral. Anenomes, adonis, hyacinth, clematis: all the windflowers of my girlhood turned their yellow eyes toward me. I fell to my knees and buried my face in them so that they stained my cheeks with pollen, their narrow petals crushed beneath my fingertips.

I cried as though my heart would break as the wind stirred the blossoms and a few early greenflies crawled along their stems. I could see Philip there beneath them. His hair had grown, twining with the white roots of the anemones and pale beetle grubs. Beneath rose-veined lids his eyes twitched, and I could see each iris contract then swell like a seed. He was dreaming. He was beautiful.

I wiped my eyes. I picked up my satchel, careful not to step on the flowers, and got out my easel and brushes. I began to paint.

Anemones, adonis, hyacinth, clematis. I painted flowers, and a man sleeping, and the black scaffolding of a city rising from the ruins. I painted in white heat, day after day after day, then took the watercolors home and transferred what I had seen to canvases that took up an entire wall of my flat. I worked at home, through the spring and into the first weeks of summer, and now the early fall, thinking how any day I will have to return to the pool in the Grunewald, harvest what remains of the windflowers, and set him free.

But not yet.

Last week my show opened at the gallery in Akazienstrasse. Anna, as always, did her job in stellar fashion. The opening was well-attended by the press and wealthy buyers. The dark winterscapes were hung in the main room, along with the nudes I had painted for those seven years. I had thought the nudes would get more attention than they did—not that anyone would have recognized Philip. When I look at those drawings and paintings now, I see a naked man, and that's what everyone else sees as well. Nothing is concealed, and these days there is nothing new in that.

But the other ones, the windflower paintings, the ones where only I know he is there—those are the paintings that people crowd around.

I'm still not certain how I feel about exposing them to the world. I still feel a bit unsure of myself—the shift in subject matter, what feels to me like a tenuous, unsteady grasp of a medium that I will need to work much harder at if I'm to be as good as I want to be. I'm not certain if I know yet how good these paintings really are, and maybe I never will be sure. But the critics—the critics say they are revelatory.

"SEEDS"

LISA L. HANNETT AND
ANGELA SLATTER

It passed with mortals none the wiser.

The daylight hours darkened and there were storms; many silver-shod hooves were heard ringing against the vault of the sky. Thunder and lightning ruled, for a time, and humans lifted nervous eyes to the unseasonal display, clouds colored gold one moment, red and blue the next. They watched as balls of fire fell and burst before they hit the ground.

Above the earth, Bifrost was sundered. Óðinn lay dead and Fenrir raged in the halls, devouring godly corpses and shitting them out only to begin the process anew the following day. Hel wandered, wondering what she might do next, then began to forget who she was. Frost giants, released from hatred and need, melted away. Fire giants burnt low and collapsed into stone embers. Cowards fled. The great serpent relaxed its coils and simply went back to sleep.

Miðgarðr remained otherwise untouched. Ragnarok was an apocalypse for the gods alone.

Gudrun Ælfwinsdóttir, Fragment from *The Forgotten Sagas*

"Little man," sneers Bjarni Herjólfsson as the passenger emerges from the ship's hold. "Little man, what is under that cover?"

He squints and leans over the hatch. In the darkness below, four thin blond men, all armed, huddle amid bales of homespun fabric, barrels of honey and bundled furs. Heavy air reeking of musk and damp wool issues from the hold, thick enough to choke. The pale swordsmen show no signs of discomfort. Expressionless, they surround a dome-shaped object, perhaps two feet in height and a foot in circumference. A cloth of oiled hide, its hem embroidered with silver thread in a pattern of vines twined around runes, is tucked tightly about the thing. The quartet sit facing outward, sharp ivory blades unsheathed across their folded knees. Poised and alert. Ready—but for what? Bjarni has no idea. The merchant is no slaver; he is not accustomed to ferrying live cargo, nor the odd ways of men stowed too long below decks.

The strangers have not shifted in days. At first, they would surface to relieve themselves over the strakes, or to stare up at the sky as though divining secret, cumulus messages. But after the sun rose thrice on their journey, as the ragged coastline diminished at their backs, the men were scarcely seen. When one did appear, the beardless foreigner, Snorri, left his post at the top of the stairs and took his place. The rest of the time, the runt trudged up and down the narrow steps, bringing food, hot drinks. Fussing as if they might be children liable to catch a chill. Though short, as he wended around cargo and men, he was forced to stoop to avoid crowning himself on the hold's low ceiling.

It is Snorri who speaks when required, who had negotiated their fare and the conditions of their passage, who'd paid the three marks of silver Bjarni demanded. Snorri who'd hefted the group's packs onto the ship. Snorri who whispered as the hours of watching turned to days, forever chanting under his breath.

And it is Snorri who now faces Bjarni with a fierce kind of courage, the courage of a small man protecting a large secret.

"Answer!" Bjarni's voice rattles from deep in his chest. "So sly and sharp-witted. What mischief have you hidden in my ship's belly?"

Snorri stares at the captain, lips pursed. "Growl all you like, Bear. When I hired you, it was on the condition that no questions be asked. I'll thank you to stick to the terms of our agreement."

Bjarni laughs as Snorri turns and scurries back down to his charges, but he feels a chill when four blond heads simultaneously turn his way, their blue eyes flashing silver. A warning, he thinks, cursing himself for accepting the commission. It isn't greed that has guided the group's coins into Bjarni's purse. He's worked hard for the silver that funds his expeditions, and will travel far to get it. Constantinople, Rus, Frisia, Iona—his keel has tasted the salt of many seas, and his fair dealings have earned him the respect of kings.

No, it isn't greed that drives him westward, but lengthening nights and the cloak of frost settling firm on the shoulders of day. Winter drains even the frugal man's storehouse; soon the seas will be too rough for trade. One last trip to Northumbrian shores, he's calculated, and his household will eat well until summer. Bjarni casts an eye to his sailors, their broad backs and strong arms more fit for mowing hay than fussing with rigging. He shakes his head, lifts his gaze skyward. Tries to ignore the two empty benches where Guthrum and Sihtric should be.

There had been a squall like no other not long after they left harbour. Fair winds had turned foul, and the sea boiled as if Niflheimr was bubbling up from the underworld. At midday the sky had been black, and some of the men swore they saw women in the clouds, armed and helmed, riding horses with flaming eyes and smoking nostrils. Bjarni himself had seen no such thing, but he wasn't a believer and that often made him blind to what others took for granted.

When the waters had finally subsided, his two sister-sons were missing, washed overboard by the temper of the waves. This storm was not natural, the survivors whispered; Njorðr, their friend these many years, had turned his back on seafarers. Something, they'd said, had angered their god. Eyeing the hatch, many thought *or someone*.

Seven nights, no more, sly Snorri had promised, as he paid Bjarni three times what anyone else would have. Transport to the ship's furthest port and a place to stow their goods undisturbed. The conditions were simple, and easily kept. *Stigandi*'s sail was robust, her rudder true: the *knörr* was in her element in a stiff breeze and had once made the journey in five turns of the moon. But her captain had not counted on the men's curiosity, nor on the strange events that had plagued them since their departure. Last night, two more of his crew disappeared. And on this, their sixth morning at sea with at least four yet to go, the ship is becalmed. It bobs aimlessly while a carpenter scrambles to repair the mast, snapped under the force of northerly winds. The gale had ambushed them at dawn, dying down almost as quick as it had roared to life.

It was Ran with her nets, the youngest ones murmur. *Weeds dripped from her bloated arms as she rose from the deeps, whirling her knotted webs overhead. Spinning them like horseshoes at* Stigandi's *post, intent on drowning us all.*

Bjarni paces between the benches, silencing the men's gossip with his presence. Quiet but not chastened, they sit rigid with halberds kept close, iron swords lodged in the planks at their feet. "Swing your hammers, not your jaws," he barks, even as his palm warms the hilt of his dagger. "The sooner our lady's mended, the sooner we'll be away."

Even with all hands contributing, it is late afternoon by the time the mast is erected, the stays, spreaders and fittings reattached. A square shadow stretches across the deck as ropes squeal through pulleys, hoisting the cloth once more.

"We're in your debt," Bjarni says, clapping Erlend the carpenter's back. Once the sail is aloft, the captain takes charge of the rudder himself. He works the broad oar, maneuvering the vessel so as to face the setting sun. But no matter how he steers, the ship's bow points not at the orange horizon, but at a world turned to ash.

"Steady on, lads," he says, voice thin. Timbers creak and ripples lap against the hull, the sounds muffled. "Keep your heads. We've seen fog far worse than this."

Above them hollow rumbles roll, reverberate, setting iron amulets around the men's necks thrumming. Steel blades clank their thirst for blood. The thick mist swirls, condenses. Great chunks of sky splash into the ocean, darken, grow fins. Twice the length of a warrior, the creatures surface and dive. *Whales*, Bjarni thinks, and in the same instant sees faces, scales, rotting clothes. Teeth like white knives. Taloned fingers that grapple at clinker boards. *Not whales.*

The beasts circle the boat sleekly, hypnotically. The rhythm of their swimming draws the ship off course—Bjarni fights hard with the rudder, for naught. Damp air is expelled from blowholes, from gaping mouths, and pulls the sailors' attention down to the water. Away from the sky thickening. Thunderheads amassing, dispersing.

Exploding in a hail of black feathers.

Bjarni is deafened by the sound of beating wings.

He cannot hear the men's swords singing as they are drawn from scabbards. Nor the slice of cold metal through flesh, the *thunk* of bodies being struck down. Nor beaks clashing against helms or puncturing windburnt skin. Nor hoarse shouts as wriggling figures haul themselves from the water onto *Stigandi's* deck, adding grey slime to planks already treacherous with gore. Nor howls as sharp teeth sink into ankles, calves, thighs. The pounding of sailors against a hatch locked tight, Snorri and his charges safe and secure below. Bjarni's eyes register the scene unfolding before him. His hands, welded to the tiller, ache for the leather hilt of his blade. His feet seek purchase as the ship lists under the weight of battle. But in his ears, there is a grey whirring. The fluttering of hundreds, thousands, of birds.

A tornado of magpies, grackles and crows spins around the bondsmen. A spear tears through the whirlwind, disperses its ranks—which reassemble, numbers undiminished, almost before the shaft leaves the thrower's grip. As they spiral, so too does the fog. Or perhaps it's the ship that turns, swiftly, violently, and the world remains still around it. The vessel shudders, groans, the mast threatening to undo Erlend's hard work. Bjarni feels dizzy, and is soon heaving the contents of his stomach as he hasn't since he was a boy. Stars come out and tell him he's in the wrong place. Constellations he does not recognize guide him to realms unknown. A moment later it is day, the atmosphere tinted pink—another minute and the sun sizzles, extinguished beneath the waves. Still the men fight with edges too quickly dulled. Still the sea monsters feast on the fallen, and those about to fall. Still the flock flaps and eddies.

In the vortex overhead, the only point of calm in this unnatural storm, swoops a sleek black raven. The hardened sea captain stands, dumbstruck, as the beast descends. Now as large as a bull; now the size of a *dreki*, the span of its wings rivalling a dragonship's twenty-five oars. Round as Bjarni's wife, heavy with child, the dreadful bird darts between his smaller brethren, red eyes fixed on the ship's latticed hatch.

Bjarni does not see who threw the spear that pierces the dread raven's skull. Its cry turns his bowels to water; he finds himself ducking to avoid a swarm of beaks and claws that are no longer there. In an instant the skies clear, revealing the sun, allowing Bjarni to once again get his bearings.

Impossible, he thinks, as the raven plummets from the heavens, lands like doom at his feet.

The thing lies on the planks, its wings spread in the relaxation of death. Drops of blood spot its beak and the right eye hangs from its socket. One by one, men lower their weapons, catch their wind, and creep over to behold the creature they've felled.

Salty breezes play with the ship's rigging. Fresh spray douses the remaining men as the sail billows and grows taut. Bodies clunk against the hull; none look overboard to determine if the corpses are human or otherwise. For a time, all is quiet.

"Snorri Sæmundarsson!" yells Bjarni. Seeking out his steersman, at last he relinquishes his post. The captain's hands are stiff, curled around an invisible haft. He fumbles for a missing man's battle-axe, deeming his dagger not up to the task at hand. Spots dance before his eyes as he crosses the deck; the comfort of his disbelief in the supernatural now as dead as the abomination they'd slain. Bjarni rounds the carcass carefully as if it might turn *draugr* and spring back to life. "What have you brought upon us?"

The axe makes short work of the hatch, and Bjarni kicks the splintered wood away from the opening. From below there is only the gentle susurrus of waves and then a cry, poorly suppressed, clearly grief-stricken. It comes from the passengers. No. It comes from under the grey cover.

He lowers his eyes and meets Snorri's frightened, knowing gaze. The man's companions are all concentrating their attention on the dome and the wailing that comes from within it. Bjarni can hear them speaking in quiet tones, as if to soothe a wounded animal, but in no tongue he knows. The *sounds* are similar, they seem like ones he should recognize, but the words, the language escapes him, transformed somehow the instant it hits his ears.

Bjarni's long strides shrink the distance from stairs to sitters; before any of the quartet knows it, he has breached their circle and has a firm hold on their precious cargo. Anger fuels his movements. His footing is sure. He drags the thing upstairs and tears away the grey skin while Snorri and his companions are still fighting their way up the steps.

Beneath is a bird cage. Made of polished antler, carved and stained the hue of honey, each rail wound with silver wire. Inside, not clinging to a perch, but huddling at the bottom on a folded piece of gold cloth, is a bird.

A raven, in fact, twin to the dead one on the deck, only white, completely and utterly without pigmentation. A formidable creature that looks at Bjarni with liquid silver eyes and makes his heart clench. It opens its beak and a sound between a wail of grief and a howl of rage issues forth. Bjarni, acting on instinct, brings the axe down, driven solely by the gods-given need to destroy.

His tired arms betray him. The weapon smashes through the delicate antlers, shards flying. The silver wire becomes smoke once the spindles are broken, but the blade misses the raven altogether. As Bjarni draws back for a second blow, the bird flies at the breach in its prison, growing larger and larger as it passes through the wreckage, transmuting into something *other*.

Bjarni grunts and his grip on the axe is gone. The weapon falls with a loud crack, splitting to pieces on the deck like a dropped frost-cup.

The woman is so pale she hurts the eyes, shining with the same sheen as ancient ice. Her hair is long and silver-white, and her face . . . For the briefest of instants, her face is thin and fine, translucent as the porcelain bowls Bjarni often obtains in the East. Blue highlights accentuate her high cheekbones and in place of eyebrows are long white feathers. Her irises swirl, now snow, now mercury. Then she settles. Her features firm, fill out, become almost human, but not quite, set apart by the perfection of her beauty. But it shifts, ever so slightly, vibrating from within, as if something prevents her from holding form too tightly. She wears a long-sleeved dress of arctic hues and a tunic that glistens like woven dew. Two oval box brooches adorn her chest, one on each side, just below her slender collarbone. Delicate chains link these hinged pieces to a third ornament, nestled between her breasts.

While the first two are the finest specimens Bjarni has seen, the latter is a dull lumpen thing that looks like a stone.

She is a head taller than Bjarni, than any other man on the ship, even her four fellows, whose human guises have been discarded. They stand lithe and elongated, facial feathers worn proudly as warriors' tattoos, silver hair moving with a will of its own, expressions haughty as outcast princes.

"Mymnir," mumbles Snorri helplessly. "My Lady." She snarls at him and he cowers.

"You have failed, *vísla*."

"But, my Lady, my Queen . . ." He searches for words, eyes watering. "I gave my blood to protect your passage!"

And he had, too. In the early dawn before the ship set sail, he knelt beside the vessel and chanted to the hull. He grated his palm across barnacles encrusted there, smeared red into sea stains. Others saw him, thought it a fine idea, a good gift to the gods. Within a week, every man who set to sea sliced the fat pad of his hand and gave a little of himself to Njorðr.

"Wasn't enough, was it?" Her face fluctuates as she speaks, the brow feathers there and then gone again. She shoots him a last warning glare, then turns her gaze to the dead raven and makes her way towards it. The sailors fall back as she moves among them.

Bjarni watches, trying to rub away the pain in his sword arm; it feels like a frozen blade has pierced his flesh. He tries to speak but his mouth will not move. Like a sleepwalker, he follows the woman, stopping a few feet from where she crouches, her long hands reaching out to the heavy body. Her fingers glide across coal-black plumage, keeping contact on each stroke as long as she can, mewling all the while. Bjarni thinks he catches a name; it might be *Huginn*, but he cannot be sure, for the cold in his arm has crept upwards and is infecting his neck, face, ears. Everything sounds as if it comes across a great distance.

At last she rises, cradling the bird, its blood staining the blue of her dress. In a few steps she is at the rail. Without warning she heaves the carcass into the sea, where it bobs while the air leaves it, then sinks like unwanted treasure.

When she turns back her glare is dark as burnt wine. "Put us ashore."

"There is no land," Bjarni manages, his tongue thick in his mouth.

"There." With an imperious gesture she points behind him and he turns, looks beyond her four companions and the sniveling vassal, and sees a beach and trees. Seagulls flying, surfing, nesting on rugged rocks and cliffs. The captain takes heed. He nods to his men, who readily tack the sail. A helpful breeze springs up as if commanded and sweeps them in like flotsam on the spray. This land could be filled with the richest of kings, Bjarni muses, but for once trade does not enter his mind.

"Anchor at the ready," he yells, scouring the coastline for a likely bay in which to moor, in which to offload his passengers.

Mymnir watches as the ship pulls away, leaving the six on the coast with only their packs. She had not demanded food or drink be left, but Bjarni hadn't questioned it. *Too ill*, she imagines. The *knörr* gets smaller and smaller and, when she judges hope might *just* have entered their hearts, she raises her arms and begins to sing.

The wave is strangely silent. It does not displace the liquid around it, as if it has been made separately from the ocean, a thing apart that hammers the vessel, overturns and smashes it, sending Bjarni and his men to join the black raven on the seabed.

Mymnir nods, satisfied. Away from the presence of iron weapons, from all that damned dampening metal, her powers grow stronger. She can feel the surge through her limbs, the settling of her form. She watches until the sea calms, until only memory can claim there once was a boat there, crewed by those with souls. She turns her back to the waters, skewering her guardians with a hard stare.

One of them, Harkon, bows and speaks, his voice coldly musical. "Forgive us, Lady, we did not expect a threat from the humans."

"No indeed. Too consumed with feeling sorry for yourselves. Too concerned with what has been burned and lost. You chose to come with me, all of you, so look forward or gods help me you will look upon nothing ever again."

"Yes, Lady," Eiðr says, and they all bow, even Snorri, although he is without Fae grace and his movements are comical and clumsy. "Your brother, Lady. How did he find us?" Valdyr asks, brow creased.

"Perhaps Óðinn threw—" suggests Per, but is cut off.

"Óðinn is dead." She sets off along the shingle, toward an ascending the path that leads upwards, muttering. "I will not die. I will not lie down and accept a fate not of my choosing."

Yet she knows that her twin must have followed her, left his post and tracked her down. And if he had, perhaps *others* might have too . . . No. Theirs is—was—a connection only one god shared, and that one-eyed bastard is a rotting corpse. No, her brother came because he's prone to fits of temper. Enraged and reckless, he attacked. Enraged and reckless he died, just so she would be forever yoked by his death, forever carrying it around her neck like a stone.

When they reach the top of the cliff, a flat expanse stretches out before them. In the far distance, a great thick forest bristles; closer, a river courses toward them over meadows and fields to career off the verge in a powerful, frothing arc. Wild grapes hang on vines, thick and lush, richly purple and fat. Mymnir nods.

"This will do. For now, this will have to do."

Snorri, forgotten Snorri, puffs behind them, making it to the plateau at last. Mymnir turns her eldritch gaze upon him and smiles. She waves him forward. He takes heart from that, and obeys.

One hand she lays on his shoulder and he beams, spine straightening him to new heights; with the other, she unclasps the left box brooch from her tunic and flips the intricate clasp that holds it closed. She releases it—and it floats to the ground, the open lid remaining upright. It settles on the rich green grass and Mymnir squeezes, feeling Snorri's thin bones.

"You have been faithful, *vísla*, and for that I thank you."

"My Lady." Snorri lifts his head to stare into her eyes and does not see how the nail of her index finger lengthens and becomes white, hard as flint and sharp as hate. He barely feels it as it slices across his throat, as the blood pours over the tiny container at their feet.

Mymnir does not let him fall until he is dry. After a moment, she leans forward and whispers to the kingdom box, which shakes itself like a kitten waking after a nap then begins to hop about, struggling.

Once the first item springs from its depths—a fountain—others follow much more easily. In short order there are fine houses, more fountains, city squares, trees bearing strange fruit, horses and goats and shaggy cattle, byres and barns, a smithy, benches, paved streets and gardens and, finally, a palace, all glinting in the sun. The ground grumbles beneath their feet, then roars as stone rears from the earth. Jagged peaks push the construct up, so high its new rooftops seem to pierce the blue. Stone vines shoot from the soil, curl around the buildings, securing them to the ridge. Structures sprout granite roots, steeples and turrets are tethered to the mountainside by marble buttresses grown from sheer walls of rock. Mymnir crosses her arms, surveys her handiwork, whistling as it detaches from the continent, opening a league-wide channel between the two shores. Before the dust settles, an alabaster bridge stretches over the chasm, its railings topped with crystal orbs that catch the light, refracting rainbows up and down its length.

"Not quite Bifrost," she says, bending down to retrieve the box, which seems to gasp, exhausted.

"One last thing," she tells it and a sigh escapes the little thing. She flips it over and onto her unlined palm fall tiny seeds, silver and gold, perhaps a hundred. Mymnir exhales over them then flings them out before her.

Where each one lands a person unfurls. Maidens and lads, all Fae, all lovely and cold, and each one sinks before her into a deep bow. She nods once again.

"Home," she says. Her smile smug, regal. "For now, this is home."

"WONDER-WORKER-
OF-THE-WORLD"

NISI SHAWL

It was near the beginning of things, but it was not really right at the beginning. Life was good. The land was fat, and luscious with grass. The herds of the people were free from any sickness, for there was not yet any sickness in the world. Nor was there any strife, nor any sort of evil.

The cause of all this was the buffalo, Wonder-Worker-of-the-World. Whenever the people needed anything they would ask him for it. If a man needed a large assegai he would go to Wonder-Worker-of-the-World, and lean upon his big black shoulder, and sing:

"Ah, my father, it is from you
Comes all goodness.
It is from you
Comes this long spear."

Then he would take the assegai and go away to hunt.

Or if a woman needed a length of colored cloth she would come to the buffalo and lean upon his shoulder and say:

"Oh, my father, it is from you
Comes all goodness.
It is from you
Comes this fine cloth."

Then she would take the cloth for a body wrap.

So things went on, and for a while, Wonder-Worker-of-the-World thought that things were good, and then he saw that they were too good. "These people will never do anything," he said. "Whatever they ask I must give them, but I do not wish that they should not be able to get anything for themselves." So he went away from his people, and they were left on their own.

At first the people were confused, but then they found other ways of getting the things they needed. They found they could make spears and spin cloth and dig for metal in the ground.

And it was ever the custom, when they got what they needed, to sing:

> "Oh, my father, it is from you
> Comes all goodness."

Thus it was with most of the people. But there were those who were lazy, who thought badly of Wonder-Worker-of-the-World because he left them. They took what they wanted from those who made it and killed those who tried to keep what they had made. Murder and theft came into the world and with them many other evil things: sorrow, hunger, disease, and so forth.

Again, there was confusion among the people. Things became worse and worse. The fat land became thin and worn out with the people's struggle. The grass was trampled into bloody dust.

An old man who remembered the early, easy days said "It must be that we have offended our father, Wonder-Worker-of-the-World. He has given us everything, and we have returned nothing to him. We must give our father a most valuable gift. Then he will see that we love him, and all will be well once more."

Now this old man was quite wrong, but no one knew that. Everyone believed him. Some thought that if the people gave back to the buffalo some of what he had given them, he would take away all misery and confusion. Others thought that if the gift were great enough, their father would come to them to stay, again taking care of all their needs.

There was much discussion as to what the proper gift would be. At last it was decided that the only suitable thing would be to give him one of themselves. So they chose a beautiful, strong young maiden named Untombinde and clothed her in finely woven wraps. They put golden ornaments in her hair and on her breasts. Then she was ready and they had to learn how to send their gift to Wonder-Worker-of-the-World.

The old man told them, "You must kill Untombinde. Kill her. It is the only way she will come to our father, who is gone from among us."

Again, the old man was wrong, but again all believed him, because he was so old.

The people took up all their weapons and gathered in a circle. Untombinde stood at the center, filled with fear. The people took a step towards her and she fell to her knees. "No," she cried. "Do not kill me!" But the people with their weapons drew a step nearer, and she fell onto the ground. Then she felt a sinking feeling, and she lifted her head. She saw that she had sunk into the earth as high as her waist. She screamed again and again. The people stepped nearer and nearer, and held their weapons high to strike. She felt the earth pull her down, so that now only her head was above ground. Untombinde gave one final scream, and down came the knives and death clubs. But they did not kill her, for she was safe under the earth.

Untombinde was riding on the back of an enormous buffalo.

She knew it was her father, Wonder-Worker-of-the-World. At first everything was black around her, but gradually she came to see. The road was shining like starlight. The plants and trees along the way were like the moon behind thin clouds. All glowed softly with a dim beauty.

Wonder-Worker-of-the-World took her to his kraal. He said "I asked my people for no gift, but since they were so evil as to try to slay you, you will stay with me and be my wife." He showed her where they would sleep, and where the garden was, and many other things to do with their life, some of which were wonders.

The buffalo had three wells. One of them was sweet and one was salty and one was sour like beer. Untombinde had to water the vegetables from the proper wells. She had to learn songs to sing to the spirits of the garden, those which would encourage the vegetables to grow.

The buffalo had three fires: a red fire, a green fire, and a black fire. Untombinde had to tend the fires. Each needed a special fuel. Wonder-Worker-of-the-World told her that bad things would happen if the fires went out. "And if it is the black fire which dies," he told her, "it is all over for the both of us."

The buffalo had three windows. One showed the land there below the earth. One showed what happened in the land above the sky. But the third showed nothing, for it was kept covered.

The buffalo gave Untombinde three jars. In the first was a red paste. "Use this, he told her, "and polish my horns." So she did. The second jar contained a green paste. "Use this to polish my hooves." So she did that, using the green paste. The third jar was larger than the other two and was filled with a black liquid. "Use this when you brush my hide," he said, and again she did as she was bid.

Thus Untombinde lived with Wonder-Worker-of-the-World. She groomed him and cared for his garden and tended his three fires. When she was not busy she looked through the open windows and saw many strange things. She would have been very happy if not for that third window.

At first she was just bothered by the way that her husband kept it covered. She teased him and teased him. Wonder-Worker- of-the-World had never been good at refusing to give things to his people, and finally he allowed Untombinde to uncover the window. It showed her all the things that were happening on the earth.

Now that she had gotten what she wanted, Untombinde was still not happy. Far from it. For though the people had tried to kill her, she did not really believe they were evil, but only ignorant. And there they were, no better off than they had been before, while she was living a life much improved. So she watched and watched as her people suffered and she was filled with sorrow.

The sadder she became, the more time she spent looking through this window at the things that made her sad. Even when she looked through the other windows she was still seeing the wars and plagues that troubled the earth. Even when she attended to her tasks she cried for the sorrows of her people. The sweet and sour plants became weak and sickly because of the salt tears that fell constantly upon them from the eyes of Untombinde. The salty plants grew rank, like weeds, and dominated the garden.

She did not notice; she saw only the sorrows of the earth. Untombinde wept into the pots of grooming paste and ruined them.

Her husband's coat grew patchy and thin; his horns and hooves grew dull. She did not notice, for she saw only the sorrows of the earth.

But one day Untombinde looked up from her weeping and saw to her horror that her tears were drowning the black fire! Quickly she sprang up to feed it. The air grew dark around her; the land's dim light faded and she had to gasp for every breath. Groping about, she found a little bit of kindling which had not been soaked through with her tears. She placed the kindling on the smoldering black fire and blew upon the coals with her feeble breath. At last the flames shot high again and everything came back as it had been. Just then her husband dragged himself in through the door. "What happened?" he asked when he had strength enough to speak. He himself had nearly died because of her neglect.

Untombinde told him everything, and the buffalo was very sad. "It is clear that you do not belong here, but on earth where you were born," he said. "But how should I send you back to your people who wickedly would have slain you? They do not deserve to have you among them."

Then Untombinde pleaded with him. It was true she missed her people and she wished that she might be able to help them. Yet also she had come to love her husband, Wonder-Worker-of-the-World, and if he sent her back above to live, she would never be happy again.

The couple talked and talked. After many days they decided what to do.

Now some of the time Untombinde lives on the earth, and some of the time she lives below it. And sometimes she travels alone, and sometimes she rides on the back of a big, black buffalo. And if you see a beautiful, strong young maiden riding such a beast, you must lean against his shoulder and sing for me:

"Oh, my father, it is from you
Comes all goodness.
It is from you
Came this story."

"THESEA AND ASTAURIUS"

PRIYA SHARMA

"**D**addy, you're telling it wrong."

"Am I?"

Thesea looks up at her husband and daughter.

"You tell it then," he says to the child.

"King Minos prayed to Poseidon, who sent him a magic bull but Minos didn't sacrifice it like he was supposed to, so Aphrodite made Minos' wife fall in love with it."

Only the gods inflict love as a punishment, Thesea thinks.

"The bull and the queen made a baby called the Minotaur." Thesea's glad that she's too young to be concerned with the details. She bares her teeth and draws her fingers into claws. "It was a monster."

"The Minotaur had a bull's head on a man's body." Their son; older, placid, lacking his sibling's drama.

"I'm telling it. Minos made Daedalus, his inventor, build the labyrinth to hold the Minotaur. He fed it human sacrifices sent from Athens."

"Really?" her father asks.

"Yes, then Athens sent a prince called Theseus who was so handsome that Ariadne, Minos' daughter, gave him a sword to kill the Minotaur and string to find his way out of the maze."

The girl has no interest in being Ariadne. She leaps about pretending to be Theseus, imaginary sword in hand.

"Calm down," Thesea puts an arm around her and draws her in. "You've all got it wrong. Listen and I'll tell you what really happened."

Athens. Thesea is eleven. The other children are paddling in the shallows, splashing one another. The fisherman's son follows her along the shore. He won't leave her alone.

"My mother said you're going to be sent to Crete to die." He tries to grab her hand to stop her walking away.

Thesea runs into the sea and dives into the advancing wave. She holds her breath and twists about so that she can look at the churning surf from underneath.

So what she's heard is true. She's not meant for this world. Perhaps that's why she's always felt outside it. There are only these moments then. She resolves to make them last.

Thesea at seventeen. She stands apart from the cargo of weeping foundlings, looking ahead. As they approach Crete, blue is divided by yellow sand into sea and sky. The ship navigates the coast to where Minos and his men have gathered on the dock to greet the fresh meat.

The boat's close enough for Thesea to see their faces. They look like salivating dogs. She can read Minos with a glance; his smile is a yawning hole that could swallow her.

He wants the entire world. Greedy bastard.

The group shuffle down the gangplank. The Athenian crew can't look at them. Sailors on other ships stand and stare.

A girl greets them. She wears purple silk, and gold shimmers at her ears and throat.

"I'm Ariadne, daughter of Minos, princess of Crete." She takes a garland from a slave's arms and puts it around the neck of the first Athenian and kisses the boy's cheek. "We thank you for your great sacrifice."

Thesea's the final one in line. Ariadne stares as if trying to get the measure of her. The garland tickles Thesea's neck. Then she feels cold metal slipping down the front of her gown.

Ariadne kisses her and whispers, "Run. Run *into* the labyrinth." She steps back and smiles, the dimple in her cheek revealed. "Come, we've prepared a feast for you."

They're mad. Thesea follows them to the tables. *Every single one of them.*

Thesea's spent her life expecting death at the Minotaur's hands or teeth or trampled underfoot.

The rest of the Athenians have been sacrificed and there's not a monster in sight. Only Minos and his men. Thesea's witnessed it. Sex and blood, all at once.

"Your turn."

She's untied. A hand clamps her wrist. She's not agreed to this. This isn't sacrifice for the greater good. It's rape and murder. She pulls the knife from her dress and plants it in the man's neck. He has a soldier's reflexes. His sword bites her arm.

Ariadne's plan doesn't seem so stupid now. Run. Whatever is in the labyrinth can't be worse than this.

"Get her."

"No," Minos calls from the heart of the carnage, "leave her. She'll starve in there. Or he'll find her. Let him have a live one. Poor sod deserves a bit of fun."

There's laughter. She runs faster in case they change their minds. When she looks back over her shoulder the soldiers are dragging the bodies towards the maze's mouth.

Let him have a live one.

The novelty of a warm, writhing body instead of a cold, already illused carcass. She pictures the bull-headed giant sitting on a throne of bleached bones, tearing the flesh from a human leg with his teeth.

Thesea feels like a bucket of hot water has been poured down her arm. It's slick down to her wrist. There's a relentless drip from her fingertips. Her heart thumps to compensate. A contrary feeling, making her weak and energised all at once. She tears the hem from her gown and binds her arm.

The labyrinth's endless corridors of white marble. Blind endings. Steps and turns. Arches and pillars. It's baffling. Thesea turns a corner to find a fountain, the water making music. In a courtyard there's an altar laid with roses. Elsewhere a lyre nailed to a wall. Smells without source—jasmine, fire, and cooking fish. These anomalies don't help her to orient.

Thesea remembers being lost in the forest as a child. The tree's pretense of familiarity. The maze is the same. Alive. When she leans against a wall it moves beneath her skin as if breathing her in.

I'm going mad.

I'm going to die.

She lays down, head on the ground. Stone shifts beneath her cheek, like something exhaling. Her skull trembles. Vibrations announce the Minotaur's approach.

There's a roar that could shatter rock.

She pulls herself up to a sitting position.

Let him come. I was bred for death.

The Minotaur's an abomination. Union of earthly woman and divine bull. His outline fills the corridor. His horns throw long javelin shadows on the floor. He lowers his head and breaks into a run.

The Minotaur halts beside her. Thesea tries to be calm as he picks her up. She's cradled in his arms. He smells, she thinks, like the summer rain on warm earth.

She's being carried along a corridor. Its proportions are less grand than the rest of the labyrinth. The Minotaur's bellowing is no longer just sound, it's becoming speech.

"Daedalus! I've found one. She's alive!"

The workshop's around the next corner. Daedalus looks up from his bench. Thesea sees a frowning mouth, crooked nose, a pair of goggles and a flash of grey hair. He sheds the goggles to reveal blue eyes.

"Quick, on here."

Daedalus clears the bench with a single sweep of his arm, his tools shrapnel flying to the floor. Thesea's laid down, a body on a slab. She's heard of this Daedalus, dubbed *the cunning worker*. His constructions are wonders. He's so complicated that his king is his patron *and* enemy and he's ended up imprisoned with a beast in the jail that he was commissioned to make.

Will he convert her into a terrible machine or will the pair of them sit down to feast on her?

"Fetch my medicine chest."

The Minotaur looks about in panic. The workshop's a mess of prototypes and parts. It smells of grease and metal. Boxes spill maps, sketches, cogs and wires. Others are sealed with triple padlocks.

"The leather one, there."

Thesea feels a cold ring of metal on her chest. It's connected to tubes that Daedalus puts in his ears. He tells her the name later. *Stethoscope.* Daedalus checks the integrity of her bones. Lays a flat hand on her abdomen. Then he unwraps the binding on her arm.

"It's just a flesh wound. She's lost some blood though. Get me the Glenrothes."

The Minotaur holds out a bottle of amber liquid but Daedalus is too busy with needle, syringe and vial. He nods to the Minotaur, "Pour me a glass."

"It's not to clean her wound?"

"Single malt? Are you joking? That's for me. We'll use the cheap stuff on her arm."

The Minotaur fusses over her so much that Daedalus sends him away.

"Can you feel this?" He prods at the edges of the wound with a needle. "No? Then we'll begin. Look away."

Thesea refuses. She watches the needle pierce numb skin.

"What's your name?"

"Thesea."

"Greek?"

"Yes." Of course Greek. Where else? "Minos. I didn't know . . ." Her sentence collapses.

"He's as crazy as a sack of snakes."

They lapse into silence. Behind Daedalus there's a lit candle in a niche. It illuminates a painting of a young man lying on a rock, his complexion ashen. The sky behind him is red, the horizon a dark line. White nymphs reach for him with pale hands.

A pair of enormous wings are strapped to his arms.

"What's that?" she asks.

"A gift from the Minotaur."

"He's an artist?"

"No. He just thought I should see it. It's called 'The Fall of Icarus'."

"I don't understand."

Daedalus finishes his embroidery. Flesh is reunited.

"We'll talk later." He drops the needle into the bowl. "You should get some rest."

Thesea's mouth is dry when she wakes. Daedalus dozes in a chair. She looks at his sketches but can't fathom their purpose. She helps herself to water from the jug. Slices cheese onto bread.

She looks into an alcove, then realizes it's a balcony. The Minotaur's below her, in a vast field. He waves.

"Feeling better?"

"Much."

She recognizes now that the stretched mouth is a smile.

There are bodies laid out in a row. Ariadne's flowers are tangled with torn clothes. She recognizes a wave of black hair. A scarf. A necklace. They remind her that mauled flesh was someone she once knew.

The Minotaur's stripped to the waist, shovel in hand, knee deep in a hole. Behind him markers stretch down the hill and out of sight.

He's burying them, she thinks. *Each in their own grave.*

"I'm going for a walk." Thesea stretches, trying to lengthen her muscles.

"Sure," Daedalus rummages in a box, "you're not a prisoner. Take this string and use it to find your way back."

"Call if you get lost. I'll come." Then the Minotaur adds, "If you feel faint put your head between your knees."

"How will you find me?"

"I will."

Daedalus follows her down the corridor and whispers in her ear. "Be careful. He's different, depending where he is in the maze."

"He can't always speak, can he?"

"Not just that. He's not always so affable."

"How will I know?"

"You'll know."

Her walk exhausts her. The Minotaur lays a blanket over her knees when she returns and fetches extra cushions. She watches him work the bellows for Daedalus and together they shape metal. Flames and fatigue bring sleep but not for long. Thesea sits upright, wet faced, choking on a scream.

"You're safe." The Minotaur kneels before her, clutching her hand.

"You've no idea."

"I do."

"I'm sorry, of course you do." He dignifies the dead with burial.

The Minotaur reaches into his pocket and brings out a brass ring. "Minos gave me this when I was a boy. His captain held me down while he put it through my nose. Daedalus was kind enough to remove it."

Daedalus tells her everything later. How Minos sniggered as he threatened to castrate the Minotaur when he reached manhood. How they branded the delicate flesh of his inner thigh.

"I'm not an animal," the Minotaur tells her.

"No, I know you're not."

Thesea is holding *his* hand now.

Thesea cries less in her sleep. She walks farther each day using her string as a guide. Daedalus won't let her chalk arrows on the floor. *Just in case we get unwanted visitors.*

The Minotaur accompanies her when he can.

"What's your favorite place?"

"The beach near where I grew up. Not far from Athens."

"Why?"

"Because I've never been anywhere else."

"I want to show you something."

She follows him deep into the maze on a bewildering journey from which she'd never return without him.

"Here." He puts his palms against a wall in a tentative gesture. "Yes, here will be perfect."

The Minotaur pries at the stone with his fingertips, pulls out a few blocks and lays them carefully on the floor. He peeks through and once satisfied, he enlarges the hole. The blocks become a stack. Thesea tries to put her hand through but she can't. It's as if there's a hidden barrier. The Minotaur reaches in with ease.

"Why can't I?"

"I don't know," he shrugs. "Daedalus can't either. It frustrates him too, knowing I can wander around out there. Now, take a look."

There's a room on the other side. What stuns her is the view from the window on the far wall. She knows by instinct the slow-turning jewel out there is home, even though she's ignorant of astronomy. That the blue is ocean after ocean. Brown is the ground that should be beneath her feet. She can't reconcile this paradox. That labyrinth is *down there* and *up here.*

"Daedalus says that's the moon," the Minotaur points to a silvery ball, part in shadow.

The moon. She can't see Diana, goddess, huntress and lunar mistress. It's just a ball of rock.

"Is Daedalus a god?"

"No. He says this is a place where men are gods."

"The gods don't exist?"

"Not always. I don't know if this is before or after."

"Is that natural?"

The Minotaur continues to stare out of the window. "I'm not the person to ask about what's natural and what isn't."

Thesea's giddy. A place where the fates and gods have no sway. They're insignificant, or will be, or were. So is she.

It's terrifying. It's liberating.

"It's that time." Daedalus looks at the calendar and shakes his head.

The Minotaur's digging again. Thesea takes him a jug of water. The bodies laid out on the ground are black skinned. The flower of Ethiopian youth.

Thesea makes an approximate count of the markers. The Athenian tribute would only occupy a corner of the graveyard.

"So many?"

"From all over the world. And more than you think. There are mass graves in the corner. It's the work of more than one man. The slaughter of innocents is a family tradition." A dynasty of psychopaths. "Luckily Ariadne's not like that, although Minos doesn't know it."

"Ariadne?" Thesea's forgotten her. The sudden warmth in his voice makes her feel jealous.

"My sister. Half-sister, really."

"Were you close?"

"We still are. I talk to her through the wall, although it's hard to catch her alone. Minos watches her all the time. He went even crazier after his wife fell in love with my father."

"What happened to your father?"

"Minos ate him."

"Oh, I'm sorry." There's not much she can say to that.

The Minotaur nods, his eyes lowered.

"Why doesn't Ariadne hide in here with you?"

"Is that what I'm doing? Hiding?" He digs as they talk. A consummate sexton.

"I'm saying all the wrongs things. I'm sorry."

"No. You're right. Minos would rip this place up looking for her. And she stays to make sure Minos treats his prisoner well."

"Who?"

"Icarus. Daedalus' son. She's in love with him."
"Icarus." The outstretched wings.

Thesea happens upon the wrong part of the maze. The Minotaur sits and seethes, his eyes embers in the gloom. Steam rises from his nostrils. He could erupt at any moment.

She backs away, afraid.

"Daedalus, which is the real Minotaur?"

"We're all made of different parts. One's not less real than the rest." He shrugs, seemingly less concerned with the semantics of the soul than she is.

"You're lying."

"I'm not." He doesn't look up from the machine that whirs in his hands.

"An omission's as bad as a lie."

"I've missed this," he smiles.

"What?"

"You remind me of my wife. She saw through me like I was water, too."

"Don't change the subject."

"That's exactly what I mean."

"Tell me or you won't get a moment of peace."

He sighs.

"She did that as well. If there's anywhere that all his parts are united it's the heart of the labyrinth."

The heart of the labyrinth is the heart of the Minotaur. Daedalus shakes a finger at her when she demands a blueprint.

"I burnt it. What do you think would happen if Minos got hold of it?"

Yet here she is, due to string and intuition. Here is the Minotaur laid bare.

Thesea's disappointed when he snorts at her but from his embarrassed look she can tell he's speechless, not dumb. There's no doubt that he's more man than animal. His body's beautiful. A giant construct of muscle slabs laid on bone. His tail, a curl of a thing, sits above his buttocks.

Thesea holds out her arms to him. His black eyes are liquid in this light. He buries his face in her palm. His nose is wet, his tongue large and rasping.

He can't kiss me, not like a man kisses a woman.

He lays his immense head in her lap. His physiognomy defies her fingers. She touches the curve of his horns.

"Your neck must hurt."

He snorts again, tilts his head one way, then the other as she rubs his neck and shoulders. She massages the knots until they soften. His bones click under her hands. He grunts, grateful.

When he pulls her down beside him, she stiffens. Brutality is all she's seen of sex. The Minotaur undoes the memory with a torrent of tenderness.

There are only these moments, Thesea thinks, *I must make them last*. But he draws her on to the next moment and then the one after.

Thesea's dream's a riot. She can see each bead of blood, each gash, each contortion. It's a churning sea of screams. A man's voice carries above it. Sweat pricks her forehead. She opens her eyes. Daedalus is shaking her awake. She can still hear the man, shouting. He's close.

"It's Minos. Hide."

"What about the Minotaur?"

"He'll know already." Daedalus shoves her in a cupboard.

Thesea kneels and peeps through the keyhole. Minos comes in, followed by a line of men. A line of human string.

"Daedalus," Minos folds his arms, "make it obey me."

"It's *him*, not *it*. And what do you want to do?"

"His duty."

"As what?"

"A weapon. I want him to march at the head of my army. I'm going to remind my dissenters who I am."

"The Minotaur's no killer."

"Then he's no use to me. Persuade him. We march at the next full moon. If he's not with me then the first place I'll come is here. There'll be nowhere to hide. I'll pull this place down brick by brick. Oh, and I'll execute your precious Icarus."

"Someone should put a knife in him."

"I've tried to persuade the Minotaur to do it while he's visiting his sister but he won't. He says it would be murder."

"Then we have to leave."

"Not without Icarus and Ariadne." Daedalus fiddles with a set of cogs. "And I don't know if the Minotaur can."

She snatches them from him.

"Explain."

"This isn't a prison. I just wanted somewhere to keep him safe."

"What have you done?"

Thesea's already guessed. It's why the Minotaur knows who's where. Why the walls breathe and the floor sighs.

"He's like his father. The stuff of gods. He can punch holes in time and space. He *is* the labyrinth. It's made from him. Don't look at me like that. This way he'd never be lost or trapped."

"And being able to travel outside?"

"An unforeseen consequence, but he can't stay away for long. I don't know what it would mean if he tried to leave for good. Part of him is in here. In the fabric of this place."

The Minotaur's out of breathe from running. "I got here as fast as I could." He stands so close to Thesea that she can feel his relief and body heat. He looks from her face to Daedalus'. "What did Minos want?"

Thesea puts her head next to his.

"I'm not trying to fight with you but we have to stop Minos."

"We can stay in here. Forever if we have to. He won't find us."

"What about Icarus and Ariadne? What about all those people?" She remembers diving beneath the surf and breaking through on the other side. From then on each moment catalogued, her life finite. She's defied fate. She's seen a future where even divinity is expendable. "We can stop him."

"How?"

"We'll need Ariadne's help."

Daedalus has kept them out of the workshop until it's ready. Thesea glances at the Minotaur. His mouth hangs open.

A copy of the Minotaur's head is on Daedalus' workbench. It's perfect, down to its eyelashes and moist nose.

"Did you find it?" Daedalus asks.

Thesea nudges the Minotaur who's still staring.

"Right, yes." The Minotaur hands him a tube. "The shopkeeper said this will glue anything together."

They all turn back to the head that's watching them.

"There are a couple of things missing."

Thesea knows right away what Daedalus means.

"Your horns." The old man nods at him. "I'll get the hacksaw."

"I'll need them in a fight." The Minotaur backs away.

"You're not going to fight."

It's only when Thesea puts a hand on his arm that the Minotaur relents. She stays but has to turn away. There's the rasping see saw sound of metal on horn.

Afterwards she uses his forelocks to cover the stumps.

"How does it feel?" Thesea asks later.

"Strange. My head's lighter."

"Will this work?"

"It has to." He curls a strand of her hair around his finger. "I feel like I was asleep before I met you."

"And before you I thought my life was forfeit and I didn't care because I had nothing to fight for."

"Thesea, if it doesn't work . . ."

"Don't say it."

"If it doesn't work, don't wait for me."

"It'll work."

"It would be all right. I don't want you to be alone."

"Shut up and kiss me."

"You should know my name. It's Astaurius."

Sword, shield, and helmet have transformed Thesea into Theseus. Girl into boy. She carries the fake head in a bag. It's heavy.

As she and Daedalus leave, the labyrinth walls dull as if a light's going out. She pauses and presses her lips to the stone but it's devoid of life. It's as they planned. The Minotaur's reversing Daedalus' design. Taking the god-given power of Olympus back within himself. If he's got it right, he'll use it to make one final door and come out somewhere else, nothing remaining of him in the stone to tether him there.

The ground shakes beneath their feet, a subtle tremor spreading out from deep within the maze.

Astaurius.

Daedalus is as encumbered as Thesea. He looks hunchbacked because he's wearing a folded set of wings beneath his cloak. He hefts the second pair in a sack.

There's another rumble. Behind them there's the distant sound of collapsing masonry. The maze is a construct that can't withstand the world without the Minotaur.

"Hurry." Thesea takes the spare wings from Daedalus.

Ariadne's waiting for them. The watchman lies at her feet. Blood stains his tunic. Ariadne is Minos' daughter after all. Thesea tries to hide her shock with a question.

"Is that what you're wearing?"

"It would look a bit odd if I was dressed to travel rather than for a party, wouldn't it?" She looks at Thesea like she's a simpleton. She's planned revels to distract the court. "At least this way I'll be able to take some things of value for us to live on."

Ariadne wears silks, too many layers considering the mildness of the day. Her yellow hair's bound up in an elaborate coil, studded with gems. Gold bangles tinkle on her arms.

"Clever girl," Daedalus laughs. "Where's Icarus?"

"Here's a map. He's at the top of this tower. Father has the only key. I couldn't get it."

"Leave that to me." Daedalus, lover of locks, will tease out its secrets. "What about the guard?"

"I took him a cup of wine." Her smile makes Thesea shudder. "Icarus knows where we're meeting. Tell anyone who asks about the wings that you're part of the entertainment. Are you sure those things will work?"

"Certain."

A shockwave escapes the labyrinth.

"What's that?" Ariadne asks.

"Your brother. We best go. He's going to attract a lot of attention." Daedalus squeezes Thesea's hand. "Goodbye dear."

"We'll go this way." Ariadne pulls Thesea away. She takes one last look at the maze. Another quake nearly floors them but Ariadne just laughs like it's an adventure. "There's an Athenian ship in dock. I can play the distressed captive but can you be a convincing kidnapper?"

Crete gets smaller. Thesea's still holding up the Minotaur's head. The ships in port bear witness to the feat. The Minotaur's dead. The gods are no longer on Minos' side. The news will carry around the world on the tide.

Minos is a speck on the dock. Thesea can feel his eyes burning into her, even at this distance but he won't risk his darling girl. Ariadne's played her role so well that Thesea wonders at the upbringing necessitating that kind of skill.

Once they're safe on open sea, Thesea goes to the prow to be alone, cradling the Minotaur's head in her arms.

The sun's a red ball shrouded by fog. Thesea waits for Astaurius on the beach.

He'll come. Any day now.

She listens to news of Daedalus' escape and the nations refusing Minos' demands. He's forced into unwinnable wars on too many fronts.

Gulls' cries carry over the water. There's the lonely lap of waves. A figure walks up the shore towards her. He looks familiar.

"It's you," he says.

Thesea takes up a fighting stance, sword in hand.

"Don't you know me?"

It's the fisherman's son, the one who used to plague her. She lowers the sword a fraction.

"I live up there, with my family. Remember?" He points to a house high on the cliff. "These are for you."

A generous gift of line and net. A loaf of bread. "If you want to fish, come and ask. I needn't be the one to teach you. My mother or sisters can show you."

When Thesea eventually knocks at the door it's his mother that answers. The promise holds true. The women cluck about her, teaching her to fish and forage, to cook delicacies in the embers of a fire.

She sits with his mother one evening, learning how to repair nets. She admires the older woman's dexterity.

"I was pregnant before I wed. By another man."

Thesea looks up but her teacher's intent on her task.

"My husband knew. He was good to me. I came to love him very much. There's many who'd judge me, not knowing my story." She sniffs. "It's no one else's business. It's a hard thing bring up a child alone. How far gone are you?"

Thesea's startled. Her stomach only show's a slight fullness. She blushes.

"My boy didn't eat for weeks after you were taken away. He's loved you since he was a child. He loves you, no matter what."

Thesea doesn't want to listen. She feels like her reclaimed life is over without the Minotaur.

Astaurius, why don't you come?

"So that's what happened. Come and kiss me goodnight."

Helena comes first, still posturing and playing out the tale. Next, Astaurius, unusually tall and strong for his age. When they laid him on her belly she didn't know if she was disappointed or relieved that he didn't have horns and a tail.

"Are you coming?" her husband asks.

"One minute. You go ahead." She tidies the platters away, folds up a pile of clothes.

When she's sure she'll be left alone she takes out a key. It unlocks the chest in the corner, which is hers alone. The Minotaur's head looks up at her. She raises the lamp and light animates the liquid eyes. Daedalus' work was a marvel built to last.

Her husband's dozing. She blows out the lamp and lies down beside him. Her throat thickens and she tries to swallow the tears. He rolls over and a gentle hand wipes her face. She takes it and kisses it.

Her husband says, "I wonder what happened to Daedalus."

Daedalus and Icarus. Flight is so much more certain with polyurethane resin than with wax.

The sun is dazzling. They soar.

"FOXFIRE, FOXFIRE"

YOON HA LEE

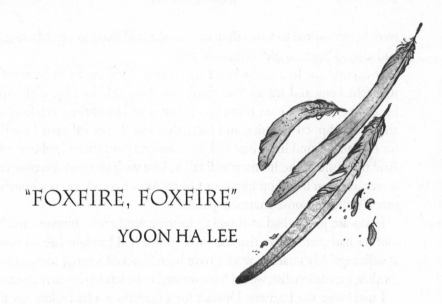

If I'd listened to the tiger-sage's warning all those years ago, I wouldn't be trapped in the city of Samdae during the evacuation. Old buildings and new had suffered during the artillery battle, and I could hear the occasional wailing of sirens. Even at this hour, families led hunched grandmothers and grandfathers away from their old homes, or searched abandoned homes in the hopes of finding small treasures: salt, rags, dried peppers. As I picked my way through the streets tonight, I saw the flower-shaped roof tiles for which Samdae was known, broken and scattered beneath my feet. Faraway, blued by distance, lights guttered from those skyscrapers still standing, dating to the peninsula's push to modernization. It had not done anything to prevent the civil war.

I had weighed the merits of tonight's hunt. Better to return to fox-form, surely, and slip back to the countryside; abandon the purpose that had brought me to Samdae all those years ago. But I only needed one more kill to become fully human. And I didn't want to off some struggling shopkeeper or midwife. For one thing, I had no grudge against them. For another, I had no need of their particular skills.

No; I wandered the Lantern District in search of a soldier. Soldiers were easy enough to find, but I wanted a nice strapping specimen. At the moment I was posing as a prostitute, the only part of this whole affair my mother would have approved of. Certain human professions were better-suited to foxes than others, she had liked to say. My mother had always been an old-fashioned fox.

"Baekdo," she had said when I was young, "why can't you be satisfied with chickens and mice? You think you'll be able to stop with sweet bean cakes, but the next thing you know, it will be shrimp crackers and chocolate-dipped biscuits, and after that you'll take off your beautiful fur to walk around in things with buttons and pockets and rubber soles. And then one of the humans will fall in love with you and discover your secret, and you'll end up like your Great-Aunt Seonghwa, as a bunch of oracle bones in some shaman's purse."

Foxes are just as bad at listening to their mothers as humans are. My mother had died before the war broke out. I had brought her no funeral-offerings. My relatives would have been shocked by that idea, and my mother, a traditionalist, would have wanted to be left to the carrion-eaters.

I had loved the Lantern District for a long time. I had taken my first kill there, a lucky one really. I'd crept into a courtesan's apartment, half-drunk on the smells of quince tea and lilac perfume. At the time I had no way of telling a beautiful human from an ugly one—I later learned that she had been a celebrated beauty—but her layered red and orange silks had reminded me of autumn in the forest.

Tonight I wore that courtesan's visage. Samdae's remaining soldiers grew bolder and bolder with the breakdown in local government, so only those very desperate or stubborn continued to ply their trade. I wasn't worried on my own behalf, of course. After ninety-nine kills, I knew how to take care of myself.

There. I spotted a promising prospect lingering at the corner, chatting up a cigarette-seller. He was tall, not too old, with a good physique. He was in uniform, with the red armband that indicated that he supported the revolutionaries. Small surprise; everyone who remained in Samdae made a show of supporting the revolutionaries. Many of the loyalists had fled overseas, hoping to raise support from the foreign powers. I wished them luck. The loyalists were themselves divided between those who supported the queen's old line and those who wished to install a parliament in place of the Abalone Throne. Fascinating, but not my concern tonight.

I was sauntering toward the delicious-looking soldier when I heard the cataphract's footsteps. A Jangmi 2-7, judging from the character-istic whine of the servos. Even if I hadn't heard it coming—and who couldn't?—the stirring of the small gods of earth and stone would have alerted me to its approach. They muttered distractingly. My ears would have flattened against my skull if they could have.

Superstitious people called the cataphracts ogres, because of their enormous bipedal frames. Some patriots disliked them because they had to be imported from overseas. Our nation didn't have the ability to manufacture them, a secret that the foreigners guarded jealously.

This one was crashing through the street. People fled. No one wanted to be around if a firefight broke out, especially with the armaments a typical cataphract was equipped with. It was five times taller than a human, with a stride that would have cratered the street with every step, all that mass crashing down onto surprisingly little feet if not for the bargains the manufacturers had made with the small gods of earth and stone.

What was a lone cataphract doing in this part of the city? A scout? A deserter? But what deserter in their right mind would bring something as easy to track as a cataphract with them?

Not my business. Alas, my delicious-looking soldier had vanished along with everyone else. And my bones were starting to hurt in the particular way that indicated that I had sustained human-shape too long.

On the other hand, while the cataphract's great strides made it faster than I was in this shape, distances had a way of accommodating themselves to a fox's desires. A dangerous idea took shape in my head. Why settle for a common soldier when I could have a cataphract pilot, one of the elites?

I ducked around a corner into the mouth of an alley, then kicked off my slippers, the only part of my dress that weren't spun from fox-magic. (Magical garments never lasted beyond a seduction. My mother had remarked that this was the fate of all human clothes anyway.) I loved those slippers, which I had purloined from a rich merchant's daughter, and it pained me to leave them behind. But I could get another pair of slippers later.

Anyone watching the transformation would only have seen a blaze of coalescing red, like fire and frost swirled together, before my bones re-settled into their native shape. Their ache eased. The night-smells of the city sharpened: alcohol, smoke, piss, the occasional odd whiff of stew. I turned around nine times—nine is a number sacred to foxes—and ran through the city's mazed streets.

The Lantern District receded behind me. I emerged amid rubble and the stink of explosive residue. The riots earlier in the year had not treated the Butterfly District kindly. The wealthier families had lived here. Looters had made short work of their possessions. I had taken advantage of the chaos as well, squirreling away everything from medicines to salt in small caches; after all, once I became human, I would need provisions for the journey to one of the safer cities to the south.

It didn't take long to locate the cataphract. Its pilot had parked it next to a statue, hunched down as if that would make it less conspicuous. Up close, I now saw why the pilot had fled—whatever it was they were fleeing. Despite the cataphract's menacing form, its left arm dangled oddly. It looked like someone had shot up the autocannon, and the cataphract's armor was decorated by blast marks. While I was no expert, I was amazed the thing still functioned.

The statue, one of the few treasures of the district to escape damage, depicted a courtesan who had killed an invading general a few centuries ago by clasping her arms around him and jumping off a cliff with him. My mother had remarked that if the courtesan had had proper teeth, she could have torn out the general's throat and lived for her trouble. Fox patriotism was not much impressed by martyrs. I liked the story, though.

I crouched in the shadows, sniffing the air. The metal reek of the cataphract overpowered everything. The small gods of earth and stone shifted and rumbled. Still, I detected blood, and sweat, as well as the particular unappetizing smell of what the humans called Brick Rations, because they were about as digestible. Human blood, human sweat, human food.

A smarter fox would have left the situation alone. While dodging the cataphract would be easy, cataphract pilots carried sidearms. For all I knew, this one would welcome fox soup as an alternative to Brick Rations.

While cataphract-piloting didn't strike me as a particularly useful skill, the pilots were all trained in the more ordinary arts of soldiering. Good enough for me.

I drew in my breath and took on human-shape. The small gods hissed their laughter. This time, when the pain receded, I was wrapped in a dress of green silk and a lavender sash embroidered with peonies. My hair was piled atop my head and held in place by heavy hairpins. The whole getup would have looked fashionable four generations ago, which I knew not because I had been alive then (although foxes could be long-lived when they chose) but because I used to amuse myself looking through Great-Aunt Seonghwa's collection of books on the history of fashion.

I'd hoped for something more practical, but my control of the magic had slipped. I would have to make the best of it. A pity the magic had not provided me with shoes, even ugly ones. I thought of the slippers I had discarded, and I sighed.

Carefully, I stepped through the street, pulse beating more rapidly as I contemplated my prey. A pebble dug into my foot, but I paid it no heed. I had endured worse, and my blood was up.

Even in human-shape, I had an excellent sense of smell. I had no difficulty tracking the pilot. Only one; I wondered what had happened to her copilot. The pilot lay on her side in the lee of a chunk of rubble, apparently asleep. The remains of a Brick Ration's wrapper had been tossed to the side. She had downed all of it, which impressed me. But then, I'd heard that piloting was hungry work.

I crouched and contemplated the pilot, taut with anticipation. At this distance, she reeked worse than her machine. She had taken off her helmet, which she hugged to her chest. Her black hair, cropped close, was mussed and stringy, and the bones of her face stood out too prominently beneath the sweat-streaked, dirty skin.

She'd also taken off her suit, for which I didn't blame her. Cataphracts built up heat—the gods of fire, being fickle, did an indifferent job of masking their infrared signatures—and the suits were designed to cool the pilot, not to act as armor or protect them against the chilly autumn winds. She'd wrapped a thermal blanket around herself. I eyed it critically: effective, but ugly.

No matter what shape I took, I had a weapon; there is no such thing as an unarmed fox. I wondered what the magic had provided me with today. I could feel the weight of a knife hanging from my inner sash, and I reached in to draw it out. The elaborate gilt handle and the tassel hanging from the pommel pleased me, although what really mattered was the blade.

I leaned down to slit the pilot's throat—except her eyes opened and she rolled, casting the helmet aside. I scrambled backwards, but her reflexes were faster, a novelty. She grabbed my wrist, knocking the knife out of my hand with a clatter, and forced me down.

"Well-dressed for a looter," the pilot said into my ear. "But then, I suppose that goes with the territory."

I had no interest in being lectured before my inevitable addition to a makeshift stewpot. I released human-shape in a flutter of evanescent silks, hoping to wriggle out of her grip.

No such luck. Almost as if she'd anticipated the change, she closed her hands around my neck. I snapped and clawed, to no effect. I had to get free before she choked the life out of me.

"*Gumiho*," the pilot breathed. Nine-tailed fox. "I thought all your kind were gone."

My attempt at a growl came out as a sad wheeze.

"Sorry, fox," the pilot said, not sounding sorry in the least.

I scrabbled wildly at the air, only half paying attention to her words.

"But I bet you can speak," she went on as I choked out a whine. "Which means you're just as likely to snitch to my pursuers as something fully human."

She was saying something more about her pursuers, still in that cheerful conversational voice, when I finally passed out.

I woke trussed up as neatly as a rabbit for the pot. The air was full of the strange curdled-sweet smell of coolant, the metal reek of cataphract, the pilot's particular stink. My throat hurt and my legs ached, but at least I wasn't dead.

I opened my eyes and looked around at the inside of the cockpit. The blinking lights and hectic status graphs meant nothing to me. I wished I'd eaten an engineer along the way, even though the control systems were undoubtedly different for different cataphract models. I'd been tied to the copilot's seat. Cataphracts could be piloted solo if necessary, but I still wondered if the copilot had died in battle, or deserted, or something else entirely.

The cockpit was uncomfortably warm. I worked my jaw but couldn't get a good purchase on the bindings. Worse, I'd lost the knife. If I couldn't use my teeth to get out of this fix—

"Awake?" the pilot said. "Sorry about that, but I've heard stories of your kind."

Great, I had to get a victim who had paid attention to grandmothers'-tales of fox spirits. Except now, I supposed, *I* was the victim. I stared into the pilot's dark eyes.

"Don't give me that," the pilot said. "I know you understand me, and I know you can speak."

Not with my muzzle tied shut, I can't, I thought.

As if she'd heard me, she leaned over and sawed through the bonds on my muzzle with a combat knife. I snapped at the knife, which was stupid of me. It sliced my gums. The familiar tang of blood filled my mouth.

"You may as well call me Jong," the pilot said. "It's not my real name, but my mother used to call me that, after the child and the bell in the old story. What shall I call you?"

I had no idea what story she was talking about. However, given the number of folktales living in small crannies of the peninsula, this wasn't surprising. "I'm a fox," I said. "Do you need a name for me beyond that?" It wasn't as though we planned on becoming friends.

Jong strapped herself in properly. "Well, you should be grateful you're tied in good and tight," she said as she manipulated the controls: here a lever, there a button, provoking balletic changes in the lights. "The straps weren't designed with a fox in mind. I'd hate for you to get splattered all over the cockpit when we make a run for it."

"So kind of you," I said dryly. Sorry, I thought to my mother's ghost. *I should have listened to you all those years ago.* Still, Jong hadn't eaten me yet, so there was hope.

"Oh, kindness has nothing to do with it." The cataphract straightened with a hiss of servos. "I can't talk to the gods of mountain and forest, but I bet you can. It's in all the stories. And the mountains are where I have to go if I'm going to escape."

Silly me. I would have assumed that a cataphract pilot would be some technocrat who'd disdain the old folktales. I had to go after one who knew enough of the lore to be dangerous. "Something could be arranged, yes," I said. Even as a kit my mother had warned me against trusting too much in gods of any kind, but Jong didn't need to know that.

"We'll work it out as we go," she said distantly. She wasn't looking at me anymore.

I considered worrying at the bonds with my teeth, even though the synthetic fibers would taste foul, but just then the cataphract shuddered awake and took a step. I choked back a yip. Jong's eyes had an eerie golden sheen that lit up their normal brown; side-effect of the neural interface, I'd heard, but I'd never seen the effect up close before. If I disrupted the connection now, who knew what would happen? I wasn't so desperate that I wanted the cataphract to crash into uselessness, leaving me tied up inside it while unknown hostiles hunted us. Inwardly,

I cursed Jong for getting me involved; cursed myself for getting too ambitious. But recriminations wouldn't help now.

For the first hour, I stayed silent, observing Jong in the hopes of learning the secrets of the cataphract's operation the old-fashioned way. Unfortunately, the closest thing to a cataphract pilot I'd ever eaten had been a radio operator. Not good enough. No wonder Great-Aunt Seonghwa had emphasized the value of a proper education, even if I had dismissed her words at the time. (One of her first victims had been a university student, albeit one studying classical literature rather than engineering. Back then, you could get a comfortable government post by reciting maxims from *The Twenty-Three Principles of Virtuous Administration* and tossing off the occasional moon-poem.) The ability to instantly absorb someone's skills by ingesting their liver had made me lazy.

"Why are they after you?" I asked, on the grounds that the more information I could extract from Jong, the better. "And who are they, anyway?"

She adjusted a dial; one of the monitors showed a mass of shapes like tangled thread. "Why are they after anyone?"

Not stupid enough to tell a stranger, then. I couldn't fault her. "How do I know you won't use me, then shoot me?"

"You don't. But I'll let you go after I get away."

Unsatisfying, as responses went. "Assuming you get away."

"I have to." For the first time, Jong's cheerfulness faltered.

"Maybe we can bargain," I said.

Jong didn't respond for a while, but we'd entered a defile and she was presumably caught up making sure we didn't tumble over some ledge and into the stony depths. I had difficulty interpreting what I saw. For one thing, I wasn't used to a vantage point this high up. For another, I couldn't navigate by scent from within the cockpit, although I was already starting to become inured to the mixed smells of grubby human and metal.

"What bargain can you offer?" Jong said when she'd parked us in a cranny just deep enough in the defile that the cataphract wouldn't be obvious except from straight above.

I wondered if we had aerial pursuit to worry about as well. Surely I'd hear any helicopters, now that the cataphract had powered down? I knew better than to rely on the small gods of wind and storm for warning; they were almost as fickle as fire.

Jong's breathing became unsteady as she squinted at a scatterfall of glowing dots. She swore under her breath in one of the country dialects that I could understand only with difficulty. "We'll have to hope that they're spreading themselves too thin to figure out which way we've gone," she said in a low voice, as though people could hear her from inside the cockpit. "We'll continue once I'm sure I can move without lighting up their scanners."

Carefully, I said, "What if I swear on the spirits of my ancestors to lead you where you need to go, with the aid of the small gods to mask your infrared signature?" This was a guess on my part, but she didn't correct me, so I assumed it was close enough. "Will you unbind me, at least?"

"I didn't think foxes worshiped ancestors," Jong said, eyeing me skeptically. She fished a Brick Ration out of a compartment and unwrapped it with quick, efficient motions.

My mouth watered despite the awful smell. I hadn't eaten in a while. "Foxes are foxes, not gods," I said. "What good is worship to a fox? But I remember how my mother cared for me, and my other relatives. Their memory means a lot to me."

Jong was already shaking her head. A crumb of the Brick Ration fell onto her knee. She picked it up, regarded it contemplatively, then popped it into her mouth.

A ration only questionably formulated to sustain humans probably wouldn't do me much good in fox-form, but it was difficult not to resent my captor for not sharing, irrational as the sentiment was.

"I need a real guarantee that you'll be helpful, not a fox-guarantee," Jong said.

"That's difficult, considering that I'm a fox."

"I don't think so." Jong smiled, teeth gleaming oddly in the cockpit's deadened lights. Her face resembled a war-mask from the old days of the Abalone Throne. "Swear on the blood of the tiger-sages."

My heart stuttered within me. "There are no tiger-sages left," I said. It might even have been true.

Jong's smile widened. "I'll take that chance."

When I was a young fox, almost adult, and therefore old enough to get into the bad kind of trouble, my mother took me to visit a tiger-sage.

Until then, I had thought all the tiger-sages had left the peninsula. Sometimes the humans had hunted them, and more rarely they sought the tigers' advice, although a tiger's advice always has a bite in it. I'd once heard of hunters bringing down an older tiger in a nearby village, and I'd asked my mother if that had been a sage. She had only snorted and said that a real sage wouldn't go down so easily.

Tiger-sages could die. That much I knew. But their deaths had nothing to do with shotguns or nets or poisoned ox carcasses. A tiger-sage had to be slain with a sword set with mirror-jewels or arrows fletched with feathers stolen from nesting firebirds. A tiger-sage had to be sung to death in a game of riddles during typhoon season, or tricked into sleep after a long game of *baduk*—the famously subtle strategy game played upon a board of nineteen-by-nineteen intersecting lines, with black stones and white. A tiger-sage had to consent to perish.

We traveled for days, because even a fox's ability to slice through distance dwindled before a tiger-sage's defenses. My mother was nervous than I'd ever seen her. I, too stupid to know better, was excited by the excursion.

At last we approached the tiger-sage's cave, high upon a mountain, where the trees grew sideways and small bright flowers flourished in the thin soil. Everything smelled hard and sharp, as though we lingered dangerously close to the boundary between *always* and *never*. The cave had once served as a shrine for some human sage. A gilded statue dominated the mouth of the cave, lovingly polished. It depicted a woman sitting cross-legged, one palm held out and cupping a massive pearl, the other resting on her knee. The skull of some massive tusked beast rested next to the statue. The yellowing bone had been scored by claw-marks.

The tiger-sage emerged from the cave slowly, sinuously, like smoke from a hidden fire. Her fur was chilly white except for the night-black stripes. She was supposed to be the last of the tiger-sages. One by one they had departed for other lands, or so the fox-stories went. Whether this one remained out of stubbornness, or amusement at human antics, or sheer apathy, my mother hadn't been able to say. It didn't matter. It was not for a fox to understand the motivations of a sage.

"Foxes," the tiger rumbled, her amber eyes regarding us with disinterest. "It is too bad you are no good for oracle bones. Fox bones always lie. The least you could have done was bring some incense. I ran out of the good stuff two months ago."

My mother's ears twitched, but she said only, "Venerable sage, I am here to beg your counsel on my son's behalf."

I crouched and tried to look appropriately humble, having never heard my mother speak like this before.

The tiger yawned hugely. "You've been spending too much time with humans if you're trying to fit all those flowery words in your mouth. Just say it straight out."

Normally my mother would have said something deprecating—I'd grown up listening to her arguing with Great-Aunt Seonghwa about the benefits of human culture—but she had other things on her mind. That, or the tiger's impressive display of sharp teeth reminded her that to a tiger, everything is prey. "My son hungers after human-shape," my mother said. "I have tried to persuade him otherwise, but a mother's words only go so far. Perhaps you would be willing to give him some guidance?"

The tiger caught my eye and smiled tiger-fashion. I had a moment to wonder how many bites it would take for me to end up in her belly. She reared up, or perhaps it was that she straightened. For several stinging moments, I could not focus my vision on her, as though her entire outline was evanescing.

Then a woman stood where the tiger had been, or something like a woman, except for the amber eyes and the sharp-toothed smile. Her hair was black frosted with white and silver. Robes of silk flowed from her shoulders, layered in mountain colors: dawn-pink and ice-white and pale-gray with a sash of deepest green. At the time I did not yet understand beauty. Years later, remembering, I would realize that she had mimicked the form of the last legitimate queen. (Tigers have never been known for modesty.)

"How much do you know of the traditional bargain, little fox?" the tiger-woman asked. Her voice was very little changed.

I did not like being called little, but I had enough sense not to pick a fight with a tiger over one petty adjective. Especially since the tiger was, in any shape, larger than I was. "I have to kill one hundred humans to become human," I said. "I understand the risk."

The tiger-woman made an impatient noise. "I should have known better than to expect enlightenment from a fox."

My mother held her peace.

"People say I am the last of the tiger-sages," the tiger-woman said. "Do you know why?"

"I had thought you were all gone," I said, since I saw no reason not to be honest. "Are you the last one?"

The tiger-woman laughed. "Almost the last one, perhaps." The silk robes blurred, and then she coiled before us in her native shape again. "I killed more than a hundred humans, in my time. Never do anything by halves, if you're going to do it. But human-shape bored me after a while, and I yearned for my old clothing of stripes and teeth and claws."

"So?" I said, whiskers twitching.

"So I killed and ate a hundred tiger-sages from my own lineage, to become a tiger again."

My mother was tense, silent. My eyes had gone wide.

The tiger looked at me intently. "If the kit is serious about this—and I can smell it on him, that taint is unmistakable—I have some words for him."

I stared at the tiger, transfixed. It could have pounced on me in that moment and I wouldn't have moved. My mother made a low half-growl in the back of her throat.

"Becoming human has nothing to do with flat faces and weak noses and walking on two legs," the tiger said. "That's what your people always get wrong. It's the hunger for gossip and bedroom entanglements and un-fox-ish loyalties; it's about having a human heart. I, of course, don't care one whit about such matters, so I will never be trapped in human-shape. But for reasons I have never fathomed, foxes always lose themselves in their new faces."

"We appreciate the advice," my mother said, tail thumping against the ground. "I will steal you some incense." I could tell she was desperate to leave.

The tiger waved a paw, not entirely benevolently. "Don't trouble yourself on my account, little vixen. And tell your aunt I warned her, assuming you get the chance."

Two weeks after that visit, I heard of Great-Aunt Seonghwa's unfortunate demise. It was not enough to deter me from the path I had chosen.

"Come on, fox," Jong said. "If your offer is sincere, you have nothing to fear from a mythical tiger."

I refrained from snapping that 'mythical' tigers were the most frightening of all. Ordinary tigers were bad enough. Now that I was old enough to appreciate how dangerous tiger-sages were, I preferred not to bring myself to one's attention. But remaining tied up like this wasn't appealing, either. And who knew how much time I had to extract myself from this situation?

"I swear on the blood of the tiger-sages," I said, "that I will keep my bargain with you. No fox tricks." I could almost hear the tiger-sage's cynical laughter in my head, but I hoped it was my imagination.

Jong didn't waste time making additional threats. She unbuckled herself and leaned over me to undo my bonds. I admired her deft hands. *Those could have been mine*, I thought hungrily; but I had promised. While a fox's word might not be worth much, I had no desire to become the prey of an offended tiger. Tiger-sages took oaths quite seriously when they cared to.

My limbs ached, and it still hurt when I swallowed or talked. Small pains, however, and the pleasure of being able to move again made up for them. "Thank you," I said.

"I advise being human if you can manage it," Jong said. I choked back a snort. "The seat will be more comfortable for you."

I couldn't argue the point. Despite the pain, I was able to focus enough to summon the change-magic. Magic had its own sense of humor, as always. Instead of outdated court dress, it presented me in street-sweeper's clothes, right down to the hat. As if a hat did anything but make me look ridiculous, especially inside a cataphract.

To her credit, Jong didn't burst out laughing. I might have tried for her throat if she had, short-tempered as I was. "We need to"—yawn—"keep moving. But the pursuers are too close. Convince the small gods to conceal us from their scan, and we'll keep going until we find shelter enough to rest for real."

Jong's faith in my ability to convince the small gods to do me favors was very touching. I had promised, however, which meant I had to do my best. "You're in luck," I said; if she heard the irony in my voice, she didn't react to it. "The small gods are hungry tonight."

Feeding gods was tricky business. I had learned most of what I knew from Great-Aunt Seonghwa. My mother had disdained such magic herself, saying that she would trust her own fine coat for camouflage instead of relying on gods, to say nothing of all the mundane stratagems she had learned from her own mother. For my part, I was not too proud to do what I had to in order to survive.

The large gods of the Celestial Order, who guided the procession of stars, responded to human blandishments: incense (I often wondered if the tiger I had met lit incense to the golden statue, or if it was for her own pleasure), or offerings of roast duck and tangerines, or bolts of silk embroidered with gold thread. The most powerful of the large gods demanded rituals and chants. Having never been bold enough to eat a shaman or magician, I didn't know how that worked. (I remained mindful of Great-Aunt Seonghwa's fate.) Fortunately, the small gods did not require such sophistication.

"Can you spare any part of this machine?" I asked Jong.

Her mouth compressed. Still, she didn't argue. She retrieved a screwdriver and undid one of the panels, joystick and all, although she pocketed the screws. "It's not like the busted arm's good for anything anymore," she said. The exposed wires and pipes of coolant looked like exposed veins. She grimaced, then fiddled with the wires' connectors until they had all been undone. "Will this do?"

I doubted the small gods knew more about cataphract engineering than I did. "Yes," I said, with more confidence than I felt, and took the panel from her. I pressed my right hand against the underside of the panel, flinching in spite of myself from the metal's unfriendly warmth.

This is my offering, I said in the language of forest and mountain, which even city foxes spoke; and my mother, as a very proper fox, had raised me in the forest. *Earth and stone and—*

Jong's curse broke my concentration, although the singing tension in the air told me that the small gods already pressed close to us, reaching, reaching.

"What is it?" I said.

"We'll have to fight," Jong said. "Buckle in."

I had to let go of the panel to do so. I had just figured out the straps—the cataphract's were more complicated than the safety restraints found in automobiles—and the panel clanked onto the cockpit's floor as the cataphract rumbled awake. The small gods skittered and howled, demanding their tribute. I was fox enough to hear them, even if Jong showed no sign of noticing anything.

The lights in the cockpit blazed up in a glory of colors. The glow sheened in Jong's tousled hair and reflected in her eyes, etched deep shadows around her mouth. The servos whirred; I could have sworn the entire cataphract creaked and moaned as it woke.

I scooped up the panel. Its edges bit into my palms. "How many?" I asked, then wondered if I should be distracting Jong when we were entering combat.

"Five," she said. "Whatever you're doing, finish it fast."

The machine lurched out of the crevice where we'd been hiding, then broke into its version of a run. My stomach dropped. Worse than the jolting gait was the fact that I kept bracing for the impact of those heavy metal feet against the earth. I kept expecting the cataphract to sink hip-deep. Even though the gods of earth and stone cushioned each stride, acting as shock-absorbers, the discrepancy between what I expected and what happened upset my sense of the world's equilibrium.

The control systems made noises that had only shrillness to recommend them. I left their interpretation to Jong and returned my attention to the small gods. From the way the air in the cockpit eddied and swirled, I could tell they were growing impatient. Earth and stone were allied to metal, after all, and metal, especially when summoned on behalf of a weapon, had its volatile side.

The magic had provided me not with a knife this time but with a hat pin. I retrieved it and jabbed my palm with the pointy end. Blood welled up. I smeared it onto the cataphract's joystick. *Get us out of here*, I said to the small gods. Not eloquent, but I didn't have time to come up with anything better.

The world tilted askew, pale and dark and fractured. Jong might have said something. I couldn't understand any of it. Then everything righted itself again.

More, the small gods said in voices like shuddering bone.

I whispered stories to them, still speaking in the language of forest and mountain, which had no words except the evocation of the smell of fallen pine needles on an autumn morning, or loam worked over by the worms, or rain filling paw prints left in the mud. I was still fox enough for this to suffice.

"What in the name of the blistering gods?" Jong demanded. Now even she could hear the clanging of distant bells. Music was one of the human innovations that the small gods had grown fond of.

"They're building mazes," I said. "They'll mask our path. *Go!*"

Her eyes met mine for a moment, hot and incredulous. Then she nodded and jerked a lever forward, activating the walk cycle. The cataphract juddered. The targeting screen flashed red as it locked on an erratically moving figure: another cataphract. She pressed a trigger.

I hunched down in my seat at the racket the autocannon made as it fired four shots in rapid succession, like a damned smith's hammer upon the world's last anvil. The small gods rumbled their approval. I forced myself to watch the targeting screen. For a moment I thought Jong had missed. Then the figure toppled sideways.

"Legged them," Jong said with vicious satisfaction. "Don't care about honor or kill counts, it's good enough to cripple them so we can keep running."

We endured several hits ourselves. While the small gods could confuse the enemies' sensors, the fact remained that the cataphract relied on its metal armor to protect its inner mechanisms. The impacts rattled me from teeth to marrow. I was impressed that *we* hadn't gone tumbling down.

And when had I started thinking of us as "we," anyway?

"We're doomed," I said involuntarily when something hit the cataphract's upper left torso—by the I'd figured out the basics of a few of the status readouts—and the whole cockpit trembled.

Jong's grin flickered sideways at me. "Don't be a pessimist, fox," she said, breathless. "You ever hear of damage distribution?"

"Damage what?"

"I'll explain it to you if we—" A shrill beep captured her attention. "Whoops, better deal with this first."

"How many are left?"

"Three."

There had been five to begin with. I hadn't even noticed the second one going down.

"If only I weren't out of coolant, I'd—" Jong muttered some other incomprehensible thing after that.

In the helter-skelter swirl of blinking lights and god-whispers, Jong herself was transfigured. Not beautiful in the way of a court blossom but in the way of a gun: honed toward a single purpose. I knew then that I was doomed in another manner entirely. No romance between a fox and a human ever ended well. What could I do, after all? Persuade her to abandon her cataphract and run away with me into the forest, where I would feed her rabbits and squirrels? No; I would help her escape, then go my separate way.

Every time an alert sounded, every time a vibration thundered through the cataphract's frame, I shivered. My tongue was bitten almost to bleeding. I could not remember the last time I had been this frightened.

You were right, Mother, I wanted to say. Better a small life in the woods, diminished though they were from the days before the great cities with their ugly high-rises, than the gnawing hunger that had driven me toward the humans and their beautiful clothes, their delicious shrimp crackers, their games of dice and *yut* and *baduk*. For the first time I understood that, as tempting as these things were, they came with a price: I could not obtain them without also entangling myself with human hearts, human quarrels, human loyalties.

A flicker at the edge of one of the screens caught my eye. "Behind us, to the right!" I said.

Jong made a complicated hooking motion with the joystick and the cataphract bent low. My vision swam. "Thank you," she said.

"Tell me you have some plan beyond 'keep running until everyone runs out of fuel,'" I said.

She chuckled. "You don't know thing one about how a cataphract works, do you? Nuclear core. Fuel isn't the issue."

I ignored that. Nuclear physics was not typically a fox specialty, although my mother had allowed that astrology was all right. "Why do they want you so badly?"

I had not expected Jong to answer me. But she said, "There's no more point keeping it a secret. I deserted."

"Why?" A *boom* just ahead of us made me clutch the armrests as we tilted dangerously.

"I had a falling out with my commander," Jong said. Her voice was so tranquil that we might have been sitting side by side on a porch, sipping rice wine. Her hands moved; moved again. A roaring of fire, far off. "Just two left. In any case, my commander liked power. Our squad was sworn to protect the interim government, not—not to play games with the nation's politics." She drew a deep breath. "I don't suppose any of this makes sense to you."

"Why are you telling me now?" I said.

"Because you might die here with me, and it's not as if you can give away our location any *more*. They know who I am. It only seems fair."

Typically human reasoning, but I appreciated the sentiment. "What good does deserting do you?" I supposed she might know state secrets, at that. But who was she deserting *to*?

"I just need to get to—" She shook her head. "If I can get to refuge, especially with this machine more or less intact, I have information the loyalists can make use of." She was scrutinizing the infrared scan as she spoke.

"The Abalone Throne means that much to you?"

Another alert went off. Jong shut it down. "I'm going to bust a limb at this rate," she said. "The Throne? No. It's outlived its usefulness."

"You're a parliamentarian, then."

"Yes."

This matter of monarchies and parliaments and factions was properly none of my business. All I had to do was keep my end of the bargain, and I could leave behind this vexing, heartbreaking woman and her passion for something as abstract as *government*.

Jong was about to add something to that when it happened. Afterwards I was only able to piece together fragments that didn't fit together, like shards of a mirror dropped into a lake. A concussive blast. Being flung backwards, then sideways. A sudden, sharp pain in my side. (I'd broken a couple ribs, in spite of the restraints. But without them, the injuries would have been worse.) Jong's sharp cry, truncated. The stink of panic.

The cataphract had stopped moving. The small gods roared. I moved my head; pain stabbed all the way through the back of my skull. "Jong?" I croaked.

Jong was breathing shallowly. Blood poured thickly from the cut on her face. I saw what had happened: the panel had flown out of my hands and struck her edge-on. The small gods had taken their payment, all right; mine hadn't been enough. If only I had foreseen this—

"Fox," Jong said in a weak voice.

Lights blinked on-off, on-off, in a crazed quilt. The cockpit looked like someone had upended a bucket full of unlucky constellations into it. "Jong," I said. "Jong, are you all right?"

"My mission," she said. Her eyes were too wide, shocky, the red-and-amber of the status lights pooling in the enormous pupils. I could smell the death on her, hear the frantic pounding of her heart as her body destroyed itself. Internal bleeding, and a lot of it. "Fox, you have to finish my mission. Unless you're also a physician?"

"Shh," I said. "Shh." I had avoided eating people in the medical professions not out of a sense of ethics but because, in the older days, physicians tended to have a solid grounding in the kinds of magics that threatened shape-changing foxes.

"I got one of them," she said. Her voice sounded more and more thready. "That leaves one, and of course they'll have called for reinforcements. If they have anyone else to spare. You have to—"

I could have howled my frustration. "I'll carry you."

Under other circumstances, that grimace would have been a laugh. "I'm dying, fox, do you think I can't tell?"

"I don't know the things you know," I said desperately. "Even if this metal monstrosity of yours can still run, I can't pilot it for you." It was getting hard to breathe; a foul, stinging vapor was leaking into the cockpit. I hoped it wasn't toxic.

"Then there's no hope," she whispered.

"Wait," I said, remembering; hating myself. "There's a way."

The sudden flare of hope in Jong's eyes cut me.

"I can eat you," I said. "I can take the things you know with me, and seek your friends. But it might be better simply to die."

"Do it," she said. "And hurry. I assume it doesn't do you any good to eat a corpse, or your kind would have a reputation as grave-thieves."

I didn't squander time on apologies. I had already unbuckled the harness, despite the pain of the broken ribs. I flowed back into fox-shape, and I tore out her throat so she wouldn't suffer as I devoured her liver.

The smoke in the cockpit thickened, thinned. When it was gone, a pale tiger watched me from the rear of the cockpit. It seemed impossible that she could fit; but the shadows stretched out into an infinite vast space to accommodate her, and she did. I recognized her. In a hundred stolen lifetimes I would never fail to recognize her.

Shivering, human, mouth full of blood-tang, I looked down. The magic had given me one last gift: I wore a cataphract pilot's suit in fox colors, russet and black. Then I met the tiger's gaze.

I had broken the oath I had sworn upon the tiger-sage's blood. Of course she came to hunt me.

"I had to do it," I said, and stumbled to my feet, prepared to fight. I did not expect to last long against a tiger-sage, but for Jong's sake I had to try.

"There's no 'have to' about anything," the tiger said lazily. "Every death is a choice, little not-a-fox. At any step you could have turned aside. Now——" She fell silent.

I snatched up Jong's knife. Now that I no longer had sharp teeth and claws, it would have to do.

"Don't bother with that," the tiger said. *She* had all her teeth, and wasn't shy about displaying them in a ferocious grin. "No curse I could pronounce on you is more fitting than the one you have chosen for yourself."

"It's not a curse," I said quietly.

"I'll come back in nine years' time," the tiger said, "and we can discuss it then. Good luck with your one-person revolution."

"I needn't fight it alone," I said. "This is your home, too."

The tiger seemed to consider it. "Not a bad thought," she said, "but maps and boundaries and nationalism are for humans, not for tigers."

"If you change your mind," I said, "I'm sure you can find me, in nine years' time or otherwise."

"Indeed," the tiger said. "Farewell, little not-a-fox."

"Thank you," I said, but she was gone already.

I secured Jong's ruined body in the copilot's seat I had vacated, so it wouldn't flop about during maneuvers, and strapped myself in. The cataphract was damaged, but not so badly damaged that I still couldn't make a run for it. It was time to finish Jong's mission.

"OWL VS. THE NEIGHBORHOOD WATCH"

DARCIE LITTLE BADGER

When Nina first met Owl-with-a-capital-O, harbinger of death, destruction, and despair, He resembled *Athene cunicularia*, a wee burrower. Owl perched on a twig outside her bedroom window as Nina toiled over seventh grade geometry homework. Between questions eleven and twelve, she glanced outside; yellow eyes met brown.

Owl tilted His head, as if puzzled.

That night, Nina fell asleep on a pile of pencil shavings and graphing paper. She dreamed that somebody replaced her nerves with puppet strings. The unseen puppeteer resisted every move she made, and Nina was still ensnared when sunlight tickled her eyes open. For weeks, her actions lagged, leaden, as if cement thickened in her marrow, her skull, and her heart-bearing chest.

Later, Nina learned the puppeteer's name: Depression.

Owl returned before the next depressive episode as *Bubo virginianus*, great horned owl. His yellow eyes were crowned by cowlick tufts. "Mom warned me about you," Nina said. "She says you appeared before Dad almost died. Don't visit anymore. Leave me alone!" She whisked the curtains shut.

Flower-printed cotton was an ineffectual shield against misery.

A year later, Owl came as *Strix nebulosa*, great gray. Dagger-sharp talons encircled the thickest branch outside her window, and His bulbous head blocked the moonlight. In His shadow, Nina whispered, "God. My God."

"Am I really?" Owl wondered. His melodious voice could belong to bird or man.

Nina gasped.

"Am I? Really?" He repeated. "Am I God?"

She screamed.

Nina's doctor prescribed mood stabilizers and warned her to get immediate help if birds spoke to her again.

"It's not a delusion," she said. "Owl comes with trouble. He's the flash of light before thunder. Stop treating Apache beliefs like they're superstitions. Would you tell a Christian that angels don't exist?"

"Have angels spoken to you recently, Nina?" Dr. Grigory asked.

"No!"

She never discussed Owl around doctors again.

During college—four-year, private, double major in biochemistry and philosophy—she rented an apartment in downtown Austin. The nearest tree branch grew a block away from her bedroom window. Maybe that's why it took a year for Owl to find her there. He arrived on two feet, His human-shaped disguise betrayed by round, yellow, too-large eyes. Owl-as-a-Man loitered outside her apartment, barefoot. From toes to brow, a white feather pattern rippled up His brown skin. The ghostly hospital gown He wore—*why a hospital gown?* Nina wondered—seemed at once too baggy for His body and too skimpy for the winter chill that night.

She opened her second-floor window and leaned outside. "Not now," Nina said. "Classes are going so . . ."

A waste of breath, pleading with Owl. Better spent sighing and crying. She exhaled a dissipating cloud above His upturned face.

"So what?" Owl asked. "Going so what? Poorly? Well?" When she did not answer, He laughed, a tittering sound, and strolled away. Owl rarely lingered.

As a new professor, Nina bought a house in forested Middle-of-Nowhere, Filly Lane. The neighborhood had owls, mostly *Tyto alba*, barn owls without barns. For a few years, Owl kept His distance.

One portentous night, restlessness swarmed through Nina's anthill-busy brain, down her spine, and through her veins. She paced. It wasn't enough. Nina slipped into a reflective jacket, grabbed a mini flashlight, and went jogging. Outside, a waning moon helped light her steps across the uneven dirt.

They who lived on Filly Lane, a winding, unpaved Appalachian road, shared little but a street name. Nina knew her neighbors by their mail-box labels and outdoor habits.

First, she passed the Kilpatrick home. The married couple, empty nesters, had a splendid lawn. Daily, Mrs. Nancy Kilpatrick worried over their roses and bluegrass, allaying the drought with a tin watering can. She rarely missed a chance to comment on the weather when Nina passed her in the garden.

Next lived Gorey: single man, forties. Nina rarely saw him.

Vaude: family of five. Matriarch Vaude, Patriarch Vaude, and their young daughters shared a two-story Victorian-style house that was built in 1980. The girls often played in the gigantic oak in their front lawn. A hammock and tire swing dangled from its boughs.

Wordsmith, two fathers and their son, occupied the last house on the lane. The teen walked his German Shepherd before and after school. Both boy and dog were exceptionally polite.

Nina saw few signs of life during her midnight jog. Moths battered against the Kilpatrick porch light. A raccoon scampered under the Go-rey jeep. One window in the Vaude household—second story, half-con-cealed by the oak—was bright, its light filtered by a pink curtain.

Filly Lane spilled down a tilted valley between two mountains. The incline accelerated Nina toward a dead end; where the road terminated, a narrow footpath plunged through the forest. When she first joined the neighborhood, Nina had investigated this trail. It went on for a quarter-mile and ended at a natural clearing peppered with empty beer cans and paintball shells. The desolation made her uncomfortable, so she had never returned.

Owl-as-a-Man stood at the threshold between forest and road, His eyes reflecting the flashlight beam. Recoiling, Nina mentally listed all the tragedies that might befall a jogger at night. "What have you come for?" she asked.

"I live in the beech tree."

"The beech tree?"

She'd seen several beeches near the clearing: old, branchy trees that probably supported dozens of bird species. "Since when?" she asked.

"Tonight. What are you doing here, Nina-I-Rarely-See-Anymore?"

"Filly Lane has been my home for *years*."

"Pity." Owl smiled, but the expression did not reach His eyes. None did. "I'm inclined to stay."

"Why? Are we in danger?" Nearby, the German shepherd barked, as if disturbed. She'd barely whispered the question; maybe the dog had keen ears. Or maybe Nina and Owl weren't the only ones outside. She swept her flashlight up the road: empty.

"Probably," Owl said.

"You can't be more specific?"

He tilted His head. "Supper time. Good luck, Nina." As Owl returned to the forest, His unfastened gown fluttered in a breeze that ran up the valley. The rippling pattern on His back resembled feathers.

"Don't need your kind of luck," Nina said, "*Schadenfreude* Featherface."

At home, she brewed coffee and listed catastrophes in her spare laboratory notebook.

One: contamination. Heavy metals, carcinogens, or toxic chemicals might poison the dirt and water. Unlikely, but easy to rule out.

Two: natural disaster. A tornado, flood, or wildfire could devour five houses in one violent sweep.

Three: human malice. Serial killers had to live somewhere.

Four: plague. Lyme disease was named after Lyme, Connecticut. What maladies bred in Filly Lane?

Five: something strange. Alien abductions, ghosts, goatmen.

"Might as well include meteors and evil clowns," she said, noticing a familiar silhouette beyond her bedroom window. "Right, Owl?"

"I do not understand the question."

Nina peeked through the half-cracked venetian blinds. Owl lounged on her ornamental balcony, snug between potted chrysanthemum plants. His hospital gown and face were sullied with blood, black speckles trailing from lips to chest.

She asked, "Why me?"

"Why anybody?"

"I've seen you a dozen times since seventh grade!" She snapped the blinds shut. "It's excessive! This is harassment!"

"At least I warn you," He cooed. "I warned you. I did. I warned you . . ." The voice became distant, a whisper that flew with the wind up Filly Lane.

"You didn't warn me. You teased me." How could one woman stop a plague, a serial killer, a forest fire? Mania, depression? Why did she always try?

Her zero-win record did not bode well for Filly Lane.

Maybe she should take a vacation until doom blew over. It was Memorial Day weekend, a perfect time for traveling. Unfortunately, Nina was haunted by four names: Kilpatrick, Vaude, Wordsmith, and Gorey.

How could she prepare them for a yet-unknown disaster? They weren't her undergraduate students; Dr. Nina Soto could not lecture the neighborhood about safety protocol.

She had to get creative.

Nina parked in front of her computer, opened a word processor and search engine, and typed:

Disaster preparedness
Ctrl-c
Ctrl-v
Forest fire safety
Ctrl-c
Ctrl-v
Emergency phone numbers
Ctrl-c
Ctrl-v
FBI most wanted
Roadside accident procedure
Common household risks
Snake bite treatment tornado flood first aid constitutional rights self-defense
carbon monoxide ammonia+bleach CPR lightning strike real zombies CDC

By sunrise, toting homemade educational booklets, Nina took to the street; a horn bleated furiously, and gravel sprayed her legs. She'd been one step away from death by Goodyear tire under the Kilpatrick minivan. "The limit is twenty-five miles per hour!" she shouted. "Twenty! Five! Not fifty!"

Why the hurry?

Murderer, burglar, car theft, trunk full of silverware and corpses? Either that, or one of the lovely Kilpatricks drove like a street racer.

Nancy was working in her garden, which ruled out the car theft theory. She clipped wilting roses from a hedgerow bush, dressed in overalls, white gloves, and a pink bandana.

"Good morning!" Nina called.

Nancy closed her shears and walked to the edge of her driveway. "You're awake early."

"It's strictly business." Nina held out a booklet. "I'm spreading safety protocol for the neighborhood watch preparedness initiative."

"We have a neighborhood watch?"

"Sure do! Any questions?"

Nancy flipped through the papers, her eyebrow cocked. "Fire safety. Emergency numbers. The proper way to sneeze?" She laughed. "You cover all the bases."

"If only that were true! Can I bother you for a soil sample?"

"Hm?"

"We're screening for toxins."

"Go ahead." She gestured to her lawn with the shears. "Just don't make a mess."

One sample later, Nina approached the next household. As she slipped a booklet in the red-paint-on-tin mailbox, the front door swung open. Gorey leaned outside, wearing nothing but a checkered bathrobe. He hollered, "That's a federal crime!"

"I just—"

"Not goddamn interested!"

"I'm your neigh—"

"Don't touch my mailbox!" He charged across the porch, and Nina fled before Gorey could pull a gun—or something worse—from his robe. She dropped his booklet on the curb; littering might be a crime, but was it a *federal* crime?

Thankfully, the rest of her neighbors were quiet, with one exception; the Wordsmith German shepherd barked when Nina approached his family's mailbox. She much preferred his outburst to Gorey's.

A lab tech from the university took the soil samples later that morning. "What am I looking for?" he asked.

"Everything," Nina said. "Lead, mercury, arsenic, cadmium, chromium, DDT, DDE, DDD, PCBs, TCE—"

"You live in a rural neighborhood, no known contact with commercial, industrial, or agricultural sources of contaminants. Don't expect much."

"What's the ETA?"

"Thursday," he said, "at the soonest. Dr. Soto, are you . . . is everything all right?"

She rubbed her eyes. "Just tired. Thanks for meeting me here."

"Any time." He chuckled dryly. "Wouldn't want to disappoint your neighborhood watch."

In the empty-handed, idle lull after the drop-off, Nina wondered how safety booklets and a soil test could accomplish any good whatsoever. She ordered hash browns and coffee from a McDonald's near campus and brooded over her breakfast.

How could she defy Owl's intuition? How could anyone? If, like the flash of light before thunder, Owl was inextricable from disaster, she was attempting the Sisyphean. Nina felt the piles of her hope collapsing. Desperate, she called the only number on speed-dial. After two rings, a groggy voice asked, "Honey? Are you okay?"

"Hi Mom. I need a favor."

"Oh no . . ."

"Nothing big! Remember when you saved Dad's life? Can you tell me about it again?"

A pause. "Are you hearing birds talk? Should we call somebody?"

"Christ. No."

"Right." She did not sound convinced. "I wish you'd visit more often. I'm cooking pancakes for brunch."

"Work has been hectic. Next weekend. Promise. Pancakes sound fantastic." Nina dabbed grease from her hash brown with a napkin. "Now, about Dad . . ."

"What do you want me to say? He got carbon monoxide poisoning in the garage. I left work early and saved his life."

"Why did you leave work early?"

"I never should have told you about—"

"Owl, right?"

"A bird landed on the fence outside my office window. Coincidences happen."

"That's not what you said fifteen years ago."

"Oh?"

"Owl's pupils were like holes in the fabric of your life, a reflection of the dismal future He foresaw. Dad did not answer the phone when you called. Something was wrong. You sped home, opened the garage door, and dragged his limp body outside. Another minute, he would've died."

"If you know the story so well, why call?"

"Maybe I just wanted to hear your voice."

Another pause. "It's good to hear yours, too."

"Next weekend."

"We'll be expecting you."

"Mom?"

"Yes?"

"I love you."

As Nina returned to Filly Lane, she drove past the Wordsmith teen and his dog. Slowing to a crawl she called, "Afternoon!" through her cracked window.

"Afternoon, Ma'am!" He pointed at a single gray cloud over the forest. "Looks like rain! Bad news for Memorial cookouts, right?"

Nina thought: *worst drought of the century, the earth is kindling, barbeque overturns, neighborhood burns.* "It's smart to move everything indoors. There's nothing worse than soggy burgers."

"Yes, ma'am!"

She parked in her driveway and staggered inside. The all-nighter grogginess had transformed into a headache; left untended, it might reach migraine territory. She curled on her queen-sized bed. A nap usually helped.

Would the terrible thing happen as she dreamed?

Would a migraine render her helpless?

Would the terrible thing come during daytime?

Or, like Owl, would it emerge at night?

She should set an alarm. But she was already sleeping.

Six hours later, Nina woke to inquisitive knocks against her windowpane. Red streaks marked the glass and hovered in front of Owl's faux human face. Nina opened the window wide. "Come in," she said.

Owl hopped over the window ledge, His head swiveling side-to-side. His hands were bloody from fingertips to wrists. No blood on His mouth tonight; maybe the prey escaped.

"Why do you insult me and your mother?" He asked. "She all but begged you to visit. Pancakes are delicious, Nina."

"How do you know that?"

"Pancakes? I once—"

"No. Our conversation was private."

He pointed at His ears. "Every scream, every whisper."

"So you *are* God."

"There are no gods. I'm certain. Or I'd hear their voices, too." He par-
odied a smile. Eyes too round, mouth too wide. "While we're sharing
secrets: your father should have died thirty-four years ago."

"You'd love that, huh?"

"It's what he wanted."

"Dad's very happy now."

"Ha!" Owl wiped His hands on His formless cotton smock.

"Why do you wear a hospital gown?" Nina asked. "It looks ridiculous."

"It's a uniform of infirmity. Nina, your ancestors never asked such
obvious questions. They barely spoke to me at all! When did you forget
to be afraid?"

"I am afraid," she said, "of the badness you precede."

"What if," He said, "badness and I are one and the same?"

"Are you?" she asked. "That's the only secret I need to know."

Thunder cracked. The doorbell rang.

"It begins," Owl said, and He fell into the night.

"Thanks." Nina slipped into tennis shoes, grabbed her mini flashlight,
and ran downstairs. Half the neighborhood stood on her porch. Nancy,
Teen Wordsmith, the Wordsmith fathers, the German Shepherd, both
Vaude parents, and the two youngest Vaude girls. At least none carried
pitchforks. "Can I help you?" Nina asked.

"Have you . . . has the neighborhood watch seen Abigail?" Nancy asked.

"Abigail?"

Father Vaude held out his phone to show Nina a photograph of a
ten-year-old girl with blond curls. "My daughter," he explained.

"She's missing? How long?"

"Abby went to her room after supper, around seven. We just noticed
she's gone."

"Three hours," Nina said. "Maybe less."

"Her phone is missing, too!" Mother Vaude added.

"Well, have you seen her?" Nancy asked.

Nina rubbed her forehead. It felt bruised, and the ruckus threatened
to revive sharper aches. "I . . . the neighborhood watch hasn't noticed
any unusual behavior tonight."

"What use are you, then?" cried Mother Vaude. Her daughters
clutched her knitted cardigan sleeves, their eyes wet. Nina felt moisture
on her face, too; it was drizzling. A wall of strobe-light-flashing, rumbling clouds drenched the forest as a thunderstorm spilled up the valley.

"Call the police," Nina said.

"Is Abby lost?" One of the children asked, her voice hitching from meek distress to wailing dismay between "Abby" and "lost."

"What's their number?" Nancy rummaged in her pink fanny pack.

"It's in here." Teen Wordsmith flipped through the safety booklet Nina had distributed earlier.

"Nine-one-one!" Mother Vaude shouted. "This is an emergency!" As both children wept, thunder hummed through Nina's skull. Frankly, she was surprised that the German shepherd wasn't howling.

He barked earlier that day, when Nina approached the Wordsmith mailbox.

He also barked the night she met Owl.

"Quiet!" Nina said. "I need to think! Please, shh!"

Whether influenced by her tone or respect for the neighborhood watch, everyone, even the children, hushed.

"What makes your dog bark?" Nina asked Teen Wordsmith.

"Doorbells, vacuum cleaners, the mailman—"

"Intruders. He never barks when I jog past your house, but the moment somebody crosses property lines . . . Does Abby have a treehouse in the forest? Maybe in a beech tree?"

"No," Father Vaude said. "We don't allow her to play there."

Teen Wordsmith raised his hand. "I've seen one near the fire pit. It was just old planks wedged between branches. Something a kid might build. Maybe she sneaks out?"

"She'd have to cut across your backyard to reach the forest. Hm. The neighborhood watch has good reason to believe that Abigail does that often." No time to waste: Nina sprinted toward the maelstrom. Wind-muffled voices called her name, demanding an explanation; half the mob followed her down the street. Was she leading them to the death Owl foresaw? Abigail's death? Their own deaths?

Nina lengthened her strides to outpace them all. It was easy; she'd been training since seventh grade, driven by screaming thoughts, less escaping than coping. Running helped. Her pills did, too. She had to believe that she could help Abigail.

The forest met her like a wall. Its canopied bodies muffled the wind, the rain, the distant voices, and the pulsing thunder. "Abby!" she shouted. "Abigail! Can you hear me?" The storm responded with a mocking shriek. She leaped over a branch that had fallen across the path; its twigs brushed her legs, grasping. Thunder cracked. A flash quickly followed.

The lightning was near.

Across the clearing, near a beech tree, lay a pink-clothed body. Abigail: face-down, soaked, her blonde hair tangled with loam and cloying blood. "She's hurt!" Nina shouted, running to the child. "Can anybody hear me? Help!" Aside from quick, wheezing breaths, Abigail did not move, and Nina was afraid to jostle her, lest she worsen a neck injury. It looked like Abigail slipped and fell from the ramshackle treehouse.

"Can you hear me, kiddo?" Nina asked. "Your family's coming. Everything will be fine."

That's when she saw them: three punctures on the back of Abigail's neck. As if she'd been attacked by a beast with claws. Or *talons*.

"Owl, why?" Nina asked, turning, finding Him waiting there, behind her, dressed in His human skin and hospital gown. The rain had washed the blood from His hands.

"Will you save a life tonight?" He asked. Bristling feathers unfurled from His skin. Black talons filleted His wide feet as they emerged. "*Yes?* Then why am I here?"

His eyes moons, His feathers knives, Owl enveloped Nina and Abigail with circus tent wings. The forest trembled, bent. Nina saw her reflection in His pupils; the blackness swallowed her.

Rain still pattered against her upturned face.

"You're just a bird," she said. "All this time."

Nina hefted Abigail over her shoulder and sprinted through Owl's swollen, bladed chest. It parted like mist. She crossed the clearing. Paused to look over her shoulder.

Athene cunicularia, a wee burrower, huddled on the ground, nearly buried by slick leaves. He winked.

Cr-ACK!

Light engulfed Him. The lightning that struck the beech tree was so close, its voice and flash reached Nina nearly simultaneously.

In the silence that followed, Abby whispered, "I fell."

"It happens," Nina said. "You survived."

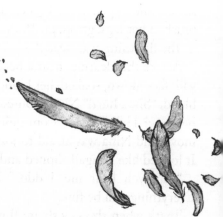

"HOW TO SURVIVE
AN EPIC JOURNEY"

TANSY RAYNER ROBERTS

———————————————— Fill my cup with wine, girl. Pass the
honey cakes, and I shall tell you a tale of
adventure and heroes. I was there. I knew them all.

(1)

Meleager liked to think it was for his sake that I ran away from home
and joined the crew of the *Argo*. Ours, he believed, was the kind of epic
love that bards sing about from one age to the next.

He even believed this sober.

I loved him well enough, but I had no illusions about how our song
would end. He had a wife at home, for all he pretended otherwise.

No matter. With Meleager warming my side at night, the rest of the
crew kept their hands to themselves, and I was able to make the most
of the adventure I stole for myself.

I signed my name to that enterprise for love, yes, but not love of a
man. I fell in love with a ship: the *Argo*, a beautiful lady in the hands of
a captain who never deserved her.

Jason is remembered as a hero, and I do not dispute that. But I think
perhaps the definition of the word "hero" has shifted over the years.

We all know men like Jason. He was tall and muscled and golden: it
was easy to believe he was favored of the gods.

The gods have shit taste when it comes to picking favorites.

I should have known there was something wrong with him from the
first—you can tell a man's worth by how he treats his servants. Our

Jason was busy flogging an oarsman when Meleager first led me to the dock at Iolcus.

Young and thirsty for adventure, I ignored the warning signs. By the time I had the full measure of Jason as a captain and as a man, I had already fallen for the *Argo*: hook, line and sinker. I would have put up with any amount of bullshit to be part of her maiden voyage.

Jason ruined everything for his crew: the quest, the prize, even the legend that followed. We hoped to do great deeds, and be remembered as ...

Yes, all right, I'll say it. Heroes.

Instead we ended up as supporting characters in Jason's tragic romance with himself. Sometimes, we are not even that. I myself am often cast out of the Argonaut legend because the idea that Jason might have allowed a woman on board a ship is beyond the pale. (Hesiod, I'm looking at you.)

Everything that Jason did, all those stories testifying to his selfishness and excess, and you fucking poets think risking a maid's virginity is where he might have drawn a moral line?

I am Atalanta of Arcadia, and I was there. My life map allowed two possible roles: to be a spinster princess or a married princess. I chose a third.

I chose to be an Argonaut.

(2)

I did not care a wet fart about the Golden Fleece. To sail and to fight, to be a comrade alongside my fellow adventurers, was all I ever wanted. The Fleece was an excuse, a story to sail ourselves into: it could as easily have been a monster to slay, a crown to collect, or a stable to scrub clean.

It was Jason who believed that the treasure gave us purpose.

As the *Argo* neared Colchis, we rescued four sailors from a wreck and they asked us whither we were bound. We told them, and they were surprised.

"You know the king of Colchis is an eccentric host," said one.

"He claims to be son of Helios," said another, with a smirk that suggested he did not believe the tale. "And he punishes those who challenge that claim."

"You're not mocking the gods, are you?" my shipmate Perseus demanded. He was one of at least three sons of Zeus on the voyage, not including Herakles who had abandoned us weeks earlier.

"Nay, friend, but when a king wears a golden hat with spikes and regularly descends into his throne room on a string and pulley so as to pretend he is the sun itself . . ."

We all agreed that it would be hard to keep a straight face with such antics going on.

"My crew and I are on a quest to steal the Golden Fleece so that I can reclaim my father's throne," Jason declared proudly.

The four sailors stared at him a long while and then, in unison, laughed so hard they were nearly sick.

This did not bode well for our quest.

(3)

Jason claimed that Herakles jumped ship in pursuit of a lover. We knew better than to believe our captain's lies by then.

There had been blazing rows between the two heroes, and not only when they were in their cups. Herakles believed a hero should do more than collect shiny trinkets and kiss up to royalty. (This was rich, frankly, coming from him.)

Jason, as royalty himself, took those insults personally, and insulted Herakles in turn for his treatment of women. (I know. Believe me. The hypocrisy did not go unnoted.)

A crew cannot survive with two captains. We owed Jason our loyalty even if most of us agreed that Herakles would make a better leader.

So Herakles left and the boy Iolaus scurried after him. The *Argo* was lighter and quieter with them gone. No one argued with Jason for a while, and the next time we slew a sea monster, we toasted the name of our good friend, Herakles the hero.

He met a bad end, of course, but not before Jason met his.

(4)

Let me tell you about this hero of ours, captain of the beautiful *Argo* (seriously, that ship was spectacular, it breaks my heart the way she ended).

On the isle of Lemnos, Jason seduced the local queen, only to abandon her with a thickened waistline. I don't mean that he baked her a nice cake before we stole out in the dead of night without paying for a winter's worth of bed and board. I mean he knocked her up.

It was a terrible winter. Our mast cracked in two places, and there's only so much you can do to repair wind damage to sails before there's nothing left of them at all.

Thus we arrived on Lemnos: the isle of women, surrounded by a stormy sea. All their men had left, in boats that never returned.

While Jason negotiated for us to winter on Lemnos, our heroic Argonauts joked that it was the women's hairy legs, or their smell, that sent their men packing. This was a fishing island, and I can tell you now that the smell of fish scale and bone had nothing to do with the women.

We could have been happy there, Meleager and I. We learned to fish, and it was easy enough to forget about my lover's own abandoned bride while we were so far from home. But adventure called, spring awoke, and thanks to Jason's honeyed promises to the queen (who still believed they would marry before her babe was born) we had to slide the *Argo* into the water under cover of darkness and make away in secret.

Jason laughed that night about his narrow escape, and I seethed at him in silence. For love of the *Argo* and the quest ahead of us, I said nothing.

No hero ever claimed to be a good person.

(5)

Let me explain more about Jason.

You would think he had been born to the crown, that his childhood was all pomp and silk cushions and "your Majesty" and sweetmeats, every inch of wealth and privilege ever extended to a child. A life like the one I ran away from, as fast and far as I could.

In truth, Jason was raised far from all that. The son of a usurped king, he was hidden as a baby, raised by peasants or by centaurs, depending on which story you believe.

My money is on centaurs. There was nothing humble about our Jason: he was all piss and arrogance. Every step he took was in the expectation of an embroidered carpet sliding beneath his foot. No peasant-raised creature would ever behave thus.

When he came of age, Jason presented himself to the kingdom of Iolcus in Thessaly to claim his father's throne, armed with fairy stories and a sharp sword. This was inconvenient for everyone, not least his uncle Pelias who was enjoying the job of king.

Jason had lost a sandal on his journey while helping an old woman (possibly the goddess Hera) across a river. Clytius of Troy reckoned it was more likely Jason lost the sandal while shagging a wine maiden. You can guess for yourself which version sounds more authentic to my ear.

An oracle had warned King Pelias he would be killed by a man with one shoe, so he was never going to embrace his nephew in friendship. Destiny and paranoia collided.

"What would you do, dear boy, if a man came before you whom the oracles had foretold would be your murderer?" the wicked uncle asked Jason over a cup of wine.

Jason, never the quickest ship in the fleet, wiped wine off his mouth and said "Give him an impossible task that will see him killed; or at the least, out of your hair for a year or three."

How they laughed.

The next day, Jason was sent on his epic voyage to claim the Golden Fleece, and prove his worth.

Would I have joined the crew if I knew our quest was deemed impossible long before I even reached Thessaly? Hells yes. I would have fought a dragon for a chance to fly the *Argo* across the waves. I would fight a dragon for that ship still, if she was prepared to wait a little longer for me to lay my old-lady cane down and ready myself.

If she still sailed; the *Argo* never got a chance to become a crone like me.

Putting up with Jason was a price worth paying, or so I thought back then. I had no idea how steep the price would rise.

(6)

So, there we were in the waters of Colchis, finally. We arrived, tired and hungry, presenting ourselves as friendly travelers seeking royal hospitality from a dangerous king. Our mission: to steal his most precious and beloved treasure.

I know what you're thinking right now. You're thinking, "What is the worst possible thing Jason could have done to sabotage this difficult and sensitive task?"

How exactly did Jason of Thessaly fuck it up?

I present the following evidence: The King of Colchis had a daughter. A young, barely marriageable and voluntarily chaste daughter.

The epic poem writes itself, doesn't it?

Medea reminded me of myself. She was a princess who would rather be anywhere than her father's palace. She wanted to escape, and in

Jason she saw a handsome, golden prince straight out of a children's tale. She saw a hero.

She was smart, Medea, but young, and she crumbled beneath the golden boy's charm. She became our secret weapon—we would never have got past the dragon or escaped the city without her.

Later, years later, Jason claimed that Medea's love for him was a gift from the gods; if that is true, then he is not the only one in debt to Aphrodite.

I would be dead, were it not for our quiet, dark-eyed princess and her skills of healing. Medea saved me.

If only she could have saved herself.

(7)

The worst part of that night . . .

I can't speak of it yet, give me a moment to gird my strength.

We ran, Argonauts all, back to our ship with the stolen Fleece and the stolen princess. There were shouts and cries and torches, and we knew how badly we had gone astray.

King Aëetes was going to kill and eat us all, and who could blame him?

Two hard-faced young warriors with fine clothes and expensive swords—Medea's brothers—met us at the dock, ready to kill us all. My Meleager and Perseus and the others stepped up to fight at Jason's side.

I was already hurt, having taken the kind of slow wound you don't recover from, while our fearless leader was seducing his new girl.

Our heroic crew made short work of the princes and left them bleeding out on the ground. We had to step over the bodies to make the ship ready: ropes and sails flying through our hands.

I dragged the Fleece aboard, wretched and foul-smelling thing that it was.

Medea stood on the docks, wrapped in her shawl. Jason hovered on the gangplank of the *Argo*, his hand outstretched and faltering. Did she want to join us or not?

"We should bring the bodies," she said finally. "My father is a superstitious man. If we separate their limbs and scatter them in the seas, our pursuers will be delayed by trying to restore the bodies of the princes."

We all stared at her. What a mind she had, to come up with such a plan: devious and devastating.

"Make haste!" Jason cried, hauling Medea aboard. He gave the orders to seize the bodies and bring them on deck.

It was foul work that we did, butchering those corpses and dropping the pieces one by one in the waters of the shallow shores of the Aegean.

True to Medea's prediction, the men of Colchis collected our grisly gift, piece by piece, and risked drowning to plunge after the pieces that floated further and further away.

We sailed to safety.

"A strange people," Jason said later, his eyes on the princess as she worked on my belly, smearing the neatly stitched wound with a poultice that stung my eyes with its fumes. I would not die after all. Her hands were cool as she worked; her face professional.

Medea had served Hekate since she was six years old. Her skills went beyond a talent for potions and creams. She was witch, sorceress, priestess. She was more dangerous than anyone on our ship.

Jason saw only a girl that he wished to possess.

I lay back on the ship's deck, in a haze of sweet-smelling drugs and the smell of my own blood, while Medea saved my life. Through my heavy eyelids, I observed the princess, that angry, powerful, dead-inside witch, and I thought: that girl needs a friend.

(8)

Never let Meleager tell you the story of the golden apples, especially when he's drunk.

It is not his story to tell.

The story of the apples belonged to a younger, prettier man: Hippomenes of Thebes. Hippomenes Fleet-Foot. Hippomenes Sharp-Wits.

I had already run away from home once by the time I was sixteen. I joined the great Hunt for the Calydonian Boar, a monster set upon the world by a vengeful Artemis. This was my first taste of what it was to be a hero: the Hunt was full of men desperate to earn a line or two for themselves in an epic ballad.

Men, and me.

King Oeneus of Calydon called for heroes to save his kingdom from the rampaging beast; he forgot to specify that those heroes be male. When I arrived with my bow and leathers, many so-called adventurers refused to join the hunt if a woman came along. Meleager, son of King Oeneus, was in charge of listing our names, and he thought it a grand old joke to let me play.

It was less of a joke when my arrow found the Boar first: fourteen of us brought the creature down in the final battle, but I had made first touch and thus, when the spoils were divided, I won the hide.

Meleager placed it around my shoulders and winked at me; I lifted my chin and thought myself dignified because I did not let him charm me into his bed. (Not then, at least, not yet.)

My furious father dragged me home to Arcadia. He demanded I marry like a proper princess, or dedicate my chastity to the gods—anything but live the life of adventure I had barely begun to taste.

Over-confident with the smell of fresh-killed boar hide still lingering in my hair, I pledged to my father this: I would marry any prince who bested me in a foot-race.

No prince was that fast.

I saw off dozens of suitors, all embarrassed and limping by the end of their travails, but it was Hippomenes who got the better of me.

This is the story that Meleager tells (that all men tell, when they repeat it): Hippomenes tossed golden apples before me as we ran, and thinking myself unbeatable, I allowed myself to be distracted by the pretty trinkets.

A princess after all: soft and weak for beautiful objects, for the gifts of the gods.

In truth: he did not throw apples, but rocks. There was no godly work in this. He broke my leg.

I never saw my father so furious as when he exiled Hippomenes from the kingdom; never saw him so guilt-ridden, so completely on my side.

So I asked a boon of him: to let me have my quest, as all heroes do, before they settle down. I almost had him convinced. But my father could not imagine a world in which a woman was a hero without being raped and ruined. He refused me.

Once my leg healed good and straight, I stole myself all over again. This time, my father did not catch me. I found Meleager, and Jason, and the *Argo*.

Atalanta of Arcadia sailed into adventure, and never looked back.

(9)
Ours was no grand romance. Meleager and I simply fell in with each other. I liked his wit; he liked the swing of my hips and my bold talk.

He thought himself in love; I did not challenge the notion.

If Meleager were not married already, I might have given in to the notion of being a wife: I liked the idea of a husband who could be friend and travel companion. His hands were warm and clever in the dead of night, while our friends slept around us on the deck. A future together would have been amiable.

But he was not free, and I was no Medea; there would be no poisoning of my lover's wife.

(That horror was still in her future, as the *Argo* creaked around us, carrying us home.)

Medea made a good companion. She charmed the men with cheerful prophecies of their noble futures. She made a herbal soup that made us all merry and filled our bellies with cheer.

As my mortal wound healed, I watched Medea blossom into the role of Jason's wife. Happiness suited her.

We faced monsters on the way back to Thessaly. Medea hypnotized them, and made them bleed. We grew comfortable and lazy as her powers steered us safely home.

She was heavily pregnant by the time we stepped ashore in the city where it all started. Pregnancy did not slow her down in the least; her fierce loyalty meant that she was already calculating how best to support her man.

There was a parade in Iolcus for the returned prince: Jason was given the people's ovation. He waved the Golden Fleece with one hand, and clutched his stolen princess with the other. We followed in his wake, his Argonauts, waiting for the pomp to end so we could escape.

He had promised his ship to us. He would need the *Argo* no longer, when he replaced his uncle as king. We stayed for every feast and celebration, while King Pelias grew harder of face and stiffer of shoulder.

Meleager danced with me, wine on his breath and hands warm on my hips. "We're not getting that ship," he whispered, and I saw that his eyes were not as glassy as I had believed. "We have to leave, tonight."

"But he promised us the *Argo*," I replied in my own furious whisper.

"Jason's going to need her to escape with his life," Meleager whispered back. "Look at them all."

Above the celebrations, King Pelias and his daughters watched a would-be usurper dance his way across their banquet hall.

I loved the *Argo*, but I wasn't stupid enough to die for her. "You're right," I conceded. "We don't want to be here for what happens next."

(10)

Here is what happened to Meleager: after many adventures: animals hunted, monsters slain, treasures found, he begged his lover Atalanta to return home with him and be his mistress while he filled his wife with a new generation of royal babies.

Atalanta refused politely, and they parted on good terms.

Meleager died many years later, in a fire that may or may not have been a curse from the gods. His family line continued. He had allowed his daughter to learn the bow and the knife; a better choice on whole than when he arranged for his sister Deineira to marry Herakles.

Heroes make the worst husbands.

What of Atalanta?

I took my own share of the spoils we won together and went to Argus, builder of the original *Argo*, and one of our former shipmates. I commissioned a ship: the *Calydonian Boar*. She was a splendid craft, small enough to manage with a minimal crew.

I sailed into adventure.

Sometimes, I heard word of the Argonauts: of Herakles and his labors; of Laertes, father of Odysseus, of Perseus and Castor and Deucalion and all the rest.

The stories of Jason and Medea were the worst: they left murder and misery in their wake. King Pelias' daughters became convinced that Medea's herbs and spells were enough to heal their father of his silver hair and the pains of age, when in fact the best choice for his health would have been to give up the throne and live in comfortable retirement.

Medea's spells went wrong; Pelias died. The anger of the people sent Jason and his witch wife into exile. They went to Corinth, I heard. Corinth, a bright and prosperous city which had need of a new king, as long as he did not mind setting Medea aside to marry a nubile young princess.

Jason, you will be shocked to learn, did not mind that in the least.

(11)

Long after the fellowship of the *Argo* ended, there were times when I missed Medea. It might seem strange to you, that I liked the woman; she was clearly a monster. And yet, there were many who thought the same of me.

We lived in a world that did not allow women to breathe; how could we be anything but monsters?

Medea saved my life. She sang songs that made the wind catch the sails faster. Her soup was delicious. I could use a witch like her on my crew, were she not busy with her children and her errant failure of a husband.

Years passed, and I did not hear from her. I hoped she had found happiness.

I had my own happiness: wind in my hair, wood firm under my feet, salt in my teeth. I had a crew willing to take orders from a female captain as long as I paid them well and looked the other way when they spent my gold on whores and wine.

One day, I received a letter that broke my heart. It said: *My children are dead, and Corinth wants me dead too.*

I went to rescue Medea. Of course I did. That's what friends do.

Jason's new bride Creusa was murdered. The method was a poisoned dress: a wedding "gift" to the woman who stole Medea's husband. The people of Corinth hounded Medea out of the city. They hurled stones at her that did not find their mark, because she had doused herself in hasty protection spells.

The stones rebounded on her children.

Now she was alone and heart-sick, a prisoner of her own grief.

She was a monster, they said, for of course the city claimed that she had killed the children herself, in vengeance against Jason.

"I did not expect you to come," she said when I broke open the lock on her prison door. "I do not deserve to survive this, Atalanta."

"Suffer if you must," I told her calmly. "But don't do it here. I have need of a witch on my crew. The pay is decent, and you will be far from that ass you once called husband."

Medea frowned at me, as if she did not quite understand. "They failed to kill me. I thought you might do it. You were always the noble one, of that whole crew. Your arrows fly the straightest."

I rolled my eyes at her. "If you must die, do it battling a monster or facing down an endless whirlpool of terror, like a normal person."

"Like a hero," Medea scoffed.

I took her hand, and led her out into the sunshine. "If Jason counts as a hero, anyone can."

(12)

This is the story of the *Argo*, and how she died.

Of all Jason's failings, this is the worst: he let his ship rot. She could have survived for generations if he took proper care of her, but without children to carry on his blood, Jason grew bitter and more selfish.

He lived out his later years deep in his cups, allowing the greatest ship of our age to fall to wrack and ruin.

We grew old too, Medea and I; past the age of motherhood, we settled for being sailors and adventurers. The *Calydonian Boar* wintered on Circe's island every year, so that Medea could learn from her aunt, the greatest sorceress who ever lived. It helped, I think. Circe gave Medea a peace she had never known, the forgiveness of her last surviving family member, and the companionship of a woman who knew how to read and write and think deep thoughts.

I spent those winters wandering the island during the day, gamboling with sheep and goats, and reading epic poetry. In the evenings, we drank wine, ate cake, and told stories of our adventures to entertain our hostess. Sometimes a boat would deliver supplies from the mainland: honey, oil, spices, and the snippets of news and gossip that Circe was always keen to pay for.

I had heard about Meleager's own untimely demise exactly like this, three winters earlier.

Now Medea read aloud to us by candlelight. "Jason's dead," was all she said and then: "Oh, the *Argo*," as if her heart was breaking.

I have never loved her more.

Circe snatched the parchment from her niece. "Her mast was rotted through," she said in disapproval. "That sounds highly unsafe."

"Clearly," said Medea. "As it fell on Jason's head."

We drank wine and shared a moment of silence for the ship that Medea and I had both loved so very much. Our first taste of freedom and adventure. We would always be Argonauts.

"If Jason is dead," I said a moment later.

"It changes nothing," said Medea instantly. "We should sail the *Boar* further south this summer, if you're willing? I've always wanted to find a dragon."

I grinned back at her. "When have you ever known me to say no to an adventure?"

"SIMARGL AND THE ROWAN TREE"

EKATERINA SEDIA

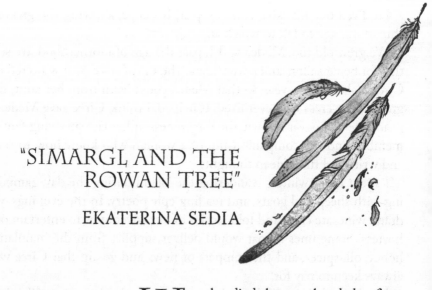

When he died, he was handed a fiery sword and an absinthe spoon. He tucked the former under his leather belt, and gave the latter a careful looking over. No doubt, the spoon in question was his own, the very instrument of his demise. He run his fingers over the feathered slots of the antiqued silver, and thrust the spoon into the back pocket of his jeans, his elbow encountering an unexpected obstacle in the shape of a pair of wings. He then turned to the faceless luminous figure that endowed him with the accoutrements of the afterlife.

"What do I do now?"

"You guard heaven," the figure said, and gestured vaguely in the direction of the endless azure expanse, where a golden chariot idled, waiting. "Your name is Simargl. Follow Ra."

That explained the wings, then.

Simargl nodded his agreement, and headed down a steep aurora borealis to the waiting chariot that cradled a giant, glowing orb. A man in a hawk mask, the driver of the chariot, gave him a slow nod. "You must be our new Simargl. Welcome."

"What happened to the old one?"

"Nobody lasts forever. Even I am getting old." The sun god heaved a sigh. "So, I presume you have killed yourself by fire?"

"It was an accident," Simargl replied, the spoon in his back pocket flaring hot at the memory. "But I suppose it was self-inflicted."

Ra clucked his tongue, and the chariot started to move, slowly at first but soon gaining speed, forcing the new Simargl to trot after it. "This is what Simargls are," Ra said. "Suicides by fire."

The day went on, as the chariot arced through the blue plains. As he trotted along, Simargl noticed that running was much easier on all fours, and that a fiery aura had grown around him. As far as he could guess, he looked more like a winged dog than a man. Just as Simargl started to fear that the azure void would never end, a green glittering jewel caught his eye. When they got closer, the green turned into a fresh meadow, studded with white and yellow flowers, sliced through by a sparkling stream. A cow—a gleaming white cow, and the most beautiful creature Simargl had ever laid eyes on—grazed among the flowers sagely.

"This is the Celestial Cow Zemun," Ra said, and pointed at the wide berth of tiny white stars that stretched above the meadow. "That's the Milky Way—she made it."

"Hello," Simargl said.

The cow smiled, with a mischievous twinkle in her emerald eyes. "Ah, good. It is about time you got here. Just make sure you do your duty, and don't give into the lure of the middle world."

"I apologize for my ignorance—" Simargl started.

"I forget that you've just got here," Zemun interrupted. "You're in the upper world—not because of virtue, but as a result of the manner in which you died, understand. The middle world, Yavi, contains the living and the lesser beings—banniks, domovois, rusalki . . . they are not enemies, but don't be distracted by their charms. And then there's Navi, the land of the dead and Chernobog, and his general Viy." The cow gave a thunderous sigh, and her eyes moistened. "My daughter Dana is married to Viy's son, who stole her from me."

"I'm sorry," Simargl said.

"Don't be," said Zemun. "Just watch over us, so that Navi's evil doesn't seep through to heaven."

And so Simargl did. He followed Ra's chariot all day long, and at night they usually arrived somewhere else—Zemun's meadow, Belobog's tall castle, or Veles's forest. But wherever he went, he found his gaze straying downward, to the middle world. His vision became such that when he focused on an object, no matter how remote, it stood before his eyes, diminutive but in perfect clarity. He could watch children playing in the gardens, the rusalki swimming and frolicking in the cool waters of the autumn streams, and the bird Sirin's solemn flight, as it sought to harvest souls and carry them to Navi. At night, he never slept but watched the wonders that unfolded in the lower worlds.

It was only the matter of time before his attention was returned. One of the rusalki, a gaunt girl with transparent eyes, the soul of a drowned virgin, looked up at him and smiled.

"Simargl," her voice whispered, disembodied and hollow, ringing out in the empty heaven, "come to our feast, come to our rusalii . . . we will play and sing all day, and we will wind long garlands of the water lilies. Come and dance with us, fire dog with the golden fur."

"I can't," Simargl said. "I am guarding heaven."

The girl sighed. "Oh, surely you can sneak away just for one night?"

"I wish I could," Simargl said. "Besides, I don't know how to get down."

"That's easy," the rusalka said. "Just find the rowan tree and climb down the trunk."

"Maybe some other time."

The rusalka's transparent eyes stared upwards, straight at him, but he wasn't sure if she could really see him. "Tell me about heaven," she pleaded.

He did. He felt bad for her, for how much she longed to be up there, but was instead bound between the world of the living, and the cold riverbed that was her grave.

She whispered about the rustling sound the small stones made when the current of the river rubbed them against each other, of the long strands of algae that entangled in her hair, of the small curious perches that came to peck at her dead eyes, and cried. "Why can't I see heaven?" she said between sobs.

"I died too," he told her. "I was a man once. But I died by fire, and ended up here . . ."

"It's a painful death," she said. "Perhaps this is why you went to heaven and not me. Perhaps I did not suffer enough." Her eyes glistened. "Tell me how you died."

He explained to her about the absinthe ritual, of how one poured bitter liquor over the sugar lump cradled in the spoon, and lit it on fire. He told her of the sizzling sputter of caramelized sugar, of the slow drip of liquor and melted sweetness through the slots of the spoon. He should've been more careful, he admitted. His balance was already affected by his previous intake, and his motions grew languorous and clumsy. He knocked over the silver goblet and the spoon that rested atop it, spilling the flaming, sticky sugar and absinthe mix over his clothes. It burned through his clothes and his couch, caught on the curtains, and the sizzling he heard all around him smelled of charred flesh.

He spoke to the rusalka, whose name was Kupalnitsa, every night. But he never ventured downward. His presence in heaven seemed too important, even though he did keep his eye out for the trunk of the rowan tree stretching between the worlds. He found it one day, when Ra stopped for the night. It seemed that with every day their trips were getting shorter, and Ra hunched more in his chariot. He rarely spoke.

Their resting place that day was a forest, deep and cool, buzzing with mosquitoes. Ra sighed and dismounted from his seat in front of the chariot, leaving the sun in its cradle parked in the narrow opening between tree trunks. He lay on the cushion of moss under a tall spruce, and closed his eyes.

Simargl watched his companion sleep, surprised and saddened to notice how old he had grown. With a heavy heart, he turned away, and decided to take a stroll to take his mind off Ra's decline. Among the tree trunks, he meandered, never fearing to lose his way, since the sun shone brightly like a beacon in a dense forest. And then he saw another source of light—a column of pure white, streaked with red and yellow.

It was the rowan—the world tree, and its branches studded with ripe red berries stretched above his head, and its trunk pierced the forest floor and continued down, deep below through Yavi, all the way to Navi, the underworld. It was dark there, and the fur on his back prickled: even from this distance, he saw the misshapen creatures that shifted in the darkness, he heard the weeping of the dissolute dead, he smelled the stench of the foul river that carried the dead souls to their destination. And then he saw Viy.

Viy's eyes were concealed by the eyelids so long they brushed the black sand under his clawed feet, and his fingernails scraped and tore the ground with every step, as they dragged along. Simargl's upper lip curled and he gave a low growl of warning. Viy heard him, and motioned for his attendants, who carried iron pitchforks, to come closer and lift the terrible weight of his eyelids so he could look.

Simargl jumped away from the tree, uncertain what would happen to him if Viy's stone eyes met his; he regretted his interest in the underworld, and decided to confine his attention to heaven and Yavi only.

Still, the weight in his stomach told him that he had made a mistake by drawing the attention of evil he thought to repel from heaven.

Ra was getting worse. He was barely able to climb to his seat in the mornings, every joint of his desiccated body creaking with the effort.

"That's enough," the Celestial Cow decided when one night they spent their rest time in her meadow. "You son can take up your work."

"But I can do it!" Ra protested.

"No you can't," Zemun said, and looked to Simargl for support.

He had no choice but to growl in agreement. "Every day, we're traveling less. The day in Yavi is getting shorter and shorter. It's only December, and their nights are longer than days."

Ra slumped. "If that is to be my last day as the sun's guardian," he said, "I want to die. I don't want to be a useless old man. Zemun, old friend, lift me up on your horns."

The Celestial Cow lowered her mighty head obediently, and with a single toss the old god soared high on her horns. He bled from the wounds where Zemun's horns had broken his skin, and his blood flowed freer and wider, changing from almost black to clear. As the blood—water—flowed, Ra shrunk, and soon there was nothing left but a calm wide river, spilling from Zemun's meadow all the way down into Yavi.

"Ra-river," Zemun said. "It is better this way."

The two of them stood, watching the immobile sun reflect in the calm surface, and then they drank from the river. With every sip, Simargl felt the secret knowledge stirring within him, growing like a tree from its tiny seed until the order of the world stood clear before his mind's eye. Then, he summoned Khorus, Ra's son.

Khorus was young and strong, and he didn't want Simargl's help. So Simargl found himself free to wander as he pleased, and he took advantage of it. His fiery sword in his paw, he walked across heaven on two feet, making sure that evil did not seep through. He spent most of his time in the forest near the world tree. There, he could talk with Kupalnitsa as if she were right there, next to him, and he could see her clear eyes as if they were level with his face.

She cried and pleaded, and begged him to come down to Yavi, to dance at her pretend wedding; she would never have a real one. She whispered of the dark desires that blossomed in her chest—terrible urges to steal the babes from their cradles, and to lead the passersby astray. Crying, she confessed that she was with the other rusalki when they found a child, lost in a wheat field, and tickled him to death.

"I can't come to your wedding," he said.

"Navi would be better than this!" she cried.

"But maybe I can help you." He reached up to the branches of the rowan tree with his clawed paw, but still the berries hung too far. He picked up his fiery sword and swung, and the berries fell into his open palm like drops of blood. From his drink of Ra-river, he learned that the berries had many mysterious powers. "Take these. They can cleanse the smudges of sin from human souls."

He opened his paw and watched the berries roll down the trunk, and fall one by one into Kupalnitsa's cupped hands. All but one—a single berry avoided her, and kept rolling, all the way into the darkness of Navi, where it disappeared like a stone in a deep well.

"Thank you," Kupalnitsa whispered, and swallowed the berries. Their effect was instantaneous—her eyes gained color, the palest blue of the autumn sky, and her gaunt face lost its hungry look.

Simargl sighed with relief—he could not take her to heaven, but he could help her battle whatever darkness was taking her over. Berries seemed like a small price to pay for saving her from the terrible fate of the rusalki, and he tried to ignore the nagging worry about the single berry that rolled into the underworld.

He patrolled heaven as usual, nodding to Khorus who occasionally crossed his way on his repetitive trip, and to Zemun, whom he visited often. The Celestial Cow was the one who brought it to his attention that things were not the way they were supposed to be.

"Something stirring in the underworld," she said one night, as they were playing one of their frequent games of marbles.

"How do you know?" Simargl asked.

"Just a feeling I have," Zemun said. "The same one I got when Viy abducted Dana for his son." She pushed the bright yellow marble with her muzzle, and it collided with Simargl's favorite, a clear one with a blue spiral inside. "I didn't pay attention then, but now I do. The only thing worse than an old fool is an old fool who doesn't learn. I know Viy is up to something."

"It's probably nothing . . ." Simargl's regretful gaze followed his favorite marble as Zemun swallowed it. "But I accidentally dropped one of the berries from the world tree into the underworld."

The Celestial Cow gave him a troubled look. "Is that so? Oh Simargl, you may have caused a misfortune! Why did you touch the world tree?"

Stumbling over his words, he told her about Kupalnitsa and her plight, of her fear and hatred of her nature.

The Cow nodded. "I understand. Your gesture was noble, but it had an unintended consequence. You must rectify it."

"What can I do?" Simargl sat up, huffing, the game forgotten. "Besides, maybe nothing will happen. And if Viy had got that berry and ate it, I have no way of retrieving it. The best I can do is to keep my eyes open and guard heaven."

"Perhaps," the Celestial Cow said. "But know this: the berries have strong magic. If you wait too long, the problem might be greater than what you can handle."

"I'll go tomorrow," Simargl said with a sigh.

"Good. Ra-river will lead you. And drink of its water on your journey—Ra will make you wise. Rest now."

When Simargl awoke the next morning, he noticed that something was amiss. He rose to his hind legs and stretched, as Zemun slept peacefully in her meadow. It was cold; colder than he could ever remember. Moreover, it was dark, and Simargl worried that the evil had struck.

His suspicions were correct. When he resumed his vigil, not a few steps away from Zemun's meadow, he found Khorus, his mask splattered with dark blood and his throat slit. The empty chariot rested next to him.

Simargl cried over the dead god's body, his heart rent by guilt—there was no doubt in his mind that Viy was able to enter heaven with the help of the berry, legitimately, and this was why Simargl did not sense his presence. When his sobs had died down, he returned to the meadow, and told Zemun of what had happened.

Without words, the Celestial Cow broke off one of her horns, and it became a large barque, with richly decorated hull of mahogany and amber, and the sails spun out of silk. The masts of the barque, the tallest of cedars, seemed to pierce the low, leaden sky.

"Follow the Ra-river," the Celestial Cow instructed, "until it leaves Yavi and flows into the river of the dead. Keep a look out for Viy's fleet."

"I'll bring the sun back," Simargl promised, and set on his journey. His only provisions were the jug of Ra-river water and a handful of rowan berries.

The barque floated down the river, slowly as it traversed heaven, and speeding up as it approached the precipitous drop off its edge. The barque stood at the top of the waterfall for one tremulous moment, and then plunged downward, falling among the froth and sparkling waves all the way to Yavi.

Simargl caught his breath when the barque righted itself and resumed its dignified progress down the Ra-river. Its waters darkened, and he felt uneasy under the leaden sunless skies, boiling with angry clouds.

The inhabitants of Yavi shared his discontent—he saw them all along the river, people and demonic creatures, their gazes turned to the sky, their faces lined with unease. Men and women, children and old people keened and complained. The bowlegged satyrs and the green-haired mavki, domovois and leshys, banniks and kikimoras all gnashed their teeth and cursed those who were responsible for the missing sun.

Their anger and grief touched Simargl, but there was only one face he searched for. Kupalnitsa was not among her sisters. Once or twice he thought he glimpsed her pale face underwater, and wondered if his visions resulted from guilt and longing. Still, he called out her name a few times, but no answer came. He looked at the water, trying to glimpse her again, but the river had turned muddy and foul, and slow menacing shapes moved below the surface—skeletal fishes and undead whales trailing threads of slime and rotting flesh.

When Simargl looked up, he realized that he was underground; the light was the same as in Yavi orphaned by the sun, grey and cold. The stone ceiling cupped low over the barque's masts, and dangling beards of lichen and mold soiled the white sails a putrid green. He remembered Zemun's warning when he noticed long sleek shapes darting in and out of the rolling fog upstream—the Viy's fleet, a flotilla of long sleek boats fashioned from dead men's nails.

"Simargl," ominous voices whispered all around him. "Turn back, turn back, fiery dog. Navi will swallow you, drink your blood, splinter your bones . . . there's no fire here to protect you."

The hairs on his back stood on end, and a low growl pulled back his lips. Still, Simargl stood on the prow, the fiery sword clenched tightly in his paws. His gaze tried to pierce the darkness of Navi, to find the hidden sun and its abductors, but the stone walls and hissing in his ears rendered him almost blind. He could only clutch his sword and keep his eyes on the Viy's ships.

They approached, slowly, cautiously. Simargl discerned the dead who manned the oars, and small demons that tittered and rolled around, and leapt high. On the prow of the main ship sat the bird Sirin, its feathers sparkling green and blue. The bird had the face and breasts of a woman, and it sang.

Sirin's song was the most beautiful thing he had ever heard—it rolled and trilled like a brook born of snowmelt running over stones, it promised and reassured that happiness was close. He needed only to close his eyes and give into the sweet voice. His knees weakened under him, and his hands lost their grip on the hilt of the sword. He fell into her words like a stone into a well, welcoming oblivion and sleep. Sleep was happiness, and he only had to close his eyes, to lie down, and he would be home, away from the sunless sky and dead eyes of the demons. As he sunk to all fours, his front paw touched the blade of the sword, and he hissed in pain—the blade burned deep into his skin, jolting him to awareness.

Simargl took a quick gulp of the water from the jug, and felt the calm wisdom of Ra radiate through his mind, clearing his head of the curse. He chewed on the berries, their tart and bitter taste fortifying his weakened body, and sprung to his feet. The flaming sword in his paw flared brightly, sending the demons scuttling for cover and whimpering in fear.

Sirin stopped her singing and hissed in frustration, and the ship that carried her swung around and disappeared into the fog. Simargl followed the fleeing ship, until he came to the beach covered in black sand and empty shells of hermit crabs. Simargl leapt out of the barque, and chased after the shapes that laughed and skittered in the dusk of the underworld.

"Simargl," came a tiny whisper from behind him, "wait."

Kupalnitsa, her face stained by the foul water but unmistakable, smiled at him as she swam to the shore.

"Where did you come from?"

"I latched onto the keel of your boat as you passed through Yavi," she said.

Her words about Navi being better than her fate were fresh in his memory. "Will you stay here?"

She shrugged, and twisted the hem of her long linen shirt to squeeze out water. "I want to see it first."

She followed Simargl as he left the black beach and entered the forest of phosphorescent, leafless, weeping trees. Their crooked branches entwined over their heads, forming a cupped canopy.

Simargl kept peering through the dense entanglement of trees and black brambles. He noticed a weak beam of light penetrating through the growth, and turned toward it. But the light did not come from the stolen sun; in a forest clearing, covered with yellow grass, a fine red cow chewed her cud.

"Dana?" Simargl said.

The cow nodded.

"I'm friends with your mother," Simargl said.

Dana's brow furrowed. "Mother?"

"The Celestial Cow Zemun. Don't you remember?"

Dana shook her head.

"Give her a berry," Kupalnitsa said.

Simargl offered the cow a berry that glowed bright red, like a ruby. Dana swallowed it, and her eyes went wide.

"Do you remember now?" Simargl said.

Dana smiled. "And I miss her. Can you take me with you to visit her?"

"If I get the sun back," Simargl said.

"I can help you!" Dana pointed with her hoof. "Over there, it is hidden in Chernobog's castle. Viy guards it. But please, do not hurt his son, Pan—he is my husband. And remember, you can't hurt Viy with iron."

Chernobog's castle loomed atop a cliff that jutted from the forest like a giant thumb. The building itself seemed like an ugly growth on the rock. At the foot of the cliff, Viy was waiting, his attendants at his side, ready to lift his terrible eyelids. At the sight of him, Kupalnitsa gave a little cry and covered her eyes with her pale hands.

Gripping the hilt of his sword, Simargl approached the monstrous general.

Even though Viy could not see him, he spoke in the gravelly voice. "You came for the sun, guardian of heaven. And you've bested Sirin."

"Yavi and heaven needs the sun," Simargl said. "And the murder of Khorus and Dana's abduction will not be unpunished. Prepare to fight, Viy."

Viy's laughter, quiet but unsettling, scratched Simargl's very soul. "I'll fight," he said, and snapped his fingers, grating his nails. "Attendants, lift my eyelids!"

Kupalnitsa gasped. "Not his eyes! Simargl, he turn anyone into stone with his gaze!"

Simargl lunged at the attendants, his sword at the ready. He tried to chase them away, but as he swung the sword, he severed one of Viy's eyelids. No longer held down by its weight, it started to rise. Simargl shielded his eyes with one paw, and thrust at Viy with the fiery sword.

"To the left," Kupalnitsa yelled from behind him. With only one eye open, Viy could only pay attention to Simargl. "Careful, he's got an axe!"

Something metal, of great weight whistled close to Simargl's floppy ear, and something warm trickled down his fur. He felt suddenly dizzy, and took a stumbling step back.

Kupalnitsa cried out directions, and he followed them blindly, thrusting his sword this way and that, and ducking whenever she told him to. He swung, and felt the burning blade encounter something solid. Foul blood spilled from Viy's wound, and he uttered a slow, halting hiss that froze Simargl's heart. The dark liquid pumped over the blade of Simargl's sword, and it hissed and sputtered, and then its fire went out—it was just a regular iron sword now.

You can't hurt him with iron, Dana said, and Simargl cast away the useless weapon. As Viy advanced on him, injured but still strong, Simargl retreated blindly. He was going to die again, and stay in Navi forever—not as Simargl, but as one of the countless grey souls that inhabited the underworld. The memory of his first death overwhelmed him, and he felt as peaceful as when Sirin was singing to him of quiet surrender, of wordless happiness. He heard the crackling of fire all around him, and felt a burning in his pocket.

The silver absinthe spoon was still there, and he grabbed it just as Viy's bulk pressed against him. He thrust the spoon at the quavering belly of the general, and Viy gave the most terrible of cries anyone had ever heard, and stepped back. Where the silver touched his warty black skin, a fresh wound bloomed, spreading open, growing wider with every minute. Viy's flesh sputtered and recoiled from the contact with silver. Simargl chased after him, all the way up the steep steps of the castle. At the doors, Viy turned around, and Simargl flinched and covered his eyes. He pushed the spoon at Viy's throat, drawing a deep moan from his chest.

"You won," Viy told him, his lone eyelid brushing the ground. "You can have your sun back."

Simargl walked through the Chernobog's castle, and found the sun in the throne room. The dark god himself scowled at him from his throne chair, made of skulls and thighbones.

Simargl bowed to the god, but his gaze was on the sun, sitting bright and unharmed in the middle of the bone floor, spilling its light through the narrow windows.

"Don't burn yourself," Chernobog mocked.

Simargl picked up the sun, but it didn't burn him, and instead clung to him like a child ready to go home.

Simargl carried the sun outside and placed it into the barque. Meanwhile, Kupalnitsa ran to fetch Dana, and the two of them sat in the barque with him.

"I missed heaven so much," Dana said. "I'm going to visit my mother often, now."

Kupalnitsa sighed. "I wish I could see it too."

Dana's blue eyes turned to Simargl. "What say you, guardian of heaven? Didn't this girl earn the right to leave Yavi?"

"I suppose," Simargl said. "I'll ask Zemun if Kupalnitsa can stay in heaven."

The barque left the black shores of the underworld and glided upstream, serene like a swan, until the caved stone ceiling of Navi and undead whales fell far behind. The inhabitants of Yavi greeted the return of the sun, and paid no mind to the fiery dog, a red cow, and a pale drowned girl who sat beside it in the marvelous barque built by the Celestial Cow.

"THE TEN SUNS"

KEN LIU

The prairie stretched in every direction as far as the eye could see. The sparse grass, yellow-tipped and dotted with purple and white flowers here and there, resembled an enlarged version of the tattered carpet that lay on the ground in Headman Kiv's tent. To the east, a few hundred bumps poked out of the carpet like mushrooms after rain—except that the mushrooms wriggled slowly.

A herd of taurochs.

With Primus high in the sky, this was the hottest hour of the day. The light summer coat of the taurochs shimmered in the sun as though each wore a rainbow, and their triple horns rose and dipped from time to time as they grazed lethargically. The animals would become livelier once Primus had set, and the temperature had cooled a bit with only Secundus in the sky.

Aluan, sitting atop his stallion at the head of the band of hunters, waved his arm decisively. "Charge!"

Forty whips fell against forty horses, and the thunder of pounding hooves filled the riders' ears. The men and women of the hunting band rushed towards the herd like an arrow made of flesh and blood, with young Aluan in the lead: the taurochs represented food, shelter, clothing, thread from sinews, tentpoles from bones, kefir bags from stomachs. The hunters took their bows from their shoulders.

The animals looked up, their long triple horns glinting in the sunlight. Sleep faded from their dark eyes like a receding tide, replaced by terror.

As one, the herd began to run, first slowly, then faster and faster. But a few older cows and young calves fell behind.

Quintus, Sextus, Septimus, and Octavus—none as bright as Primus—hung high in the sky from west to east like a strand of pearls. It was only a little cooler than when Primus shone alone.

Around the bright and warm bonfire, people danced, their movements loosened and their laughter made louder by bowls of kefir, were each accompanied by four shadows at their feet. Beyond the ring of dancers, racks of meat smoked.

"Not bad for your first time leading a hunt," said Ly. She had just stepped out of the ring of dancers to sit down on the ground next to Aluan. "We should have enough food to last a full month."

Aluan nodded perfunctorily.

Ly detected a lack of real joy in the gesture. "What's bothering you?"

"The animals are so lean and small. Have you ever seen a bull as fat as the one your grandfather said he killed when he was your age, heavy enough to need twenty men to lift it off the ground?"

"He was probably just exaggerating. Old men like to tell tall tales."

Aluan said nothing. After a few moments, he pulled out a handful of grass next to him and handed it to her. "Chew on this."

The taste was bitter, acrid.

"It's too dry," said Aluan. "Don't you remember how thick the grass used to be on the prairie when we were kids, and how sweet it tasted? No wonder the taurochs are not fattening up or reproducing as they used to."

She spat out the grass. "We always think things used to be better when we were little. But that's just because the world seemed new to us then."

Aluan laughed bitterly. "How many more hunts are left before there will be no more taurochs? You know I'm right, but you're afraid to agree with me. No one wants to talk about the truth. We'd all rather drink kefir and pretend things have always been the same—"

"It *has* always been the same." A few of the other hunters, sitting a bit further away, looked over at her raised voice. She looked back and smiled in a way that suggested this was just a lovers' spat. The others smiled in understanding and returned to their own conversations.

Before Aluan could answer her, the chants began around the bonfire. "Aluan! Aluan! Aluan!"

"It's time to retell the legends," said Ly. Her face looked anxious, and she gave Aluan a shove. "Don't mess it up. This is your first time. My father agreed that we can get married if you show yourself to be as proper in your beliefs as you are skilled as a hunter."

Aluan stood up, sighed, and walked towards the middle of the ring.

This is a story of how people came to be in our world: We were not born here, but were brought.

Long ago, before the time of the Five Kings and the Three Councils, before the time of the Fire and the Flood, before the Killings and the Separation, the world was a bare rock, cold and devoid of life.

Then the Zyxlar, the Bringers of Judgment, scattered the seeds of life into the world. It is said that the Zyxlar ruled over many worlds and held the power of life and death over many different forms of life: some had bodies made of stone; some had bodies made of insubstantial gas; some had hard carapaces like insects; some had leathery limbs like the creatures who crept in the grass; and still others were like you and me.

No one knows why the Zyxlar seeded this world with our ancestors, and the ancestors of the Saurians, Chitters, Silicates, and Methenes. They brought forth grass and trees, lakes and prairies, deserts and salt flats, the birds that fly in the air and the rockleech that swim in the water, the taurochs and devourers, the tumblebugs and stonerays. To give everything heat and light, they placed ten suns in the sky.

Now, there are many stories of the days when the ancestors of the Five Races lived together with, and served, the Zyxlar. They lived in a place called the City, where the houses were as tall as mountains. They could soar in the sky on giant mechanical birds and roam the earth on beasts made of metal that obeyed their will.

It is also said that they were not always hunters who lived like migrating wolves on the edge of starvation; in fact, there was a time when the world was not so dry, and our ancestors lived by the magic of agriculture, tending to plants that sprung out of the rich, wet soil, heavily laden with grain and fruit. It was then possible for a couple to have as many children as they wished, and all would have plenty to eat—

"That's enough, Aluan!" Headman Kiv cried out. "I've tried to tolerate your insistence on heresy, but you seem to treat my forbearance as weakness. How dare you repeat these lies! There is no such thing as 'agriculture.' We have always lived as proud hunters following the taurochs herds."

"Father!" Ly came up and stood by the side of Aluan. She glanced at Aluan, her eyes filled with annoyance and worry, but then she turned to look at Kiv with a placating smile. "Aluan has had too much to drink after a victorious hunt. You don't need to be so angry with him."

"I'm not drunk at all." Kiv's public reprimand only made Aluan more defiant. He shook off Ly's restraining arm. "How can you speak of 'always' when living memory can extend no further back than three generations? But what I spoke of are ancient stories, whispered from mother to son, generation after generation. If they are lies, why are you so afraid?"

"You speak heresy! Foolish stories lead men's hearts astray and threaten our people's survival. The Zyxlar made this world for us and assigned us the task of praising their name. How dare you suggest that they were not perfect and that the world has declined from some golden age? You'll never lead another hunt. Ly, step away from that fool. You're forbidden from speaking to him again."

"Dad!"

Aluan stepped in front of Ly. "She's sixteen. She may choose who she wishes to speak to. Think about it: your anger confirms what we all suspect is the truth—that the world is not perfect, that something has gone wrong. The Zyxlar made us the lords of this land, but foolish headmen have led us astray and lack the courage for change."

Kiv's face was so red that his head seemed on the edge of explosion. "I should never have taken you in as an orphan and raised you like my son. Doren, Sy, Klaiten, seize this fool and whip him until he confesses his error."

Aluan stood still, his face obstinate.

But Ly pulled on his arm. "Run, run! His anger will dissipate faster than your body can heal. I swear: I won't come to visit you if you are whipped because you're too stubborn to listen to me tonight."

Reluctantly, Aluan turned and ran with Ly towards the horses.

Kiv's men gave pursuit for a while, but Ly and Aluan had taken two of the fastest horses. Besides, they were also Aluan's friends and chased rather half-heartedly. Eventually, the men disappeared below the horizon.

Aluan and Ly loosened the reins and slowed down. Only Nonus and Decimus remained in the western sky. Primus was about to rise. After a day of hunting and hard riding, both riders and their horses were tired.

On the shore of a tiny lake, they crested a small hillock that blocked the wind a bit. "Let's camp here."

Since they had escaped in a hurry, all they had in their packs for food were just a few strips of smoked meats. Ly went to fish while Aluan started a campfire.

Freshly grilled noodlefish, even unsalted and spiced only with hunger, was tasty. After the meal, Ly and Aluan lay down on the grass and looked up at the blue, cloudless sky.

"You really think that the world has changed?" Ly asked.

Aluan laughed bitterly. "Ly, did you see that cairn we passed half an hour ago? The one with ten red stones at the base?"

The migrating tribes left cairns on the prairie to mark their passage and to indicate the boundaries of their territories to strangers. After years of bloody wars long lost to lore, the Five Servant Races had claimed separate parts of the world in the Great Separation.

Six years ago, on her tenth birthday, Aluan and Ly had spent a full day collecting red rocks from all over the grasslands to build a cairn to celebrate. Red was her favorite color.

—*So that's ten stones, one for each year you've lived, and one for each of our ten suns.*

—*That makes no sense. How can a stone stand for both a year and a sun?*

—*Ly, do you know why there are ten suns in the sky?*

—*Dad says it was because Zyxlar had the Five Servant Races and that there was a heaven and a hell for each.*

—*So each sun would be a different world?*

—*I guess so.*

—*Maybe. But I think it's because the Zyxlar were lazy. Instead of making one big sun, they made ten little ones. It's like how it's much harder to bake one large flatbread that's cooked evenly throughout, but much easier to bake ten little ones.*

—*Hahaha . . . Aluan, you're being ridiculous. Be careful not to let my father hear it, or you'll get whipped again.*

—*Why should I get whipped? My story is just as likely to be true as his.*

In the intervening years, others passing by seemed to have added to the cairn, but left the red stones exposed at the base, perhaps because they looked so distinct.

Aluan's voice pulled her back into the present. "Remember, we built it on the shore of a lake."

This lake. For half an hour, they had ridden over ground that had once been covered by water.

"But lakes grow and shrink all the time." Ly said. "That's no proof that the drought is getting worse or that our people once lived differently."

"Your father isn't around. You really believe that?"

Now it was Ly's turn to say nothing. She picked up another stalk of grass and chewed on it. It was bitter.

"Even if what you say is true, what can we do about it? The Zyxlar left us long ago. They had the power and magic, not us."

"Why *can't* we do something about it? There are also stories of our people being great heroes from before the time of the Zyxlar. There was Hercules, who fought a god. There was Neil the Strong-Armed, who walked in the heavens—"

"—those are myths! More heresy! Would it kill you to just worry about what you can see and touch?"

Aluan looked at her, a smirk turning up the corners of his mouth. "You wouldn't like me much if I did that."

"Ha! Who says I like you much now?"

"You're here with me, aren't you?"

Ly blushed and decided to change the subject. "My father raised you like a son, hoping you'd be my right arm when I take over one day. I'm sure his anger will have ebbed in another few days. We'll go back and apologize."

"I am not apologizing! How can I help lead our people if I'm not allowed to say or think what I want?"

"What makes you so certain you're right?"

Aluan gazed back at her. His face held an expression she had never seen before.

"Tell me!"

"I don't hate your father. I know he's trying to keep the tribe focused on the task of survival, instead of . . . fantastical stories that have no use. He's only become so orthodox because the drought seems to have no end. If you go back now, your father will forgive you. But if I tell you . . ."

"How can I decide what to do if you can't trust me to know what you know?"

Aluan blew out a breath. He nodded. "All right. Let's wait until Primus is up, and I'll show you what I've found."

They woke up after Primus had climbed about a quarter of the way to the zenith.

They washed with the clear, cold water of the lake, and then, while Aluan dressed and cooked a hare he had shot, Ly faced Primus, closed her eyes—staring at the glory that was Primus, even for a few seconds, would have blinded her—and sang her morning prayers.

Giver of Light, First Among Equals. You are the warmest, brightest, most life-giving of ten brothers. We give you thanks, Lord Primus. May our Headman lead us as wisely as you lead the suns of Zyxlar.

She noticed that Aluan refused to join in the prayer or to even pause his work. *Has he really grown so full of pride?* Her anger grew. *He doesn't know everything. No one does. Haven't the Wandering Sages of the Grasslands always taught that the Terrans are meant to be ignorant about much of the world, lest we become as the Zyxlar?*

After the meal, as they washed their hands and faces by the lake, Aluan said, "Would you try to hunt for some supper by yourself? I need time to prepare something to show you."

Ly nodded, preoccupied with thoughts of how to reconcile her father and Aluan.

By the time Ly returned to their campsite, Primus was nearing the western horizon, and Secundus and Tertius were rising in the east. She had a pair of rock-shelled voles hanging from her saddle and a dozen prairie gaswing eggs, a delicacy, packed in soft grass in her pouch. Aluan had been a malnourished little boy when he had first arrived in their tent, and for years, her father had saved all the prairie gaswing eggs for him. Maybe the sight would guilt him into agreeing to return home with her.

Aluan, sweaty and exhausted looking, was working on some contraption. By the looks of it, he had been at it all day. It was possible that he had skipped lunch and even his nap.

"Hey, time to eat."

He looked up and smiled at her. "I'm almost finished. I have to get this done before Primus sets."

She sat down next to him and brought the fire back to life. She set the eggs to boil in a bark-pot and began to dress the voles, peeking at what Aluan held in his hand.

He had constructed a long, rectangular box out of skins wrapped around a frame woven from the tough reeds growing at the edge of the lake. One end of the box was covered by the soft, supple skin of a young fox, stretched taut across the opening. There was a tiny hole in the middle of the skin, apparently poked by a sharpened reed.

"What are you making?"

"You'll see." He flipped the box over to show her the other end. She gasped. A translucent, pale white, thin screen covered the opening of the box.

He had collected the gossamer threads spun by the spiders whose silken balloons drifted across the prairie in spring whenever there was a breeze. The threads were so thin that he must have spent all day painstakingly picking up each strand with a reed stalk to carefully lay it across the box opening. It was the most beautiful thing she had ever seen.

She frowned. "That's a lot of effort for something that will fall apart with a puff of breath." On the grasslands, effort had to be conserved and survival was tenuous. The amount of effort he had spent on something like this could have been spent on hunting. She lamented the waste.

"Then don't blow at it." He held the box up so that the end with the tiny hole in the fox skin faced Primus, and the end with the gossamer screen was in front of her face. She looked and gasped again.

On the screen was an image of Primus, about the size of the palm of her hand. It was another shade of white, much brighter than the screen itself. But unlike staring at Primus itself, it wasn't painful to stare at this echo of Primus.

"What kind of magic is this?" she asked.

"It's not magic," he said. "The box is light-proof—"

Ly shuddered. The world was never without light from one or more of the ten suns. Lightless places, where the sun could not shine, existed only in caves deep under water, in snake nests hidden underground, in stone houses where murderers and witches were left to die in darkness. To construct a light-proof thing was to brush against evil.

But Aluan went on, oblivious. "—and through this pinhole, only a thousandth of Primus's strength can pass through. That light, falling against the screen on this end, forms an image of Primus. But because

the image has only a small amount of the strength of Primus, it's possible to look at it without hurting your eyes. I call it the sun-gazer."

"That's very clever," Ly said. She marveled at the image on the screen,
the first time she had ever been able to truly see what Primus looked like.

Instead of the perfect outlined circle she had always imagined, she
saw a disk with fiery, indistinct edges. Curling tongues of flame shot
out from the disk, reminding her of the tiny swimming legs of the gigantic jade-jellyfish drifting in the lakes. And the disk itself was hardly
like the surface of a pearl. Dark patches, like impurities drifting in a
cup of kefir or pimples on a youthful face, dotted the white surface and
marred it.

*But Lord Primus was without flaws. Unlike earthly objects, Primus was
heavenly and contained no impurities.*

"Hardly perfect, is it?" asked Aluan. She could hear a kind of weariness
as well as relief in his voice. "But that's not even the most interesting part.
Try to memorize the pattern of the dots." Aluan then moved the box so
that the pinhole end pointed at Secundus. "Tell me what you see."

Secundus was not nearly as bright as Primus, and the image on the
screen was far dimmer as well. It took a few moments for Ly's eyes to
adjust. Once again, there were the curling tongues of flame reaching
out from the edge of the disk and the scattered black spots across the
surface: here's a bunch that reminded her of the shape of the rocks poking out of the lake's surface; there's a bunch that she thought looked like
the hundreds of cairns snaking across Tannerjin, the holy site where all
the tribes gathered every year . . .

Wait!

She grabbed the box from Aluan's hand and looked back at Primus,
and then at Secundus again. Then she turned to Tertius, and then back
to Primus. Finally, she put the box down and stared at Aluan.

His face was completely expressionless. Not even a muscle twitched.
He was waiting for her to say what she thought before he would react.

Her voice trembled. What she had seen was too incredible, too
strange. She was sure she was hallucinating. "Secundus and Tertius . . .
looking at them is like looking at Primus . . . in a mirror."

Whatever Ly had been expecting from Aluan wasn't what she got: he
whooped and roared with laughter; he did a cartwheel; he came up to
her and kissed her, hard.

She was too stunned to speak.

"Finally, finally!" He put his hands on the sides of her face and touched his forehead to hers. "I've been unable to share what I've seen with anyone. For the longest time, I thought I was crazy, mad, that I hallucinated. I made sun-gazers and then destroyed them, only to rebuild them again. But you see it, you see what I see! It's true."

"But what does this mean?"

"I don't know! I've been observing the suns in secret for years. The patterns have been getting denser." He took out and unfolded a large sheet of the thinnest tauroch skin, cured and scraped and worked until it was as soft as a newborn's nose. It was filled with dense drawings of disks with patterns of black dots. "The patterns of dots shift over time. It's always the same: whatever shows up on Primus can also be seen on Secundus, Tertius, Quartus . . . but backwards, so that what's east is west, and west east."

Ly looked at him, terror in her eyes. "I don't understand. Are you saying that the nine suns other than Primus are illusions? That they don't exist?"

Aluan shook his head. "I don't have answers. But I do know that the stories your father insists on are not true. The ten suns are not each unique; the drought has been getting worse; we used to have more and bigger game to hunt, and maybe we once didn't need to hunt at all. I don't know how these things are connected, but I do know that I can't make myself believe in lies anymore." He nodded at the sun-gazer in Ly's hand.

Ly thought about what she had seen on the translucent screen. It was true. Once she had seen the flares curling away from the edge of the image of Primus, it was impossible to believe in the perfectly smooth, unchanging flow of her father's stories.

But she was reminded of one particular story her father had once told her after he had drunk too much kefir, a story that he had laughed at and said contained no truth at all.

"It's an old myth of Earth," he had said, "just a made-up story."

No one knew what "of Earth" meant—whether it was the name of a place or person or god. Ly knew only that it meant this was a story from before the time of the Zyxlar, brought from the womb of the Terrans. And the story had frightened her.

Long ago, when the universe was young and the Terrans still lived on our home world, there were ten suns.

The suns did not come out all at once. Instead, they slept beneath the world, and each day, a different sun rose from the east, heated and lighted the world, and set in the west to bring forth night.

—Ly, what's "night?"

I don't know, and my father didn't explain. But since the suns only came up one at a time, I guess night is when there is no sun.

— But there is always at least a sun, or a few suns, in the sky.

Let me finish the story. One day, the ten suns grew bored, and decided to all come out and play at the same time. The combined heat of the ten suns was unbearable. Water boiled from the ocean and the lakes; the exposed riverbeds cracked with the heat; plants wilted and animals panted with thirst; those laboring in the fields fell down—

—What does "laboring in the fields" mean?

I don't know!

There were lots of things my father said that didn't make sense.

What happened next was that a great hero, whose name was Hou Yi, came to save the Terrans. He climbed the tallest mountain, and, from its peak, demanded that the suns resume their orderly course.

The suns refused.

And so Hou Yi took off his bow, which was made from the horns of the strongest, biggest bull taurochs, and he notched an arrow, which was made from the sharpest reed growing by the shores of the Yellow River and the longest wing feathers of migrating wild gaswing. Hou Yi pulled the bow until it was as round as the disks of the suns themselves. Then he let go.

The arrow struck one of the suns, and it dove into the ocean and sank beneath the waves like a fiery bird shot out of the sky.

One by one, Hou Yi shot down nine of the suns. The last sun, terrified, promised to rise and set every day as regularly as the swings of a pendulum, and that was how the great hero restored balance to the world.

Aluan pondered Ly's story. Then he opened his eyes.

The determination in Aluan's eyes both excited and frightened Ly.

"What have you decided?" Ly asked.

"I must become Hou Yi and shoot the suns down. I must go to the City. It's the only way to save our people."

"You're crazy—"

Aluan smiled at her. "Why do you think I'm the one who's mad? Isn't it even more mad to go on pretending year after year, decade after decade, that nothing is wrong, that nothing has changed, that we can do nothing?

"But now we know what our people are capable of—"

"—it's just a myth—"

"—but myths can become true. Would you have believed that you could gaze at the face of Lord Primus one day without being blinded? Would you have believed that the other suns are but mirrors for Lord Primus? Had I told you these things but yesterday, you would have dismissed them as myths, too!"

Ly's heart felt uplifted. His faith was like the light of life-giving Primus. "Then I'm coming with you."

Our ancestors once lived with the Zyxlar in the City, far to the north. There, the mountain-houses were so dense that they formed a forest. Thousands, perhaps even millions, lived in the forest, along with metal beasts and machine birds.

—That's not even remotely possible, Aluan.

Don't talk to me of possible and impossible. Haven't we already reached the edge of the grasslands, supposedly endless? Haven't we already seen animals you've never imagined? Haven't we already been journeying in this land where there's nothing but sand for days? Haven't we seen the Silicates and Saurians scurry out of our way even though we were told that violating the Separation would surely bring us death?

Back to the story. One day, the Zyxlar decided to abandon our ancestors and left them on their own. Without the Zyxlar, the magic that kept the City running died.

—I'm going to die of thirst if I don't get a drink of water.

Here you go.

—Why aren't you drinking?

I'm not thirsty.

— Liar! That was our last bit of water, wasn't it? You should have taken it yourself. You haven't drunk anything for a whole day.

I told you. I'm not thirsty.

—Our horses are dead. We're never going to get out of this place, are we?

Of course we will. Didn't Hou Yi have to climb the highest mountain? Didn't Neil the Strong-Armed have to endure a house of darkness propelled by a pillar of fire? We will make it.

—Finish telling me the story. I'm not so thirsty when the story gets good.

The lights in the mountain-houses dimmed. The stale air inside the City became suffocating. The metal birds fell out of the sky, killing those who rode on them. The metal beast no longer obeyed. The Terrans had to leave the City to survive, and the City fell silent and disappeared from our memories.

But it's there Ly, I know it's there, and I will find it. That is where I will find the bow that will shoot down the suns that are drying this world and killing us.

The rain came like a solid sheet of water descending from the sky. The two of them were drenched in minutes. Still, they lifted their faces to the sky and drank and drank.

All the suns, even Primus, were hidden behind thick layers of clouds. Light seemed to come from everywhere.

The country they were in now was mountainous, and the water, more water than they had ever seen, coalesced into rivulets, collected into rivers, and thundered through the valleys into some misty distance. The mountains, steep, hard, and soilless, supported no vegetation. Any seeds that tried to take root would have been washed away.

"Do you think that's where the *ocean* is?" Aluan asked.

"Perhaps." Ly was no longer able to doubt anything, no matter how fantastic.

"No matter how hard it rains here," Aluan said, "the water doesn't seem to be able to cross the desert before it's boiled away. It rains hard where there's too much water, and it doesn't rain where the ground is thirsty."

When the rain stopped, they emerged from the valley.

The City loomed before them, a forest of towering steel skeletons that seemed to reach for the sky. At their feet were piles of rubble like giant cairns. As Ly and Aluan made their way through the City, broken shells of metal beasts, some with stiff wings like dead birds, lined the wide avenues. Beds, chairs, tables and other strangely shaped furniture whose purpose eluded them were scattered here and there, crumbling to dust at one touch.

"So, it's all true," whispered Ly. It was so quiet save for the occasional twitter of a bird or the scrabbling of some animal's feet. The place felt unwelcoming; everything seemed alien.

They headed for the center of the City, where a gigantic domed structure rose out of the rubble, the only intact building left.

The build had heavy metal doors that slid on rails. They were stuck, semi-open. Beyond the opening was darkness.

Ly hesitated.

"Hou Yi would not be afraid," said Aluan, even though Ly could tell that he was terrified. Nonetheless, he took a deep breath and stepped inside.

Immediately, a booming, disembodied voice whose tone betrayed no emotion spoke: "Access denied. Unaccompanied members of the Slave Races must be authorized."

The heavy doors came to life can began to slide towards each other. Aluan tried to back out but his right leg was caught between them. He fell to the ground and began to scream. The doors groaned and the sound of rusty, ancient machinery drowned out his screams.

Ly rushed over and tried to pull him out, and then she tried to push the doors back. It was like struggling against a mountain. Aluan's leg slowly deformed in the crushing grip of the doors, and then they heard it break. He screamed again. But the doors still would not let go.

Ly prayed to Lord Primus, she called out to the Zyxlar. She shouted for her father's help. But no one answered her.

Then she saw a row of five impressions on the surface of the door, one of which was in the shape of a hand. Without thinking, she put her hand in it. She felt a sharp stab of pain, and when she pulled her hand out, she saw beads of blood at the tips of her fingers.

"Identity of authorized Terran confirmed," said the disembodied voice. "You may enter."

The doors scraped even more loudly in their rails as they slid back open.

Ly cradled Aluan's head in her arms and kissed his face. "Oh thank Lord Primus. I thought I had lost you!"

Aluan gave her a wan smile. "Thank yourself. The bloodline of the Headmen flows through you. The Zyxlar authorized you."

A second set of doors slid open, and they were bathed in milky white light.

Inside, the domed building was just one massive circular hall. Ly had splinted Aluan's leg, and slowly, with Aluan's arm over her shoulder, the pair climbed up the long, spiraling stairway along the wall on three legs. It was like being inside a mountain.

A great chandelier hung suspended from the apex of the dome. As they passed clusters of strange machinery along the wall, full of levers and buttons and blinking lights, the strange voice would speak up as they passed each:

"Terraforming Station Fifty, Solar Observation: heightened solar activity exceeding safety levels. Recommend decrease in illumination."

"Terraforming Station Forty-four, Hydrology: water table depleted in temperate zone."

"Terraforming Station Twenty-one, Meteorology: extreme weather patterns in progress. Recommend decreasing global temperature."

Aluan and Ly took everything in, without being certain of anything.

At last, as they were about to collapse from exhaustion, they arrived on the platform at the top. A great globe hung in front of them, and on it was a mottled pattern of green and brown, dotted here and there with some blue patches. The globe spun slowly. Some distance away, a blindingly bright lamp illuminated half of the globe. Close to the globe, on the side away from the lamp, hovered a semi-ring made of nine circular mirrors that reflected the light from the lamp onto the half of the globe that would have been in shadow.

The voice spoke again, "Terraforming Station One, Solar Energy Collection: all reflectors operational."

Ly and Aluan understood without needing to say anything.

They looked around and saw another station marked with the image of a rising arrow atop a pillar of flames.

"Planetary Defense Station: Authorized personnel only."

Ly placed her hand, like before, into the impression by the station. She winced as more blood was taken from her.

"Identity confirmed. Weapons systems fully operational. No invading spacecraft identified within range."

In front of them was a screen, a much bigger version of the one on Aluan's sun-gazer. Below it was a stick. As Aluan pulled and pushed at it, the view on the screen seemed to change, and eventually, the pale image of a disk filled the screen.

"Target is Reflector Number Two. Are you certain?"

Aluan and Ly looked at each other and smiled.

"Are you ready?" he asked.

She nodded. "Let's be Hou Yi."

Aluan pressed the button. There was a thunderous roar that shook the building and the two of them fell to the floor. By the time they scrambled up, Secundus had disappeared from the screen.

"One down, eight more to go," said Ly.

When they emerged from the building, they were greeted by darkness.

Ly clutched Aluan's hand. "Is this night?"

Aluan squeezed her hand.

They seemed to hear again the emotionless voice that had accompanied them as they descended the great, spiral stairs.

"Terraforming Station Thirty-One, Temperature: All reflectors offline. Global temperature decreasing."

"Look," Aluan said, pointing up at the sky. Flickering sparks drifted high above them, the broken bits of the mirrors that had once made this world one without night. As some of them fell, they turned into bright meteors.

But behind them were more steady pinpricks of light that studded the dark heavens like nourishing dewdrops on the prairie, like bright pearls scattered around a black crown, like hope emerging from desperation.

"I wonder what Dad is telling everyone," said Ly. Instead of terror, she felt awe and beauty.

For the first time in millennia, the Terrans on this planet saw the stars.

"ARMLESS MAIDENS OF THE AMERICAN WEST"

GENEVIEVE VALENTINE

There's an armless maiden in the woods beyond the house.

She doesn't wail or weep the way you'd think a ghost or a grieving girl would. Her footsteps are heavy—sometimes she loses her balance—but that's the only way to hear her coming.

It happens in plenty of time that you can grab the bucket of golf balls you're collecting (the golf course buys them back for beer money) and get out of the woods before she reaches you.

If you do see her, it's because you lingered when the others ran, and you hid behind the largest oak, the one you and your dad once built a fort under, and waited for her.

The first thing you see is that her hair is loose. That strikes you as the cruelest thing, that whoever did this to her couldn't show even enough mercy to fasten her hair back first, and cast her into the forest with hair so long and loose that it's grown into corded mats down her back. The knots at the bottom are so twisted and so thick they look, when she's moving, like hands.

(No, you think, that's the cruelest thing.)

But her face is clean, as these things go. You imagine her kneeling beside the creek that runs all the way out past the golf course, dipping her face in the water.

There are dark stains down the sides of her dress, all the way to the ground, where she bled and bled and did not die after they cut her arms off at the shoulders.

The armless maiden has hazel eyes, or maybe brown.

She says, "Hello."

There's no telling what the armless maiden did.

It doesn't matter now. To her father, it was offense enough to warrant what happened. To anyone else, what happened was a crime beyond measure; what happened to her was a horror.

(Where they were when her father picked up the axe, there's no telling.)

She's been living in the woods as long as you can remember, though no one talks about it much where you are. Live and let live. If she stays off the golf course, no one minds her.

Nobody in town talks about her to strangers, but still, word gets out.

Sometimes one of the news crews from a bigger city would get wind of her and send a crew to do a story about the woman who haunts the woods. Usually it was Halloween, but sometimes it was International Women's Day, or something horrible had happened to a woman where they were from, and they wanted to find as many crime victims as they could to round out the story so it could last.

Once someone came all the way from Indianapolis to write her up; she asked if anyone had caught her, like she was a rabbit or a disease. The station could pay for testimonials, she said. She gave a dollar number that meant Indianapolis was serious about it.

She left empty-handed. The neighborhood didn't like the implications.

The armless maiden has never spoken, that anyone has ever said, and someone would have said. There's no need to tell strangers from Indianapolis about her, but she belongs to the town, sort of, and it's nothing strange to talk about your own.

Suzanne from the hairdresser's talked sometimes about how she couldn't imagine how that poor girl was looking after herself, and how she'd go out to the woods asking if the maiden needed anything, except that it would be butting in. Usually she said this when she was cutting your hair; she said, "I hear she's a blonde," and then there was no sound in the whole place but her scissors, and you watched your hair falling and held your breath.

At least once every year, someone from the PTA stood up in a meeting and asked if she was still of the age where she needed to be in school, even though she'd been in the woods so long that even if she'd started out that young, she wasn't now.

Tommy from the motel told everyone about the time the bird watchers came down to look for some warbler that was hard to find except in the forested region where they were, and ran into her, and got so frightened they left town without paying their bill. But they left most of their things in the room, too, so he sold the binoculars and the cameras and it came out all right.

He told the story like it was funny, how scared they had gotten, like any of them had ever really seen her and there was something to compare.

You start to think that you're the only one who has ever seen her.

It's a terrible thing to think, and you hope for a long time that it isn't true, but in all the stories people tell about her, no one says a word about seeing her themselves. Maybe she's just the kind of person whose privacy people respect, you think.

(But you know already, long before you admit it, that you're the only one who's ever seen her, and that she must be so lonely it makes your stomach hurt.

When she said hello, you've never heard anyone so surprised.)

That year, a researcher comes.

She isn't like the newscasters, with their navy or pastel skirt-suits, and their hair that got blonder the farther south they came from, and their camera crews who said nothing and tipped poorly.

She comes alone, with a roll-along suitcase that Pete from the diner said was mostly just full of notes and books and a laptop. She read papers the whole time she ate, Pete said, and after she paid the bill she asked him if the rumor was true.

"I'm studying armless maidens of the American West," she said. "I hear there might be one in the area. If anyone has any information about her, I'd like to meet her."

Pete said it like she was the weird one, but some of the people he told the story to thought she sounded different.

Meet, she had said, which sounded very civilized, and which none of them, the more they thought about it, had ever really done.

You kind of hate Pete for not asking more about it. You worked Wednesday through Saturday; if she had come in a day later, you would have asked her plenty.

Because it was as though no one heard the part you hear, the part that sends you down to the motel after work Friday to leave a wadded-up note with Carla, who does the night shift, and who would be more likely to actually pass the word along. (Tommy works days, and he'd let it get lost out of spite, because some guys are just nothing but spite, aren't they?)

She had said, armless maidens.

There are more.

There's comfort in an armless maiden.

In the stories about one armless maiden or another, her suffering is finite; because she is a girl of virtue—or was, before her father got to her, but allowances are made—we know she won't always wander the forest, bleeding and solitary.

While she does make the forest her home, angels part the water for her to walk through, so she'll never drown, and drape their heavenly cloaks on her, so she'll never freeze. It's a comfort.

The birds drop berries into her open mouth, and the rain falls past her grateful lips, so that when the prince finds her she won't be starved (princes in stories don't like maidens whose bodies are eating themselves).

The comfort of the armless maiden is how well you know she's being cared for; how easy it is to understand which parts of her are not whole.

When the researcher actually calls you back, you're surprised.

"It was kind of you to contact me," she says. "And yes, I'm still very interested in speaking with her, if it's possible."

You ask, "Why?" like she was the one who left you a note instead.

She says, "I'll show you the structure of the study, if you want. It's very respectful of privacy. It's still at the research stage at the moment—we're a little low on funding—but I hope that we're doing important work."

The guys at the golf course probably do important work, and you hope she's after something besides golf-course money. (You feel like you wouldn't even know what really important work was.)

"Sure," you say.

The armless maiden is alone.

Even in dreams, no one comes near her; even if there are forests teeming with armless maidens, each one is in a world only she knows for certain.

If the woods were teeming with them, the armless maidens wouldn't believe it, somehow; they would pass by and pass by, each thinking of the others, What a lonely girl, how like a ghost.

(In the good dreams, the world of an armless maiden is a world of silence; it's a world filled with rings of silver; it's a world where the axe couldn't hold.)

The researcher comes in on a Thursday night with her rollalong, looking just like Pete described her, and orders a cup of coffee, and asks you to have a seat.

There are some people who stopped off on their way to the antique fair, so you can't right away, but you stop by to refill her coffee about a dozen times, and finally she pushes a document toward you.

You flip open the first page, standing right there at the table because you can't wait any longer to know what's going on.

You scan the page quickly—the corner booth ordered omelets and the toast gets stone cold if it sits out for more than ten seconds.

It reads, "The armless maidens of the American West are not, despite the title of this study, a geographically-defined phenomenon. The concentration on this region merely allows for a reasonable sample size to be defined and, if possible, interviewed."

Then, farther down, "For purposes of this study and in the interests of maintaining privacy for participants, all names have been changed."

Then there are lists of names; there are charts and graphs full of more data points than you ever thought were possible to gather about anything.

(One axis is labeled "Age at Dismemberment." You can't breathe.)

Next to her, there are stacks of paper fastened with clips, with names like ANNA or CARLIE or MARIA written in large block letters across the front, maybe so they're easy to find.

They're not real names; you wonder if she picked them, or they picked their own.

"What happened to them?" you ask, finally, after you've decided there's not enough money in the world to make you pick one up and read it.

(Your fingers are still resting on CARLIE. Underneath her name it reads: AGE 13.)

She considers her answer, like she doesn't want to frighten you.

She says, "Different things."

That's sort of worse—you had tried to take comfort in the old story that only a father did this kind of thing. Your dad was okay; you thought you were fine.

You swallow. "Are they—are they all right?"

"Some of them," she says. "It depends a lot on what happens to them afterward—who they know, how much they feel they have support to rejoin the world. Sometimes their arms even grow back, eventually, depending."

You guess a little bit about what that depends on, but it's not hard; the armless maiden has been around a long time, and nothing has healed, and everybody you know says things about her but never to.

"I'd like to speak with her, if you know where to find her," she says. "It's a good starting point. The more we talk to them, the easier it is to take note of their progress."

Progress.

There could have been progress already, if someone had ever walked out past the golf course and looked her in the eye, just once.

You don't want to talk about this anymore.

"I'll get your check," you say, and fill her coffee cup too full, and clock out for your smoke break twice in a row by accident because your hands are shaking.

You suck the cigarette down to the filter, making up your mind about it.

You go back out to the woods, late in the day, when no one is likely to be on the course.

(You don't like the golfers. They never come into the diner, even though it's right down the highway and they have to drive past it, and it seems more trouble to avoid it than to stop.)

You wait near the tree. You've brought some things that make you feel stupider than you've ever felt, including the time you had to give an oral report on the French Revolution in history and blanked, and Tommy never let you hear the end of it.

(You've brought scissors, a comb, vitamins, a dress with sleeves.

You want to be prepared; when you tell her about the researcher, she might say yes.)

Near dark, just before it's really night, she comes by all the same, with careful footfalls.

When she sees you, she stops.

"Hello," says the armless maiden.

You say, "Hello."

"GIVE HER HONEY WHEN YOU HEAR HER SCREAM"

MARIA DAHVANA HEADLEY

In the middle of the maze, there's always a monster.

If there were no monster, people would happily set up house where it's warm and windowless and comfortable. The monster is required. The monster is a real estate disclosure.

So. In the middle of the maze, there is a monster made of everything forgotten, everything flung aside, everything kept secret. That's one thing to know. The other thing to know is that it is always harder to get out than it is to get in. That should be obvious. It's true of love as well.

In the history of labyrinths and of monsters, no set of lovers has ever turned back because the path looked too dark, or because they knew that monsters are always worse than expected. Monsters are always angry. They are always scared. They are always kept on short rations. They always want honey.

Lovers, for their part, are always immortal. They forget about the monster.

The monster doesn't forget about them. Monsters remember everything. So, in the middle of the maze, there is a monster living on memory. Know that, if you know nothing else. Know that going in.

They meet at someone else's celebration, wedding upstate, Japanese paper lanterns, sparklers for each guest, gin plus tonic. They see each other across the dance floor. They each consider the marzipan flowers of the wedding cake and decide not to eat them.

Notes on an eclipse: Her blue cotton dress, transparent in the sunlight at the end of the dock, as she wonders about jumping into the water and swimming away. His button-down shirt, and the way the pocket is torn by his pen. Her shining hair, curled around her fingers. His arms and the veins in them, traceable from fifty feet.

They resist as long as it is possible to resist, but it is only half dark when the sparklers are lit, from possibly dry-cleaned matches he finds in his pocket. She looks up at him and the air bursts into flame between them.

They are each with someone else, but the other two people in this four-person equation are not at this wedding. They know nothing.

Yet.

In the shadow of a chestnut tree, confetti in her cleavage, party favors in his pockets, they find themselves falling madly, falling utterly, falling without the use of words, into one another's arms.

Run. There is always a monster—

No one runs. She puts her hand over her mouth and mumbles three words into her palm. She bites said hand, hard.

"What did you say?" he asks.

"I didn't," she answers.

So, this is what is meant when people say *love at first sight*. So this is what everyone has been talking about for seven thousand years.

He looks at her. He shakes his head, his brow furrowed.

They touch fingertips in the dark. Her fingerprints to his. Ridge against furrow. They fit together as though they are two parts of the same tree. He moves his hand from hers, and touches her breastbone. Her heart beats against his fingers.

"What are you?" he asks.

"What are *you*?" she replies, and her heart pounds so hard that the Japanese lanterns jostle and the moths sucking light there complain and reshuffle their wings.

They lean into each other, his hands moving first on her shoulders, and then on her waist, and then, rumpling the blue dress, shifting the hem upward, onto her thighs. Her mouth opens onto his mouth, and—

Then it's done. It doesn't take any work to make it magic. It doesn't even take any *magic* to make it magic.

Sometime soon after, he carries her to the bed in his hotel room. In the morning, though she does not notice it now, the hooks that fasten her bra will be bent over backward. The black lace of her underwear will be torn.

This is what falling in love looks like. It is birds and wings and voodoo dolls pricking their fingers as they sing of desire. It is blood bond and flooded street and champagne and O, holy night.

It is Happily Ever.

Give it a minute. Soon it will be After.

So, say her man's a magician. Say that when he enters a forest, trees stand up and run away from their leaves, jeering at their bonfired dead. Say that in his presence people drop over dead during the punchlines of the funniest jokes they've ever managed to get through without dying of laughing, except—

Like that.

So, say he knew it all along. This is one of a number of worst things itemized already from the beginning of time by magicians. This falls into the category of What To Do When Your Woman Falls In Love With Someone Who Is Something Which Is Not The Least Bit Like The Something You Are.

The magician shuffles a deck of cards, very pissed off. The cards have altered his fingerprints. Scars from papercuts, scars from paper birds and paper flowers, from candle-heated coins, and scars from the teeth of the girls from whose mouths he pulled the category Things They Were Not Expecting.

Turns out, no woman has ever wanted to find a surprise rabbit in her mouth.

He finds this to be one of many failings in his wife. Her crooked nose, her dominant left hand, her incipient crow's feet. He hates crows. But she is his, and so he tries to forgive her flaws.

His wife has woken sometimes, blinking and horrified, her mouth packed with fur. No one ever finds the rabbits. His wife looks at him suspiciously as she brushes her teeth.

Sometimes it hasn't been rabbits. When they first met, years and years ago, she found her mouth full of a dozen roses, just as she began to eat a tasting menu at a candlelit restaurant. She choked over her oyster, and then spat out an electric red hybrid tea known as *Love's Promise.* By the end of evening, she was sitting before a pile of regurgitated roses, her tuxedoed magician bowing, the rest of the room applauding.

She excused herself to the bathroom—golden faucets in the shape of swans—to pick the thorns from her tongue. And then sometime later, what did she do?

She married him.

The magician continues to shuffle his cards. He clubs his heart, buries said heart with his wife's many diamonds, and uses his spade to do it. Some of those diamonds are made of glass. She never knew it.

In their hotel room, the lovers sleep an hour. He's looking at her as she opens her eyes.

"What?" she asks.

He puts his hand over his mouth and says three words into it. He bites down on his palm. She reaches out for him. It is morning, and they are meant to part.

They do not.

This is meant to be a one-night love story not involving love.

It is not.

They stay another day and night in bed. They've each accidentally brought half the ingredients of a spell, objects rare and rummaged, philters and distillations, words that don't exist until spoken.

They get halfway through a piece of room service toast before they're on the floor, tea dripping off the table from the upended pot, a smear of compote across her face, buttered crumbs in his chest hair.

They think, foolish as any true lovers have ever been, that this is so sweet that nothing awful would dare happen now.

They think, *what could go wrong?*

Right.

And so, say his wife is a witch. A cave full of moonlight and black goats and bats, housed in a linen closet in the city. Taxicabs that speak in tongues and have cracked blinking headlights and wings. An aquarium full of something bright as sunlight, hissing its way up and out into the apartment hallway, and a few chickens, which mate, on occasion, with the crocodiles that live in the bathtub.

Like that.

Say she knew about this too, from the moment she met her man, foretold the mess in a glass full of tea, the heart-shaped, crow-footed face of this woman who is nothing like the witch.

The night the two true-lovers meet, his wife is sitting in their shared apartment. Coffee grounds shift in the bottom of her cup. A yellow cat streaks up the fire escape, shrieking a song of love and lamentation. The witch's hair tangles in her hands, and she breaks the knot, tears the strands, throws them from the window and down into the neighbor's place, where he, wide-eyed, elderly, and stoned on criminal levels of pot, drops the witch's hair into the flame of his gas stove and leaves it be while it shoots fireworks over the range and sets off the smoke detector.

The witch looks for allies. There is one. He's a magician. Typically, she works alone, but she suspects her skills will be blurred by sorrow and fury.

She sees him in her coffee grounds, shuffling a deck of cards and crying. He pulls a coin from beneath his own eyelid. A white rabbit appears in his mouth and then climbs out, looking appalled, dragging with it a rainbow of silk scarves and a bouquet of dead roses. The magician lets the table rise beneath his fingers, propelled by the rattling ghosts of other magicians' wives.

The witch has no patience for any of this. She spills milk so that no one needs to cry over it anymore. There. It's done. It's happened. After a moment, though, the waste begins to irritate her, and so she unspills the milk and pours it into her coffee cup. She sweetens it with a drop of her own blood, and drinks it.

She's strong enough to kill him, but she doesn't want to kill him.

She is not, unfortunately, strong enough to make him fall out of love. Making someone fall out of love, particularly when it is the kind of love that is meant to be, is much harder than murder. There are thousands of notoriously unreliable spells meant to accomplish just this. Typically, they backfire and end up transforming eyebrows into tiny, roaring bears, or turning hearts inside out and leaving them that way.

Once, when attempting something similar, the witch found her own heart ticking like a timebomb. This was expensive to fix, and in truth, the fixing did not go well. Her heart is mostly made of starfish these days. At least it could regenerate when something went wrong.

When the witch first fell in love with her husband, she showed him all of her spells, a quick revue of revelations.

She crouched on the floor of the apartment, and opened her closet full of cave, let the bats and goats and ghosts come pouring out into the room, and he laughed and told her she might need an exterminator. She crumpled herbs from ancient hillsides, and in their dust she planted seeds shaken carefully from a tiny envelope. She watched him as the flowers bloomed up out of nothingness. Each flower had his face. She wasn't sure he'd noticed. She pointed it out, and he said, "Thank you."

She worried he was not impressed enough. They stayed together.

At night sometimes, she took down buildings brick by brick, all over the city, but left their bedchamber untouched.

The witch is busy too. She has things to accomplish. She has no time for fate. She doesn't wish to let her man go off into his own story, giving *fate* as his reason.

Fate is never fair. This is why there is such a thing as magic.

The witch picks up her phone and calls the magician. She monitors him in the coffee grounds as he answers. He's dressed in a full tuxedo and most of a sequined gown. He's sawed himself in half, and is carefully examining the parts. The witch could have told him that this'd yield nothing in the way of satisfaction. Years ago, just as she met this man and learned about the other woman in his future, she dismantled her own body, and shook it out like laundry, hoping to purge the urge to love. It hid, and when she replaced her skin with cocoa-colored silk, the urge to love got loose, and hid elsewhere.

She never told him about the woman he's meant to meet. Men were often blind. He might miss her.

Love was blind too, though, and this was the witch's mistake. Had he been blind and deaf and mute, he'd still have met the other woman, in the dark, in the silence.

This doesn't mean there isn't something to be done.

"Meet me," she says to the magician. "We have things to do together."

Together, the lovers walk through a cemetery holding hands, laughing over the fact that they are tempting fate by walking through a cemetery holding hands.

Together, they walk through a torrential storm, heads bent to look at each other's rain-streaming faces.

Together, they have faith in traffic.

Together, they fuck in the stairwell, on the floor, against the book-shelves, on the couch, in their sleep, while waking, while dreaming, while reading aloud, while talking, while eating takeout first with chopsticks and then with fingers and then from each other's fingers, and then?

Lover's arithmetic: test to see how many fingers can be fit into her mouth, how many fingers can be fit inside her body. Test to see how many times she can come. They chalk it up on an imaginary blackboard. She lays still, her hair spread across the pillow, and comes simply by looking at him.

Together they compare histories, secrets, treasures.

Together, they're reduced to cooing and whirring like nesting birds, junketing on joy.

Together, they try to doubt it.

It's no use. There are too many ways to break a heart. One of them is to tear that heart in half and part company. And so, they don't.

"Fate," he says. And it is.

"Magic," she says. And it is.

"*Meant to be together*," they say, together. And it is.

Careful. There need be no mention of star-crossing, not of Desdem-ona and Othello, nor of Romeo and Juliet. Not of any of those people who never existed, anyway. Someone made those people up. If any of them died for love, it's someone else's business.

Together, they compare fingerprints again, this time with ink. He rolls her thumb over his page, and looks at the mark, and they memo-rize each other's lines.

Together, they say, "Forever."

Look. Everyone knows that *forever* is, and has always been, a magic word. Forever isn't always something one would choose, given all the information.

And so, the magician and the witch hunch over a table in the neutral zone of a Greek diner, brutalized by a grumpy waitress and bitter cof-fee. Outside, the sky's pouring sleet. Inside, the ceiling's streaming flu-orescent light. The witch's taxicabs patrol the streets, crowing miserably, wings folded. Too nasty out there to fly.

The magician is in formal dress, including top hat. The witch is wearing a fleece blanket that has sleeves and a pocket for Kleenex, and though she's managed lipstick, it's crooked. She's wearing fishnet stock-ings, which the magician suspects are an illusion.

Neither witch nor magician are in top form. Both have head colds, and are heartbroken. Each has a sack of disaster.

The witch coughs violently, and removes a tiny, red-smudged white rabbit from between her lipsticked lips. She holds the rabbit in her hand, weighing it.

The magician stares steadily at her, one eyebrow raised, and after a moment, the witch laughs, puts the rabbit back into her mouth, chews, and swallows it.

The magician blinks rapidly. A moment later, he chokes, and tugs at the neck of his tuxedo shirt, where his bowtie was, but is no longer.

He glances sideways at the witch, and then fishes a black bat from his own mouth. The bat is wild-eyed and frothing, its wings jerking with fury. It has a single black sequin attached to its forehead.

"Are you ready to stop fucking around?" asks the witch.

"Yes," says the magician, humbled, and the bat in his hand stops struggling and goes back to being a bowtie.

The waitress passes the table, her lip curled.

"No animals," she says, pointing at the sign. She sloshes boiled coffee into each of their cups.

"What do you have for me?" says the witch.

"What do you have for *me*?" says the magician. "I love my wife."

"We're past that. You're not getting her back, unless you want half a wife and I want half a husband. Look."

She pulls an X-ray from her bag. It's a bird's-eye skeletal of two people entwined in a bed, her back to his front. In the image, it's appallingly clear that their two hearts have merged, his leaning forward through his chest, her heart backbending out of her body, and into his.

"How did you get this?" the magician says, both fascinated and repulsed.

The witch shrugs.

She hands him another image, this one a dark and blurry shot of a heart. On the left ventricle, the magician reads his wife's name, in her own cramped handwriting. "Hospital records from forty years ago," she says. "None of this is our fault. He was born with a murmur. Now we know who was murmuring."

She passes him another photo. He doesn't even want to look. He does.

His wife's bare breasts, and this photo sees through them, and into the heart of the magician's own wife, tattooed with the name of the witch's own husband.

"What's the point, then? Revenge?" he asks, removing his tailcoat, unfastening his cufflinks, and rolling up his sleeves. There's a little bit of fluffy bunny tail stuck at the corner of the witch's mouth. He reaches out and plucks it from her lips.

"Revenge," she repeats. "Together forever. That's what they want."

She pulls out a notebook. When she opens the cover, there's a sound of wind and wings and stamping, and a low roar, growing louder. Something's caged in there, in those pages. Something's been feeding on *forever*.

The magician smiles weakly and pours out the saltshaker onto the page. He uses his pen to carve a complicated maze in salt. He feels like throwing up.

"Something like this?" he says, and the witch nods. She feels like throwing up too. No one ever wants things to turn out this way. But they do.

"Something like that. I'll do the blood."

"I could do it if you don't want to," the magician volunteers, not entirely sincerely. That kind of magic's never been his specialty.

"No, I owe you. I ate your rabbit."

He rummages in his sack of disaster and brings out a pair of torn black lace panties. A bra with bent hooks. A photograph of a woman in a blue dress, laughing, giddy, her eyes huge, her hair flying in the wind. He looks at the crow's feet around her eyes. Side effect of smiling. Crows walk on those who laugh in their sleep. He tried to tell her, but she did it anyway.

He pushes his items to the witch's side of the table. The witch rummages in her own sack and removes a razor, a T-shirt ripped and ink-stained, a used condom (the magician suppresses a shudder), a gleaming golden thread. She suppresses the urge to smash the T-shirt to her face and inhale. She suppresses the desire to run her wrist along the razor blade.

She signals to the waitress. "Steak," she says. "Bloody. I don't normally do meat, but I get anemic when I do this. And a martini."

"Two," says the magician.

"We don't serve steak," says the waitress. "You can get a gyro, if you want a gyro. That's probably chicken."

The magician flicks his fingers, and the waitress pirouettes like a ballerina.

A moment later she returns with a white damask tablecloth, and two lit candles. Two plates of prime float out of the kitchen, smoking and bleeding. The fluorescent lights flicker off. The witch and the magician raise their glasses in a toast.

They toast to "Forever."

And even when *they* say it, it is, as it always has been, a magic word.

The monster, newly uncaged, runs hands over new skin. The monster opens a new mouth and learns to roar.

She fell asleep holding his right hand in her left. She wakes up alone. There's a playing card stuck to her left breast. It is not the Queen of Hearts. It's a two of spades.

She's in a hospital.

Her husband is a magician. Her lover's wife is a witch. She knew better than to do this, this forever. But here she is, and here's a nice nurse who asks her what she thinks she's doing when she asks for the return of her shoelaces and belt and purse strap.

"I don't belong here," she says, in a very calm voice.

"Then why do you think you are here?" asks the nurse, in a voice equally calm.

Her wedding ring is missing too, but she doesn't miss it. Her mouth tastes of rabbit and overhandled playing card. Where historically she has felt sympathetic to her husband, to his oddities, to his pain, she now begins to feel angry.

She looks down at her left hand and feels her lover still there. She looks at her ring finger, and sees something new there, a bright thing in her fingerprint.

A red mark. A movement, spinning through the whorls, slowly, tentatively. Someone is there, and the moment she thinks *someone*, she knows who it is.

She brings her fingertips closer to her face. She looks at them, hard. She concentrates. One does not spend years married to a magician without picking up some magic.

His eyes open. He's freezing. His blood's turned to slush and he remembers that time, when he did his girlfriend a significant wrong via text message. She salted him, limed him, and then drank him with a straw for seven hollow-cheeked minutes.

Last night, he held his lover in his arms, and kissed the back of her neck. She curled closer to him, pressing her spine into him.

He heard the crowing of taxicabs in his dreams.

There are looping, curving walls on either side of him. Above him, far above, the sky is dazzling, fluorescently white.

A flash across the heavens of rose-colored clouds. They press down upon him, soft and heavy. They depart. A rain of saltwater begins, and splashes through the narrow passage he inhabits. He hears his love's voice, whispering to him, but he can't find her. Her voice is everywhere, shaking the walls, shaking the sky.

"I have you," she says. "You're with me. Don't worry."

But he can't see her. He's frightened.

Something has started singing, somewhere, a horrible, beautiful, sugary roar. He's suddenly hit by a memory of fucking his wife, on the floor surrounded by flowers that had his face. They both failed to come, bewildered by lack. It was years after the beginning, back then, but still nowhere near the end.

"I have you," his beloved whispers. "You're safe with me. I know the way." He wonders if he's imagining her.

The walls shake around him. He can feel her heartbeat, moving the maze, and his own heart returns to beating a counterpoint, however tiny in comparison.

He opens his hand and finds a ball of string in it.

The witch and the magician fumble in the car on the way to her place. Her sleeved blanket is rumpled. His top hat and tuxedo have turned to ponytail and hoodie. He may or may not be wearing a nude-colored unitard beneath his clothes. Old habits.

"Unbelievable dick," she says, not crying yet. "He deserves this."

"Believable," he says. "Some people are idiots. *She* deserves this. I think maybe she never loved me."

He's looking at the witch's black curls, at the way her red lipstick is smeared out from the corner of her lip. He's thinking about his rabbit, working its way through her digestive tract. She's still wearing the fishnet stockings he'd thought she conjured.

"It's hard to make fishnets look right," she says, turning her face toward his. Her eyelashes are wet. "They're complicated geometry."

He pulls an ancient Roman coin from behind her ear, clacking awkwardly against her earrings. She looks at him, half-smiling, and then pulls a tiny white rabbit from out of his hoodie. He's stunned.

"It seemed wasteful to let it stay dead," she says.

He puts his shaking hand on her knee. She moves his hand to inside her blanket. He takes off his glasses. She takes off her bra.

There are still people in madhouses and mazes. There are still monsters. Love is still as stupid and delirious as it ever was.

The monster in the middle of the labyrinth opens its mouth. It starts to sing for someone to bring it what it wants, its claws trembling, its tail lashing, its eyes wide and mascaraed to look wider, its horns multiplying until the ceiling is scratched and its own face is bloody.

The monster screams for honey, for sugar, for love, and its world comes into existence around it. Bends and twists, dead ends, whorling curves and barricades and false walls, all leading, at last, to the tiny room at the center of the maze, where the monster lives alone.

The other thing that's always being forgotten, the other thing that no one remembers, is that monsters have hearts, just as everyone else does.

Here, in the middle of the maze, the monster sings for sweetness. As it does, it holds its own heart in its hands and breaks it, over and over and over.

And over.

"ZHUYIN"

JOHN SHIRLEY

The only reason they went into Burned Oak, California, on that smoldering summer day was because of Logan's thirteenth birthday. Bridey was taking Logan for a birthday hamburger and shake in town, which is what Logan asked for. Logan was excited about it, in her quiet inward way, because she and Bridey—her mother—had spent most of the summer on the farm, with only the animals and the occasional visit from the livestock veterinarian. Bridey was reluctant to come to town. She made excuses; she even went to the considerable expense of having groceries delivered.

Bridey parked the old Toyota pickup across the highway from Meaty Mary's Café. She turned off the engine and climbed out with a certain weariness. She was wearing her yellow sunglasses and sunhat and a yellow sundress.

Logan got out in a hurry. She wore her San Diego Padres baseball cap, shorts, thongs, and a white blouse. The sweat started on her forehead the instant she stepped onto the baking road. Blinking in the hot sun, Logan flapped along in her thongs close behind her mother.

Logan noticed a pretty blond teenage girl sitting on the shaded stoop of the hardware store next to Mary's. The girl was frowning at her smart phone. Her rather strident makeup had been selected to match her very short blue and red flower-print dress. She glanced up, and her smirking inspection made Logan feel she should have worn sneakers and a nicer blouse, maybe even a dress. She only had one dress that still fit her, and she'd only worn it one time since school.

Bridey and Logan got across the highway just ahead of an enormous double-trailer truck carrying boron from the mine; the semi rumbled by, not fast but so weightily Logan felt the wooden walkway shiver under her at the café's door. Burned Oak tried to keep an old-fashioned veneer, with false front buildings and wooden walkways. The little town, sparsely edging the Southeastern California highway, was aware that it was rustic and, perhaps, tourists could be encouraged to regard it as quaint.

To the left of the café's front door a noisy air conditioner drooled rusty water. To the right, a big Sunshine Orange Soda thermometer was screwed to the wood.

Logan followed her mom into Mary's. The café was almost cold after a ride in a truck with a broken AC. It was Sunday afternoon and there were a good many people—miners and shopkeepers and their wives—all looking at Bridey and Logan as if remembering they were from around here but not sure exactly who they were. Her mother was a modishly attractive brunette with short hair and large dark eyes, and she was a magnet for curious looks.

Logan and her mother sat at the counter because Bridey believed Logan liked to watch the shakes being made, an impression outdated by ten years.

A Mexican cook looked at them from behind his service window. He pointed to Logan's baseball cap. "Hey, the *Padres!* I used to go see the Padres play, back in San Diego! Nice ballpark there."

Logan smiled and gave him a thumbs up. "Padres!"

She and Dad had gone six times to see the team at Petco Park. He loved baseball more than he'd loved the Padres. Maybe still loved it, if he was alive. There were no more tickets to major league games after they moved out here to be near the Sierra Butte Army base. Just the two of them, then, her and Dad at the farm—which wasn't really a working farm, though there was a milk cow, a bull, and some horses who were supposed to breed colts. Logan had been there most of a school year, Dad working on his classified project at the base. She didn't mind making her own dinner, or the interminable bus ride to the middle school in Quarryville, miles and miles with a bunch of kids who never talked to her. True, there was that girl Brinda, with the big wine-mark on her face, and that spotty-faced boy, Erwin, who liked to tell her, breathlessly and cluelessly, about how he was breeding some kind of Japanese cattle for the FFA. Nice kid, anyway.

But then, Dad . . .

Don't think about Dad today, she told herself. *Birthday stuff. Seeing town with Mom. Think about that.*

Meaty Mary's waitress was an elderly white lady with bright red lipstick and vividly dyed orange hair caught up in an old fashioned waitress's cap. She had arching, drawn-on eyebrows. "How you doing, honey?" she said, setting her little notebook on the counter. She smiled at Logan. There was some lipstick on her dentures. *Lana* was embroidered on her blouse.

"Okay." Logan hoped that Bridey wouldn't mention the birthday.

The waitress looked at Bridey. "Ma'am? Getcha something?"

Bridey ordered for both of them and Lana wrote it down. Then she looked Logan and Bridey over, and screwed her mouth up like an early television comedy actress, her head cocked. "You'd be . . . Bridey? Married to Harve Kelly?"

"I would be her, yes," said Bridey dryly, taking off her sunglasses. "Except that Harve has passed on."

"He's *missing in action*," Logan corrected, voice low but firm. "Overseas. In Tunisia."

"The Army says . . ." Bridey let it trail off, and shrugged. "He's missing in action."

"Oh my gosh, I'm so sorry, sweetie!" Lana said, her cartoon eyebrows knitting. "He's . . . I thought he was stationed over here on some research thing? They put him into combat overseas?"

Bridey adjusted her silverware. "Field testing something over there—I don't know what exactly." Her voice was almost inaudible.

Lana patted Bridey's hand. "I'll get your burgers and fries . . . and I won't forget those shakes. One vanilla, one strawberry."

They ate and drank in silence, Logan stealing a glance now and then at Bridey.

Since the day Bridey had shown up at the farm, Logan had never, ever called Bridey "Mom" or "Mother." An ambitious lawyer for a while, Bridey had broken up with Dad when Logan was small. Apart from Christmas presents shipped from an internet site, she had been out of Logan's life for years until Dad went missing. Just didn't come home one day. She called the base, they said they'd look into it—and after three days alone at the farm, Bridey showed up with some papers from the Army and told her that Dad was overseas and hadn't come back from a mission and, "As your mother, it's my responsibility to take care of you, so . . . here I am."

To be fair, she'd only said it that cold way because Logan had been crying and yelling at her and saying she wanted to talk to her dad on the phone and she didn't believe he would leave without telling her he was going, she could take care of herself and she didn't even *want* Bridey to take care of her.

But Bridey had stayed, and Dad hadn't come home.

Two months of Bridey working from the farm, using the internet, some sort of legal consultant now, with Logan keeping to herself and Bridey sporadically dating a middle-aged Army captain from the base, a guy named Miles Winn. And sometimes a young sergeant named Chris something.

Then the word had come that Dad was listed officially MIA in some unspecified North African military disaster, possibly an encounter with an Islamic State spin-off.

Bridey wasn't dating Miles now—coming home one night she muttered something, about a fight with him. "He was hounding me. Hassling me about dating Chris." That was all she'd say. But a button was torn from her blouse, a small hole ripped where it had been.

Bridey preferred Chris anyway—only, Chris hadn't been around in weeks. Which was maybe part of why Bridey was so pensive and silent lately.

Finishing her shake, Logan mentally rehearsed the speech for the ride home. *I can live with Aunt Tracy in Riverside, we talked online and she said I could stay with her. I don't want to stay here and you won't have to take care of me and I'll give the Army my contact information for when they find Dad.*

Maybe she was tired of trying to "do the right thing." Maybe she'd let her leave.

The sun was still blazing when they returned across the highway to the truck. They climbed in, sweating in the even hotter pick up. Bridey frowned over her purse as she looked for the keys.

"Can we go to the library, on the way?" Logan asked.

"The library? I doubt it's open." Bridey put the key in the starter and turned it. The key made a doleful clicking sound.

"I doubt it's *not* open, Bridey. It's air conditioned. I want to see if they got the book I ordered."

Bridey's frown deepened as she tried the key again. The engine wasn't turning over. *Click, click, click.* "You have a book to return, before you can check anything out."

"I have the book here, it's under the seat."

"Logan, hush—the car won't start. I need to figure this out . . ."

She tried again. Nothing but clicking.

"Take the key out and put it in again," Logan suggested.

"It's not like rebooting a computer." But she did try it. The starter still just clicked. "We have half a tank of gas, so it's not that. *Shit.*"

They tried for a few minutes more, and then heat drove them out of the truck. They went back into the café, where Bridey, scowling now, called the tow truck at Milburn's Car Repairs.

It was after five before Bridey let her walk down to the library. She got there just as Erwin was coming out, a few hefty books unsteadily tucked under his skinny arm. "Oh, hi Logan." At school he'd been fairly cheerful, now he had the expression of someone in a hospital waiting room expecting bad news.

"Hi. Are they closed?"

He nodded. "Closing right now." He looked glumly at the ground.

"Are you . . ." Logan broke off. She didn't know him well enough to ask him why he was so upset. She nodded toward his books. "Are you reading about, um, animal husbandry?"

"No. About predators." He looked out toward the hills overlooking the town. "California predators. Migration of cougars and like that. My cattle . . ." His mouth buckled and he looked close to crying.

"Something attacked those cows . . . the cattle you were raising?"

He gave a single quick nod. "Yeah. Something killed them all."

"*All* of them?"

"Didn't even leave much behind. Tore them up, ate 'em. Could be coyotes, even wolves—but no tracks." He took a deep breath. "I got to catch the last bus home."

"Sure. I'm walking up to the garage." Logan dropped her book in the "Return" slot. "If you're going that way."

Erwin walked with her up to Milburn's Car Repair, both of them silent, squinting against the maliciously angled sunlight. Her thongs seemed extra noisy on the sucking soft asphalt. When they got there he turned, smiled shyly at her—a touch of gratitude in that smile—and walked on.

Logan went into the cluttered, oil-redolent garage office. Bridey was standing by the window, chewing her lower lip and looking anxiously out at the empty street.

"Library was closed," Logan said. "I dropped off the book."

Bridey gave the faintest of nods.

Logan sat in an old wooden chair—and almost at the same instant, Miles came in. Miles Winn. He was loosening his tie, carrying his Army captain's jacket over the other arm.

Bridey turned him a cold, heavy look. "Just to make the day complete."

Miles was a round-faced man, a little plump, with sweat on his wide forehead. He took off his cap, wiped his face with a sleeve and said, "Wow. Still hot. I saw your truck in the garage there . . ."

"Yep, there it is," Bridey said, voice tinder dry.

Miles nodded pointlessly. "I talked to Milburn. He doesn't think you'll get it fixed today. You need a ride?"

"I don't, no," Bridey said, her voice clipped. She looked out the window again.

He turned his hat in his hand. Logan was surprised at the way he was looking at Bridey—sucking air through clenched teeth and staring at her without blinking. Then he turned briskly away and walked out without a word.

"Damn," Logan said. "What happened with you guys?"

"He's been harassing me, is all. I'm going to report him to his commander. Don't worry about it."

"But—"

Milburn came in, then, wiping grease from his hands with a red rag, his incomplete smile stretching his thin red face. "Well, we got to order a part. New distributor. Don't have it for that model."

"How soon?" Bridey asked, getting wearily up from the plastic chair.

"Maybe tomorrow afternoon. If they have it in Quarryville."

"I can give you a ride after work," he went on. "But that'll be after seven-thirty, or so."

It was eight-thirty before they were bouncing and swaying along the curving country road, all three of them in the tow truck's big front seat. Milburn was still wearing his coveralls; his blackened fingers left marks on the steering wheel. Logan was glad she was sitting by the window. She didn't feel comfortable around Milburn.

She looked out across at an uncultivated field thick with a tall yellow-flowered weeds. The sun was barely down; the western horizon was still a brooding scarlet.

They were still half an hour from the farm when Milburn said, "You know, that distributor—looked like someone cut those wires."

Bridey stared at Milburn. "*Cut the wires?* Why didn't you tell us this back at the garage, that someone cut the wires? I'd have called the sheriff!"

"Because—" He licked his lips. "Captain Winn told me not to say anything. Said he'd take care of it. He thought it was somebody pranking you. He wanted to handle it."

Logan gaped at him. "Miles told you not to *tell* us?"

"He—Miles is not a guy you cross. People in town, we learn that." He shook his head.

Bridey swore under her breath. Then she asked, "Christ, Milburn—couldn't you have just . . . I don't know . . . *spliced* the wires or something?"

He grimaced—he had a scowl as big as his grin. "No ma'am, you wouldn'ta been sure to get all the way home, with spliced wires. Now, what I'm thinking—"

"There's something in the road!" Bridey said suddenly, pointing.

Logan clutched at the dashboard as Milburn hit the brakes. They swerved to a stop about fifty feet from a big tree-trunk lying across the highway. In the headlights it looked glossy black. Maybe the bark had been removed, Logan thought.

Both ends of the trunk stretching across the road were hidden in shadow under the fringing oaks.

"Oh god, a fallen tree!" Bridey said. "That figures. That just fits right goddamn *in* with this whole damn day. Can you drive around it?"

"Well now, I don't know, with that woods there. Maybe I could tow it out the way. Gotta have a look." He switched off the engine, pocketed the keys, and climbed out of the truck.

Logan watched Milburn walk into the overlapping circles of headlight glow. He stopped and stared, looking right and left along the tree trunk.

The tree wouldn't be easy to move even with the tow truck—it looked to Logan like it was four feet in diameter.

Milburn shook his head and turned toward them, shouted something. "*I don't think it—*"

Then the tree trunk started to move.

It was sliding, right to left, across the road, very slowly, with the thick sluggishness of a lava flow.

"Is something pulling it or . . . ?" Bridey asked. "No. It's . . ."

Logan's mouth was dry. It was hard to talk. "It looks like . . . it's *moving itself.*" What was making her heart pound, her mouth dry, was the fact that the tree trunk was *slithering*, weaving very slightly from side to side, as it went. It was supple, and it was big, and it was sliding along on its own power, shimmering in headlight glow with the motion. Milburn was gawking at the big, sliding black form. He backed away, still gaping.

"Didn't even leave much behind. Tore them up, ate 'em. Could be coyotes, even wolves—but no tracks."

"Bridey?" Logan heard herself say. "What is that?"

"I don't know. Is it *really* . . . ?"

Now the thick, tubular sliding thing was changing directions. Its middle was rippling toward the truck, where Milburn had backed up against the grill. There was a whickering sound, and a kind of heavy white static that rattled the windows with its intensity. And then the black trunk suddenly looped, in a motion almost too fast to follow, and nosed around Milburn, looping, gripping him, squeezing . . .

Killed them all, Erwin had said.

Milburn's head popped off his shoulders. Blood splashed thickly on the hood of the tow truck.

Logan screamed and Bridey clapped a hand over her mouth to smother a scream of her own.

The slitherer was dragging Milburn's limp, headless body closer . . . It reared up, over the left side of the car—Logan couldn't see it up there, but Bridey could.

With an odd mix of hissing and grumbling the thing was sliding onto the truck cab. The windshield began to crack on the left side; then the roof started to buckle downward.

"Oh no," Bridey said. "Logan—get out of the truck!"

"No! We're safe in here!" She tried to huddle under the dashboard.

"No, dammit, Logan listen to me! That door's going to fly open, it's going to come over there! *Get out!* We need to get out that door!"

A sharp authority in Bridey's voice stirred her; Logan opened the passenger side door, and wriggled out. She saw something dark looming over them . . .

"Run back toward town!" Bridey shouted, her voice cracking.

Panic washing over her, Logan ran. She plunged blindly down the curving road, into the night; after a time she stepped into a pothole, lost a flip-flop from her right foot, kicked the other one off, ran barefoot, on and on.

Bridey . . .

Breathing hard, her feet hurting, Logan stopped, turned to look for her mother.

She couldn't see anyone—just the empty highway, the truck hidden beyond the curve. She was afraid to call out, afraid it might bring the thing that killed Milburn right to her. Moaning, Logan turned back toward town, and went on. But the town was a long ways away.

Was that a car, coming toward her?

Lights lanced the dark, vanished behind trees, then reappeared about a half-mile off.

Logan heard a noise from behind. She spun around, squealing with fear—a dark figure rushed toward her.

"Logan!" It was Bridey's voice.

Bridey's arms clasped Logan, pulled her close. Logan let her mother hug her, and they both panted with relief.

Then Logan caught her breath and pulled back, whispered, "Is it coming?"

"I don't know!"

"There's a car coming. We could wave to them . . ."

Headlights washed over them. Bridey took Logan's arm, drew her to the side of the road. The sedan pulled up—it was an olive-colored government vehicle, with a number on the door.

Chris was at the wheel, ducking his head to look at them. He was a sergeant, in uniform, with buzz-cut blond hair, a clipped blond mustache, a slightly weak chin, gray eyes that usually squinted as if at some private amusement. Right now his mouth was grimly compressed. The window hummed down. "Get in! Quick!"

They climbed in, Logan in the back. Bridey had scarcely gotten the front passenger door closed before Chris gunned the engine, spinning the car to head back toward town.

"You know about it, don't you," Bridey said, looking at him. "That thing back there."

"I . . . yeah I do, Bridey. Lana said you were going out here with Milburn—and the thing is out there tonight."

"It killed him," Bridey said huskily. "Milburn."

"Figured when I saw you."

"If you know about it . . ."

"I've been trying to figure out how to talk to people about it, who to go to. The right chain of command and—I wasn't sure I could do it without some Green Machine clean-up crew punching a hole through my head."

Logan stared at Chris. Was he saying the Army might *kill* him?

"I should have left the farm before now," Bridey said. "I should have taken Logan away."

"Why didn't you?" He was driving rapidly but carefully, slowing more than he needed to when he came to a curve. Like he was worried about what might be around the bend.

"Miles. He said if I stayed, he'd find out exactly what happened to Harve. If I left—no soap. I'd never know. Logan would never know. And . . . he just made me feel like it wasn't *safe* for me to leave."

"Christ. You still seeing him?"

She shook her head. "No. He calls me. Texts me. Way too much. He's . . . I'm scared of Miles."

"He knows exactly what happened to Harve. And that implied threat stuff . . ." Chris smacked the palm of his hand on the steering wheel. "That's the real Captain Winn! Just under the crust of 'officer regular guy,' that's the real Miles: a prick." He glanced in the rearview at Logan. "Sorry about the language."

"I thought he was a prick too," Logan said. "Can't we call the sheriff?"

Chris took a phone from his uniform shirt pocket, and passed it to Bridey. "Give it a try. I'm not optimistic. Wasn't working ten minutes ago. I came out here following the captain and . . . I think he saw me."

Bridey tapped the phone. She listened. "Emergency number's not ringing."

"Try the base's number."

She tried, and shook her head. "It's all fuzzy. Just static."

"Yeah. He's got the damper on the area now."

"Then—just get us back to town, Chris. Please. Fast!"

Logan leaned forward. "Where's my dad, Chris? You said Miles knows. Do *you* know?"

Chris slowed for a curve—slowed a lot. "I just found out for sure. It's a hard thing to tell anybody. That thing—it's all about the big snake." He shook his head. "It's called Zhuyin." He pronounced the name *zou-heen*. "Zhuyin was . . . It's a myth from China. Giant snake with a man's face. It was supposedly a god who brought daylight by opening its eyes, night by closing them. For us it's the Zhuyin Project. What's more elastic, more camouflaged, more subtle, more adaptable to terrain, more under the radar . . . what's got more stealth . . . than a snake? They're powerful, terrifying to the enemy. Make them big enough and responsive enough, armored enough—an exquisitely effective weapon." He added in disgust, "Miles tested it on some of the local cattle . . ." He brought the car to a jolting stop. "Oh no, no, that's . . . Jesus, that thing is *fast!*"

The shiny black oozing thing had cut across country. As they watched, it nosed out ahead of them, weaving across the road into the headlight glow.

Logan saw it clearly now. *Zhuyin*. It was a snake—a snake sixty feet long, thick as a considerable tree, tapering at the tail, scales as big as cup saucers, jet black except for two rings of white back of its jaws, and what looked like a blister of glass and metal on the very top of its head, just above and behind the eyes.

Zhuyin reared up in the headlights' glow and turned to look at them. Its face, a living bas-relief on the diamond shaped head, was made of scales, and was proportionate to its body, but it was did not have a snake's eyes, nor quite a snake's muzzle.

In a rough way, it was a man's face. A man's eyes.

Its visage was black-scaled and too large, but still human. It had eyes like a man's, though larger than normal; the nose was a bit flattened; it had scales over its flattened lips.

It shifted, catching the light differently—and she recognized the face. It was her father.

She screamed and Bridey sobbed and Chris swore.

He put the car into a grinding reverse, looking over his shoulder as he backed the vehicle up. He spun into a turn, roared off down the road, and left the gigantic serpent in the shadows.

"I guess . . ." His voice was hoarse. "It cut across country. And it's going to have a chance to do it again."

Logan felt unreal, distant from everything. The only clear feeling she had was a sickness in the pit of her stomach. She was distantly aware they were driving alongside a ravine lined by dusty, twisted oaks.

"It wasn't really him," Bridey said, between two angry sobs.

"Yeah," Chris said. "It was."

A car was blocking the road ahead. Chris hit the brakes; Logan had to grab the headrest on the front seat. Their car squealed to a halt.

"Is it?" Chris murmured, then added, "yeah," as someone got out of the car blocking their way. "It's Miles."

As if something were breathing on neck, Logan turned to look behind her—and saw a pair of eyes gleaming red in the taillight's glow, as it slithered rapidly after them. It was coming fast, unthinkably fast.

"It's coming . . ." Logan could barely get the words out.

"Just drive around the son of a bitch," Bridey said coldly. "Or over him if you have to." She hadn't heard Logan.

"I'll try to deal with him," Chris was saying. "But—"

"*It's coming!*" Logan screamed.

Zhuyin came slamming down on the car, so that the thin steel roof dented in, then cracked—the back window exploded outward into diamond-like fragments and the back door next to her popped open. Logan threw herself down behind the front seats.

The car twisted against the ground, like a trapped animal struggling to get free of a boa constrictor, tires spinning as Chris jerked the steering wheel and stepped on the accelerator and Bridey shouted wordlessly—

Then the car lurched free, and seemed to leap up . . . and abruptly it dove down.

Logan was slammed against the back of the seats, obliquely saw a branch smash in through a side window as the car plunged down through a sickening series of bounces.

They jolted to a stop in a cloud of dust and smoke.

"Out!" Chris yelled. "*Out!*"

Logan felt dazed, incapable of deciding what to do. This wasn't a time to move; it was a time to lay still, to play dead, to hope it would all pass over them . . . To hope that Zhuyin would slide over them and away, in search of fresh prey.

She felt something tugging on her feet and she screamed and tried to writhe away.

"Stop fighting me, Logan, let me help you get out!" Bridey yelled.

Logan looked, saw that Bridey had hold of her ankles, was trying to pull her out the popped-open door.

Logan let her pull, got her feet on the ground, and clambered out the rest of the way on her own.

She stumbled, coughing, out of the smoke, with Bridey clasping her arm.

They found themselves in a dry creek bed choked with leaves and sticks. Chris was nearby, with a small flashlight in his left hand, and one of those big square-barreled pistols in his right hand. He turned them both to point up the hill.

A whickering and the static sound came from up there. Something was sliding down toward them.

The car started howling then, making Logan shriek in reaction—it was a car horn blaring. She turned, saw their car was crunched into a tree stump, its front end twisted; small blue flames flickered under the crumpled hood.

"Come on!" Chris yelled. "Get away from the car—fast!"

Logan and Bridey stumbled after him, Logan's feet smarting, the car horn howling warningly from behind them; they tripped over roots, barely kept to their feet as they went down the creek bed at the bottom of the ravine. Trying to keep up with Chris, they followed the creek bed as quickly as they could.

The car horn stopped. Logan heard a dull thump and caught a flash of light, looked back in time to see the wrecked car engulfed in blue-yellow flames.

And the living black enormity was coming out of the flame whipped shadows, its eyes catching the firelight, glowing blue-red now. It was a quivering S-shape towering over the fire, looking toward the flames as if hypnotized. *Zhuyin.*

The face turned toward Logan . . .

She sobbed and looked away, hurrying awkwardly on, her feet crackling through dry leaves, and layers of twigs. Chris had stopped, his flashlight, pointing at something.

Logan caught up with Bridey, and saw Chris was pointing his gun now too—the sparse flashlight beam picked out Miles Winn, who was skidding down the slope from the road. He was still in his uniform, but without the jacket and cap, and wearing a headset like something the boys in San Diego wore when they were playing co-op videogames.

There was something in his hands—hard to see clearly in the uneven red light. Then she knew. It was an assault rifle, and it was aimed at Chris.

Up above, the Army captain's car was angled partway into the ravine, its lights on, spotlighting the two men.

Logan stumbled closer—but Chris waved her back, never taking his eyes off Miles. "Logan, stay with your mom."

Logan backed up, and felt Bridey's arms close around her. "It's coming!" Logan called out. "It's behind us."

"He won't come any closer, unless I tell him to," Miles said, skidding a little farther down the dirt of the slope.

He. Miles calls it a he.

Miles was about ten feet from Chris now. "I can talk to him, Chris. He knows my voice. He's wired to obey that voice. Only that and nothing else."

"You weren't supposed to go this far with it. You weren't supposed to hybrid *anything* but chimps."

"He volunteered."

"Not for this, Miles. He didn't volunteer for this."

"Captain. Call me captain, Sergeant Eckhardt."

"I don't recognize your authority," Chris said. "You're a fucking criminal. You planning to keep Bridey in building twenty-three? What's the plan for the girl—hybridization?"

"They can both be useful. And there's a very unusual form of hybridization you may not be—"

Chris broke in, "They're not going to let you turn building twenty-three into your personal dictatorship!"

"I was given full—"

"They did not give you permission to do this to Harve!"

"Dear God, it *is* him, it's *him*, it's *him*. . . ." Bridey muttered. "Harve."

Miles chuckled. "I told you. Harve volunteered."

"He volunteered a sample of his *DNA*," Chris grated. "Not his body, and not his *brain*, Miles! You set him up! You obsessed on Bridey and you needed Harve out of the way! You're a fucking psychopath!"

Bridey caught her breath.

"I need what I need," Miles said equably. His smile was light and pleasant, but his eyes, in the uneven glare, were dark pools. "And the Army needs what it needs. All we've done is make one soldier more like all soldiers should be—how they will all become. What's the difference if . . . inside becomes outside?"

From behind them came the whickering sound, the waves of static . . . and a long, exhaling hiss. Logan thought she heard pain in that hiss.

There was a growing crackling sound too—and the smell of wood and leaves burning. It had been so hot, so relentlessly hot; it had been dry for so long . . .

Miles was looking past them. "Your car's started a fire. That fire'll spread fast. We don't have much time." He looked at Bridey. "You should have trusted me, Bridey! I control him. You come with me, and I'll make sure he doesn't hurt you! You'll be with me and all will be well!"

"You pretended that Harve was dead ... overseas ..." Bridey's voice was hoarse now.

"He was never more than twenty miles from you!" Miles said, with a mocking tone of apology. "He *is* dead though—he wasn't cooperating. And we used some of him. We needed to bioengineer something that had human memory. Fuse it with some very special reptilian genetics ... And glory is upon us! *Zhuyin!*"

Logan tried to grasp it all. *Daddy. Violated. Dead. Reborn into ...*

"You crossed the line a million years back, Miles," Chris said, raising the pistol and aiming.

"Chris!" Bridey shouted. "Don't! He'll—"

Chris and Miles fired at the same time.

Miles staggered ... and Chris, taking three rounds in the chest, sank to his knees, and coughed blood.

Logan started toward him—Bridey dragged her back, whispering, "Get ready to run, just follow me ..."

Miles shifted his rifle to one hand, touched his left side, grimacing. "Just a crease. You choked, Chris ..."

Chris tried to stand—and then pitched over on his left side.

"Chris!" Logan yelled. He didn't respond. His legs twitched. *Dead. Chris is dead.*

"Run!" Bridey cried.

Bridey tugged at Logan and the two of them ran into the darkness, out of the shine from Miles' headlights.

"Bridey—!" Logan called, tripping—almost falling headfirst, then catching herself, staggering on. They were running toward the wildfire; toward the giant black serpent waiting somewhere close by. "Bridey—that's the wrong way! That thing is down there!"

"He controls it!" Bridey shouted between harsh breaths. "He won't let it kill me!"

Was that true? Maybe he would punish Bridey for running away from him, Logan thought.

Maybe he would tell Zhuyin to kill them both.

As they ran from the man with the gun, the wildfire's flames seemed to be running toward them, as if to meet them, to embrace them.

Then, Zhuyin was there—she saw it peripherally, shimmering off to their left, its whickering sound mixed in with the crackling of flames ...

Smoke billowed toward them, as they ran, and they coughed. "Up the hill, Logan, we—" Bridey broke off, coughing.

Logan tried to follow her up the slope, slipped down the steep loose dirt of the hill. She found herself on her hands and knees, and turned to look at the black, serpentine hulk of the Zhuyin limned in flame. She saw it was coiled like a cobra but turning attentively back toward Miles. Clearly it was listening to him.

Black smoke drifted in front of her, itself like a Chinese spirit serpent, and she lost sight of it.

"Logan!"

She got up, coughing, reached out to Bridey's offered hand and caught hold. They struggled up the hill . . . but the flame was there before them.

A thick bank of Madrone and scrub pine burst into flame up ahead, as if it had been dipped in kerosene—prepped by the endless drought the dry half-dead foliage ignited, and in seconds there was a wall of flame blocking the way.

One hand raised against the heat and glare, Bridey seemed to hesitate, as if despairingly stunned by all that had happened. *The serpent. Miles cutting Chris down. The fire. Harve. Zhuyin.*

Eyes stinging from smoke, Logan looked around, and thought she saw a way out up to the right. "This way!" She tugged on Bridey's arm.

Bridey turned to follow, and staggered. She fell to her knees, shaking her head. "I don't know what to do, I don't understand what's—" The rest was swallowed in a coughing fit as smoke swirled more thickly around them.

It wasn't just the brush. The very ground under the plants was burning: "dead fuels" they called it, fallen twigs, desiccated plant matter, the ground's coating becoming an instant carpet of flames. The world was filling with crackling and the hissing of living white static.

The flame rushed toward them. Bridey turned and embraced Logan, covered her as if to take the fire on herself.

"Mom! Mom, we have to go back to Miles—maybe he—"

But as she spoke Logan looked toward Miles, and saw the dead fuel catching fire up the dry creek bed, like ignition running along a fuse. It was filling the valley, and closing in around them, rippling sinuous heat waves and stealing oxygen as it came.

Logan felt a thump on the back of her legs, a hard push, unstoppable and weirdly cunning, and Logan was suddenly up in the air, Bridey clinging to her. Both of them were hoisted up, now too weak from the smoke to resist, and Logan saw that they were just behind the head of the Zhuyin. They had been lifted up by the enormous snake.

Bridey started to slip off—she would fall into the fire that closed in around them. She clawed at the slippery scales. But Zhuyin writhed purposefully in place, shifting so that Bridey remained aboard its wide serpentine back just behind Logan. Then the great serpent swayed upward, raising them above the flames, and went sailing toward Miles like a water snake, skating atop a lake of red and blue fire, until it had passed clear, out of the smoke and spreading flame.

Twenty seconds more—they had were getting close to Miles who was partway up the hill, backing away and coughing.

Logan clung to the scaly body just behind the Zhuyin's cold head, clinging to her sanity at the same time, rasping and gasping between sobs.

Something gleamed on its head—the glass node, a small transparent hemisphere impregnated with hyper-attenuated wires that pulsed with reflected firelight.

She looked past it and through smoke-teary eyes Logan could see Miles, closer now, talking into his headset with a fierce pertinacity. The Zhuyin slithered closer to him . . .

Take it off me. Take it off me. Take it off me.

Whose voice was that? *Take it off me.* Arising out of the white static sound, the hissing, the crackling, the whickering, all of it together, and somehow bound into it: a voice.

A voice Logan heard in her mind.

Take it off me. Take it off me. Pull it off. Take. It. Off.

Logan gripped the serpent with her legs, and reached with both hands to claw at the glass node.

Yes. Take it off. Tear it away.

It was implanted into the Zhuyin's scaly black head—and into what remained of her father. She couldn't get a good grip on the glass node. Her fingers were slippery; the glass offered no purchase.

Take it off. Tear it away.

Logan dug her fingers under scales near the node, and ripped at it with all her strength . . .

The effort threw her off balance and she fell, sliding off the Zhuyin, thumping heavily onto dirt and gravel.

Flame cooked up, close by . . .

"Mom!" Logan shouted. Feeling the bloody glass thing in her hand. She'd torn it from the Zhuyin.

Bridey slipped down beside her. She put her arms around Logan, helped her stand.

Zhuyin was flowing along beside them, toward Miles, who was backing away, shouting at it.

"Go back! Pick them up, both females, and bring them to me!"

Zhuyin bore toward him . . .

There was a black flash, and Miles yelped.

Zhuyin was rearing up with Miles clasped in its widening jaws—jaws unhinging to make more room. The assault rifle was rolling away down the slope.

Zhuyin tossed Miles screaming into the air—caught him, headfirst, gulped him partway down. Then it turned, and slithered toward the rushing wildfire. Which was spreading, charging up the hill like a herd of translucent yellow-red beasts, surrounding them . . .

Zhuyin didn't look at Logan, or Bridey. It glided past, toward the heart of the fire, undulating a little left and a little right, left and right, the whole long length of it wending back to the inferno . . . and it spat. It flung Miles into the flames.

Smoke rose thick and black, and there was screaming and hissing behind a roiling, thickening curtain of smoke. Logan couldn't see the great black serpent now.

Bridey tugged Logan away, and up the gravel scree toward Miles' car. They were almost at the top, and then Logan slipped and fell, rolled yelling for Mom, her mama, not Bridey anymore, Mama now . . .

Smoke closed around her. Fire burst through. Somewhere Bridey called her name. Then the shining eyes . . .

A week later, Bridey was driving a rented pickup smoothly along the highway between wide, blackened stretches of landscape, a no-man's land that had almost consumed their farmhouse. It was a cooler day, clouds had blown in from the north, bringing a soft faintly damp breeze. She wanted to turn back. But she made herself go on, her mouth dry, her stomach fluttering. She kept going.

There—the ravine.

Bridey slowed and pulled over. Hands trembling, she got hesitantly out, and thought, I shouldn't look. The Army had used canine teams to find what little remained of Captain Miles Winn, Sergeant Christopher Eckhardt, and Logan Kelly. Forensics experts identified them from DNA and dental records.

Or so they said. But she didn't trust them.

Bridey sighed and walked stiffly onto the cold ashes, so very black, toward the edge of the ravine. Puffs of ash rose up around her footsteps.

She paused at the edge and looked down into the small, ashen valley.

It took her a few moments to make out the wreckage of the government car they'd crashed into the tree. There it was, in the old creek bed, so blackened that at first she'd thought it was a boulder.

Then she saw something else, along the edge of the burn, past the burned out car, on the other side of the ravine. The breeze was exposing it, now. Blowing ash aside . . .

The numb thought came to her that it must be what was left of Zhuyin. Maybe that was its skin, its skeleton. Or Logan's.

At the very end Logan had called her *Mama*.

Bridey skidded down into the ravine. Hesitated. Then went a little closer. She stared.

There were no bones. But on the edge of the burned, blackened earth, was an empty snakeskin. It was an impossibly big snakeskin, big as an ancient myth. She knew the look of it, she had seen shed snake skins many times.

It was the shed skin of Zhuyin, parts of it slightly charred. And nearby, a long ashen track was pressed into the ground, where something big had slithered off, up the slope, and into the countryside.

She clambered up along the snake track, a mark big as the print of a semitruck's wheel. The grade was steep, and sometimes she had to claw her way up, coughing from disturbed ash.

Sweating, she got to the top, her hands and knees black with ash . . .

Nothing. Just countryside. And the track fading as it approached the thick growth. Unburnt close-growing copses of Sierra shrubbery and small trees; bitterbrush, deer brush, buck brush, sage, Manzanita. Dense and dark.

Hissing, rustling . . .

Then—something reared up, shedding petals from the flowering buck brush. It was a serpent—with two heads, one a little more petite than the other.

Another kind of hybridization, Miles had said . . .

There were two faces forking from the serpent's body. Her ex-husband's. Her daughter's. Faces flattened, scaly, faintly recognizable. There was a deep hiss, a soughing of static . . . and she heard a voice in her head.

I love you, Mama . . .

And then Zhuyin turned and slid away, into the shadows within the shadow-woven, fragrant underbrush. She could see its outline, a purposeful motion rippling the top of the bushes. That direction . . .

Goodbye. Hungry now.

And Bridey knew just where Zhuyin was going. It was heading straight for the Army base.

"IMMORTAL SNAKE"

RACHEL POLLACK

Long ago, in a time beyond memory, Great Powers owned the land, the water, and even the air. Of all these empires, the strongest was a land called Written In The Sky. The soldiers of this land, who called themselves the Army of Heaven, traveled in rolling multi-level engines covered in sheets of black glass so that pillars of darkness moved across the earth.

And yet, despite the strengths of its forces, the true power of the country lay in the wisdom of a group called Readers, priests trained to follow the tracks of heaven known as God's writing in the sky. The priests lived in an observatory called the Kingdom of God, high above the palace of the country's ruler. Every night they watched and calculated the slow movements of the stars, and the swifter movements of the planets. If any clouds dared to obscure the night, the Readers let loose their white bulls, whose bellows of rage cleared the air of rebellious vapors.

Through their perfect knowledge the Readers could tell the Army of Heaven where to strike, or the owners of mines where to dig for copper or gold, or the creators of spectacles what grand images of beauty and desire would entice audiences to love them and long for them.

Most of all, however, the Readers studied the sky for the greatest of all messages, the secret that caused the finger of heaven to stroke Written In The Sky with power—the death of its ruler.

Though the merchants and slave traders managed the empire's wealth, and the Army commanded obedience, all power officially belonged to the ruler who lived in a palace in the central circle of a city called The

Nine Rings of Heaven and Earth. The name of this man was always the same, no matter who it was that sat on the Throne of Lilies. They called him Immortal Snake.

During the time of his reign, each Immortal Snake enjoyed more delights than any single person could imagine. Whole teams of people worked beyond exhaustion to devise new pleasures for him to experience. And everyone loved him. Every house contained portraits of him, and figurines to set above the bed, and there were statues in even the smallest towns. Children were taught to write letters to him, grateful for his love and protection. In every wedding the bride swore love to Immortal Snake and then her husband, who in turn declared himself a stand-in for the beauty and devotion of the ruler.

And yet, all of it, all the adulation and the pleasure, could end at any moment. For as the Readers insisted, it was only the willing death of the Snake—the "shedding of the skin"—that convinced God of the country's worthiness.

No one knew when it would happen, but a night would come when all the stars and planets locked into place. Then the Readers would put on their purple hoods and march through the city, blowing copper trumpets blackened by age, and driving their herds of white bulls maddened by loneliness, through the streets of The Nine Rings of Heaven and Earth. All through the city people doused their fires, even the lanterns in their kitchens, and then locked themselves in rooms without windows or chairs.

At the beginning of his reign each Immortal Snake chose a male and female "companion," two people who served only one function. They died first. The Readers alone knew the exact manner of their death, but their hearts and lungs and genitals went into a dish cooked in a stone pot. Every Immortal Snake knew something very simple. If he wanted to live he must resist the food the Readers brought to him. It was so easy. But lights flashed in the bubbles of steam; and the smell excited tiny explosions all up and down his tongue; finally, like every Immortal Snake before him, he would tell himself that just a taste, just a drop, could not possibly harm him.

When he had eaten the entire dish he would begin to vomit. All his insides would pour out, even his bones, which the food had turned to brightly colored jelly. When nothing but the skin remained the Readers would drape it over a wooden cross they then would carry through the city back to the vaults underneath their observatory. And then, from the directions written in the sky, they would choose a new Immortal Snake. And everyone would celebrate.

In front of the Kingdom of God the Readers would hoe a small patch of earth, into which the new Immortal Snake would plant a seedling tree. As the tree grew the people would take seeds from it to plant in their own villages, a promise that they would never go hungry. When the new Snake in turn would shed his skin the priests would uproot the tree, then prepare the ground for the next planting.

So it happened once again, after so many times. The man who had ruled for a span of years and months that no one was allowed to count (for according to doctrine there was only one Immortal Snake, and his reign was eternal) vanished into a torn skin flapping on sticks. A new ruler emerged, a young man called Happier Than The Day Before. When the Readers came to tell him of his ascension he shouted with joy, for he could hardly imagine all the gifts and pleasures that would pour into his life at every moment. When they left him he stood on tiptoe, stretched his arms out to the sides, and spun around until he fell down laughing. "Immortal Snake," he said out loud. "I'm Immortal Snake. I'm the ruler of the world!"

And indeed, over the next weeks countless marvels and delights arrived from all the lands that owed tribute to Written In The Sky. There were carpets woven from the wings of butterflies. There were bottles of wine sprinkled with the tears of old women remembering the kiss of the first person who'd ever loved them. Performers and teachers from every level came to entertain and instruct the new ruler. Hermits who'd sealed themselves in caves for half a century reported on what the shapes of stalactites taught them about human longing. People marched in and announced they'd committed atrocities just so they could come to The Nine Rings and recount all the details to Immortal Snake, who laughed as he pretended to cover his eyes in horror. Poets who'd been torn apart by wild dogs and then brought back to life as babies floating on the sea arrived to solve any riddle anyone had ever devised.

The spectacle lasted fifteen days. and in all this time only two things wounded the Snake's pleasure. The first was his minister, a pinched looking man named Breath of Judgment, who insisted that Immortal Snake consider his duties, a subject that did not interest the new ruler in the slightest. As far as Immortal Snake could tell, these duties consisted primarily in choosing his male and female companions. And *that* was a subject he did not want to think about at all.

The second annoyance was his sister, an unpleasant young woman named More Clever Than Her Father and Everyone Else. Even before her brother's glorious rise the woman had always done everything to make him feel impure and trivial. She would never go to any of his parties, never laugh at his jokes, never accept the boys he chose for her. She ate only the simplest foods, drank only the smallest sips of wine, and spent her days studying ancient texts, or writing poetry, or designing elegant furniture, or filling the walls of her rooms with murals depicting the mysteries of Creation. She wore long dark dresses buttoned to the neck (though they always contained streaks or panels of intense color), and shoes made of flat soles and worn leather straps that wound round and round her ankles. When her brother and his friends staged elaborate parties More Clever Than Her Father would trace her way through the Nine Rings until she emerged into the desert. There she would spend hours watching tiny creatures scurry back and forth to no purpose.

And now that her brother had ascended to his glory, the woman strode into the throne room, rudely ignored all the acrobats, contortionists, and life-size wind-up giraffes, and simply demanded that he use the power of Immortal Snake to raise the lives of the poor and helpless.

Her smugness made him want to jump off the throne and tear her hair out. But then a better idea came to him. With a smirk he turned to Breath of Judgement. "Good news!" he said. "I've chosen my female companion."

More Clever stepped back. "No!" she said. "Don't say it. There's still time. You can stop."

Slowly, her brother shook his head so that his wide grin swept all across her. He said, "I choose my sister, More Clever Than Her Father And Everyone Else, to accompany me through all the worlds as my female companion." And then, because it sounded so good, he added, "Blessed forever is Immortal Snake."

More Clever said nothing, only marched out past the laughter of all the courtiers who hoped to become the ruler's special friend. She went to her bedroom, where she pulled out a small wooden trunk from under her bed. Shaking, she took out the strands of hair from her first haircut, done at her name enactment, along with the pale blue dress she'd worn, and the black doll in a gold dress her mother had given her as a present after the ceremony. She put these in a basket and took them to the farthest ring of the city, where a small stone building inside the walls housed the Temple of Names.

The Name priests, who all wore oversize masks carved with letters from alphabets nobody remembered, feared she might produce a dead baby from inside that basket and demand they give it a name. But the new companion to Immortal Snake only dumped her relics on the rough stone floor. "My name no longer belongs to me," she said. "I want you to take it back."

The priests tried to talk her out of it. To go without a name, they said, meant that no one could bless her when they cast stones into the Well of Life. Even her dreams would not be able to find her. She suspected what really troubled them—the enactment to remove a name required the priests to inscribe the offensive words on inedible cakes that they would have to eat so that the name would pass through their bodies and be expelled to oblivion. She said, "I don't intend to go without a name. I've found a new one. My name now is Broken By Heaven."

Sitting on the Throne of Lilies, Immortal Snake, once known as Happier Than The Day Before, continued to applaud his parade of gifts. He'd begun to open some of the rarer bottles of wine, and when the minister would ask for a decision on the male companion, the Snake would hold out the bottle as if to offer it, then take a long swallow.

At last the great show came to an end. Only one figure remained, a slave by the look of his knotted hair, his clothes that were little more than a binding cloth and a tunic tied at the waist with a red rope. But he was tall and graceful, with deep eyes and long hands, and a wide strong mouth. Immortal Snake glanced at the sheet of gifts prepared by his Office of Numbers, but all he could see at the very bottom was "slave." He said "Where do you come from?"

"Great Lord," the slave said, "I come from the Emperor of Mud and Glory." Immortal Snake smiled. The Land of Mud and Glory was a rival of Written In The Sky, but even they could not deny him his gifts.

He said, "And your name? Does your emperor allow you a name?"

"Great Lord, my name is Tribute of Angels."

"Wonderful," the ruler said. "We're making progress. Now. Tell me what treasures you bring me from Mud and Glory."

Tribute of Angels cast down his eyes. He said, "I bring no treasure, Great Lord. I myself am the gift."

Snake half rose from his throne. "A slave? Has he lost his imperial mud mind? Would he like his cities filled with the Army of Heaven?"

The minister touched the ruler's arm. "Lord," he said, "perhaps the slave carries some treasure inside his body. The formula for gold written on his bones, or a treaty hidden in his belly."

But the slave shook his head. "Your forgiveness, Great Lord. My body contains nothing more precious than blood."

The minister, fearful his ruler might order a slave's blood poured out onto the sacred floor, said quickly, "Then some talent? Some wondrous skill? What can you do, slave? What knowledge or power do you bring us?"

Tribute of Angels raised his eyes. Their dark light shone into the face of the world's most beloved and hated man. "Great Lord," he said. "I tell stories."

There was a long silence and then Immortal Snake laughed loudly. "Stories!" he said. "Wonderful." And then the Living World of Heaven inserted an idea into his head. A joke. He turned to his minister and said "You want me to choose a companion? There. Tribute of Angels will be my companion."

"Lord!" Breath of Judgment cried. "The creature is a slave!"

"Ah, but he can tell stories. On those long boring nights when you and all the others are off making lists, or whatever you do, my *companion* can tell me a story." He laughed again. "What better companion can a snake have than a storyteller?"

In the Land of Written In The Sky there was no recording of time. Immortal Snake was the Living World's extension into the world of death, a finger from the Great Above stroking the Great Below, and just as the Living World was forever and unchanging, so was Immortal Snake. He existed always, only shedding his skin when God's writing in the stars and planets told the Readers to bring the Snake to renewal. Immortal Snake was forever, and there was no before and after.

Still, time passed, or at least turned, and lesser creatures grew old and died, and the seasons replaced each other, and the Sun would return after a number of days to the same place in the sky. Though the years were not numbered their length was understood, 360 days, just like the 360 degrees of the circle, for wasn't Immortal Snake, like heaven, a great circle without beginning or end? In between the years there were five extra days, placed there by the Living World to allow people a moment outside their duties. Every four years there would be another day before the Sun could return to its place, but nothing that happened that day was ever written down, and so it did not exist.

In this manner of counting, three years passed, 1080 days plus fifteen extra, plus one that no one would remember. Through all this, Immortal Snake celebrated his power. Every night he hosted elaborate parties, with teams of competing chefs from countries conquered by the Army of Heaven. Sometimes the parties featured dramas of the Snake's glory, or paeans to his sexual potency. The guests, who often included heads of state, were given costumes to wear, or assigned various comical tasks, such as the imitation of farm animals.

During the days Immortal Snake usually slept late, and when awake would sometimes fidget, or yell at his slaves or advisors. In the early days he liked to stare at the crowns and jeweled swords presented at his ascendancy, or play with the puppets or mechanical animals given along with the more traditional gifts. Over time, however, these things began to bore him. He even tired of the slave girls' adoration and turned, to everyone's surprise, to his ministers, and the dry voices he used to ridicule. He began to ask questions and every now and then make suggestions. Then, at night, satisfied with his contributions, he would give himself to parties.

In this same period Broken By Heaven stayed almost entirely within her official rooms in the second ring of the Nine Rings of Heaven and Earth. She'd painted grey paint over the murals that once filled the walls, she'd removed the lacquered tables, the carved chairs, the gold and enamel plates, the bed that had stood high in the room under a canopy painted with clouds. Heaven had broken her and she'd ordered the bed destroyed, replaced with a simple mattress on a low wooden platform. She would eat only the plainest food, boiled vegetables and rice without sauce, served on lumpy white plates.

Every morning the young women who attended her laid out elaborate dresses for her in hope that some heroic god might have entered her dreams to drive away the demons who had possessed her ever since her brother had become Immortal Snake. She ignored them and dressed only in white, the color of emptiness.

And Tribute of Angels? The storyteller who was simultaneously slave and companion to the Ruler of the World spent his days alone, in a

small chamber at the edge of the slave quarters. No work was assigned
to him, hardly anyone spoke to him. Sometimes at evening, the slaves
who collected rainwater from the cisterns on the roof would see him
standing on the edge of the world, his face as empty as the sky.

Three years passed, and then one night the Living World placed two
thoughts in the head of Immortal Snake.

The first was this: *I'm going to die.* The trumpets would blare in the
night, the people would lock themselves in their windowless rooms, the
bulls would run through the streets, and then the Readers would feed
him that stew of death that no Immortal Snake had ever resisted.

He looked around at all his splendor, the ornamental swords he had
never learned to use, the jeweled mechanical lions and butterflies, the
two beautiful nameless women asleep in his perfumed bed. Useless. All
his ministers, useless. The terrible Army of Heaven, useless. They too
would hide their faces, they would shut away their black engines of war,
for when the Readers declared that God's writing in the Sky demanded
the skin of the Snake, nobody challenged them.

That was the first thought. The second one was this: *That storyteller.
My companion. Maybe he can distract me.*

Though the Snake could not remember the storyteller's name, he
knew it would be listed as the final gift from the Emperor of Mud and
Glory, and of course, as his official companion into death.

Should he summon the slave now? He could wake up his steward,
who would wake up the Chief Minister, Breath of Judgment, who
would do something or other. No. He decided he wanted to enjoy the
story in the proper setting. He went back to bed where he pushed aside
the two women so he could stretch out, and fall asleep. When he awoke
he ordered Breath of Judgment to prepare the storyteller, for that night
the gift of Mud and Glory would entertain the Snake and all his court.

It took some time to locate the gift and companion, but at last Tribute
of Angels was brought to the inner rings, where the Wardrobe Minister
For The Snake's Amusement bathed, oiled, and dressed him. It was a
challenge; the minister was not used to dressing men, at least for this
version of Immortal Snake. At least the slave simply did whatever was
asked of him, with a look on his face that was not exactly empty, yet
impossible to read. He would say only "The Living World wills it." The
minister did his best, and by evening Tribute of Angels was ready to
perform his task.

The storyteller arrived in the great Hall of Precious Happiness at the beginning of the feast, when the slaves were about to bring the first dishes and pour the first glasses of wine. Music announced him, reeds and drums and flutes. According to tradition, God gave these to the first musicians when Immortal Snake descended from the Great Above to the Sad Below. Since then, countless musicians had lived and died, servants of the eternal song, for a musician is nothing more than a body in this world of suffering and death, while music itself, like Immortal Snake, is unending, the voice of the Living World. There were no trumpets, however. These belonged to the Readers.

The Snake looked at his Companion and was startled to see how beautiful he was as he stood among the torches. Tribute of Angels was taller than the Snake remembered. His hands were long, with tapered fingers. His hair had been tied in a slave knot the only other time the ruler had seen him; now it was brushed back and decorated with tiny purple stones. Its color was a coppery gold, but there were black strands as well, dark streams in a river of light. His face was both strong and delicate, as if angels flowed into his body. He wore a tunic of yellow and blue silk, perfectly fitted yet not too ostentatious for a slave.

For a long time the Snake just stared at that graceful body, that serene face. But then the smell of lamb cooked in figs returned him to his feast, and he laughed happily. "Come," he said, and patted a cushion near his feet. "Come tell us your story."

"Great Lord," his slave and Companion said, "your command is my blessing." He sat down, his back straight, his hands in his lap. Immortal Snake raised his wine glass, painted with peacocks and lions. All the guests raised their glasses at the same time, for it was impolite to drink before Immortal Snake, who waited for the opening words of the story before that first cup of wine would delight his mouth.

Tribute of Angels began to speak, his voice soft yet somehow touching every ear, like perfumed smoke. They listened and closed their eyes, and slowly they put down their glasses and leaned back in their chairs. The slaves stopped serving and sat down on the floor; there was no harm, for no one was eating. The musicians set down their instruments, and everyone closed their eyes and smiled. Tribute of Angels' voice wound through them like the river that once flowed from Paradise until it became lost in the dark woods of human suffering.

It was a tale of a boy and girl who swear their love for each other, only to be separated just as they are about to kiss; separated first by the boy's uncle, for there was no dowry, and then by demons jealous of their beauty. At last, after decades of trials, they find each other in old age and discover that their long-delayed first kiss restores them to the perfect moment of their youth.

Immortal Snake, and all his guests, and his slaves and his musicians and his dancers and his cooks all closed their eyes, and smiled, and floated away. When they opened their eyes again, thinking that a few moments had passed, they discovered it was morning. All the food was cold, and all the wine was dull. It didn't matter. Each one got up and silently left the room, leaving Tribute of Angels on his cushion at the feet of the Snake, his legs underneath him, his back straight, his head slightly bowed, his face serene. For a long time Immortal Snake looked at him, then the Snake too got up and walked alone to his bed.

The next evening the ruler once more summoned his companion to the Hall of Precious Happiness. "Ah, but tonight," he said, and waved a finger, "you will tell us your tale *after* we have eaten. Otherwise, all our food will rot and we will all become as skinny as slave children taken into the Army of Heaven." He laughed at his own joke and waved his companion to a red cushion at his feet.

"As you wish, Great Lord."

They ate, but quickly, and sipped their wine without the proper intervals to allow the alcohol to flow lazily through their blood. It made no difference. If they were drunk, or dyspeptic, or agitated, or sleepy, that all changed the moment Tribute of Angels began to speak.

He told of Lover Of Wheat, an ancient Goddess who ruled over all the plants and animals that feed the world. The Goddess had a daughter who every morning played among the flowers that sprang up at her approach. One morning the girl saw a shadow on a rock wall, and she found that she could not help but stare at it, until a breeze stirred the flowers, and the movement of color distracted her. The next morning there was the shadow again, and this time it took the form of a man, handsome and tall. Lover of Wheat's daughter stared at him a long time, her face dry and hot, her fingers trembling.

The morning after that she ran outside without eating. Frightened, Lover of Wheat followed her, but the daughter was swift, and by the time the mother reached the field the daughter had taken the hand of Shadow and walked into a darkness in the rocks.

The girl found herself on a stone stairway that went deep into the earth. When they reached the bottom, Shadow put his arm around her, and stroked her face with long fingers, and touched her shoulders, and her back, and finally her lips. She trembled, and closed her eyes, and let him hold her, and kiss her, and when he whispered "Be my bride," she whispered back, "Yes. I am your bride."

While she stood there, and gave herself, soft voices gathered all around them. When she opened her eyes she discovered she was in the Land of the Dead. Great crowds of shadow-people surrounded her. "Shining In Darkness!" they shouted, and when she looked at her arms she discovered it was true, light pulsed from her with every breath. She turned to Death, her dark husband, and turned back to look at the hungry faces who already longed for the joy only she could bring them. That was when she knew, she would love her husband deeply, but she would love the dead as well.

In the world above Shining In Darkness, her mother, Lover of Wheat, wailed and waved her hands. At first the Gods tried to soothe her, but then they grew angry. "Why should you complain?" they told her. What better husband could there be than Death, for he was always constant, and his subjects endless?"

Lover of Wheat would not be consoled, only cried louder until the King of the Gods, whose name was Voice In The Sky, ordered her to stop that terrible noise. She fell silent then, but only for awhile. She found the empty shell of a dead turtle and attached to it the neck of a swan who, like the turtle, had gone down to dwell with her daughter's husband. Next she attached long sinews of the muscles of dead cats. Now she strummed her lyre, an instrument born out of death, and she began to sing.

Down below, Shining In Darkness lay next to her great and terrible lord, when suddenly she felt a shock in her heart. A song was riding over her, verse after verse, a song of her return and the world's joy at greeting her. "All the lions will stand roaring . . . all the owls will fly in moonlight . . . all the trees will wave their branches . . . six black horses will come running . . . *all the dead will rise up singing . . .*"

"No!" she cried, and Death woke up to stare at his beloved. "Help me," she begged, for the song was pulling her. Already she could feel herself fading from darkness. Her husband tried to hold her, all the dead crowded round to protect her. They shouted to drown out the song but it was no use, the melody filled her and lifted her, she pulsed between shadow and light. "Six white horses . . ."

At the last moment, Death reached into his own body and took out his heart. The dead rushed up to it and it opened like a pomegranate of darkness, with a thousand seeds. Just before she vanished, while her fingertips still touched her husband and their endless tribe, Shining took three seeds and swallowed them.

An instant later she stood again in the breezes and smells of life, in a field of flowers, so bright with such an excess of color, she could not bear to look at them. Her mother stood there, tall and strong. Lover Of Wheat dropped the lyre and held out her arms, but when she saw her daughter's face filled with grief she whispered "What have I done?"

Shining In Darkness said to her mother, "As you are to the Living, so I was to the dead."

"Oh my blessed child," Lover of Wheat cried. "I have done a terrible thing." They wept together, and at last the Daughter embraced the Mother, for sorrow had overcome her anger. When they stepped back Lover Of Wheat said "Now tell me. Did you eat anything in the Deep Below?"

Shining nodded. "Yes," she said. "I ate three seeds of my husband's heart."

Her mother smiled, with love and sadness. "Then you are free to return to him for one third of every year. In the season of the lion and the season of the swan you will remain with me, but in the season of the serpent you may join your husband and all your children."

This was the story told by Tribute of Angels on the second night of his service to his master, Immortal Snake. All those who heard it never knew exactly when the story ended, for they floated down strange and glowing rivers until finally the dawn came and they discovered themselves back in the Hall of Precious Happiness. Silently they left the room, careful not to look at each other until only the Snake and his companion remained.

Tribute of Angels sat with his hands in his lap, his eyes cast down. The Snake whispered "Come again tonight."

"As you wish, Great Lord."

"No. Not my wish. My life. Your voice is my breath. Your stories are my blood. I was dead and you have brought me alive."

Tribute of Angels raised his head now, and for the first time his eyes met the eyes of the Snake. "Yes," he said. "I will come again this evening."

"Thank you," said the ruler.

That afternoon, four women dressed as deputy ministers came to the slave room of Tribute of Angels. Their disguises were not very good, really, despite their false beards and mustaches, and hair pinned up under a minister's three-cornered hat. They giggled when Tribute of Angels inclined his head and said "My lords. How may I serve you?"

In a deep breathy voice the one who wore the highest rank announced "We have come to take you to your new quarters."

Tribute of Angels stood up. "As you wish."

They marched from the outer to the inner rings of the Nine Rings of Heaven and Earth until they came to a wide set of rooms with high ceilings. There were subtle tapestries on the walls, and carpets that mimicked a summer lawn. Lacquered chairs and tables were draped with clothes, from shimmery robes with striped collars to shoes with long toes that turned up in spirals. In the inner chamber a large bed was piled high with pillows and blankets of every color.

The minister smirked as she waved a long graceful hand whose fingers were each painted a different color. "Do you like it?" she said.

The storyteller said "It is all very beautiful."

"Our lord Immortal Snake ordered that we prepare these rooms for you."

"My gratitude is beyond words."

They giggled again, nearly overcome at the idea of anything beyond the words of this blessed being. The minister said "I chose the clothing myself." She inclined her head sweetly toward the inner chamber. "For you and for the place of rest. And pleasure."

Tribute of Angels bowed his head. "Your taste is exquisite. I hope you will not consider me ungrateful if I ask for a small change."

"Of course. Our lord said to give you whatever you desire." She smiled, and the others stared at the floor.

"I have only one need. A smaller bed." As the women stared he said "I am a slave. My only joy is the service of my lord. I will live here, and wear the clothes Immortal Snake wishes for me, but I would sleep in a slave's bed, narrow and hard."

She tried another smile. "Ah, but what if you desire company?"

"In that case, my lord, I am sure the proper setting will reveal itself."

The imitation ministers left without further comment. In a short time workers came to remove the bed that would have housed the storyteller and all four of the women. Tribute of Angels was not there, and gone were the bed linens and most of the clothing. He had taken them to the outer rings, to distribute among the slaves and the poor.

That night his story was a sad one, about a woman who gives birth to a phantom. Those who heard it found themselves under a gray sky, with only streaks of rose and violet colored lightning to guide them. Though the listeners blinked open their eyes at dawn with the belief that they had wept for a hundred years they still sent rings and paintings and marvelous toys to the storyteller's bare and lavish rooms. He gave away everything but one painting, a miniature of a black and yellow bird perched at the top of a golden tree.

During all this time, the three years that were officially the same moment in the never ending life of Immortal Snake, his sister and companion, Broken By Heaven, remained in the small empty room she had chosen for herself. Her servants lived more lavishly than she, for they were ladies of the court, and she had given them her gray-washed rooms and moved into the servant's room. Despite the pleas of her young ladies, who longed for romance and intrigue, she refused to go anywhere or see anyone. There was no point, for at any moment the trumpets might sound and the white bulls trample the stone streets. And then the Holy Readers would cut her throat, and cook her into their poisonous stew.

So she sat quietly, often just staring at the wall, or occasionally writing poetry, in complicated forms, in a large leather book that had once belonged to her grandmother, using very black ink to write over the supposedly wise and sacred teachings that covered the pages. Should she kill herself? It would end the terrible waiting, and if nothing else it might disrupt the calculations of the Readers. Just for that reason, she knew they would never allow it. Along with the chattering ladies two men stood guard at her doorway. They told her that the Snake had sent them to protect her, but she knew why they were there, and whose orders they followed.

Sometimes the young ladies teased the guards and pretended to seduce them. Oddly, Broken By Heaven never seemed to mind their silliness. In the days when she was More Clever Than Her Father she detested such women, whose heads contained nothing but powder and kohl. Now, however, she enjoyed their laughter and their whispers, their heartbreaks that never seemed to last more than a few days, even their occasional pouting. They were alive, and eager, and no one was waiting for the right moment to murder them. They were all she had, and she loved them.

So it was that one day, after noticing them even more breathless and twittery than usual, she asked what had so excited their interest. One of them, a bright young lady named Flower Of Her Brothers, clapped her hands and said "Oh mistress, last night we went to hear Tribute of Angels. It was so marvelous. You must go." The others joined in, "Yes, please please go."

Broken By Heaven smiled at her. "And what exactly does this Tribute of Angels do? Is he a singer? A love poet?"

"Oh no," Flower said, and all the ladies laughed at the thought that there was anyone, anywhere, who did not know of this wonderful man who was a very gift of God. She said, with a certain pride, "Tribute of Angels is a storyteller."

Broken By Heaven closed her eyes. She remembered now. She had heard how after she'd walked out on her wretched brother he had taunted his ministers by choosing a storytelling slave to be his male companion. Soon—at any moment—she and this slave would bubble and cook together in a bowl of death. She said "I would like to hear this man. Do you think he will perform again tonight?"

The girls jumped up and down with excitement. "Yes, yes," they proclaimed, "he tells his marvels every night. There's a feast beforehand. We can dress you and—"

Broken held up a hand. "I think the storyteller will be enough for me. What time does he begin?"

She entered the Hall of Precious Happiness just as the guests finished the final glass of wine, the last dates coated in exotic jellies. She wore a white dress, cut too large and made of thick cloth so that it appeared she had no body, only a head riding on clouds. She might as well have worn burlap from head to toe with only a single webbed eyehole for all the difference it made. Or, for that matter, a dress of light spun from the mouths of stars. Tribute of Angels' head rose up as if pulled by wires the moment she entered the room. She saw him and staggered backwards. After that neither moved, but only stared with frozen faces, as if they would hold that moment forever.

Immortal Snake took no notice, only said "Well? We're done eating. We're ready. Blessed God, you haven't run out of stories, have you?"

Tribute of Angels lowered his eyes. "No, Great Lord. The well of stories is inexhaustible, for every moment more stories are born than anyone can tell."

"Well, then you better begin."

"The fulfillment comes before the wish."

That night Tribute of Angels told of a king, an alchemist, who had discovered that he could live forever by drinking the blood of young women. He had no shortage of sacrifices; he was rich, and powerful, and the poor offered their daughters to him. But he was also alone, and he longed for a queen who could rule alongside him. One day he heard of a woman more beautiful than the birds, more perfect than the morning star. He sent his nephew to bring her back for him. "Tell her," he said, "that she will never die, for I will not take her, but instead we will share our blood, and together we will drink the milk of paradise."

The king lived on an island, and so the nephew sailed away in a marvelous round boat guided by songs; he would sing to the sea, and the currents would carry him. When the woman heard the king's message she agreed to go with the nephew, for all her life she had never allowed herself any pleasure or desire, fearful that a fever or a random arrow or a hungry beast would take her away from whatever happiness she might possibly find. She traveled with him, and they were in sight of land, when a whale breached against the side of the boat, pitching them against each other. The nephew had his mouth open and it happened that his teeth fell against her neck, so that he, and not his uncle, was the first to taste her blood.

Nothing sweeter had ever flowed down the throat of any creature, human, or angel. And for her, the puncture of his teeth was like the burst of a bubble that had hid from her all the glory and wonder of the world. He told her that if she joined with him she would give up immortality, for only his uncle knew the secret of turning blood into life. It made no difference, she said. Quickly he bared his neck, and she bit him, and they were bound together.

The tale went on to tell of the king's rage, the lover's flight, how they found themselves, after years of hiding in caves, in a lost sanctuary known as the Garden of the Two Trees. Once, in the early days of the world, this garden had been a sheltered place, but now the roots of the Trees had withered, and all the leaves had turned to stone. Here they would die, they said, for above them they could see the king's ravens and knew he would be upon them in days. They had reached the end, and no longer wanted to run.

Long ago, the Living World had sent an angel with a flaming sword to guard the entrance to the Garden. As the Trees withered, however, the angel had fallen asleep, and now when the king arrived, he found the sword lying on the ground. He picked it up and raised it over his head, eager to destroy his traitorous nephew and the woman who had turned down immortality for the life of a fugitive. The two made no attempt to hide, but only sat in peace, ready for the blow.

As the king lifted the sword, however, it struck a stone wall, and sparks of fire scattered on the ground. The sparks burned a hole into the earth and out of it came the ghosts of all the women whom the king had killed. In moments the ghosts surrounded him and pulled him down into the Land of the Dead, where he still remains, the only living being among the shadows of Death.

The nephew and the lover were free. When he kissed her, then bit her neck, two drops of blood fell onto the roots of the great Trees. They heard a sigh, and then, slowly, the roots filled out, fresh leaves grew on the branches, and light and fragrance filled the air.

When the story ended everyone had fallen asleep but the Snake's two companions. Broken by Heaven walked through the scattered bodies, never looking down, never missing a step, drawn to Tribute of Angels like a shooting star pulled down to Earth. The storyteller stood with his body tilted towards her then stepped towards her so that they were both moving at the moment they met, like butterflies mating in the air.

They kissed until the end of the world, until the Readers all died out and their observatory crumbled, until her brother and all the Immortal Snakes had wandered off into caves to meditate and dream, until the Moon and Sun merged together. So it seemed, but when she finally let go and opened her eyes she saw it was still night, and her brother and all his guests and servants and slaves still sat in their chairs, or lay on the carpets, or stood propped against pillars of marble and onyx—and every one of them asleep.

Tribute of Angels said "I have no place."

"I know of one," she told him, and took his hand. She led him through rooms and corridors until they came to a mahogany door that opened into the bed chamber of Immortal Snake. They spent the night there, deep in each other's bodies, until just before dawn when they returned to their places in the Hall of Precious Happiness. Soon everyone awoke and left the room.

That day, Broken By Heaven surprised her ladies by asking for color in her clothes. After several consultations and dashes to seamstresses they presented to her a violet dress shot through with swirls of yellow and green. Their suggestion of a special haircut was met with a single upraised hand, so they settled for taking turns brushing her hair, ten strokes each, with a silent prayer for their mistress's happiness at the start of every stroke.

The dress fit so well, and her hair shone so brightly, that Immortal Snake did not even recognize her until his eyes had followed her halfway into the Hall of Precious Happiness. When he realized this was his sister he blushed, then made a face, thinking she had come to lecture him for wasting his time with stories. He braced himself for a fight, lining up in his mind all his recent efforts to persuade his ministers to help the poor. When she said nothing, only smiled (he could hardly remember the last time that had happened), and took a seat at his right, not far from the storyteller, he was surprised to discover he was disappointed. He almost wanted her to scold him so he could show her how wrong she was.

The tale that night was like a drug, a smoke or an oil that first delights the senses, and then carries one away down a river of color and sound, and wave after wave of pleasure. It was not really sleep it brought, and not really a dream, but in a short time they were all gone. All but the storyteller himself, and one of his listeners. Broken By Heaven stood up, and Tribute of Angels rose beside her. They kissed a long sweet time, certain that no one would disturb them. Then once again she took his hand and led him to the wide bed of the ruler of the world.

They continued this way for a week until one night, as the dawn approached, and Tribute of Angels began to gather his clothes to return to the Hall, his love began to cry. He said nothing, only kissed the flow of tears on her face. Finally she looked at him and she said, "I don't want to die."

"No," he said.

"They will come today, or tomorrow, or next week—do you know what they will do to us?"

"Yes."

"*I don't want to die.*" He held her now, his arms and legs around her, his head on hers, as if the force of his love could shield her from heaven and earth. Then, to his astonishment, she laughed. When he unwound from her it was like unwrapping a present. "I have an idea," she said.

That afternoon the female companion to Immortal Snake, dressed in the simple clothes of a minor lady of the court, made her way through the intricate streets of the Nine Rings to a hill beyond the edge of the city. There were no trees on this path, only the single fig tree at the top of the hill, that her brother had planted when he became Immortal Snake. Here and there crosses stood alongside the road, hung with tattered clothes like pieces of skin. Broken By Heaven knew what they were, of course, the symbols of the dried out skins of all the Immortal Snakes who had gone before her brother, and whose actual skins remained in the vaults underneath the observatory. Beyond the road, in large black pens, the white bulls snorted and scratched at the ground, as if they themselves were only waiting for the moment when they could tear her to pieces. She stopped a moment and stared at one of them, his shoulders like earthquakes, his eyes like tornadoes. He stamped the earth and she almost lost her balance but she held fast, and when the bull looked away, the female companion of Immortal Snake laughed and continued up the path.

The Kingdom of God was a large square building with a glass roof. There were four doors, one for each season. At dawn on the equinoxes and solstices the Readers of God would step out the door of that time of year and sound the trumpets, as if they themselves commanded the sun to show itself. Broken By Heaven took a breath and entered the gray door of winter.

A consultation was taking place, and Broken By Heaven stayed back while the Reader told a jewelry maker the best day to open a new shop in a colony city. When the jeweler had placed the proper fee in a toad-shaped box made of gold and jade, and then hurried out (for no one stayed longer than necessary in the Kingdom of God) Broken by Heaven stepped into the light of the wide room.

At first the Reader allowed shock to open his face, for it was no secret what the Snake's companion thought of the Readers and their sacred duty. Quickly he recovered and crossed his arms over his chest as he inclined his head. "Mistress," he said, "how may this servant of God help you?"

She looked around. The ceiling was high, and painted with stars and animals running through the sky. Along the walls stood more of the tattered effigies on crosses but now the rags were made of gold leaf. Broken By Heaven said "I've never been here before."

"No, Mistress."

She smiled to see his nervousness. Though he wore the yellow and purple robe of his office the fabric looked a little thin, the snake amulet around his neck made of bronze instead of gold. She said "I wonder if you might ask the head of your order if he wouldn't mind talking with me a moment. I have a question I would like to ask him."

"Of course," the man said, and hurried away, eager to let someone else answer her questions. They could not deny her. The Snake's companions into death were due every honor, every request granted but one.

The master was a larger version of the underling, broader, thicker, with gray hair grandly swept back, a bushy beard with eyebrows to match, a thick nose and scarred hands. Broken By Heaven had heard he was once a wrestler. His robe was thick and luxurious, his talisman almost large enough to be a breastplate. Gold, it depicted a snake wound around a tree whose fruit was stars. "Great light of our heart," he said. "You fill this hard-working temple with joy."

"Thank you," Broken By Heaven said, and nodded. Then, "Lately I find myself awake at night, curious beyond curious with a single question."

She could see his shoulders tense, the head tilt down slightly. Carefully he said "My lady, some things we cannot know in advance. All we can do is give ourselves to the sacrifice when God reveals the moment."

Broken pretended to be startled, amused. "Oh no," she said. "I would never—that would be like cheating, wouldn't it?" She smiled sweetly at him.

"Please forgive me, mistress, I wasn't saying—"

"To be honest, my question is not practical but philosophical." He said nothing. "Tell me. What is God's greatest gift to the world?"

He laughed. "What you ask is too easy. Certainly God's greatest gift is the writing in the sky. Through this one benevolence we know everything—when to plant, when to harvest, when to attack or defend, when to build homes or compose songs, when to dig a well or begin a marriage—everything."

She nodded. "What you say is of course true. But God has given Tribute of Angels the power to tell stories in a way that has never been equaled."

For a moment he stared at her, outraged. Then his breathing calmed and he said "You are not suggesting that a storyteller can surpass God's writing in the sky?"

"No. I am saying that this life on earth is a greater wonder than all the calendars of heaven. And the voice and stories of Tribute of Angels are the doors to understand this."

"Forgive me, Lady, but what you say is nonsense. God's writing lasts forever." He did not add "And the voice of the storyteller ends the moment we kill him."

She said "The writing in the sky, the moon and the stars, you know these things. Have you listened to Tribute of Angels?"

"Of course not."

"Then how can you judge? Only come tonight, you and all your brothers. Come this one time, and then you may decide."

The old battler crossed his arms. "We will be there, but I warn you, we will not stay. God's writing is a gift that renews itself every evening."

"Thank you," she said. "I look forward to your presence in our company."

When Broken By Heaven returned to her room she wrote a short note on a piece of blue parchment, sealed it with a stamp of a boy and girl holding hands in a garden, then gave it to Flower Of Her Brothers, the least frivolous of her servants. She said "Take this to Tribute of Angels."

The storyteller bowed his gratitude to the breathless young woman, then waited till she left before breaking the seal. "They come tonight," the note said. "Be ready."

When he first saw the Readers enter his Hall of Precious Happiness Immortal Snake jumped from his chair as if he would outrun them. The guests too rushed to the side of the room, expecting bulls to charge in and trample the ruler. They soon realized that no trumpets had sounded, no orders had come for the people to hide themselves in their houses. And look, there were the Snake's companions, and neither of *them* had panicked. Carefully the guests returned to their seats.

"Great lord," the Master said, with all his crew, some twelve of them, from boys to old men, clustered behind him. "Your sister, who is beloved of heaven, took pity on our loneliness and came to speak with us." Immortal Snake stared at his sister, who looked down at her hands in her lap. He glanced back at the Reader, who did not seem to find such modesty unusual. The Readers, however, had not known her all their lives. Suddenly interested, Immortal Snake leaned back in his chair and said "My sister is a kind and generous woman."

"She told us," the Reader said, "of the wondrous stories told every night by your blessed companion, Tribute of Angels."

Now the Snake looked to his other side, where the slave too sat modestly. The remains of his panic flowed out of him now, and he raised a palm, as if in gratitude to God. He said to this man, who someday would feed him poison and mount his skin upon a stick, "The Living World honors us to have given us such blessings as Tribute of Angels. And of course my sister." He waved a hand to the slaves, who rushed forward with chairs and cushions. "Please," the Snake said. "Come sit with us. Would you like some roast pork? My cooks have stuffed it with dates and fennel."

"Forgive us, Lord," the head Reader said. "Our time is limited. The stars have already begun to show themselves, and the planets to move among them. When the moon rises we must go with it."

"Of course," Immortal Snake said.

"So if we leave before the end of the story, you will understand that we are only following our duty."

Immortal Snake noticed that his sister had abandoned demureness and was now smiling warmly at their guests. A strange excitement stirred his spine. He said "We understand." He turned to his slave companion. "You had better begin if our guests will have to leave early."

Tribute of Angels said, "Your wish creates my voice."

That night Tribute of Angels told a story of the first people. In the beginning there was only mud and stones, and the bright sky, and trees as thick as houses, and flowers in colors no one remembers. Then there were lions, and spiders, and squirrels, and nightingales, but no people. One morning a leopard came home from hunting all night to discover that an eagle had killed his wife. The leopard had no idea why the eagle would do this, only that his wife's body lay in pieces on the dirt. He roared and wept and begged her to come back to him but it was no use. After a day of sorrow he flung his wife's remains on his back and left the open fields and woods that had been their home.

The leopard walked for nine days and nights, frightened to sleep lest crows and jackals and ants take away more pieces of his wife. Finally he came to a desert, and a dream of an oasis. There was nothing there, really, but if the leopard closed his eyes he saw bright trees, and a waterfall, and herds of antelope who had never heard of leopards. He set down his wife's body alongside what he imagined was a pool and lay down next to her. Then he wept and wept until there was nothing left of him but spotted skin over a pool of tears. The tears changed the dirt to salty mud, and out of this mud the first people stood up, naked and frightened, with no idea of how they would live.

For generations people traveled from desert to forest, from islands to mountains, frightened, stealing whatever food they could from the animals, hiding in caves or the tops of trees. They traveled from the north to the south, from the east to the west, and everywhere they were hungry and helpless and hunted.

One night a woman with three sons hid in a muddy hole in the earth, a place not much different from any other except that the walls flickered with black and yellow light. Though she did not know it she had found her way back to the cave of the dead leopards. That night she dreamed of the sky.

Usually her dreams were of running, and the teeth of wild beasts, but now she dreamed that she sat upon a rock high on a mountain and looked up at a sky that flowed like blue water over the peaks of the world. In all her life she had never dared to stare up like that—what if a pack of dogs attacked her children, what if the other women picked all the roots before she got to them? But here, in her dream, she stared and stared, and the more she looked the more she could glimpse a different world on the other side.

She woke up with sorrow in her throat. All day she thought of the dream, while she dug in the dirt for worms, while she searched for bubbles of rainwater that would not make her too sick. That night she rushed to feed her sons so she could return to sleep. Lying there on the mud floor, her body sighed with pleasure as she found herself safely back in the dream.

This time she saw creatures in the world beyond the sky. Some were two-legged like people, except that they had beaks like birds, and sometimes wings that flashed out from their shoulder blades. And they stood upright, their backs straight, unafraid. There were other creatures, brightly colored bulls and horses. They looked solid yet they also seemed made of music and light.

That morning she woke up in tears and wept all day long. As evening approached she did everything possible to avoid falling asleep, for she could not bear to visit that world and wake up in this one. She could not help herself, she fell asleep before the moon rose.

Instead of sorrow, however, she found hope, for this time the dream was different. She was not alone but stood in the center of a crowd of people. Under her command the people constructed a stone pyramid that allowed them to climb close to the sky world. With stone knives painted with pictures of the sky creatures they slashed their arms and flung the blood above their heads. Hawks and eagles raced for the blood, and as they fought for it their beaks and wings slashed open the sky.

The creatures of light and music poured down into the world. They raised up the people and fed them sky food so that the people would live forever and never be hungry. They showed the people how to make buildings out of songs, graceful houses where everyone could rest comfortably, temples that spiraled up into the sky so the people could meet with the sky creatures and praise them and receive their blessings.

When the woman woke up she jumped to her feet, summoned her boys, and began a journey to tell everyone her dreams, and what they all should do to open a door for the sky people to enter their world. At first no one believed her. They chased her with rocks or tried to take her sons away to make them dig for food. Slowly, the woman's insistence began to convince people, first one or two, then larger groups. Soon she had several hundred people, enough to build a pyramid to open the sky.

Everything happened just as in her dream. When they climbed the pyramid they could see the thinness of the sky, see and hear and even smell the world beyond. They cut their arms and flung their blood upwards with great drama and energy. Sure enough, there came the birds, and they fought each other in their hunger, and the claws and beaks tore open the sky, and the creatures of light and music entered through the gash. Soon the Bright Beings stood on the pyramid, towering over the people.

And then it changed. Instead of giving instruction and blessing, the creatures of light and music began to snatch up the people and lift them to their mouths, where teeth like icicles broke them in pieces.

The people screamed and knocked each other down as they tried to run or just tumble down the pyramid. Some jumped off, for they'd rather crush themselves on the rocks, a death they understood, then be swallowed in dark ice.

The woman who had brought this disaster was in fact one of the few who escaped. She reached the ground and ran as hard as she could, slipping on blood, weaving between pieces of bodies. She kept running until she came to the shelter where she'd hidden her three sons.

If life was hard before, now it was much worse, for as well as animals and cold and sickness and hunger the people had to hide from the Bright Ones.

Time passed, and the woman did little but wail and wave her hands, so that her sons had to carry her on their backs as they moved from one hiding place to another. Finally the oldest son said "Enough! We need to fight back." On their travels he'd seen how a certain kind of rock was changed with fire to become hard and shiny, with sharp edges. Now he found some and took it to a bubbling volcano where he could heat it and then work it with other stones. Then he cooled it in the evening rain. He did this during the new moon, when power becomes strong. When the weapon was ready he stood up in an open field and challenged the Bright Beings, thinking if he could cut open just one or two they might respect the people and keep away.

It was hopeless. They broke his shiny weapon like a toy, then tore him apart, sounding laughter through the hills.

The second brother decided that the first had been a fool to challenge the Powers. He climbed a hill with his head down like a submissive dog, making sweeping gestures with his arms as if to clear away his unworthiness before he even took a step. When he reached the top he threw himself face down on the ground and called out "Great Ones! Creatures of music and light. Spare me and my family and I will show you where the people are hiding."

The red and black horses shook their manes. The golden bulls stamped their feet. The one with the head of a hawk said "Why do we need you? We can smell humans whenever we want them." And then the second brother too was torn apart.

The youngest one had heard and seen what happened to his brothers. Now he slipped quietly down to where his mother was hiding. The mother shrieked and hit the flats of her hands against the sides of her head when she realized two of her sons were gone. The youngest grabbed her wrists and leaned forward until he could feel her breath. "Be quiet," he said, "or I will cut your throat." She stared at him, then cowered silently against the wall. When he told her to give him her clothes she immediately obeyed.

With his mother's clothes under his arm the boy went to a deep cave he had discovered at the foot of the pyramid where the people had opened the sky. Using mud and ochre he painted great pictures of the bulls and horses and the bird-headed creatures. Next he found a tree that had fallen and been hollowed out by termites. He carried this with him to the cave, where he took the skins of people who'd thrown themselves from the heights and sewed them together, then stretched them over the ends of the hollow tree to make a drum. Finally he took a leg bone, cleaned it and polished it, and set it aside as a striker.

Now he put on his mother's rags and rubbed mud on his face, and went outside the cave where he hit his hands against his face and cried out "Oh! Oh! Oh! I am the most wretched woman who has ever lived. My babies are eaten, no one will help me, everyone hates me. Oh! Oh! Oh!"

The Great Ones laughed and came charging at him as he ran into the cave. When they got inside, however, they forgot all about him, for they saw the pictures and became entranced. Excited, they rushed into the scenes on the walls.

Immediately, the boy jumped up and pounded the drum. "Brightness of sky," he chanted. Bam! "Hardness of earth," Bam! "Don't leave these walls." Bam! "Through death and through birth." Bam!

The Great Ones struggled and twisted but it was no use. They were trapped in the paintings and would never get out. Once more the boy chanted and hit the drum. "Trapped in stone." Bam! "Trapped in dirt." Bam! "Feed our hunger." Bam! "Heal our hurt." Bam!

Ever since that day the people could compel the Creatures of Music and Light to help and teach them, but the Bright Ones could never escape to enslave or eat the people ever again.

This was the story told by Tribute of Angels on the night the Readers of the Sky traveled down from their observatory in the Kingdom of God to Immortal Snake's Nine Rings of Heaven and Earth. The story began at evening but no one knew when it ended. Around the time of the moonrise a few of the Readers shuddered, and pain flickered through their faces but they did not leave their places. When morning came, and the guests and servants and slaves shook themselves awake, the Readers hurried from the hall.

That afternoon Broken By Heaven once again climbed the hill to the Kingdom of God. The chief of the Readers met her at the door, his arms folded, his feet firm on the ground. They stared at each other a moment, then Broken by Heaven said "Which is greater? God's writing in the sky, or the stories of Tribute of Angels?"

"We were not ready," the Reader said. "You did not tell us." The sister of the Snake said nothing. "We will come again tonight."

Broken By Heaven bowed her head. "Your wisdom is great," she said.

All that day the Readers chanted and burned pieces of paper with prayers for strength. They tethered a young bull in their courtyard, walked around it seven times, one for each of the planetary spheres, and then slaughtered it, first cutting its fetlocks so it would topple forward, then the throat. They let the blood drain into the earth, then cut out the heart, which they burned so that the fire might carry the dead bull to the Living World. There, they hoped, the bull would tell of their devotion, and the angels would buoy them up to resist this man who claimed to be the angels' tribute.

The Readers came to the Hall of Precious Happiness that evening wearing their formal robes, with black vertical stripes cutting through the purple and yellow. They wore their bull masks, and each carried one of the crosses with tattered rags. When those symbolic skins entered the room Broken By Heaven looked at her brother. She was pleased to see that he only cringed, and just for a moment. The Readers set their burdens against the walls and sat down with folded arms. None of them spoke. After a few silent breaths Immortal Snake turned to his left, where Tribute of Angels sat on a cushion. "We seem to be all here," the ruler said. "Why don't you begin?"

The story that night was a simple one, about a boy who falls in love with the moon. Every month, as the moon wanes, he offers parts of his body to the wolves so that he might dwindle with his love until, at the dark of the moon, he lets them tear out his heart. But the moon has changed his heart to white quartz, so that the wolves cannot swallow it, and every month squirrels find it and place it in a dirt mound, and add twigs and nuts and dung to it, so that slowly it takes the shape of a boy. Finally, the light of the full moon brings him alive for he and his lover to be united for three precious nights.

The story was short, but all who heard it drifted away from the earth, carried beyond the houses and treetops, beyond the mountains, far into the region of the evening stars. Soon they were cast into a deep sleep from which not even a storm could have stirred them. All but Broken By Heaven and Tribute of Angels, for they were in the trance of love, and that is deeper even than stories.

They spent the night wrapped together in the bed of Immortal Snake. When they returned to the hall the guests were just starting to awake. Once again the Readers hurried from the room, not looking at each other, even leaving behind their effigies of cast-off skins. Immortal Snake pointed to the tattered crosses and said to a pair of slaves "Take those things away and burn them." Broken By Heaven stared at her brother.

She did not visit the Readers that day. Instead she lay on her bed while her young women darted all around her, and she thought about Immortal Snake. He was the weakest part, and therefore the most dangerous, of all her plans. Would he be ready when the time came? She had learned to expect so little from him, but he seemed different, stronger. Had the stories of her beloved Tribute changed him? Could they have rearranged his brain and heart? She smiled at the thought. A month ago she might have said it would take a miracle to change her brother. But wasn't Tribute of Angels exactly that? She closed her eyes so that her body might remember his voice, his lips, his hands, his body pressed against her, inside her. He was, she thought, the breath of God speaking through the harsh words of humans.

The next night the Readers came without announcement or ceremony. They sat in places already reserved for them, they listened and slept, and when morning came they hurried away.

So it continued. Every evening the Readers slipped into the hall, their eyes down as if they did not want to see each other, or pretend that if they did not look no one could see them. Every morning they hurried away, like a man who has a vision of God in some unlikely place and is embarrassed to let anyone know but he will make sure to come back.

A surprise came to Broken By Heaven on the day she went to her brother to suggest he think about his responsibilities to his people. She expected ridicule, or just petulance. Instead he asked her to help him, to tell him what to do. They began to work together, for the poor, the merchants, the fishermen and farmers. They even punished those who took bribes and cheated the people. They talked together sometimes for hours, and made plans to use the Army of Heaven to help people in faraway lands. What Broken By Heaven did not tell her brother was that all this work, all this change, was in fact preparation. For she was waiting for a certain event, or rather a moment, and there was no way to know exactly when that might happen.

The moment came at the beginning of Spring, when the first flowers broke through their buds to offer color to the sky and to the eternal glory of Immortal Snake. Broken By Heaven was surprised it did not happen sooner, and while she was grateful for the time to prepare her brother, she had become anxious, and had taken to staring at those early buds, or the birds annoying the sellers in the market, thinking "Too much time has passed. It should have happened by now."

Then, on a cool morning with clusters of clouds low in the sky, a man walked the path up to the Kingdom of God. He was ordinary, this man, short, fleshy, a spice dealer. It could have been anybody. He entered the temple, glanced around nervously, then placed his hands together and inclined his scraggly beard toward the lower level Reader who had come to greet him and take his money in exchange for the usual blessing or amulet.

The request, however, was more substantial. "Wise one," the man said, "my daughter is getting married and of course she cannot do so until after the middle day of the Spring festival." The reader nodded; any marriage begun in the weeks prior to the Day of Cuts would never see a single child. He nodded, but his face was strangely pale. The spice dealer continued "I have not heard any announcements of the Festival. Can you tell me, please, when it will happen so we may plan the wedding?"

The Reader stood silent a moment, then said "Please wait."

Inside, in the meeting room, he found the majority of his friends and superiors, some playing the game of Chase on a board of red and blue triangles, others sipping tea, or reading. He thought, *they're waiting for evening.* "A man asks the time of the Spring festival," he said. "What should I tell him?" Everyone looked around the room. "Who has been studying the night sky?" Now they all looked down. "Has anyone written down the progress of the moon and planets?"

One of the Readers jumped up. "Follow me" he announced. "They did so eagerly, grouped behind him as he marched past the statues and wall carpets to the private chamber of their leader. Through a half-open door they could see him standing by the window, like a man caught in a memory of a dream. He was turned in the direction of the Hall of Precious Happiness.

Fury rose in him when they told him their dilemma. "This is absurd," he said. "All we need to do is consult the book and give the man his answer." No one answered him, and when they had all climbed up the tower to the records room just outside the glass-roofed observatory, and the Master slammed open the giant gold-bound book, he too fell silent. No one came close enough to look; they all knew what they would find, blank pages since that first evening they had gone to hear Tribute of Angels. For weeks they had been using old calculations for the minor questions presented to them, but the Spring enactment was of a different order.

Finally the oldest among them, whose robe was so worn the colors had run together, spoke softly. "We were enchanted. A spell has taken us away from God's writing in the sky. Now we cannot say when the seasons call their festivals. We no longer know when to shed the skin of the Snake."

The High Reader clenched his fists. "Tribute of Angels must die."

The old man said "If the Living World has sent him it is the will of God. But if he does not come from God he must surely die, for no creature can resist him. I have looked, and even the insects cease their flight to listen to him."

The master answered "God taught us that the sky is a living book, with words written every night. Tribute of Angels has taken us away from that wonder of wonders. How could he have come from God?"

"Then he must die," the old man said.

They turned back to the stairs. Softly, the young Reader who had begun it all asked "What should I tell him? The man who asked about the festival?"

When the master didn't answer, the old man said "Tell him to be patient a short time longer, until the will of God shall reveal itself."

All that day and night the Readers built up their power. They cut the throats of three bulls, they cut their own arms and legs, they burned parchments with prayers, they burned the clothes they'd worn when they went to hear Tribute of Angels. In the morning they marched down the hill to the great city and palace of Immortal Snake.

A single figure stood at the gate. Broken By Heaven stood motionless in a long white dress, with a white jewel set upon her forehead.

The Master Reader crossed his thick arms on his chest. "Mistress," he said, "please step aside. We come as messengers from the Living World."

Broken By Heaven said "When we spoke weeks ago I told you that God's greatest gift was not the writing in the sky but life on earth, revealed in the stories of Tribute of Angels. Now, today, tell me if I lied or spoke the truth."

The Reader answered "Tribute of Angels desecrates the will of Heaven. Now he must die."

"And who will kill him?"

"That is the province of Immortal Snake, beloved of God."

"Tribute of Angels is the companion of Immortal Snake. Is it time, then, for the Snake to shed his skin?"

"We will speak with Immortal Snake directly."

"Of course. God dwells in my brother. Come with me." She turned and opened the door that led to the royal pathway of the Nine Rings. Though her skin and all organs trembled, she walked with a firm step, never looking back.

They found the ruler sitting alone in his petition room, on a chair carved with lions and swans. Broken By Heaven had told him to wait there; now she was pleased to see the formal air he struck, as if indeed the Living World would speak through his mouth.

The High Master of the Readers spread himself face down on a carpet depicting Immortal Snake raising the dead. "Great lord," he said as he rose to his feet. "Speak to us of the slave, Tribute of Angels."

"My companion in death."

"Yes, lord."

"Then I shall speak. God sent me first the terror of my dying and I was frightened as a naked child. God then sent me the memory of the slave who had come to me as a gift, by record from the Emperor of Mud and Glory, but in truth from the Living World. His voice and his spirit made me happy, and so I gave him gifts, beautiful clothes, statues, gold. He gave it all to the poor, and the people love him. He has given me something almost as precious as his tales. He has taught me to serve my people, and for this I would kiss the tips of his fingers."

The Reader said "He will destroy everything. His stories cover God's writing in the sky. Without that we cannot know when to hold the festivals, we lose the length of days and the order of the nights. We will not know when Immortal Snake must shed his skin. Yes, I speak of that too, for without the sacrifice the Living World will take back its blessing, and nothing will remain but death."

"I once cared for my life," the ruler answered, "but now I care only about my people."

"Good. Then for the sake of the people destroy Tribute of Angels."

Immortal Snake closed his eyes, and his sister held her breath. He looked again and said quietly "Since we agree that all we do is for the life of the people the people will decide." The Readers stared at him.

"Come tonight to the Plaza of Celestial Glory. Then you will tell your fears to all who wish to hear them." And with that he stood up from his chair of lions and swans and left the room.

The Plaza of Celestial Glory celebrated Written In The Sky's triumph in one of its many battles with the Empire of Mud and Glory. Formed by the facades of the palace and various ministries, its huge open square flashed with gold, rubies, sapphires, and emeralds, the colors of the sun, blood, the sea, and the plants, so that all of heaven and earth would honor Immortal Snake.

Soldiers cleared away the beggars and street merchants who usually clogged the sides of the plaza, then workers built platforms for the Readers to address the crowd, and booths for honored guests. Meanwhile, heralds traveled all up and down the Nine Rings, and beyond to the villages and farms, calling out the message that that evening Tribute of Angels would tell his stories to the people.

That afternoon, Broken by Heaven once more traveled to the Temple of Names. At sight of her the priests cringed inside their stone masks of forgotten alphabets. They still remembered the day she demanded they take back her childhood name, and they recognized the basket she carried. She'd already used it to discard her original name relics, the strands of hair, the black doll. When she turned it over this time it held only an oversize white dress of coarse cloth. "My name no longer belongs to me," said Broken By Heaven, who once was More Clever Than Her Father And Everyone Else.

The priest said "Mistress, the Living World does not like it when a woman—"

"My new name," she said, "is Wiser Than Heaven."

They did the ceremony as quickly as possible and purified themselves as soon as she left.

Thousands gathered, from farmers to ministers, beggars to generals. Even the deaf were there, for word had spread that the stories of Tribute of Angels could heal the sick, even those beyond hearing. At first no one was sure which way to look but then a great snake banner unfurled from a low palace balcony and everyone knew that that would be the source of "the Voice of God," as some were calling the Snake's companion.

Before that voice, however, there came another sound, and if the crowd had been capable of movement they might all have panicked and tried to run inside the buildings. Trumpets. The great copper horns of the Readers sounded in the evening air, and people covered their eyes, for the sound was the signal for Immortal Snake to shed his skin, a ritual no one must witness. They cowered down as best as they could, trying to hide among their neighbors, wondering when the white bulls would trample them.

Instead, they heard voices, amplified through speaking tubes. "Arise, blessed ones. The champion of heaven and earth calls upon you to watch, and to listen." Still frightened, they nevertheless dared to look up. And then a great cheer surged up from the plaza, for yes, there were the Readers, terrifying in their masks and robes, and look, they carried no effigies this time, but the very remains of previous rulers—but above them, on the royal balcony, Immortal Snake opened his arms to his people. He wore a robe of blue silk streaked with red, the colors of sunrise, and his face was painted golden, and on his head he wore a golden crown in the shape of a coiled serpent with eyes like the night sky flashing with stars.

"Beloved," Immortal Snake called out, and his voice carried across the square to bounce off the sides of the ministries. "Tonight you will give your judgment of what is true and what is false, what is above and what is below. Listen now to those who have served us through all our past glories, the Readers of God's Writing in the Sky."

The Master Reader stood at the front of the platform, with the skins of the past rulers lined up behind him. "You believe," he said, "that Tribute of Angels has come to you from the Living World. This is a lie. He and his stories have risen up from the Abyss. If this man lives, God will abandon us and all our joy and glory will fall to dust."

As soon as the Reader finished Immortal Snake spoke again. "Now hear the voice of Tribute of Angels. And then decide if he shall live or he shall die."

From inside the palace the storyteller stepped onto the balcony, wearing only his slave cloth. "I am a servant of God," he said. "All hatred in the human heart is a violent strike against the Living World. Therefore, I ask only that no one seek violence. I call for no man's death, but offer only a story. For Immortal Snake has asked that I tell a simple tale, and there is no greater joy than service to Immortal Snake."

In later years scholars would ponder and explore the stories of Tribute of Angels. They would write them all down, both forward and backward, and then add up the number values of all the words, and chart the shape of the letters, and search for phrases that appeared first in one tale and then another. But no one ever talked about the story told on the night the Readers called for the death of the teller. No one wrote it down, and everyone who was there would claim they had no memory of what he said.

He spoke softly, without the speaking tube, yet each one heard him like a whisper alongside the face. It seemed to each that he or she stood alone in a dark world, and the only light was the glow that flowed from the lips of the storyteller. In the beginning the tale was a sweet dream, soft and quiet. Then a wind came, and swept them into a storm of fire.

He talked through the night, and as the world edged toward morning his voice rose, and the story shifted wildly, one moment as joyous as the hidden doorway to Paradise, the next a lightning bolt of terror. As the first edge of dawn approached, his voice cracked open their bodies and shattered their bones.

At last it was over. The sun had not yet risen but the people discovered they could open their eyes, look around them for the first time in many hours. There, at the feet of the platform, on the mosaic tiles depicting the glory of victory, the Readers lay, every one of them face down in a great wash of blood.

In the plaza the people stared in confusion and horror. Many looked up at the sky, frightened the stars would fall to earth and crush them. On the balcony Immortal Snake had to steady himself as he looked down at the blood, so much of it, he thought he would drown in it. Alongside him, Tribute of Angels stood motionless, his head down, his arms held low, the hands clasped together.

Only his lover was able to speak. Wiser Than Heaven took the arm of her brother. "Now," she whispered, "before they can run away. Look for the white horse tethered just inside the gate. Go!" Immortal Snake stared at her a moment then he seemed to come awake and hurried inside to the stairs. Wiser Than Heaven turned to her beloved. "Walk alongside him," she said. "I will follow."

She watched him as he glided down the stairs, then she stepped onto the balcony. "Children of Immortal snake" she cried. "Beloved of the Living World. The Angel of Death has stepped among us tonight. God's will has revealed itself. Look up, look up! Do you see? The stars have not vanished, they shine so brightly you can see their faces. The stars cry out with joy. They shine for *you*, and they shine for Immortal Snake, who has descended from heaven to live on earth. And now, children of God, behold your ruler. Your servant. Your father. Immortal Snake comes among you!"

With that the great doors of the palace flung open as if by the hands of angels, and Immortal Snake rode forth on a white horse, its mane braided with diamonds. The people fell back, frightened, but they could not keep away, for he was beautiful, far more than the idealized portraits and statues. It was the beauty of a man who has ridden on the boat of stories, traveling beyond the sky night after night. The storyteller himself stood beside him, and the people bent down to kiss the dirt around his feet. Soon Wiser Than Heaven joined them, and slowly, with the Snake's male companion to his right and his female companion to his left, they moved up the hill to the deserted observatory known as the Kingdom of God.

When they reached they saw that the young tree, which the Readers had planted when the new Immortal Snake ascended to the Seat of Heaven's Grace, lay uprooted on the ground, its branches withered and dry, as if it had lain there for years. Wiser Than Heaven took a small gold-handled hoe which she had attached to the saddle and gave it to her brother. "Hoe a small place on either side of the tree," she whispered, and was thankful for the grace and elegance with which he did as she told him. Next, she and Tribute of Angels both took a handful of seeds from a green silk pouch she wore around her neck and dropped them into the hoed dirt.

"Children of the Snake" she called out to the huge crowd. "Now you must close your eyes with holy dread, for no one may witness what is about to happen." All up and down the hill people put their hands over their eyes and crouched down and buried their faces in their arms. A strange faint sound drifted through the air, the softest whisper of a breath, a scratch on the wind. Tribute of Angels was telling a story to the seeds. When at last Wiser Than Heaven called to the people to open their eyes two fully grown fig trees stood at the top of the hill. And behind them vines and flowers covered the walls and doors and windows of the Kingdom of God.

Thus ended the long rule of the Readers, who worshipped the sky and ignored the earth. No longer would they kill the Snake's companions, no longer would they lure him to shed his skin. From then on, Immortal Snake would serve his people for the length of his life.

Far to the east, in the Land of Mud and Glory, the man whom his subjects called Emperor of All the World stood in a small dark room with the seer of the imperial court. Though the Emperor was a short man and the seer was long and bony the Emperor rose high above the diviner, for he stood on stilts covered by his long robe painted with the night sky. His face was painted green and his hair was braided and waxed to stand out from his head like the rays of the sun.

Very old and thin, and dressed in a shapeless robe the color of mud, with long white hair, the seer might have been a man and might have been a woman. Not even the Emperor knew, or cared.

The two of them stared into a small three-legged cauldron where the remains of an ancient tortoise bubbled in a dark broth. "Now?" said the Emperor.

"No," the seer said. "Not yet."

The Emperor sighed. "Then it will not come in my lifetime."

"Perhaps not even in the lifetime of your son. But it will come."

"Then all is good."

Immortal Snake ruled seventeen years, dying finally after he went out in a storm to command a tornado not to attack his city. The tornado turned aside, but the ruler became ill and his lings filled with water and he drowned in his love for his people. During his reign, with his sister and Tribute of Angels beside him, he became the living breath of compassion and wisdom. And power. The Army of Heaven extended its rule over countries and provinces and peoples no one had even known existed. Every year the other Great Powers sent money and treasure to the Nine Rings, while their young men and women imitated the styles and speech and art of the land of Immortal Snake, which was no longer Written In The Sky, but had been renamed, under the direction of the ruler's sister, Mirror of God.

Tribute of Angels no longer spoke every night, but four times a year, at the beginning of the seasons, people gathered at sunset up and down the hills to the south of the Nine Rings. Tribute of Angels would sit cross-legged on top of the hill, wearing the slave clothes in which he'd first come before Immortal Snake. He spoke softly, yet each would hear him as if the Teller sat alongside and whispered in their ears. When morning came, the people would walk away slowly, their faces empty but their eyes lit with a secret fire, like someone who dreams that he has passed through the seven spheres and come upon the hidden throne of God.

When Immortal Snake died, panic rose up in the land. People burned their crops at night, for fear the sun had gone out and they would never be warm again. When day came others jumped off their roofs in the belief that divine messengers would lift Immortal Snake to heaven and they would be carried along. The world *must* end, they thought, for no Immortal Snake had ever died a natural death, and now there were no Readers to appoint a new one.

Soon, however, joy replaced terror, for the word went out from the Nine Rings that the people themselves would choose their ruler. As for the choice, no one even had to discuss it. Tribute of Angels became the new Immortal Snake. In a ceremony designed by his beloved, he lay face down on the Plaza of Celestial Glory. One by one the ministers, heads of the noble families, and even village leaders sprinkled him with rose oil, calling "Rise up, beloved of God. Rise up." Finally, Wiser Than Heaven herself took the body in her arms, like a mother sheltering a dead child. "Rise up, rise up," she said. "Awaken to your people. Rise up, Immortal Snake!" Now he opened his eyes, and kissed her, and the celebrations began.

Under the rule of the new Immortal Snake the land of Mirror of God became even more powerful, more loved and admired. Its empire now stretched across the world. When drought or locusts destroyed crops people everywhere suffered, except in Mirror of God, for they had taken the best of every nation's plants and livestock and spices.

For twenty-two years Immortal Snake, who had been Tribute of Angels, ruled his people. And then the sun hid his face, for the Snake became ill.

Day after day Wiser Than Heaven sat alongside him. He lay now on the same narrow bed he'd requested for his quarters so long ago. When she joined him, there was more than enough room for both of them, for it was if each had vanished and a single being replaced them. It had always been like this. In their glory days it was as if a star came to lie among mortals. Now it looked like the union of light and shadow, for the great storyteller was nearly gone.

She was sitting alongside his bed on the tenth night of his illness when he turned toward her and whispered "Can you see the sky?"

"Yes, of course," she said as she glanced up at the high window above the bed.

"Tell me what is written there."

She began to cry, the first time in days. "I'm sorry," she managed to say. "I don't know."

"It doesn't matter," he whispered. "It was all decided such a very long time ago." He managed to turn his head and look at her. His voice so soft she had to bend close, he said "I should never have come here. I should have thrown myself into the sea."

"No!" she said. "Don't say that. Please."

"I thought of it. The night before I arrived. I couldn't do it, even then I could feel you calling to me."

"I don't understand." Instead of answering he closed his eyes. His breath seemed to flutter in the air just above his mouth. Wiser Than Heaven cried out and pressed her mouth down on his, as if she could trap him inside his body. Too late. Tribute of Angels, who was now Immortal Snake, had returned forever to the world of story.

Wiser Than Heaven stayed with the body for three days. When they finally pulled her away she returned to the small room where she had lived before she met her storyteller.

Across the land, people rubbed their faces and even their entire bodies with ashes. Many refused to eat, while they stopped all work and recited stories from the authorized collections. There was no panic, however. It was God's will, they reassured each other, and waited for the moment when the ministers and wise men would choose a new Immortal Snake.

Only—whom would they choose?

Wiser Than Heaven had three sons. The oldest said "I am the first born. By right the land and all the power should go to me."

The middle son said "My brother only cares about himself. I have served the people all my life. The power should go to me."

The youngest said "I was my father's favorite. All power belongs to me."

Each one appealed to Wiser Than Heaven but she refused to speak with them, or to the ministers who begged her for a decision. Each of the brothers gathered allies, spread rumors, made promises. The factions began to battle each other, first through rumors, and then assassinations, and soon armed crowds were fighting each other.

Battalions from the Army of Heaven rushed home, supposedly to stop the fighting, but even before they arrived, their commanders had chosen one side or another. Civil war flashed across the land. Finally, Wiser Than Heaven realized she must do something. She summoned her sons, only to have them refuse to be in the same room with each other for fear of assassination. So she saw them separately, and pleaded with each one to give up the fight for the sake of the people. Each one explained that too much had happened, that when he began the struggle he did so for his own glory, but now he continued for the good of the nation.

The conflict was never decided. In the second year, with bodies clogging rivers, and whole cities burned, and dead children tossed into the branches of trees, an even greater calamity fell upon the people. From all sides, from the sea, the mountains, the desert, a great army invaded Mirror of God, formerly known as Written In The Sky. Made up of soldiers from all the countries Mirror of God had conquered or dominated, the Grand Coalition was led by a young Emperor of Mud and Glory. He stood on a boat with black sails, his face radiant, his body raised up on stilts, and beside him, in an ancient robe thickened with dirt, stood a bent figure who may have been a man or may have been a woman.

The Coalition slaughtered the last remnants of the once terrible Army of Heaven. They killed half the women and almost all the men, and took the children as slaves. In a short time all three brothers were executed in the Plaza of Celestial Glory. Their mother disguised herself as one of the old women who tend the fires of the dead, and threw herself on the flames of her youngest son.

The soldiers tore down the Nine Rings of Heaven and Earth, they smashed every building, every statue, they burned down farms and villages. Then they plowed salt into the cracked earth so that nothing could grow there. At the very end, the Emperor of Mud and Glory stood among the blood-soaked ashes and proclaimed "God has cursed this place forever and ever."

That was the end of the land of Written In The Sky. Once it was the most powerful of all the world's peoples. Now nothing remains of it but sand and misery and a hatred whose origin no one even remembers—that, and the secret traces of a storyteller who was both its glory and its destruction.

"A WOLF IN ICELAND IS THE CHILD OF A LIE"

SONYA TAAFFE

But I know the one there is, and this is not his story.

This is mine: I might have spent the summer in Tuscany, if my mother had visited Iceland in 1968. I could have found a boy in Siena with the face of an Etruscan faun and read him D. H. Lawrence among the vineyards and the oak-groves, olives silver in the sun; in Brittany, paced the stones of Carnac and the pine-dark tumuli and looked out for a reaper's broad-brimmed hat in the bars of Carnac-Plage and La Trinité-sur-Mer; maybe even, if I had accepted Rohit's invitation to stay a few weeks in Kyoto, shared sake and fried tofu with a girl met at the foot of Fushimi Inari-taisha, her hair as fiery cinnabar as its torii, her eyes lit amber like a fox's. In Belfast, in Brno, anyone at all. Or solitude, some postcards, a secondhand book: I could have drunk hot chocolate at the Museo del Prado and spoken to no one. Kept a diary. But my mother's stories were there ahead of me, a planted pale of anecdotes marking out the globe more strictly than capitals or date lines, and at least in Reykjavík none of them could shadow me—student riots in Paris, endlessly feuding in-laws in Bonn, opera buskers in London and missionaries in Thessaloniki and an ill-fated shortcut across the Connemara bogs. *Black,* she said when I asked among their litany for a description of Iceland, *black and white. Lava and ice,* as stark and shuttered in time as all her photographs of that year. All she had seen was half an hour of tarmac

and 707s under snowy overcast, the airport at Keflavík where every other
transatlantic flight was laid over for the weather, their passengers dispersed to hostels and *gistihús* and their own devices, but hers flew on to
Glasgow and she could only look backward at frost and fire, the earth
spilling up through the sea: not blue remembered hills, but fjords and
burning fells; unclaimed. She saw Zeffirelli's *Tosca* at Covent Garden.
She made her backpacker's grand tour of the Continent while I dreamed
sketchily of Ultima Thule, looping Sigur Rós and Thom Yorke for six
hours above the North Atlantic; she learned how to say *I am a good
girl, leave me alone* in Cretan Greek and I took a man from last call on
Austurstræti back to my room at the Hjálpræðisherinn because his hair
was a ramshackle gray and his face too young for the fine lines awled
into it and even on the dancefloor he shivered in his overcoat, crowded
up with strangers and crashing bass. Straddled under me, he looked thin
and lost, as though he could not remember where to start with hands or
hips or silence, his eyes painfully closed under drift-ice brows. I had to
snap out the lights, draw the dormer curtains before he would unfasten
his jeans, pull over his head the dark fisherman's jersey that left his hair
hackled up like winter, boyish against his bunched shoulders, and I felt
all over him the scars I could not see. I could hear him in the bathroom
afterward, throwing up. The solfatara smell of hot water came back to
bed with him, but a cold sweat was on his shoulders and his mouth tasted rusty, tongue-bitten, and the second time we fucked was something
starving: weight and nails, *aftur með gaddavír sem rífur upp gamalt gróið
sár, er orðinn ryðguð sál*. I thought he was starting to retch again, but
it was laughter. *You should try my father* . . . His eyes were lighter than
brandy, resin-yellow. My mother brought home a moleskine of names
from trams and churches, museums and pubs, and folded anonymously
with my pickup in a single bunk, asleep at all the wrong angles to one
another, I had my first nightmares since leaving Baltimore: scoria, torch-
smoke, the seethe and mutter of spattering rock; an icefield sky-bright
under freezing steam; the sun circling endlessly at the horizon's rim.
The four black paws anchored in his naked human feet, the black wolf's
head that had mimed him across the radiator, the fixtures and brackets
as he reentered the room. The walls were filled with daylight where there
should have been dawn. I woke in their Christ o'clock brightness, so cold
I thought I was alone; startled by a feverish heat when I touched the tight
bones of his back. He breathed beside me in small pants and whimpers,

a badly dreaming child. Last night's stubble showed up silvery, black-ticked, like his hair; less transparently, the old weals roped up and down his arms, streaked whitely at his throat. My Reykjavík snapshot, my *rúntur* souvenir. I left him sleeping in the inarguable sunlight, camera in hand to Hallgrímskirkja and the whale-bellied clouds. Whatever we had drunk up and down Laugavegur under the white-night neon reel, the waning daymoon, his shadow by morning rucked and splayed over the crumpled sheets, curled in on itself, nose to tail. When did it ever stop me, knowing someone's name? All I had called him that night was *shape-changer.*

I know his story; I nearly write it sometimes. The girl at the last bed-and-breakfast in Höfn named one of her sheepdogs Disraeli, after Kaori Yuki rather than Benjamin, Earl of Beaconsfield. I laugh when I find out, Váli eyes us both tiredly, un-*bishounen* in the tousling wind that shears the clouds up against the mountains, spits everyone's hair but Ásta's into their eyes. His hands are in his pockets, so neither of us can see his bitten nails; his head rises as though he has forgotten something at each yap and bark. In Sauðárkrókur, we drink store-bought *brennivín* like winos on the curbside with an archivist whose English is as flawed and fluent as his Portuguese, Icelandic, Malayalam, watching sunrise and moonset cross the same luminous sky: Váli makes a tele-scope of the bottle's black-ringed glass and repeats, dreamily cursing, the names of his nephews, fire-jawed pursuers of light. He takes ter-rible pictures of me on the Dutch-spread bed in Kirkjubæjarklaustur, camisole straps falling down and toothpaste on my fingers. I retaliate on the asphalt-colored sands of Vík í Mýrdal, where he flinches with each wave that explodes against the basalt stacks. Between his diffident hands and the confusion of flash adjustment with shutter speeds, the better shots are jags and spurs of light, seepage and clipped signals; his profile frays into the bare blue sky. We are in Breiðdalsvík, the night he finally goes out alone. Back at Pravda, he had stared at me with eyes I took for drink-dilated hazel and said doggedly, *My brother's blood is on my hands. You don't know. I watched them put my father away,* sounding more like a medieval penitent than a bragging ex-con and I thought he was lying either way. Now he crouches away from me in the bedside light, a wet holly spray in his frost-rick of hair, scarlet-spattered across his winter-haunted face, his coat's hem trailing as darkly as the shadow that whines and worries at his heels, and when at last I have gathered him trembling into my arms, all ribs and elbows, hot as a hawk, I can hear his heart hammering the black miles of Surtshellir. Egilsstaðir, Seyðisfjörður with its ferries and nineteenth-century clapboards and the tide rolling green up to green-springing turf, we run the ring round the island that makes a crime scene's chalk of glaciers and it is not the last night he comes home with blood in his teeth. Sheep-killer, I think. Not hikers, backpackers: lovers some bored or aching hour under the pale sun-stifled sky. Are there girls in black mackintoshes and emptied throats, cast up under the birches of Skaftafell? Boys with surprised, wind-roughed faces billowing like ghosts in the white water of Barna-foss? The next butcher's mess he chokes up into the sink or the shower stall, in a ditch or a byre somewhere, laid open to the heavens and the Allfather's single eye. *I am not your brother*, I whisper into his sleeping mouth. He kisses me goodbye at the terminal with almost the same dazed, curious submission, as if he never bit me, or I fucked him till both of us bled. You think of these things at half past three in the morning, when the streetlight filters through frozen rain on the windows, a dead tintype wash you can just read by. Maybe it ends when he kills me. A brief mortal interlude, getting on for Götterdämmerung. Or maybe I introduce him to my mother. I shouldered my bag off the carousel at JFK and—travel-stickered, slightly hungover and still on Greenwich Mean Time—declared nothing more than a bottle of *svarti dauði*, duty-free, two novels in translation and a roll of unshot film. He was gone by the time I came back from the cathedral, only the sun reflecting on the very clean walls, my bruises slowly fading in; a smell of sex and iron in the sheets, as of chains cankered by the sea.

One day, the one you love will tear your throat out. One day, the sun and the moon will fall to their wolves. The earth will flash to clinker in the red-giant rush of stellar evolution, the universe drift to static and silence resolved, and the gods walk quietly across wind-hushed Iðavöllr. One night I dreamed of his father under the earth and the ice, burning in his chains at the core of the world, and I had no answers from him, either. He watched me with eyes the color of white wine, flickering softly as if a candle's flame bobbed and drew before him. I had imagined him slight, sly and sharp-edged, not sinewy as old yew and taller than his lean-boned son, but his hair was spiky, cindery, cider-red, and the same untraceable light shadowboxed in it; I had been asking him questions, but even in the dream I could not remember what he had replied. He should have been skinned bones and screaming. No one had knelt ministering at his side in years. (She left him in 1938, when Grímsvötn's fissures boiled over and the ice of Vatnajökull smoked, bucking in blind agonies as the earth ran. I knew this from the dream, as I knew I would never see the serpent that hung above us in coils as black as the frostbitten dead, the venom that still trickled and dropped, fire-gold, sweating a sticky sundew light, the plain, ash-wood, palm-worn bowl she had set down, carefully, to kiss her husband on the mouth where he could not feel it for the poison running from his eyes like tears. Tall as a Valkyrie, a fair-haired woman with stiffened, scarred hands, never lowering her gaze. I imagined her in Oslo or Copenhagen, looking at Viking ships or the paintings of Edvard Munch; alone of her family, looking as though she moved through time. Her eyes were not blue, but the fine gray of gulls' wings. I do not know if any of this is true.) But the echoes of his voice had crackled to silence against the dark undercurve of stone, the smallest sounds of snowfall and settling ash; all that remained was the smile twisting among the runestone lines of his face. Implicit, inextricable. The vulnerable, catching flame. Not for the son haunting Reykjavík's nightlife like a half-recalled *einheri* or the son whose guts were shackles on his father's skin, for the wolf or the world-serpent or the daughter half-frozen in the dark, but because I had smiled so easily back, I said for the last time, "Why?" and his smile only deepened, or did not change at all.

"Why does fire burn the hand that holds it?"

I whispered, "Your son isn't fire."

Sudden as delight, I saw his real smile, hair and eyes and scars all the same swift leap, flaring up like cinnabar, in their afterimages all the shapes he had once taken and the ones he never would, even at world's end. "*Megir mínir*," he said softly. I expected to hear a salmon's slick flip in it, a mare's whinny or the snapping stems of mistletoe. The roar of the volcano was only the stutter of blood in my ears; the plumbing in that ward-white room on Kirkjustræti had been louder. I heard his son, asking me nothing in the middle of the night.

"All of you are."

I woke in the winter dawn that silvered rather than warmed, ash-gilding book-spines, jewel cases, a saltgrass-streaked set of sake cups.

The clock radio on the floor by the chipped green dresser was playing Radiohead, so appositely I knew it had been seeping into my dreams. I wanted sex with someone. I settled for gunpowder tea, drunk scalding in the poured-out, brightening air as the studio's raddled heating whistled and pinged to life around me. *We are accidents waiting, waiting to happen* . . . A little before New Year's, Rohit called me from the last payphone in D.C. with two suitcases, no gloves, and enough change for cab fare; still the same chapter and a half from the end of his dissertation, broken up with a bunraku puppeteer, he slept on my fold-out couch with the last four volumes of the OED until he could get hold of the conservationist at the Freer and Sackler who had once offered him an internship, digitizing kabuki playbills. Ásta e-mailed me weekly until suddenly she stopped, and then in early February I checked my departmental mail in Gilman and found a postcard of the harbor at Höfn, Prussian blue under brightly painted sailboats and a lyme-grass fringe, the clouds plumed like Eyjafjallajökull. I sent my mother photographs from the trip. *Ragnarök is always coming. How else could we get on with our lives?* One day, I will hold my hands out to be burned, and burn back. And I do not dream of either of them, anymore.

ABOUT THE AUTHORS

Steven Barnes is a *New York Times*-bestselling, award-winning novelist and screenwriter who is the creator of the Lifewriting™ writing course, which he has taught nationwide. He recently won an NAACP Image Award as co-author of the Tennyson Hardwick mystery series with actor Blair Underwood and his wife, Tananarive Due.

Aliette de Bodard writes speculative fiction: her short stories have garnered her two Nebula Awards, a Locus Award and two British Science Fiction Association Awards. She is the author of the Dominion of the Fallen series, set in a turn-of-the-century Paris devastated by a magical war, which comprises *The House of Shattered Wings* (British Science Fiction Association Award, Locus Award finalist), and its standalone sequel *The House of Binding Thorns* (European Science Fiction Society Achievement Award, Locus award finalist). She lives in Paris.

Brooke Bolander writes weird things of indeterminate genre, most of them leaning rather heavily towards fantasy or general all-around weirdness. She attended the University of Leicester studying History and Archaeology and is an alum of the 2011 Clarion Writers' Workshop at UCSD. Her stories have been featured in *Lightspeed, Strange Horizons, Nightmare, Uncanny,* and various other fine purveyors of the fantastic. She has been a finalist for the Nebula, the Hugo, the Locus, the Theodore Sturgeon, and the World Fantasy awards, much to her unending bafflement. Her debut novella with Tor.com Publishing, *The Only Harmless Great Thing*, was published in 2018.

Anya Johanna DeNiro lives and writes in Minnesota. Her short fiction has appeared in *Asimov's, One Story, Strange Horizons, Persistent Visions,* and elsewhere, and she's been a finalist for the Theodore Sturgeon

Award. DeNiro is the author of the collections *Skinny Dipping in the Lake of the Dead* and *Tyrannia and Other Renditions* and the novel *Total Oblivion, More or Less*.

Tananarive Due is the recipient of the American Book Award and NAACP Image Award. She is the author or co-author of twelve novels, a British Fantasy Award-winning collection, and a civil rights memoir. Due has a BS in journalism from Northwestern University and an MA in English literature from the University of Leeds, England, where she specialized in Nigerian literature. Due currently teaches creative writing in the MFA program at Antioch University Los Angeles. She lives in Southern California with her husband, novelist, and screenwriter Steven Barnes.

Bestselling author **Neil Gaiman** writes books for readers of all ages. He is listed in the *Dictionary of Literary Biography* as one of the top ten living post-modern writers and is a prolific creator of works of prose, poetry, film, journalism, comics, song lyrics, and drama. His fairy tale *Stardust* was turned into a 2007 movie while the layered novel *Coraline* became an Oscar-nominated, BAFTA award-winning animated film. In 2017, Gaiman's novel *American Gods* was also adapted into a television series on the Starz network. *Good Omens*, a miniseries, based on the novel of the same name he wrote with Terry Pratchett, will debut on Amazon Prime and air on the BBC in the UK in 2019.

Elizabeth Hand is the author of fourteen cross-genre novels and four collections of short fiction. Her work has received the World Fantasy Award (four times), the Nebula Award (twice), the Shirley Jackson Award (twice), and the James M. Tiptree Jr. and Mythopoeic Society Awards. She's also a longtime critic and contributor of essays for the *Washington Post*, *Los Angeles Times*, *Salon*, and the *Village Voice*, among many others. She divides her time between the Maine coast and North London.

Lisa L. Hannett has had over seventy short stories appear in venues including *Clarkesworld*, *Fantasy*, *Weird Tales*, *Apex*, *The Dark*, and *Year's Best* anthologies in Australia, Canada, and the US. She has won four Aurealis Awards, including Best Collection for her first book, *Bluegrass Symphony*, which was also nominated for a World Fantasy Award. Her debut novel, *Lament for the Afterlife*, was published in 2015. A new collection of short stories, *Little Digs*, is coming out in 2019.

Maria Dahvana Headley is a *New York Times*-bestselling author and editor, playwright, and screenwriter, most recently of *The Mere Wife*, a twenty-first century update of the epic poem *Beowulf.* She is the author of young adult fantasy novels *Magonia* and *Aerie*, the dark fantasy/alt-history novel *Queen of Kings*, and the internationally bestselling memoir *The Year of Yes*. With Neil Gaiman, she is the #1 *New York Times*-bestselling editor of the anthology *Unnatural Creatures*, benefitting 826DC. With Kat Howard, she is the author of the novella *The End of the Sentence*—one of NPR's Best Books of 2014. Her Nebula, Shirley Jackson, and World Fantasy Award-shortlisted fiction has been anthologized in many year's bests, and appeared in *Lightspeed*, *Uncanny*, *Nightmare*, *Tor.com*, *Shimmer*, *Apex*, *Clarkesworld*, *The Journal of Unlikely Entomology*, *Subterranean Online*, *The Toast*, as well as many anthologies and "year's bests."

Ann Leckie is the author of the Hugo, Nebula, and Arthur C. Clarke Award-winning novel *Ancillary Justice*, *Ancillary Sword* (British Fantasy Society Award-winner), and *Ancillary Mercy*. Each novel won the Locus Award and was nominated for the Nebula Award. Her novel *Provenance* is set in the Imperial Radch universe of her trilogy, but is not a sequel. *The Raven Tower* will be published in 2019. She has also published short stories in *Subterranean*, *Strange Horizons*, *Beneath Ceaseless Skies*, and *Realms of Fantasy*. Her story "Hesperia and Glory" was reprinted in *Science Fiction: The Best of the Year, 2007*, edited by Rich Horton. Ann has worked as a waitress, a receptionist, a rodman on a land-surveying crew, and a recording engineer. She lives in St. Louis, Missouri.

Tanith Lee was born in London in 1947. She died peacefully after a long illness in Hastings, East Sussex in 2015. After grammar school, she worked at a number of jobs, and at age twenty-five had one year at art college. Then DAW Books published her novel *The Birthgrave*. Since then she was a professional full-time writer. Publications include approximately ninety novels and collections and well over three hundred short stories. She has also written for television and radio. Lee has won several awards including two World Fantasy awards for short fiction. In 2009 she was made a Grand Master of Horror and was honored with the World Fantasy Convention Lifetime Achievement Award in 2013. She was married to the writer/artist John Kaiine.

Yoon Ha Lee is a Korean-American writer who received a BA in Math from Cornell University and an MA in Math Education from Stanford University. Yoon finds it a source of continual delight that math can be mined for story ideas. Yoon's fiction has appeared in publications such as *The Magazine of Fantasy & Science Fiction, Tor.com*, and *Clarkesworld*, as well as several year's best anthologies. Some short stories have been collected in *Conservation of Shadows*, and *The Foxes Tower and Other Shadows* collects some flash fiction. The space opera trilogy, The Machineries of Empire (*Ninefox Gambit, Raven Stratagem*, and *Revenant Gun*), will be followed by *The Hexarchate Stories* in June 2019; the middle-grade Korean mythology space opera, *Dragon Pearl*, was published in January 2019.

Charles de Lint is a full-time writer and musician who makes his home in Ottawa, Canada. He was named as a Lifetime Achievement Award recipient by the 2018 World Fantasy Convention. The author of more than seventy adult, young adult, and children's books, he has won the World Fantasy, Aurora, Sunburst, and White Pine Awards, among others. Modern Library's Top 100 Books of the 20th Century poll, voted on by readers, put eight of de Lint's books among the top hundred. De Lint is also a poet, artist, songwriter, performer, and folklorist. He writes a monthly book-review column for *The Magazine of Fantasy & Science Fiction*.

Darcie Little Badger is a Lipan Apache geoscientist and writer. Her short fiction, nonfiction, and comics have appeared in multiple publications, including *Love Beyond Body, Space, and Time, Strange Horizons, Lightspeed*, and *Deer Woman: An Anthology*. She also contributed to *Moonshot: The Indigenous Comics Collection Volume 2*. She currently lives on both coasts but will always be home along the Kuné Tsé.

Ken Liu is an author of speculative fiction, as well as a translator, lawyer, and programmer. A winner of the Nebula, Hugo, and World Fantasy awards, he is the author of The Dandelion Dynasty, a silkpunk epic fantasy series (*The Grace of Kings, The Wall of Storms*, and a forthcoming third volume), and *The Paper Menagerie and Other Stories*, a collection. He also wrote the Star Wars novel *The Legends of Luke Skywalker*.

Rachel Pollack is the author of forty-one books, including two award-winning novels, *Unquenchable Fire*, winner of the Arthur C. Clarke

Award, and *Godmother Night*, winner of the World Fantasy Award. She has also written a series of books about Tarot cards known around the world, a book of poetry (*Fortune's Lover*), and has translated, with scholar David Vine, Sophocles' *Oidipous Tyrannos* (*Oedipus Rex*) under the title *Tyrant Oidipous*. She designed and drew her own Tarot deck, The Shining Tribe Tarot. With artist Robert Place she has created two more decks, The Burning Serpent Oracle, and The Raziel Tarot. She has taught and lectured on four continents. For eleven years she taught in Goddard College's MFA writing program. Rachel lives in New York's Hudson Valley.

Before earning her MFA from Vermont College of Fine Arts, **M. Rickert** worked as kindergarten teacher, coffee shop barista, balloon vendor at Disneyland, and in the personnel department of Sequoia National Park where she spent her time off hiking the wilderness. She now lives in Cedarburg, Wisconsin, a small city of candy shops and beautiful gardens. She has published numerous short stories and two collections: *Map of Dreams, Holiday*, and, most recently, *You Have Never Been Here*. Her first novel, *The Memory Garden*, was published in 2014, and won the Locus Award for Best First Novel. Her first collection, *Map of Dreams*, was honored with both the World Fantasy and Crawford Awards.

Tansy Rayner Roberts is an award-winning writer of science fiction, fantasy, feminist essays, and humor. She lives in Tasmania, Australia, with her husband and two superhero daughters. She is a co-host of *Galactic Suburbia* and *Verity*, and also has her own weekly fiction podcast, *Sheep Might Fly*, where you can listen to her reading fiction serials. She has a PhD in Classics, and still obsesses about ancient literature when she isn't busy obsessing about superheroes, musketeers, and fictional hockey.

Sofia Samatar is the author of the novels *A Stranger in Olondria* and *The Winged Histories*, the short story collection *Tender*, and *Monster Portraits*, a collaboration with her brother, the artist Del Samatar. Her work has won several awards, including the John W. Campbell Award and the World Fantasy Award. She teaches African literature, Arabic literature, and speculative fiction at James Madison University.

Ekaterina Sedia resides in the Pinelands of New Jersey. She has written four critically acclaimed and award-nominated novels: *The Secret*

History of Moscow, The Alchemy of Stone, The House of Discarded Dreams, and *Heart of Iron.* Her short stories have appeared in *Analog, Baen's Universe, Subterranean,* and *Clarkesworld,* as well as numerous anthologies, including *Haunted Legends* and *Magic in the Mirrorstone.* Some of her short fiction has been collected in her short-story collection, *Moscow But Dreaming.* Sedia is the editor of the anthologies *Paper Cities* (World Fantasy Award winner), *Running with the Pack, Bewere the Night, Bloody Fabulous,* and *The Mammoth Book of Gaslit Romance and Wilful Impropriety.* She also co-wrote a script for *Yamasong: March of the Hollows,* a fantasy feature-length puppet film voiced by Nathan Fillion, George Takei, Abigail Breslin, and Whoopi Goldberg, to be released by Dark Dunes Productions.

Priya Sharma's fiction has appeared in venues such as *Interzone, Black Static, Nightmare, The Dark,* and *Tor.* She's been anthologized in several of Ellen Datlow's *Best Horror of the Year* series, Paula Guran's *Year's Best Dark Fantasy & Horror* series, Jonathan Strahan's *The Best Science Fiction & Fantasy* 2014, Steve Haynes' *Best British Fantasy* 2014, and Johnny Main's *Best British Horror* 2015. She's also been on many Locus Recommended Reading Lists. "Fabulous Beasts" was a Shirley Jackson Award finalist and won a British Fantasy Award for Short Fiction. A collection of some of Sharma's work, *All the Fabulous Beasts,* was released in 2018.

Nisi Shawl's collection *Filter House* was a James Tiptree, Jr. Award winner. Her stories have been published in *Strange Horizons, Asimov's, Clarkesworld, Apex, Uncanny, Lightspeed, The Year's Best Fantasy and Horror,* and both volumes of the Dark Matter series. She co-authored the renowned *Writing the Other: A Practical Approach with Cynthia Ward* and co-edited the nonfiction anthology *Strange Matings: Science Fiction, Feminism, African American Voices, and Octavia E. Butler.* Shawl's Belgian Congo steampunk novel *Everfair* came out in 2016. She also edited the anthology *New Suns: Original Speculative Fiction by People of Color,* which was published earlier this year.

Author, screenwriter, and musician **John Shirley** is the author of more than forty novels including the classic cyberpunk Song Called Youth trilogy; the horror novels *Cellars, Wetbones,* and *Demons;* and the Western historical novel *Wyatt in Wichita.* Many of his numerous shorter works have been gathered in nine collections, including the Bram Stoker Award-winning *Black Butterflies*. He resides in Washington state near Portland, Oregon, where he performs and records with his band, the Screaming Geezers.

Angela Slatter is the author of the supernatural crime novels *Vigil*, *Corpselight*, and *Restoration*, as well as eight short story collections. She has won a World Fantasy Award, a British Fantasy Award, a Ditmar, an Australian Shadows Award, and six Aurealis Awards. Angela's short stories have appeared in Australian, UK, and US "best of" anthologies. She has an MA and a PhD in Creative Writing, and is a graduate of Clarion South 2009 and the Tin House Summer Writers Workshop 2006.

Emma Straub is from New York City. She is the *New York Times*-bestselling author of the novels *Modern Lovers*, *The Vacationers*, and *Laura Lamont's Life in Pictures*, and the short story collection *Other People We Married*. Her fiction and nonfiction have been published in *Vogue*, *New York Magazine*, *Tin House*, *The New York Times*, *Good Housekeeping*, and the *The Paris Review Daily*. She is a contributing writer to *Rookie*. Straub lives with her husband and two sons in Brooklyn.

Peter Straub is the author of nineteen novels, which have been translated into more than twenty languages. They include *Ghost Story*, *Koko*, *Mr. X*, *In the Night Room*, and two collaborations with Stephen King, *The Talisman* and *Black House*. He has written two volumes of poetry and six collections of short fiction, and he edited the Library of America's edition of *H. P. Lovecraft's Tales* and the Library of America's two-volume anthology, *American Fantastic Tales*. He has won the British Fantasy Award, eight Bram Stoker Awards, two International Horror Guild Awards, and three World Fantasy Awards. He was named as a Grand Master at the World Horror Convention, is a recipient of the HWA's Life Achievement Award and the Barnes & Noble Writers for Writers Award by *Poets & Writers*. The World Fantasy Convention has honored Straub with a Life Achievement Award.

Rachel Swirsky holds an MFA from the Iowa Writers' Workshop where she, a California native, learned about both writing and snow. Last year, she traded the snow for the rain of Portland, Oregon, where she roams happily under overcast skies with the hipsters. Her fiction has appeared in venues including *Tor.com*, *Asimov's*, and *The Year's Best Non-Required Reading*. She's published two collections: *Through the Drowsy Dark* and *How the World Became Quiet*. Her fiction has been nominated for the Hugo Award and the World Fantasy Award, and twice won the Nebula.

Sonya Taaffe reads dead languages and tells living stories. Her short fiction and poetry have been collected most recently in *Forget the Sleepless Shores* and previously in *Singing Innocence and Experience*, *Postcards from the Province of Hyphens*, *A Mayse-Bikhl*, and *Ghost Signs*. She lives with her husband and two cats in Somerville, Massachusetts, where she writes about film for Patreon and remains proud of naming a Kuiper belt object.

Catherynne M. Valente is the acclaimed author of *Space Opera*, and a *New York Times*-bestselling author of over two dozen works of fiction and poetry, including *Palimpsest*, the Orphan's Tales series, *Deathless*, *Radiance*, and the crowdfunded phenomenon *The Girl Who Circumnavigated Fairyland in a Ship of Her Own Making*. She is the winner of the Andre Norton, Tiptree, Mythopoeic, Rhysling, Lambda, Locus, and Hugo Awards. She has been a finalist for the Nebula and World Fantasy Awards. Her most recent collection of short fiction is *The Future Is Blue*. She lives on an island off the coast of Maine with a small but growing menagerie of beasts, some of which are human.

Genevieve Valentine's first novel, *Mechanique: A Tale of the Circus Tresaulti*, won the 2012 Crawford Award and was nominated for the Nebula. Subsequent novels include the speakeasy fairy tale *The Girls at the Kingfisher Club* and the political thriller *Persona* and its sequel *Icon*. She has written Catwoman for DC Comics and Xena: Warrior Princess for Dynamite. Her short fiction has appeared in *Clarkesworld*, *Strange Horizons*, *Journal of Mythic Arts*, *Lightspeed*, and other venues, as well as anthologies such as *Mad Hatters and March Hares*, *Infinity Wars*, *The Starlit Wood: New Fairy Tales*, *The Doll Collection*, and *Fearsome Magics*. Stories have been nominated for the World Fantasy Award and the Shirley Jackson Award, and have appeared in over a dozen "year's best" anthologies. Her nonfiction has appeared at NPR.org, The AV Club, *Strange Horizons*, io9.com, *LA Review of Books*, Vice, Vox, *The Atlantic*, and the *New York Times*.

ABOUT THE EDITOR

Paula Guran is an editor, reviewer, and typesetter. In an earlier life she produced weekly email newsletter *DarkEcho* (winning two Stokers, an IHG award, and a World Fantasy Award nomination), edited magazine *Horror Garage* (earning another IHG and a second World Fantasy nomination), and has contributed reviews, interviews, and articles to numerous professional publications. This is, if she's counted correctly, the forty-sixth anthology Guran has edited. She has four fabulous grandchildren she would be happy to tell you about. Guran still lives in Akron, Ohio, but has moved from the crumbling family manse into a condominium apartment. Even though she got rid of a great many books, she still has far too many. Of course she has a cat.

ACKNOWLEDGEMENTS

Special thanks to C. C. Finlay, Gordon Van Gelder, and more than three dozen authors who contacted me through Facebook and Twitter with suggestions.—*PRLG*